REDEMPTION

A CASSIDY KAIN SUPERNATURAL THRILLER
BOOK 1

STEPHEN WERTZBAUGHER

BROKEN MIRROR PRESS, LLC

First Edition 2025

Printed in the United States of America.

Cover design by Jake Caleb | jcalebdesign.com

Editing by: Nan Sampson Bach | Emily Burch Harris

ISBN - Paperback: 979-8-9994443-1-8

ISBN - eBook: 979-8-9994443-0-1

Visit the author online: stephenwertzbaugher.com

For Kathy
Thank you for the trust, encouragement, and patience. Without you this would never have been possible.

PROLOGUE: VENGEANCE IS A DISH BEST SERVED COLD

THE OPEN NEXUS, cloaked in a shimmering waterfall of sable and quicksilver fire, flickered across the center of a cracked and crumbling stone basement wall beneath the Warrens. The chameleon-like fire cast a dull glow on the grimy, moonlit shadows, revealing a fae-daemon Ebony Dust fueled sooty mist that crept across the dirty, debris and bone-littered floor. Drenched in sweat, his scraggy body trembling with an unquenched yearning, Gideon Silos, crouched in the crawling vapor, coal-blackened strands winding up his arms as he carved the final runes of restraining into the maimed cement floor to close the warding circle.

Jessie Colemann stood nearby, her gaze fixed on the undulating flames flitting over the crumbling brick. She tapped out a steady rhythm on her assault rifle, watching the distant shadow of the Juzarine fae-demon witch with whom she had bargained trudge across the desolate and broken landscape of the Nether Realm toward the shimmering doorway that opened into the human world. She swallowed the bitterness clinging to her mouth. Exiled by their own hellish kind, the Otherkind, the Juzarine were the vilest enemies of humanity. And yet, the necessities of her vengeance had brought her and the Juzarine together for a common cause.

The enemy of my enemy.

Jessie twitched a smile, her soul leaning into the lustful caress of the Medusa Mirror cocooned in the leather satchel dangling from the witch's belt. Chaos magic. Fae-daemon Otherkind power, twisted and distorted, wrenched and warped into a reflective glass prison to hold a human Essence. Food for the fae-daemon monsters and their fiendish alchemy and witchcraft.

Behind Jessie, three human tweens, two girls and a boy, draped in ragged and dirty clothing, huddled together for warmth beneath a frost-glazed window. Jaundiced moonlight leaked through the ice-grimed glass, falling in tatters at their battered and filthy feet. The sour stench of their unwashed bodies hung heavy and still in the frosty air, manacled to their terrified whimpers.

Jessie clenched her jaw, murdering a shudder of disgust. She glanced over her shoulder at the children and scowled at the disavowed and excommunicated Order of the Four Chasseur, a man once responsible for protecting children recovered from the Nether Realm, guarding them. His name skipped across the surface of her memory, vanished beneath the choppy surface. Better she didn't remember. What he'd done to children the Order of the Four rescued from fae-daemon captivity in the Nether Realm, made her twinge in disgust.

But for only an instant.

"Shut them up or you'll be going to the Nether Realm with them," she said.

His face twisting with frustration, the man knelt and gagged them using oily cloths he snatched from the floor nearby.

Peter Oliver stood beside her, watching, white-knuckling his assault rifle. "What we're doing is unholy."

"It is."

"Then why?"

"Did you bring Tansy?"

Rage flashed. His expression darkened. "I won't—"

"You will," she said, watching the fury churning through his deep charcoal-brown eyes. She reached over to stroke his cheek, grinned when he flinched away from her touch. "Or should Cassidy discover your betrayal and complicity in her excommunication?" she asked, pleasure rippling through her as his rage wilted into fear.

"I didn't assassinate your fiancé."

"But you were there when Cassidy murdered Wynn," she said, her voice edged with ice. "To make sure of it." She studied him. "You might as well have been standing beside Cassidy when she pulled the trigger."

Silence.

Lightning cracked the storming air behind the fiery waterfall. The shadowy figure drew closer, its footsteps ragged and uneven against a howling wind.

"It's done." Silos pushed himself to his feet, his eyes feral and hungry, exhaustion carved into the grit-smeared lines of his face. "Once through crosses the Nexus, the barriers will activate, imprisoning the Juzarine."

Jessie studied Silos, her mind turning over his crimes. His lack of remorse when confronted with the damning evidence. His eventual excommunication from the Order of the Four. Touched. Manifested. A sociopath. Each dangerous by itself. Together, a lethal concoction. And the reason she'd recruited him.

"The wards will hold?"

Silos pursed his lips, his eyes flashing dangerously in the yellow-tinged moonlight. "They'll hold."

"And if they don't?"

"They will."

She scrutinized him, then glanced over her shoulder at Peter Oliver. "Bring Tansy."

He didn't move, and for an instant, she thought he would refuse, the hackles on his scruples raised, their claws dug deep into the moral ground he'd torched when he watched Cassidy murder Ellis Wynn. Her heart stuttered. Memories churned, knotting her stomach with grief and rage.

"Tansy isn't part of this," he said. "Go after Cassidy but leave Tansy out of it."

Jessie snorted. "Ellis was innocent. Did Navarro or you or Cassidy leave him out of it?" She stepped toward him, her gaze fuming as she glared up at him. "Cassidy ripped my heart out when she killed Ellis. I'm using Tansy to return the favor."

Peter sucked in a ragged breath, nodded curtly. He disappeared into the shadowed gloom toward the stairs, the creeping fog swirling across the floor in his wake.

The Ebony Dust mist brushed against the ankle of her boot.

Subtle fae-demon power teased her mind, making her tremble, and enticing her with the promise of longed-for nuclear-enriched euphoria. She licked her lips and squeezed her eyes closed, her body clenching as the magic lit her nerves on fire. The flames danced through her blood, attempting to scatter her thoughts.

Stay on mission.

She ground the power to pulp beneath the heel of her will.

The enchantment died, its beguiling iron shackles falling to the floor in pieces.

Jessie let out a quiet breath, reached up to wipe away the glimmer of sweat from her forehead.

A soft thud made her turn.

Peter stood a few steps back, his teeth grinding beneath his close-trimmed beard, eyes blazing with a new rage. And behind it, a pulsing fear.

The wraith-like form of a late-teen girl wrapped in dark, sagging fleece slouchy shorts, filth-slimed white crew socks, and a grime-stained T-shirt sat on the floor in front of him, gangly legs clenched to her chest, girded by slim arms, a slender chin resting on her knobby knees. Tawny, bramble-snarled hair hugged her narrow face, tumbled in tangles behind her shoulders and down her back, shrouding the hazy glow from her sun-browned skin where the moonlight kissed her flesh. She stared into the midnight shadows, her dull, sea-green eyes clotted with fae-daemon Ebony Dust, the fire of consciousness muted.

"Where are the clothes I gave you?"

Peter threw a ragged pile of shredded clothing at her feet. "She refused to wear them. Tore them off faster than we could force her into them." He grimaced. "We had to jack her up with the rest of the Ebony you gave us to sedate her enough to get her into what she's wearing now." He paused. "What we shot her up with should have ripped her mind to shreds."

Jessie hid a smile and nodded, watched the way Tansy's Ebony dusted gaze roamed the haze, stopping every few seconds to stare where the moonlight glittered off the inky, swirling surface, and watching it shoot silver-gray sparks into the empty air before drifting her eyes to the next sparkling sea. The fog clung to her, crawled up her limbs, leaving behind a dirty, coal-black slime trail that shimmered in the uncertain light. The girl shivered, her face twisting into knots of longing and desire.

Jessie unmasked her smile.

Tansy stared into the midnight abyss, her slender lips contorting into a broken grin that echoed Jessie's growing anticipation.

Peter stared at Tansy, his lean, angular expression twisted in disgust and disapproval. He looked at Jessie, rage burning in his gaze. "This isn't right," he said. "You told Brandt we found his daughter in the Nether Realm."

"And we have."

"Not in the way he believes. You should have told him—"

"What?" She fixed her eyes on him, watching the impotent anger dance across his face.

"That Stephanie is dead."

She threw a negligent gesture toward the open Nexus. "I wouldn't call what the Juzarine is bringing dead."

"No, you're right," he said. "That isn't dead. It's worse."

"Then perhaps Cassidy should have made sure of it before she abandoned Stephanie's body to the Juzarine."

Peter scowled. He stared at Tansy where she huddled in the thickening swirl of black mist.

Jessie watched him shudder, one corner of her mouth twisting upward.

He shook himself, looked away.

The frosted air behind Jessie crackled, spitting a bitter and pungent odor of ozone into the shadows.

She hammered Peter with one last hard glare before turning to face the shimmering obsidian and quicksilver waterfall slithering down the cracked and crumbling wall. The pulsing light spat showers of crimson sparks into the moon-pale darkness that dropped stonelike into the rippling midnight mist, sizzling as they evaporated into the sooty haze.

A shadowed phantom stood beyond the threshold of the Nexus, a squirming rawhide pouch, its mouth close-fisted by a skin thong, dangling from a black belt.

Watching the satchel with anticipation, Jessie tightened her grip on her assault rifle and nodded.

Quiet stillness answered, followed by whispered words spoken in an alien language, its dissonant syllables raising the hackles on her neck. She clenched her jaw, tasted blood.

The surrounding air shuddered, grew thick. She sucked in a ragged breath as the cloying murk disintegrated into a tiny firestorm that burned a hole through the wavering, incandescent light.

The Juzarine witch stepped through the Nexus.

The sound of raised assault rifles rattled the quiet stillness.

A low throaty chuckle slid from the cloaked silhouette as it lowered its hood.

Glowing crimson eyes stared out from a lean, silver-frosted face that narrowed into a chiseled, arrowhead chin, framed by shoulder-length, electrified raven-black hair, hinting at faded memories of the human Essence that had once inhabited the body. Long, icepick-slender fingers whispered against the hem of the cloak's mantle for a few seconds before sliding down to join their sisters at its waist.

Jessie suppressed a shudder, tightened her grip on her rifle as she studied the Juzarine before shifting her eyes to the satchel hanging from its belt. Impatient longing for what crouched inside the pouch whispered into her ear.

The Juzarine grinned, its lips slithering over gleaming ivory white teeth. It met Jessie's appraising stare, grin widening for an instant as it focused on the rifles and slid the toe of its boot across the floor, touching the arcing line carved into the concrete. Indigo and crimson sparks spat upward, pulling a shimmering, circular curtain around it.

The witch inclined its head, unhooked the bag from its belt. "Well played," it said, the words clumsy and unfamiliar. It held out the sack. "What you bargained for."

Fae-daemon power throbbed.

Jessie pursed her lips, shook off the seductive call.

Behind her, she heard the scrape of bare flesh against the floor, felt the coiling mist at her feet shudder. And smiled.

The witch glanced past her, its grin faltering. When its gaze returned, the crimson eyes held a razor's edge. "You are more than a fool if you believe you can control the Daemonrie Chimera."

Jessie snorted. "What makes you think I intend to control it?"

Uncertainty flashed for an instant. The hand holding the satchel retreated. "And if we refuse to give you the Medusa Mirror?"

Jessie raised her rifle. A gunshot reverberated through the closed space, spitting splintered rock and cement through the air behind the witch's head.

The Juzarine flinched, hissing an angry breath. It unsheathed a dagger from its belt, the polished bone blade glinting in the shadowed light, touched the point against the side of the pouch.

Jessie stiffened. A Juzarine dagger, its blade carved from an adult human femur and cursed with fae-daemon Chaos magic meant to poison and corrupt the human Essence, eventually consuming it.

A scowl lit the witch's face as it clenched the bag to its chest. "Kill us and you lose your prize," it said. "What then becomes of your vessel?"

Jessie snorted, lowered her rifle. "Bring the tweens."

The witch frowned when they staggered from the shadows huddling beneath the window, corrupted moonlight dripping off their sallow skin. "This is not what you promised us. Where is the chieftain of your clan? The human called Navarro?"

"I am not yet prepared to deliver him to you. These are what I have brought in his stead. And what you will take."

"Then we refuse."

Jessie motioned to Silos.

He stepped forward, hands extended, muttering, his eyes blazing with emptiness.

The Nexus spat fire, flickered, and died.

Jessie fired two quick shots.

The Juzarine convulsed backward into the basement wall, hovering for an instant. It slid to the floor, staring blankly into the darkness, the satchel clutched in one hand, its dagger in the other.

Peter stepped forward, his expression blazing with shock and rage. "Are you insane?"

Soft, jarring whimpers stuttered through the jaundiced shadows, shaving bone off Jessie's spine.

She suppressed a shudder. "Get them out of here," she barked at the Chasseur, her voice low, and filled with menace.

"Where?"

"Back where you found them," she said. "Drown them in the Platte." She paused, turned a baleful glare at the man. "Throw them off the ravine. I don't care. Just get rid of them!"

She pierced Peter with an icy stare. "You disapprove?"

He pursed his lips, the sound of his grinding teeth shivering in the space between them. "You're playing a dangerous game," he said. "One that will kill us all. Or worse."

She twitched a smile. "Afraid?" Before Peter could answer, she looked at Silos and gestured toward the Juzarine. "Bring me the pouch." She grabbed the collar of another Chasseur and yanked him close. "Make sure the Numen Galére discover the Juzarine's body."

Silos shoved the bag into her hands. Jessie sighed and stole a quick glance at Tansy, watching her peer through the murky gloom, her eyes glimmering with Ebony, a savage hunger clinging to her slender face.

"Keep Brandt occupied while I prepare his daughter for their reunion."

Peter's gaze dropped to the satchel nestled between her hands. He shook his head. A moment later, the creak and groan of exhausted wooden steps echoed through the basement.

A quiet hiss breathed an anxious sigh into the nervous air. Fae-daemon power surged from the pouch, teasing Jessie's Essence with an insatiable hunger.

Tansy reached out, her expression reflecting the yearning that crept through the darkness.

Jessie yanked the pouch open and stared into smoky glass, her eyes catching streaks of pulsating Ebony Dust glaring back as she pulled the Medusa Mirror from the pouch. The indistinct and fragmented Essence of Stephanie Brandt, stripped from her dead body by the Juzarine and imprisoned inside this Medusa Mirror smoldered below the glass. Invisible tendrils snaked up, winding their putrescent tips around Jessie's Essence, and tugged. She stiffened for an instant, insatiable yearning embracing her with a lover's lust.

Memories sparked.

Jessie and Wynn; their first time together, drinking in each other with a profound passion that melted them into a single needful soul.

She shuddered. Lecherous laughter stroked her mind. Another memory surged from the darkness; Wynn's body in the morgue, his waxen face battered, bruised, and bloodied, a single gunshot through his chest. She'd discovered the text he'd sent to her later, after the deed, a single name scrawled across her phone screen: Cassidy Kain.

Jessie glanced at Tansy, the rage erupting from the depths of her shredded and threadbare grief. *You took my soulmate from me. Now I'm going to take the thing you've used to replace yours.*

"Everyone out." Jessie barked. She looked at Silos and added. "Except you."

Shadows scrambled, boots scraping broken concrete, scattering the dying charcoal-black mist. Wood groaned and creaked. A door opened on squealing hinges and slammed closed.

Tansy glanced at their passing, reached out a trembling hand, quivering fingers brushing against the swirling air.

Silence cloaked them a moment later.

Silos appeared at Jessie's side, a menacing hunger glowing in his gaze.

"Hold her still," Jessie said. "Make sure she doesn't close her eyes or look away."

Silos squatted behind Tansy, gripped her head between his soot-stained hands.

Jessie knelt down on her knees in front of Tansy, unslung her rifle, and set the Medusa Mirror on the floor between them. Psychedelic light shimmered from the mist-choked glass. Jessie drew her knife, and grasping Tansy's right hand, traced a crimson line across her palm, clenching her wrist tighter when she tried to yank it free.

Blood welled from the cut, dribbled down over the twisted Elder and Rowan frame.

Embers of fear swelled from Tansy's eyes, began to burn away the Ebony fog. Dim recognition fluttered, feeding the growing dread.

"Where am I?"

Jessie clutched Tansy's wrist, refusing to give it back.

"Jessie?" Tansy squinted, peering through the shifting shadows. Fear quivered, slowly clawing its way past her confusion. "Where's Cassidy?"

Anger and hatred constricted Jessie's chest. She shoved the emotions down, wiping them from her face as she caught Tansy's chin and forced her wandering gaze to focus. "Cass isn't here," she said. "She can't save you. Not this time."

The last of the Ebony swirling through Tansy's eyes evaporated. They went wide with sudden shock and terror as she tried to wrench herself from Jessie's grip. Blood ran from the slit in her palm, falling into the charcoal vapor writhing across the floor.

Cursing, Jessie slapped Tansy, stunning her. She flicked an angry glare at Silos. "Hold her still, damn it, or you'll replace her."

Alarm flashed through his dark eyes. He clenched Tansy's head between trembling fingers, heaving his weight down on her shoulders.

Snatching the Medusa Mirror from the floor between them, Jessie smeared Tansy's bloody palm over the glass and shoved it toward Tansy's vacant stare. She whispered words forbidden to humanity since the Creation, her quavering voice rising to an ear-shattering octave. Brute-force fae-demon power surged through the air. Jessie bit back a scream as a violent knot twisted through her chest, wrapping malevolent fingers around her mind.

Sudden horror stormed across Tansy's expression. Her eyes grew wide, her mouth contorting into a silent shriek.

A black-tinged, ruddy shade clawed out from behind the glass. Ink-black sparks lit the shadows. Skeletal, worm-like, fingers brushed Tansy's cheeks, crawling upward until they touched her eyes. A gleeful banshee cry of sudden release shook the air. The mist clinging to the broken floor exploded skyward, swirling with chaotic ecstasy.

Tansy stared into the darkness, her face etched with horror, mouth frozen open in a soundless scream. The misted strands caressed her eyes, licking the terror from her gaze.

Silence shivered through the air.

The mist shuddered, stormed into Tansy's eyes, vanishing between breaths.

Jessie let go of Tansy's wrist and set the Mirror down. She snapped her gaze to Silos. "Get out."

Silos shot backward, reverse crabbed his way across the floor until he found the basement stairs. He stared for a moment, malevolent desire chasing trepidation through his eyes. He crawled up two steps, pulled himself up, and scrambled up the remaining steps as if racing toward heaven.

Tansy slumped forward, trembling, head twitching, her body pounding out a staccato beat.

Jessie stared at her and flashed a satisfied smile. "Stephanie Brandt?"

A sucking silence embracing a fleeting doubt.

Tansy's meandering gaze convulsed and rose, a malicious leer screwing up the corners of her mouth. "Adria."

Her fae-daemon Juzarine name.

Jessie blew out a sigh, rocking back on her heels. She held up the Medusa Mirror, turning the glass toward her.

Tansy gasped, shying from her reflection. Jessie seized her arm, jerking her forward. She shoved the mirror at Tansy's face, and spat, "I am the one who freed you. And I am the Master of your Mirror." She released Tansy's arm and sat back. "I have a task for you. Complete the task and I shall grant you permanent freedom. Fail to complete your task, however—" Jessie brandished the Mirror at Tansy.

A quiet, baleful hiss. Continuing to avert her eyes, Tansy leered. "What task would you have us complete?"

Jessie closed the basement door quietly behind her. Muted conversation driven by an angry voice died at her approach.

Howard Brandt shoved Peter away, striding past a pair of twitchy Chasseurs. He came nose to nose with her, rage fuming, his hard eyes burning in a firestorm.

"Where is my daughter?"

"Step back before I do something you'll regret."

He stood his ground. "My daughter."

"The money you still owe," she said, placing her hand against his chest. "Move away."

Brandt hovered for a heartbeat before stepping back and signaling to his assistant.

Brandt's assistant nodded.

"It's done," Brandt hissed. "My daughter?"

"Stephanie is downstairs."

"In the basement? Alone?" He tried to muscle past her.

She gripped his arm. "Stephanie's been in Juzarine Otherkind captivity for over almost two years," she said. "You need to give her the time she needs to readjust to the human world." She peered at him. "Understand?"

Hesitation cloaked with uncertainty. He nodded.

She opened the basement door. Brandt shot through, pounding down the stairs. Jessie nodded at Peter as she closed the door.

Peter hesitated, flashing a sour and disgusted look before drawing a suppressed pistol and firing a round into the back of Brandt's assistant's head. He arched a brow. "My debt to you?"

"Forgiven but not forgotten after Francisco Navarro and Cassidy Kain are rotting in hell for Wynn's murder." Jessie counted to five. A shrill scream tore through the tense air. Jessie snorted and nodded toward the fidgeting Chasseurs. "Clean that mess up."

She slammed Peter with a challenging look. "After Adria finishes feeding on her dad's Essence, pump her with enough Ebony to keep her satiated then dump Tansy's body on Jonnie Hallow's doorstep."

"You know what he'll try to do to her?"

"I'm counting on it," she said, peering at him. "Would you rather I involved your sister and her sons?"

An uneasy silence stretched until it snapped. The outrage

drained from his gaze, his expression sinking into defeated resignation. His chin spasmed a curt nod.

Jessie sidled up to Peter, touching her lips to his ear. "Make sure Cleary knows Jonnie has her."

A silence filled hesitation. "He'll take Tansy to the Shining Man."

She twitched a smile. "Who will snag Cassidy into *his* web." She paused, expecting another protest, and felt disappointment when it didn't come.

"You contacted Navarro?" he asked.

She eyed him. "Last night. I'll surrender myself to him after I have Cassidy in my custody. An olive branch he wasn't able to refuse. Or are you hoping he'll execute me on sight?"

"It would greatly simplify my life."

"I was sufficiently contrite and penitent when we spoke. And the Cassidy Kain carrot I dangled was too much for him to ignore. Sorry to disappoint." She brushed his cheek with her lips. "I'll take care of Brandt's body." She stepped away from him and swept the Chasseurs with her gaze. "Move," she commanded.

CHAPTER 1
ANOTHER HAPPY CRAPPY BIRTHDAY

DECEMBER TWENTY-FIRST.

ANOTHER HOLLY-JOLLY CHRISTMAS in the Mile-High City.

Another happy crappy birthday bereft of my twin sister, Audrey, the better half of my soul.

My thirtieth above the ground; her twenty-fifth not in the ground, and not in this world.

I stared at her headstone, the shattered fingers of frozen grime clinging to the cracked and weathered marble, her name obscured behind a dusting of soiled snow. I knelt and brushed the inscription clean, wiping away a bitter tear as I read it: '*Audrey Katherine Kain. Twin Sister to Cassidy Maribelle Kain, who should have protected her.*'

Mom's words.

The old familiar pain burned through the center of my chest, lighting my heart on fire, and turning it to ash between my stuttering breaths.

"Thanks again for the understanding, Mom," I muttered as I

retrieved the bouquet of wilting yellow daisies I'd brought for Audrey and the pint of Jack for my dad, dead for twenty years by his own hand.

Ain't guilt grand?

I shivered, felt the spear tip of cold calculating eyes wedged between my shoulder blades, the fetid whisper of Otherkind fae-daemon power pricking my soul. I scanned the dark line of blue spruce and ponderosa pine ringing this part of the cemetery. Saw nothing.

Still... I knew they were there, waiting for me to leave conse-crated ground.

A tight smile creased my lips as I turned back to the ashen tombstones at my feet.

Whatever the Otherkind wanted, they'd wait until I touched asphalt and concrete before crawling from their hidey-hole to confront me. I snorted. Cemeteries hadn't been sanctified terrain in forever.

Still...

Dusk's shadows embraced the cemetery as I stooped and laid the daisies on my sister's grave.

A light snow floated down out of the darkened sky, the flakes resembling volcanic ash.

Flat, cold, and empty. Like my soul.

I tried to remember why I'd come. Or why I lingered.

With a start, I realized I held the Kain family 1928 Colt .38 Detective Special, passed from father to son until my dad used it to blow his brains out on my tenth birthday: five years after I abandoned Audrey in the Nether Realm. I guess he figured there wouldn't be any more sons in the Kain line to pass it on to.

My thumb dragged the hammer back.

Five fricking years...

I stared at the revolver's blued metallic frame. It glared back at me from the creeping darkness, angry and accusing.

Please forgive me. Dad's last whispered words to me before he splattered his blood and brains over my new birthday dress.

I shuddered and shoved the cold-stung barrel up under my chin, willing my trembling finger to squeeze the trigger. Like I'd done dozens of times over the past year.

Nothing. The same as every other time I'd tried to imitate dear old dad.

Would he be proud of me? Or ashamed?

I squeezed my eyes closed, strangling the sudden urge to hurl the Colt into the clawing darkness. Instead, I let the hammer down, shoved it back into my shoulder holster, and dropped my face into the stinging snow piling in front of Audrey's headstone.

I sat up when my skin went numb. After wiping the grasping ice from my cheeks, I shook the snow from the pile of dead and frozen daisies I left last month and tossed them away.

A long-slumbering memory stirred at the back of my mind. It woke and glared at me from the darkness. Mom had loved daisies, too. And Audrey had adored our mom. Mommy's little girl. Right?

No guilt this time about that thought, which made me feel even worse.

It'd been twenty years since dear old Mom dumped me on the steps of St. Jude's Parish, six months after Dad's suicide, and drove off without so much as an, 'I'm sorry and good luck with your life,' or a glance into the rearview as her taillights faded into the fog-shrouded morning. She hadn't stuck around. No surprise there, which meant that maybe I'd been Daddy's little girl, after all.

For an instant, I wondered if, after dumping me, she'd been able to move on and find forgiveness. Something I wished I could do. Or perhaps not. During the ten years I had known Mom, she never struck me as the forgiving type.

I turned back to Audrey's empty grave and felt a hollow, lifeless smile twitching across my lips.

And that's when I realized my hope had deserted me.

Try as I might, I couldn't see the faces of the children I'd recovered from the Nether Realm and Otherkind captivity over the past ten years. How many had there been? How many had I snatched back from the demons that had taken me and my sister twenty-five years earlier? And how many kids had I lost because I didn't get to them in time? I used to know. I used to see every one of their faces in my nightmares.

Now though...

I saw nothing. No faces. No names.

Worse. I couldn't care less.

When had I stopped caring?

Dark, ash-laced memories from the past two years fluttered on a stale wind. Had it been when I failed to stop the assassination of Ellis Wynn, my best friend's fiancé? When I'd left Stephanie Brandt for dead in the Nether Realm instead of bringing her back, no matter the cost? Or had it been when the Order of the Four cast me aside after I'd failed to rescue Stephanie Brandt from the Otherkind?

This time, the dead smile came easy. I let the tears stream down my snow-slick cheeks, accepting that they weren't tears of release or freedom. There would never be release. There would never be freedom.

My tears stopped.

Another well gone dry.

I stared into the frigid earth. "I'm sorry," I said, pushing myself to my feet, and wiping the slushy snot from my nose with the back of a cold-numbed hand.

"Happy birthday, sis." I shoved my hands into my coat pockets.

"Wish you could be here for our number thirty. Wish I hadn't deserted you."

I lingered for a moment, dumped the Jack over my dad's grave and squatted to brush the new snow from his headstone with shaking fingers. "And I wish you hadn't blamed yourself for Audrey's disappearance," I said. "It wasn't your fault... It was mine."

I shoved myself to my feet, wondered what kind of special hell God had reserved for me, thoughts of what if, and what might have been flitting like manic sparrows through my mind.

Everything I'd done to recover children I'd done because I hadn't saved my sister. Or was it because I'd saved myself instead? Was there even a difference now?

I didn't know.

A weary voice whispered to me, dredging my muck-smeared, battered and beaten hope from the sewage of despair. Through the dripping desolation, I spied a feeble glimmer. A memory of 'why.' I didn't want other families to go through the same hell mine had. I didn't want them to lose what I'd lost.

I hesitated, realizing there was something more I needed: my twin sister. To hold her in my arms again. Tell her I loved her. And to ask her to forgive me for not keeping my promise.

I needed redemption. An opportunity to make things right.

For me.

For Audrey.

Our dad.

Maybe even for our mom, the unforgiving bitch.

All I had to do was find a way to bring myself to accept it.

Another storm of tears sprang unbidden from my eyes as that stinking dead smile creased my lips again.

My phone rang.

I pulled it out. The name of Father Mike, my onetime guardian and Order of the Four mentor, scrolled across the screen.

My finger hesitated over the Decline button. I didn't have the strength. Not tonight. Maybe never.

I answered the phone.

"Yeah?"

A slight hesitation greeted me. "Where are you?"

I bit back a retort, thought about lying to him. But he'd know the truth. And though I had no problem lying, I couldn't bring myself to lie to him.

"Where the hell do you think I am?"

No answer.

I sighed. "It's Tansy. She's gone again, isn't she?"

A long, stressed silence answered me. That wasn't a good sign. "How long?"

"I'm not sure," he said. "I've been preoccupied—"

Yeah, terminal cancer will do that.

"How long?"

A drawn breath snaked through the phone. "Two, maybe three days."

That meant the trail was already cold.

But there was something he hadn't told me yet. I felt it in the tension squeezing the life from the air. "What else?"

"I found Chaos in her nightstand."

I bit back the curse for his sake.

Chaos was man-made fae-daemon Ebony dust synthesized by a brilliant alchemist named Jonnie Hallows for the Shining Man, an ancient fae-daemon Juzarine Solitary exiled from the Nether Realm and Don of the Otherkind Crime Syndicate in Denver known as the Numen Galére. Chaos promised ecstasy and enlightenment. Instead, it gave sorrow, heartache, and death.

Despite my tongue-lashing and threats of eternal damnation

and suffering, Tansy had gone to see Jonnie Hallows again, and he'd fixed her up, even though he knew what I'd do to him when I found out. Apparently, it was true that stupid is as stupid does.

I tried to unclench my jaw.

Barely seventeen and going on thirty, Tansy thought she knew everything, including that Chaos would keep her sane while she manifested. Perks from being fed a diet of Ebony by the Otherkind bastards that had abducted us and other children.

She'd begun to manifest when she turned thirteen, about the same age I'd been hit.

Father Mike had helped me to accept and control my unnatural abilities and keep me from going all batshit serial killer crazy on everyone, like too many of the Touched did when they manifested.

Tansy hadn't been so lucky. Despite Father Mike's help, her mind was cracking under the strain. And the more her mind cracked, the more desperate she became. Contrary to what the Wannabes believed, being Touched wasn't all that supercalifragilisticexpialidocious.

Unfortunately, most of us cracked like Humpty Dumpty after his fall. Way before the end.

I guess I still did care. Just a little.

It was enough.

Before I could change my mind, I said, "I'll bring her back. Kicking and screaming if I have to."

"You know where to start."

Fae-daemon power crackled and crawled across my skin like a lightning storm.

I wasn't sure if I felt relieved or pissed off.

I peered into the cloying darkness.

Two fae-daemon Otherkind Solitaries wearing fifties-era gangster glamours stood at the edge of the asphalt, the toes of their imaginary wingtips not quite touching the frozen dirt. Muscle from the Shining Man.

I mostly saw through their illusion, and shuddered at the sight, finally understanding the spear tip that had wedged itself between my shoulder blades.

After ten years of hunting and killing these things, you'd think I'd be used to their freaking monstrous Halloween good looks.

"I'll call you back. Got some business to take care of."

I shoved my phone into my jeans pocket, slid my left hand inside my coat where it found my Walther 9mm clinging to my hip.

"Can I help you boys?"

They looked at each other.

"Cassidy Kain," the Solitary on my left said.

"Depends on who's asking."

The one on my right snorted and bared its teeth behind a disdainful smirk. "No one's asking."

For an insane moment, I considered drawing the Walther and ending this impromptu meeting before it started. I stood on mythical hallowed ground, giving me the advantage in the world of unicorns and rainbows. Unfortunately, the Solitary on my left knew about unicorns and rainbows. It stepped onto the dirt path, sneered as it opened its wool overcoat to parade the Juzarine bone dagger strapped to its belt.

Despite the distance separating us, I knew one or both would close that expanse before the Walther cleared its holster. And I didn't fancy having my throat ripped out and being eaten before I brought Tansy home kicking and screaming.

With an exaggerated flourish, I pulled my left hand from my coat, clasped both hands in front of my waist and twitched a smile. "What do you want?"

The Solitary dropped its overcoat closed, inclined its head. "The Shepherd would have words with you."

The title members of the Numen Galére gave to the Shining Man.

I shuddered, resisting the urge to sluice sewage off me.

Fireballs sizzled across my skin. Eyes narrowed, I stared at them, waiting for the punchline.

The punchline never came.

Apparently, Otherkind don't have a sense of humor.

"Tell the Shining Man that it can go screw itself. Use those exact words. No interpretations."

They stiffened, their expressions darkening.

Apparently, they didn't like 'no' for an answer, either.

My fingers twitched as I snaked my hand back inside my coat to the Walther.

Before I could react further, the Otherkind standing on the edge of the path blurred into motion, stood toe-to-toe with me before my next breath rattled from my chest. It wrapped diamond-sharp fingers around my throat and wrenched me into the air, its face contorting into a feral snarl.

Choking, my dangling feet grasping for the frozen earth, I gripped its wrist, used the leverage to twist enough to draw the Walther and with practiced precision, double-tapped two rounds into its chest.

The staccato tap-tap of the sudden explosions reverberated through the snow-deadened air, echoing back from the surrounding trees and buildings.

The ground rushed to greet my dangling feet, jarring me to my knees. The Otherkind staggered away, gasping, clutching at its chest, conflicting expressions of fury and horror contorting its rippling fake human face.

Heaving frosted breath, I reeled back and tried to catch my balance as I brought the Walther up in a shaking hand.

Frozen snow crunched behind me.

I turned.

A granite-hard grip crushed my wrist, twisted my arm until the Walther fell from limp, numb fingers, my bones snap, crackle, and popping.

I screamed, felt myself tossed through the air. I slammed into the frost-covered, snow-littered ground near the edge of the dirt path and at the feet of the Otherkind I'd just shot.

It leered down at me, drew a gun-like object from inside its overcoat, aimed it at my chest.

I tried to pull the Juzarine dagger I kept from its sheath behind my back with my right hand.

I heard a faint pop, followed by the stinging bite of two tiny teeth through my shirt.

And then came the sudden concussion of fifty thousand volts slamming into my body and brain. I twisted and jerked like a landed trout as a banshee shriek tore from my throat. An instant later, two more teeth bit into my left shoulder. Another jolt careened through me, making me dance and lurch like a drunken marionette through the snow and ice. My jaw clenched. I tasted blood as agony seared through my mouth.

I struggled to push myself to my feet, but collapsed instead into a puddle of writhing, boneless flesh.

A deeper shadow fell across my swimming vision, blotting out the jaundice-tinged parking lot lights. I tried to blink away the tsunamis tearing through my eyes, quiet the thunder roaring through my ears. Why wasn't my brain working?

The horrifying visage of the Otherkind I'd double-tapped in the chest filled my fading sight. A rough hand gripped my chin, wrenched my face so that I had to look up into burning crimson eyes.

"You should have said yes," it said.

If I could have done anything besides twitch and buck in agony, I would have torn its throat out.

A third electric blast tore through me. The back of my head slammed into the stone-hard earth.

And then the lights snuffed out.

CHAPTER 2
DANCING WITH THE DEVIL

MY EYES CRACKED OPEN, my body throbbing with a slow, stabbing ache. Spears of light sliced through my blurred vision and dragged a low moan from my throat—one that nearly stilled the quiet, eager buzz swirling around me.

I slumped back in an uncomfortable cedar chair, an unpleasant scent wending its way through my stilted thoughts. I thought I had raised my arm but realized I hadn't. And I couldn't feel my legs. Where the hell were my legs and the entire bottom half of my body? A slow, burning terror rose at the thought that I was only half the girl I'd been.

Grim light shoved its way into my world, pushing away the hazy darkness. I groaned, closed my eyes, and waited for the next train.

A hand smacked the back of my head, jarring my teeth.

I tasted blood, tried to swear, but I couldn't seem to feel my tongue, either.

"Stay awake."

I didn't recognize the voice, but it sounded human and male. A hierodule, a person who had prostituted themself to the Numen

Galére. My stomach clenched, spitting bile up my throat as I imagined apocalyptic tortures for the owner of that mouth. When this
was over, whatever this was, I was going to rip his balls out through
his mouth.

A face wearing a pornographic leer dripping unfulfilled sexual
frustration shoved itself into my clearing vision.

I head-butted him.

I didn't know if I owned the lower half of my body, but most of
my top half still worked.

He fell back and roared, clenching his nose, blood spurting
from between his trembling fingers, eyes blazing as he pulled my
Juzarine dagger from his belt and stumbled toward me.

"You broke my nose."

The dagger rose.

"Enough!"

The dagger's downstroke sputtered to an uncertain stop just
before punching through my left eye and into my brain. He looked
back over his shoulder; the blade poised for a strafing run.

"Pull a weapon in my presence again without my leave, and
your nose will not be the only part of your body broken."

Hesitation. He glanced at me.

I saw the quick calculation, wondered if he would take the
double-dog dare.

Instead, he shoved the dagger into his belt, mumbled a curse,
and threw me a murderous glare, blood streaming down his lips
and chin.

I managed a weak smirk.

"Sorry, babe," I said, my tone stiff and words slurred. "Something must have slipped. Maybe next time."

I winked.

"Leave us."

A well-manicured hand appeared, thrusting a soiled cloth into his shaking hands. He pressed it against his face and slinked around me, staggering into my broken arm on his way past. I gritted my teeth and spat blood, blinked my surroundings into focus through the pain fogging my brain.

The chair I slumped in sat near the center of an oddly shaped room that churned my gut into butter as I looked around.

No windows and walls paneled in antique reclaimed elm.

A thick burgundy carpet shimmered against the baseboards, accented by a fifties-style dark leather couch standing against the wall to my right, framed by two gilded floor lamps casting jaundiced pools of light to either side. A pair of glamoured Solitaries sat on the sofa, legs crossed, wearing black trousers, conservative suit coats, and charcoal pencil ties that gleamed against the starched white, long sleeve shirts in the lamplight.

The wall behind them embraced built-in, overcrowded floor-to-ceiling bookshelves, faded and scratched hardcover book spines glaring back at me from their cramped quarters.

Two dark leather office chairs, first-cousins to the couch, conversed around a small round elm table to my left. An Irish-cut crystal decanter set with a tray and paired glasses preened on the tabletop. A lackluster yellow liquid glowed from the carafe, kaleidoscopic light swimming through the crystal, causing my stomach to lurch.

I closed my eyes, tried to lick chapped and blood-specked lips to calm the roiling.

The agitation settled.

I opened my eyes, focused on the lumbering battleship-sized scarred oak desk glaring at me from the front of the chamber. Behind it, where a dominating picture-framed window should have looked out into a rose garden, a hand-drawn map of nineteenth-century Denver hung from the antique elm paneling.

The Shining Man sat behind the wooden monstrosity. It

leaned forward, elbows planted on the surface to either side of a blotter pad, fingers steepled below an obscured squared and chiseled chin. Its dark fathomless eyes probed my face from a blue star-bright glamour that rolled and shifted with my stuttering heartbeat. What lay beneath reminded me of all the sexiest men alive covers since time began, poured into one delectable meal.

An enchantment stuffed inside an illusion crammed into a phantasm.

I must have gawked.

It smiled.

I snapped my jaw shut.

Its bottomless gaze flitted to my left.

A grim-faced Otherkind wearing a tattered forties gangster film-era charm, detached itself from the wall and strode out of my peripheral vision. The faint whoosh and click of an opening and closing door followed.

I ordered the sharp throb in the front of my skull to take a vacation. It ignored me.

"My apologies... for your treatment. But a measure of firmness was required. What went beyond, however..."

The Shining Man's silken tenor continued to caress my mind. I tried to shove it aside, but it remained for a moment longer than appropriate before sliding away on its own.

"That..." it gestured toward the door behind me with a negligent hand. "Will never trouble you again."

My lips parted to utter my appreciation.

Its smile returned. Full of intent, but bored. As if my reaction was natural. The circle of life. Predator to prey.

"Why can't I move?" I asked, my voice cracking as I bit back the sudden spearing pain in my arm and shoulder.

"My apologies once more," it said, its tone tinged with sincerity. "You are injured. Something we must rectify if you are to be of use to me." It repeated the negligent gesture.

The door in the back of the room opened, closed with the same click of finality. Someone stood behind me. Waiting.

A familiar scent touched me.

The Shining Man nodded.

A breath of air caressed the side of my face.

A shadow blanketed me, blocking my view of the Shining Man and the Otherkind map of Denver hanging from the wall. My loopy gaze focused on the face of a woman I recognized. She was in her late thirties or early forties. I could never remember her age. Her shoulder-length wavy reddish-black hair was pulled back into a low ponytail, and her intent hazel eyes swirled with emerald green as they claimed my gaze. She had a slender Roman nose, puckered lips, and thin, sunken cheeks set into a light bronze complexion. A scar scampered from her right temple to the bottom of the razor-edged chin. My gift to her on the night of my excommunication.

I sucked in a sudden breath. Andie Gosselin hadn't changed in the year since I gave her that scar. I wondered how much I had changed. Or if she'd notice.

She spared me a cold, emotionless smile, glanced down with clinical detachment, opened a bag squatting at her feet.

"Andie? What the hell?"

She didn't respond. Instead, she pulled out a 1cc syringe glowing dusky and dark in the shifting rainbow light.

I tensed, found the Shining Man ogling me over Andie's shoulder. It smiled back at me through its starlit glamour, mimicking a ten-year-old serial killer in training, waiting to see what happened when he snapped the wings off a living bird.

"Miss Gosselin is now part of my organization." It paused, caught me in the iridescent glow of its eyes. "After the unfortunate events of last year, she found herself in need of... protection. And I am always interested in her type of talent."

I slapped my gaze back to Andie. She stared at the syringe, turned her eyes on me, and grimaced.

Ebony, not Chaos. Something I never wanted floating through my blood again. Distorted and obscene memories flooded my mind, my addiction and the corrosion of my soul, my near miss with fae-daemon possession and the corruption of my Essence. Panic exploded.

I tried to push myself through the back of the chair. My panicked gaze flicked toward the Shining Man. It still wore that damned ten-year-old psycho-kid smile.

"We bound you with Gossamer. For your safety... of course."

"Bullshit." I looked up at her. "Andie, please. You're a doctor. A damned surgeon. You know what that does to us... to me."

Her eyes found mine. What I saw sucked out the warmth.

"I was," she said. "A doctor. A surgeon." Her tone dripped venom. "Before you." Hesitation. "I don't have a choice." She snatched a covert glance over her shoulder. "It's what I owe. Thanks to you." She paused, her expression rueful for an instant. "I'm sorry."

Not sorry enough.

"While your recuperative abilities are impressive, I cannot wait. I need you whole and hail. Now. Not in a week."

Andie glanced at the Shining Man. It nodded. She looked down at me, her face sullen.

I tried again to shove my way through the back of my chair, my fae-daemon chains tightening, slicing through my exposed flesh. Blood welled from the cuts.

She tied off my right arm, flicked her finger against the vein, made it pucker with a lover's anticipation. Swabbed it. Injected the Ebony in a single, swift, efficient motion.

A tingling sensation sparked inside my skin, grew into a long slow burn that bubbled the blood in my veins into steam.

Someone shrieked.

I realized it was me.

The world went black.

A football-length field of waist-high grass danced along the bottom of the low rise on which Stephanie Brandt and I stood. A ragged line of pine, fir, and spruce marched across the other side, their spidery branches grasping at the cloudless, deep blue sky. A warm breeze teased at the loose ends of my hair that escaped from beneath my weather-worn, chocolate-brown leather Fedora.

Juzarine Chaos Magic rode the back of the fitful, scented wind, reminding my fogged mind that what I stared at was an illusion and that far more dangerous phantasmagoria waited for us at the bottom of the hill.

The bouquet tugged at me, drew me in, pulled memories of home and peace from the vapor of wished forgetfulness.

"Cassidy?"

The Juniper perfumed reminiscences stuttered and died.

Stephanie stared up at me, her thin, faded cotton blouse and short denim skirt torn, ragged, and filth-grimed. Blood and slime splattered her face, bare arms, and legs. I didn't want to glance down at her feet. Worse had clumped into her close-cropped raven black hair that I regretted having to chop off when I'd found her in her Nether Realm cage.

But the tangles and mats would have snagged in the brambles, brush, and low-hanging branches during our escape from her prison.

I returned her stare and frowned.

Ebony flakes swirled through her once bright blue eyes, accentuating the growing madness buried underneath.

"Do we have to go down there?"

I glanced down at the field of death waiting for us at the base of the rise and understood her terror. I wished I could lie to her and tell her that the worst was over. That crossing the clearing would be easy-peasy lemon squeezy. But it had taken too long to reach this summit. And a swarm of Juzarine monsters waited for us, hidden below in the illusory grass.

I sensed them. A slow throbbing pain scraped at the back of my neck that crawled into my head and tore my brain inside out from its roots.

I pursed my lips. "Stay close. And don't stop. For anything." I looked at her. "Got it?"

"Cassidy?"

"Yes?"

"Why did you kill us?"

I woke with a start.

My vision swam. Thunder pounded my temples. Lightning flashed, and everything hurt like hell. I wanted to rip someone's throat out. And then I remembered.

I shot to my feet, free, wobbled, and fell into my chair with a solid thud that jarred my teeth into the back of my skull. Sweat ran down from my hair, dripping uncaringly into my eyes. I tried to blink out the stinging sludge, used the back of my left hand to swipe it out of my eyes, and paused. My left hand.

The rage rose, pounded against my chest, an alien desperate to be let loose to commit murder and mayhem.

I shoved myself up again.

Rough hands slapped down on my shoulders, shoved me down into the chair, held me in place, the sweat continuing to drip into my eyes and run down the sides of my face. I bit the inside of my cheek, allowing the sudden stinging pain to ground my mind and my thoughts. At least until I could get loose and rip out the Shining Man's throat.

Andie had vanished.

The Shining Man remained seated behind its desk. Forties film Gangster Guy stood beside it, hands clasped at its waist. My Juzarine dagger lay obediently on the ink blotter. The Shining Man looked entranced by it, but when it glanced up, its gaze was less than cordial.

It gestured toward the dagger. "How did you come by this?"

The question was innocent, but its tone held the promise of endless torture and agonizing death.

"A souvenir."

"Of course." It leaned back in its leather office chair, the springs silent. "I should have you flayed and staked out in the noonday Nether Realm sun for this." It paused. "But I have immediate need of you and the talents that allowed you to claim your... memento."

Its intent and unwavering gaze slid its own scalpel-thin blade between my ribs to prick my heart. "Your punishment for this shall have to wait until our business is concluded."

"Go screw yourself."

"So I have been told."

"Then no."

It narrowed its eyes and leaned forward, clasping its hands together just beyond the touch of the dagger. "You believe you have a choice in this matter." It nodded toward Forties film Gangster Guy. The Solitary stepped forward, lifted the dagger from the Shining Man's desk and slid it into a leather sheath. Stepped back. "You do not."

"I do not?"

"No."

I smiled, despite the iron hands restraining me and the Ebony-induced rage boiling my blood. "There's always a choice," I said. "And I choose not to be your bitch."

"And yet you do not know what being 'my bitch' would entail."

"Doesn't matter."

"No?"

"No."

It arched a brow, the smile touching its lips holding icy amusement. "Then perhaps I have offered you the incorrect choice."

It flicked its right hand.

The door behind me opened. Closed. I tried to look over my shoulder and was reminded by a sudden slap along the side of my head that what was coming was supposed to be a surprise.

Silence squeezed the room.

The Shining Man remained seated, leaning forward as I had first seen it; elbows on the desk, fingers steepled beneath its chin. The deadpan stare pinned me to my chair more effectively than the vise-like hands anchored to my shoulders. The glamour continued to tornado around it, blurring the horrific creature within.

I'd heard the stories sputtered about Juzarine Solitaries by Order of the Four archivists. Powerful. Ancient. Their appearance hideous and angelic. And rare in the human world. None had been reported for two centuries. And then the Shining Man had appeared one hundred years ago, organizing the other disenfranchised Otherkind into a Mafia-like syndicate and growing it into a criminal empire.

The silence stretched my patience to the breaking point. I needed to get out of the lion's den, burn off the Ebony bubbling in my blood. It didn't matter that my left arm was now whole. Ebony and I shared an unhealthy history; one I didn't need or want to repeat.

I knew my next words were ill-advised, but I didn't care.

"Can we get on with it? I have to be somewhere."

The Shining Man's smile twitched wider for an instant.

"Impatience will be your death one day," it said. "Perhaps sooner than even you might expect. Or suspect."

"So said my mom twenty years ago. Just before she dumped me on the steps of St. Jude's Parish and left to get a pint and a fix. She never came back. Do you want to be Mom now?"

"As intriguing as that may be, I do not. I do, however, believe I understand why your mother abdicated her parental responsibilities."

That stung more than I thought it would.

The Shining Man shackled me with its eyes. They glowed the color of iridescent honey behind its starlit glamour. Not from Ebony, but from pure power. I shivered, trying to look away.

"You spoke earlier of choice," it said, its tone silken. Hypnotic.

I caught myself falling into that bright burning chasm, crawled back into my *real* world. If anything in my world could be called *real*.

I licked my lips, used their sandpaper scrape to steady my shivering nerves, felt the hammer poised and waiting to drop, most likely through my soul. And there wasn't a damned thing I could do about it.

What the hell had I gotten myself into? 'Tell the Shining Man to go screw himself?' Girl, you've gotta get some help with your anger management issues.

"I must confess to a certain interest in how humans make life-altering choices," it said. "How far they will go. What lines they will cross. How they face and make those inevitable choices." It smiled, its expression cold, empty of compassion and empathy. It tapped the side of its head. "What drives those choices? Desperation? Logic? Calculation? Greed? Sacrifice? Sense of family? Honor? All of them? None of them?"

It continued to stare.

I swallowed past the gobbet growing in the back of my throat. "Sounds like you need a new hobby," I said, surprised that my voice sounded steady in my own ears.

The Shining Man chuckled, the sound humorless. Deep. Dark. Deadly. "Perhaps."

It stood, buttoning its black silken coat and slithered snake-like past its battleship desk, settling its lean bulk against the desk's front edge. Arms and ankles crossed.

Standing, gazing down at me from its fathomless eyes, it seemed taller than I had thought. Larger. Stronger. For an instant, I saw through the affectations into the depths where a human soul should live, and I saw absolute emptiness. A true black hole, one that sucked in and destroyed everything that came too close.

I felt the panic rise, tried to stand, but the hands clamping me down were too strong. I glanced at it, my powerlessness an amusing anecdote reflected from the dead, soulless eyes.

"Tell me, Miss Kain. Is there a limit to what you will do?" It lifted a brow. "Is there a line you will not cross?"

"What the hell? What are you talking about?"

A light flashed through its iridescent eyes. The smile twitched wider, slid behind the mask. "Please do not dissemble. It is unbecoming. Especially from someone of your unique... nature." It paused. "You know exactly what I am talking about."

I did.

Satisfaction slithered across its face.

It nodded toward the back of the room. The motion compact. Economical. Authoritative.

The door behind me opened. I heard the rustle of bodies, the rattling clank of bone chains. A muted cry answered by the crack of an open-handed slap. Silence.

I tried to wrench free from the hands pinning into the chair. A razor-edged, rough-hewn hand wrapped steel fingers around my jaw, doused my face with a hot, fetid stench. I held my breath, rammed back the sputtering gags. A barbed-wire stubbled face touched my cheek, scoring stinging scratches across my skin.

Boil-blistered lips grazed my ear, uttered, "Try to move again and you shall know true agony."

I flicked my gaze to the Shining Man. It watched me, its eyes sucking everything into the abyss.

It rose to its full height, towering over me from the distance separating us. I felt small. Insignificant. A momentary passing interest.

The Shining Man reached out, snatched the arm of a tattered, hooded, and struggling form, dragged it over. It slapped the shrouded face with the back of a powerful hand, shook it hard enough to rattle teeth. The body went slack in its grasp.

Its eyes flashed with sinister delight as it shoved the body to its knees, grasped the top of the hood in its fist, hammered me with its gaze.

"Miss Kain," the Shining Man said, its tone flat, and unemotional. "Please meet your next line to cross."

CHAPTER 3
IMPOSSIBLE CHOICES

HE YANKED OFF THE HOOD. Tossed it to the floor.

I gasped.

The hands holding me down vanished. I didn't dare move.

Tansy stared at me from bruised and bloodied eyes. Her left eye, swollen closed, glared accusingly. Dried blood crusted below her broken nose, forming a grotesque mustache above her puffy, split upper lip. More blood dribbled down her chin, stained her neck and the ragged torn collar of her T-shirt. Struggling breaths wheezed from her swollen mouth, rattled through her chest. Enraged bruises peeked through jagged tears in her fouled shirt.

What the hell?

Ebony-fueled rage rocketed me from my chair. I took a step, crashed to my knees, struggled to breathe. My mind screamed for me to move, to rip the Shining Man's heart from its chest and shove it down its throat. Piece by bloody piece.

But I couldn't budge.

A Compulsion.

My eyes found the Shining Man. It stared at me, its face masked behind that blistering multi-layered glamour, that cursed ten-year-old serial killer in training peeking through the veil, glinting with malevolent glee.

It flicked a finger.

Rustling movements converged on me. Hands grasped my arms, hauled me into the chair, vanished as quickly as they appeared. I summoned my fury, but it refused to appear, content to lie dormant and impotent, forcing me to swivel my nuclear missile glares from Tansy to the Shining Man and back.

It snorted, twitching an emotionless smile as it kneeled beside her, clenching long, sinewy fingers around her chin, compelling her to gaze into its burning demon eyes.

It examined her, licked the fingers of its free hand, and used them to smooth down tangled and clotted strawberry-blonde hair from her puffy and bloodshot eyes.

"What do you think, Miss Kain?" It stood, pulled a silk handkerchief from its suit coat pocket, and wiped its hands clean on the fabric before dropping it in front of Tansy. She winced. "What would you be willing to do? How far would you go? What line would you cross... for her?"

A low, feral growl boiled up from the pit of my stomach. My body quivered, like a rabid dog straining at the end of its leash, laser-focused on the wolf, and ready to rip its throat out.

"Release me and I'll show you just how far I'm willing to go." I strained against the Compulsion, felt my muscles begin to tear under the stress. I fell back, my strength spent, sweat dripping into my eyes.

It waved away my threat with nonchalant indifference and slid behind its desk.

"I am not responsible for her injuries," it said. "You can thank our dear friend Jonnie Hallows for those." A dead smile creased its mouth. "Genius does have its price, unfortunately." It glanced at Tansy, calculation ticking through its eyes. "I did, however, rescue her. Which means she owes me a blood debt." A dramatic pause. "Her soul."

My boiling blood froze.

"Tansy?" My voice quivered barely above a whisper. Stone-cold silence answered me. I licked my lips. "Baby Bear?"

She looked up. A lone tear rolled from the corner of her right eye.

I snapped my gaze back to the Shining Man. Did my best to hammer it with my rage. Got nothing, except for bored amusement.

"What do you want?"

It exhaled. A frustrated parent dealing with a recalcitrant child who just didn't seem to get it. No matter how many times she screwed up. "Is it not obvious?"

I glared at it. My jaw clenched, every muscle straining against the enchantment.

More sweat dripped into my eyes.

"I wish you to fail."

That punched the wind out of my sails.

I sank down, my strength sucked dry, struggling for breath that refused to come. "What?" I managed in a trembling voice.

That did amuse it.

"Your ultimate choice. The line you must decide to cross," it said. "The soul of this girl wagered against your own. To see what you will sacrifice to save her. Or yourself. Either way, I win."

"You're insane."

"Perhaps." It glanced past me. "But as much as I enjoy your company, time begins to run against you."

It raised a hand.

The Compulsion vanished.

I shot from the chair, tumbled to my hands and knees, heaved my guts out onto the floor. I wiped my mouth with the back of a trembling hand, glaring at the Shining Man from beneath my brows. It returned my stare, a bemused smile twitching the corners of its slender lips.

It stood, buttoned its coat. "A rogue from your Commandery has bargained with a Juzarine witch for a Medusa Mirror, which they have used to create a Daemonrie Chimera." It paused, watching for my reaction, a glint of humor flashing behind its eyes. "Find and destroy the Chimera, bring me the head of the rogue." It nodded toward the back of the room.

I heard the click and soft swoosh of an opening door.

"You have forty-eight hours."

It gestured to Forties Film Gangster Guy. "Please escort the two Miss Kains to their vehicle. And ensure that no other harm befalls them."

"It's Harper," Tansy said into the space separating us.

The Shining Man paused. "Yes?"

She twisted her head to look up over her shoulder, gazed at it from where she slumped on the floor. "My name is Harper." She turned back, slapping me with a knife-edged glare. "Not Kain."

The Shining Man hit me with its own gaze. "Yes. So, it is." It swept past us and out of the room, pulling the strangled starlight with it. The door clicked shut.

Forties Film Gangster Guy flicked a quick nod. Rough hands yanked me and Tansy from the floor, shoved hoods over our heads, and dragged us away.

CHAPTER 4
POP GOES THE WEASEL

JESSIE RELAXED QUIETLY in a ramshackle plastic dollar store chair, the best Jonnie Hallows used to furnish his condo, a sprawling one-bedroom penthouse perched at the top of downtown Denver's newest trendy high-rise apartment building.

Typical of Jonnie to live in luxury, but cheap out on the guest furnishings.

She sat with her legs crossed, hands clasped loosely in her lap. Jonnie paced the length of his darkened living room, weaving his way through the squad of four Chasseurs scattered around the furniture. He shoved his hands into the depths of the pockets of his custom-tailored jeans, muttering unintelligible words, eyes meandering through the gloom.

He was Jessie's perfect pawn, caught between the irresistible force of the Shining Man and the immoveable Francisco Navarro, Master of the Denver Commandery, was now pinned beneath the crushing weight of Cassidy Kain and her unslakable thirst for vengeance for what Jonnie had done to Tansy. Just one more small task to complete; make sure her pawn didn't rabbit, but stayed put, motionless and paralyzed by fear, believing that if he didn't move, he'd remain invisible to the blood-hungry predators turning their eyes toward him.

Jessie thought of Tansy and Stephanie Brandt, the chimera she'd created from them. Alastair Cleary and the Shining Man. Francisco Navarro. And Cassidy. Then she wondered if Jonnie suspected the perfect storm she'd trapped him in and what was coming for him.

Jonnie stopped, pulled a trembling hand from his pocket, slicked down greased, sweat-laden hair, slid it back in. He noticed Peter Oliver peeking out around the corner of the penthouse IMAX-sized window past the edge of the gray blackout curtain, his right hand straddling the butt of his sidearm, trigger finger nervously tapping the side of his holster. Jonnie gulped a bucket of air, swung an unnerved gaze toward Jessie.

"Peter," she said.

"What?"

"We're twenty-five floors up. Sit down, please." She indicated Jonnie as he stalked past her. "You're making Jonnie nervous."

Peter dropped the curtain's edge, turned a sidelong look toward Jonnie. He shook his head, cast one last recalcitrant glare out the window before sliding behind a ratty, threadbare beige and white thrift store couch, and crossed his arms.

Jessie watched Jonnie trudge another lap past her and sighed. "Jonnie."

He stopped, tossing a terrified glare at her.

"You called me, remember?"

"You have to get me out of here," he said, his voice cracking. "She knows."

"Who's she, Jonnie? And what does she know?"

"Kain," he said, his voice climbing an octave. "Tansy, she was here when Cleary came to collect the Shining Man's cut," his words trailed away, slid off the edge of the cliff, splattering against the rocks below.

"And where is Tansy now?"

"Cleary took her, would have taken her to the Shining Man then told Howe that he'd found Tansy here. "Oh god, Kain knows what I did."

"Calm down. Sit," she said.

He hesitated, tensed, ready to bolt.

Her patience died.

Standing, Jessie closed the distance to Jonnie in two swift, smooth steps. Backhanded him. His head snapped to the side, blood springing from his split lip. "I. Said. Sit."

He scurried away from her, scrambled into the seat she'd abandoned, stared at her, wide-eyed and frozen. As if she couldn't see him if he didn't move.

She leaned over him, planted her hands on the chair arms, and shoved her face into his personal space, trapping him where he sat. "What *did* you do?"

"You need to protect me," he said, whining. "Put me into protective custody. Get me out of Denver. Before Kain—"

She raised her hand.

He shrank back, cowering, eyes glazed, wild, and deer-like in the headlight glare of her anger.

"What. The. Hell. Did. You. Do?"

"I—" He swallowed hard, his Adam's apple jogging up and down his throat. Sweat glistened from his forehead, reflecting the prancing firelight. "Tansy...she showed up at my door. High on Ebony. I—" He stuttered to a stop, licked his lips, doe eyes darting left and right, anywhere she wasn't. Unease greased his face. "How'd she get Ebony?"

Jessie leaned in closer, strangling her disgust. "Focus," she said. "Tansy was here."

He nodded, shaking, apprehension galloping through his eyes, his throat jumping rope. "She wanted more. Said she could pay, but—"

"But you wanted a different currency," Jessie said, her voice drenched with lethal menace. "You saw an opportunity and you decided to take it, didn't you?" She brushed his cheek with her fingers. "And she asked for it, didn't she? All jacked up on Ebony, flaunting her body. She practically begged you for it, didn't she?"

Terror swam over his weasel face.

"You tried to rape her, didn't you? And when she fought back, you beat the crap out of her."

His choked silence confirmed what she'd wanted to happen. The one thing that would draw Cassidy out, force her to defend, protect, and avenge the only person alive she cared anything about other than Father Mike.

"You're a stupid, perverted prick," she said.

He dropped his gaze, stared at his small spindly hands.

Jessie shoved herself up, drew her sidearm, pressed the muzzle against the center of his forehead. "Tell me why I shouldn't blow your brains out now."

"Jessie?"

Jonnie's eyes snapped up, focused on the source of the voice.

Jessie watched Peter slide out from behind the couch, heard the hard click from his holster as he drew his weapon. "Stay out of this."

"I won't—"

"You won't what?" she said. "Allow me to end this perverted asshole?" She flicked her gaze to the pistol at his side, looked at him, saw the uncertain question wrestling across his face.

Straightening, she holstered her sidearm, reached down and pulled Jonnie to his feet by his shirt collar. "Be glad you have friends here," she said as she dropped him down into the chair.

He slammed into the seat, huffed out a loud, hard breath, his eyes wide with uncertainty and terror. "W...what about my protection?"

She ignored him. "Are you sure Cleary took Tansy to the Shining Man and not back to Father Mike?

Silence.

Jonnie scanned the room, looked at Peter, his expression questioning, imploring.

Jessie leaned down, filling his world with her fury. "Don't look at him," she said. "He can't help you. Look at me."

He focused on her eyes, wilting under her gaze. He dug a hand into his jeans pocket, pulled out a wadded-up cloth, pressed it to his forehead. "I need a drink."

Jessie slapped him. "Answer the question."

"Yes."

She grinned, patted his cheek. "Get our boy something to drink," she said. "Something strong and smooth that'll help him grow a pair."

A hand shoved a glass filled with a colorless liquid at him. He wrapped his hands around it, almost dumped it in his lap before sucking it down.

"Feeling better?"

He nodded.

Jessie ripped the empty glass from his grasp, held it for a moment before handing it off. She smiled at him. "That wasn't so hard, now was it?"

He shook his head.

"Good boy." She sniffed, wrinkled her nose, looked down at his pants where a wet spot spread over his crotch and the hard plastic seat beneath. "Did you pee yourself, Jonnie?"

Horror spread across his face, chased by a sudden flash of color.

Shaking her head in disgust, Jessie made her way to the kitchen sink. She grabbed a towel and walked it back. Threw it into Jonnie's face. "Clean yourself up," she said. "You stink." She watched him gingerly blot at the soggy spot between his legs then wipe up the excess pooling in the seat beneath him.

She wondered what the Shining Man saw in him.

A sheep?

A tool to be used and controlled, thrown away when it outlived its usefulness?

A toy to be played with until it no longer entertained?

It certainly wasn't because of his winning personality or witty table conversation. The Otherkind were perverted in their own amoral way, but Jonnie Hallows was a vile, degenerate piece of crap, engaging in activities that would make a Juzarine blush.

But he was also the best damned alchemist she'd ever seen. An artistic savant. And the only human she knew of who'd cracked the mystery of Ebony. Jonnie Hallows was a maestro, and his synthetic Ebony was his greatest symphony.

Losing her patience, she motioned to the closest Chasseur. "Take Jonnie to his room." Without waiting for a response, she dismissed him as if he were an annoying mosquito she'd decided not to crush into paste.

A pair of hands hauled Jonnie from the chair and dragged him toward his bedroom, blubbering, tears crawling down his stubbled face, snot draining sewage-like from his alcohol-reddened nose.

For an instant, Jessie caught a whiff of something fouler as he passed by. The stench followed him, circling like carrion crows waiting for their next feast. She glanced at Peter. He stared at her from the shadows, shrugged, his expression neutral, as if he truly didn't care what happened next. Hopefully, he didn't. His continuous moral dilemmas were wearing thin.

Jessie smiled. Cassidy would be taking Tansy back to St. Jude's and Father Mike by now, trapped in the Shining Man's perverted conundrum. She'd baited the trap. Now it just needed to be sprung.

An image of Navarro rose unbidden in her mind, his narcissistic and condescending manner, his hypocritical attitude toward Order rules, the way he bent, even broke them when it suited his own needs and desires, and the way he enforced them, often with deadly consequences, when he decided to bring a wayward sheep back into the fold.

Like herself.

She thought of Ellis Wynn and their last night together before Navarro had dispatched Cassidy and Peter to remind her of the consequences for rebellion and disorder. A twinge of grief made her clench her fists as she fought down the pain and rage torpedoing through her chest.

The moment passed.

Cool detachment replaced the anger and heartbreak, settling her mind.

At his bedroom doorway, Jonnie managed to shake himself free of the Chasseur. "You need to protect me from Kain."

"I don't protect rapists."

He staggered back a step, his face pale. "But—"

She sighed. "I'll post someone on the street, discreetly. After the crap you pulled it's the best you'll get."

"And if she gets past them?"

She nodded toward the Chasseur beside Jonnie. "Give Jonnie your sidearm."

Jonnie took the offered pistol, stared at it as if it might chew his arm off, and looked up.

"When she comes, lock yourself in your bedroom and hide. Then pray she doesn't come in after you." She nodded at the

Chasseur, turned as he dragged Jonnie into his bedroom, and slammed the door closed behind them.

Looking at Peter, she said, "Make the arrangements." Without waiting for his response, she snatched up her coat and gloves, stopped beside him. "Nicely played."

He nodded. "It's easy when you're dealing with a piece of crap like Jonnie."

She touched his cheek, grinned when he flinched from her touch. "Make sure Jonnie sees our man on the street. After he's satisfied and feels safe, pull him."

She let herself out, wrapped herself in quiet, subtle power and embraced the first contentment she'd felt since Cassidy had murdered Ellis Wynn almost three years ago.

CHAPTER 5
NOT SISTERS

I CLENCHED THE STEERING WHEEL, urging the Bronco through streets thick with snow from the night's storm; the morning sun was not quite willing to slip from its warm bed to light the ashen sky and begin a new day. Dark, vacant storefronts, clutched in the embrace of the early dawn, glowered as we drove past, the buildings leaning forward into the road. Grasping and claustrophobic.

Traffic was thankfully sparse. I didn't have the patience for the normal morning slush hour. Would've probably run someone off the road. And cheered.

My phone lay still and silent beside me. No messages from Father Mike responding to my call that I had Tansy, and we were on our way to St. Jude's. I glanced at Tansy. She wore her silence like plate mail; buttoned up and girded for war, arms crossed defensively across her chest, staring forward and unmoving.

She wore an old pair of mirrored aviator sunglasses I'd scrounged from the back of the Bronco that mostly hid her bruised and swollen eyes, though I didn't see how she tolerated the eyewear over her broken nose. The leather bomber jacket I'd also scrounged hid the bruises tattooing her arms. At least until we got to St. Jude's, when she'd throw them back at me. The only things I couldn't hide were the bruises around her mouth and that damned split upper lip.

The Ebony bubbling in her veins would help heal the physical injuries; in a few days, no one would be the wiser. It was the psychological effects of the Dust and the emotional wounds from her beating that worried me. Jonnie had really worked her over.

I'd take care of the pissant. On the sly. Because if Father Mike knew... well, he was a priest before he was the avenging angel parent. But in this case... maybe not. Regardless, I didn't want him involved more than he already would be.

I watched her, trying to imagine the thoughts flitting through her mind.

Every Touched manifested differently. The lucky few barely recognized they'd changed. Most, though, went psychotic serial killer batshit crazy and had to be put down. Been there. Done that. More than I cared to remember.

Me? I fell somewhere in the middle. Yeah, I had my issues. More homicidal than not, but I'd been fortunate. Father Mike had been there, whether I'd wanted him or not. And with his some-times-tough love and compassionate help, I'd managed to sort of make it through the worst of it.

Tansy came closer to the psychotic serial killer batshit crazy side but not so close that she couldn't come through it with her mind intact and a partial moral compass, however small. At least, that's what Father Mike hoped. Unfortunately, you never really knew until the deed was done.

Then there was Francisco Navarro, Master of the Four for the Denver Commandery.

So far, Father Mike had hidden Tansy's instability from Navarro.

But after last night?

If Navarro hadn't known that Tansy was coming apart, he'd know now, which meant that he'd come for her. And without Father Mike to protect her, Tansy was burnt toast.

Turned out terminal cancer was worse than a bitch.

So far, we'd hidden his decline from Tansy, thought we'd have time to ensure she'd stay off the radar and partially sane.

I guess the rotting elephant corpse in the room had other plans.

Tansy had to have learned about Father Mike's condition. She'd said nothing, but her scared-witless attitude over the past six months screamed otherwise. And though she acted the part of a rebellious seventeen-year-old daughter, she idolized Father Mike.

I had too. Still did, though no one would catch me admitting it. Especially to Father Mike.

He was Tansy's rock. And when he was gone, I didn't know how I would take care of her. Not that Tansy wanted me to.

Father Mike had his solution: Alastair Cleary. I disagreed. I'd been forced by Navarro into that wood chipper known as Alastair Cleary but believed that I was smarter and tougher than all the other girls he'd seduced before me, thought I could tame him. I'd run back to Father Mike two years later, tail between my legs, my dignity and pride shredded, had slammed that door closed behind me. Locked, bolted, and welded shut so that it couldn't be opened again. Ever.

After ten years, those emotional scars still bled when pricked. No closure there. If there was such a thing.

I wanted to save Tansy from that and putting her under that mentorship would become nuclear weapons deadly. For both mentor and mentee.

Our alternatives for keeping Tansy safe had quickly evaporated after my excommunication from the Denver Commandery and the Order of the Four. Added to that were the other bridges I'd incinerated afterwards.

I couldn't mentor her. I'd tried but didn't have the temperament or the patience. Neither did she, at least not with me.

There had been another alternative. The only and last person in the Denver Commandery I could have trusted to help me take care of Tansy when Father Mike died. But we'd firebombed that bridge in a firestorm that made the burning of Atlanta during the Civil War look like a toddler's playdate. Did I mention I was excommunicated?

Which led me back to that door I'd welded shut and swore I'd never open again.

I shuddered as the Ebony Andie had shot into my veins sloughed from my blood, pulling the frenzied high with it. I should have been elated that I'd survived mentally intact. Instead, I just felt weary.

My hands relaxed on the steering wheel. I settled a little easier into my seat, my nerves less on edge, my brain no longer screaming with total insanity.

I chanced another covert glance at Tansy, feeling suddenly like a mother hen. Wondered when that had happened. I'd never had the chance with my twin sister, Audrey; another wound that would never heal.

People who told you 'time heals all wounds' didn't know what they were talking about. Time might lessen the sting, but most wounds just scarred over, and were always there, lurking beneath the facade of well-adjusted happiness, ready to be torn open again at the slightest provocation.

Audrey was my worst failure, a wound that ran too deep ever to heal or scar. It simply bled.

Tansy was my first success. Something that should have blessed both of us with pride and gratefulness instead of the constant Biblical warfare. Yet, despite the challenges thunder-storming through our relationship, I considered Tansy as much a sister as I did Audrey.

Which meant I would do *anything* to protect her.

For an instant, I pictured the Shining Man gleaming with plea-sure at my admission.

"What?"

Tansy's sudden question startled me. Had I been staring at her?

I over corrected, and the Bronco fishtailed through the snow and ice packing the road.

"What the hell, Tans?"

"I didn't ask you to come after me."

"And I didn't ask to get tased into unconsciousness, dragged in front of the Shining Man, and extorted into eliminating a Daemonrie Chimera and killing its maker to save your butt."

I glared at her. She continued to stare forward, her eyes hidden behind the aviator glasses, sucking her lower lip between her teeth and thoughtlessly chewing on it despite the pain flinching through her cheeks.

"Father Mike found a nickel bag of Chaos in your nightstand," I said.

She cringed, grew more rigid in her seat, but didn't look at me or otherwise acknowledge that she'd heard me.

"Damn it, Tans," I said, throwing the full weight of my frustra-tion and parental anger at her. "What the hell were you thinking?" I paused, glanced at her to see if anything I was flinging across the cab at her was making an impression. "Or were you thinking at all?"

I finally shoved her over the precipice.

She looked at me, and though I couldn't see her eyes behind

the lenses of the aviator glasses, I recognized the fiery rage clenching her expression. If looks could kill.

"He had no right going through my things like that," she said, her voice edged with lethal intent.

I paused, just managed to throw back my not so compassionate retort, said instead, "You went missing. Again. And he had no idea where you'd gone. What the hell did you expect him to do?"

"He worries too much."

"It's his job, Tans."

"He's not my dad."

Crap, not this again. "Fine, Father Mike isn't your dad. He didn't knock up your mom, wasn't there for the first seven years of your blissfully unhappy childhood. Neither was the man you called *dad*. Father Mike is here now, though. And he's been here ever since your loving and caring *mother* dumped you on his doorstep."

"After you brought back her damaged little girl."

That I knew something about.

"You should have left me there after you found me. Or killed me."

"Don't!"

"Like Stephanie Brandt."

I jerked the wheel to the right, cut off a Mercedes crawling through the snow and ice, as well as a slightly more confident Land Rover. The Bronco fishtail-skidded up over the curb and across an unplowed sidewalk into an empty, snow-packed parking lot, the studs trying to bite through the ice buried beneath last night's new snow. We came to an abrupt stop when the Bronco's grill French kissed a snow pile from an earlier storm left in the middle of the lot by a plow.

"You don't have the right!" I glowered at her.

"Don't I? I never asked for this. Any of it." She crossed her arms and stared out the passenger window.

"And you think I did? You think I woke up on my fifth birthday and told my twin sister that we should go into the woods and get abducted and abused by a bunch of Otherkind demons? You think that when I escaped and had to leave her there, that when I got back, I decided to eat birthday cake, open my presents, play, and that at the end the day tell our mom and dad, 'oh, by the way, Audrey isn't coming home. Ever?' You think I ate popcorn and drank pop in the front row while I watched my dad blow his brains out five years later? And now you have the nerve to bring up Stephanie Brandt?"

I clenched my fists around the steering wheel. "You think I don't live with that blame and guilt every damned day of my life?"

"You don't understand—"

"The hell I don't! Why the hell do you think I've been so hard on you the past couple of years?"

"So I don't become you."

That smacked me in the face so hard I felt my head move.

I stared at her. She stared back at me through those damned mirrored lenses.

"Take the glasses off!"

She hesitated. Pulled them down off her face.

Tears welled from her bruised eyes, slowly dripped out and rolled down her swollen cheeks. I reached out to wipe a tear off with my thumb. She flinched away. My hand froze, suspended just beyond her face.

"Don't—"

I shrugged, pulled my hand back and gripped the steering wheel, glared out the windshield.

The motor chugged in the background, a low grumbling hum

that dragged the rage out until I felt nothing except a deep, longing emptiness.

"I don't know how you do it," she muttered.

I glanced at her. She'd put the glasses back on, stared out her side of the windshield, her hands worrying each other in her lap. I noticed the torn fingernails, the dried blood staining the ragged ends, wondered if it was hers or Jonnie's. It didn't matter. I'd make Jonnie pay for what he'd done to her. And when I was finished, he'd know the true meaning of God's wrath.

"I don't know how I do it, either. I just do it. Every damned day." I looked at her. "And most days I don't do it very well."

I threw the Bronco into reverse and gunned it. The tires spun for an instant before the studs found purchase and yanked the bumper from the snow's mouth. I slammed the brakes, skidded to another abrupt stop.

"I wish you'd just give me to the Order. At least then, when I go completely insane, they'll end it for me."

I glared at her, my heart doing a sudden triple somersault before belly-flopping into my gut.

"You don't know what you're saying," I said.

The aviator glasses turned toward me.

"This isn't my home and hasn't been since the Otherkind took me."

I threw the Bronco into gear, fishtail skidded from the lot back onto the road just in time to cut off a Smart car picking its way through the packed snow and ice.

That one I didn't feel bad about.

"It doesn't matter," I said. "You're mine until my business with the Shining Man is done. After that, we'll figure it out. Together. The way sisters are supposed to do."

She tensed, stared at her lap, then looked up at me. My reflection in the lenses glowered back. Sullen and angry. Ready to start a world war.

"We're not sisters," she whispered into the silence between us, turned her attention to the frosted scenery rolling past her window.

Something caught in my throat. I shoved it down into the abyss and tried to keep my hands from crushing the steering wheel. I wanted to scream at her that *yes, we are sisters*. And had been from the moment Father Mike brought her into our tiny heterogeneous, dysfunctional family. Despite what she thought.

Ozzie and Harriet would have been horrified. But we did our best, and we never left family behind, no matter what. We did whatever it took, sacrificed what needed to be sacrificed, to make sure everyone came home safe. Including stubborn, thick-headed seventeen-year-old girls who believed otherwise.

My jumbled thoughts turned to the Shining Man. He had known I'd cross those lines. Do whatever it took. Sacrificed who I needed to sacrifice to save Tansy. And he'd used that knowledge to trap me for his own malevolent amusement.

I heaved a sigh, resisted the urge to tell her to get with the program. Stop being such a dolt and just let it go, like the stinking song from Frozen said to do.

Maybe I should've learned to follow my own sage advice.

None of it mattered.

I'd find a way to beat the Shining Man at its own game. Save both of us.

Because she wasn't going to die.

I wouldn't let her.

CHAPTER 6
FORGIVENESS IS HIGHLY OVERRATED

I SLID the Bronco to an abrupt stop in front of the steps leading to the Rectory doors behind St. Jude's Parish.

Father Mike stood on the portico above us, bundled in a heavy wool winter overcoat and thick black wool gloves. He leaned on a cane, his body trembling from the effort, his face drawn, complexion appearing almost ashen in the slowly brightening morning winter chill. Frosted breath blew out from his slack jaw, fitful and uncertain. His once bright and intense hazel eyes were sunken, dark, and dull.

He looked like crap. No. He looked like he was dying.

I glanced at Tansy.

She stared out her window past him, unseeing, as if she were in a different world. Maybe she was. Father Mike might as well have been invisible. Maybe Tansy wished he were.

"Tans?" I whispered. She ignored me. "Baby Bear?"

Nothing.

I flung my door open, stepped into the bitter morning chill. Father Mike started to shuffle down the iced steps on his cane. Terror squeezed my heart. I skated to the front of the Bronco, and caught my balance on the steaming hood, held my hand out toward him and shook my head.

His dulled eyes flicked from Tansy to me and back. The anguish on his face tore a hole through my heart, but he stayed on the portico. I blew out a breath, glanced through the misting windshield at Tansy. She hadn't moved. Hadn't reacted. Didn't even seem to breathe.

So much for Ozzie and Harriette family reunions.

I crunched my way around the front of the car, stopped beside the passenger door, glanced up at Father Mike. A breath of wind ruffled his thinning gray hair. He stared down at me, frozen in time. I yanked the passenger door open, the hinges squealing in protest.

I leaned in slightly. "You ready?"

She graced me with my anxious reflection in the lenses of the aviator glasses. And silence.

I'd been told that kid sisters could be real hellions. I'd balked when I heard it. Not now.

"Please, just remember that he loves you and that he only wants what's best for you." My frustrated reflection continued to stare back at me. "We both do."

The ghost of an ironic smile touched the corners of her lips. "Then you'd give me to Navarro and let me find some peace," she said, her words slightly slurred. "You'd help me at least do that."

Before I could respond, she slid from her seat, forcing me to back away, and planted her boots into the snow. She found her balance, pulled the aviator glasses off and dropped them at my feet, followed by the leather bomber jacket, before brushing past me toward the steps. And Father Mike.

As she surmounted the portico, he reached an unsteady hand toward her. She deftly slid past his grasping reach, yanked the door open and disappeared into the rectory.

The door hung open in challenge for an instant before slowly swinging closed, softly clicking shut in grim satisfaction.

I snatched the aviator glasses and bomber jacket out of the snow and ice, shook winter from them, and tramped up the steps. Father Mike laid a trembling hand on my shoulder, his eyes asking the question I didn't want to answer.

"It's bad," I said. "Really bad."

Stepping past him, I yanked the door open, threw the glasses and jacket into the hallway, and offered him a hand.

He stared as if I'd offered him Ebony wrapped in a crisp, crack and meth candy coating, shoved it away, and hobbled across the threshold. I watched him, sucking back the sudden tears. Hurt and pain knotted my stomach and shoved my heart through my ribs, as I realized the cancer had decided the debate for us. The door closed behind us.

Father Mike turned and nailed me with the same damned stare he used to hit me with when I was sixteen and doing shit on the streets that he wasn't supposed to know about.

"What the hell happened?"

"Words."

"I'm a priest. Not an angel."

"Still..."

The Father Mike smile I remembered flashed. He laid his free hand on my shoulder, peered at me with dulled and rheumy eyes. "You look like shit."

I couldn't help but notice the quaver in his voice.

"Words," I said again, trying to keep the silly smile off my face.

He managed another smile of his own, shook his head. "Fine." He paused, drew in a shallow rattling breath. "You look like you've been shoved through a wood chipper and passed through the intestines of swine."

"Yeah. I look like shit. Feel like it, too."

"Thank you for bringing her back."

The tired smile I wore died as I peered into his eyes, noticing his sallow color and the skin dripping from his face like slowly melting wax. "How long?"

"For what?"

"Don't jerk me around."

He turned away. I caught his shoulder, tried to turn him back, but stubborn strength prevailed. Damn him. Damn him to hell. "We need to talk about it," I said.

"I don't want to talk about it."

"Then when?" I shot back, frustration and anger lacing my voice.

Without answering, he started to shuffle down the long hall toward his study, the cane in his right hand shaking with every awkward step, looking as fragile as he did. "Never," he said into the space between us.

Why did men act like five-year-olds when confronted with something they didn't want to face?

"And Tansy?" I threw back into his abyss. "What about her?"

He stopped, hunched over as if I'd smacked him between the shoulders.

I hoped I had.

The silence between us stretched, threatened to snap. For a moment, I feared he would tell me to get the hell out. He'd done it before, during my early days. After Mom had dropped me off and never came back, the memory of my dad blowing his brains out still burning bright and fresh.

I'd run away, thought Father Mike would find me, beg me to come back. He didn't.

After a miserable two days spent on the street, cold, wet and hungry, I'd crawled back. Begged him to take me back. He did.

Without a word. And he treated me like his own daughter after that.

We never spoke of it again.

Without turning, he said, "Go. Pay your respects. He's waiting for you. He'll take you back. If you'll let Him." He sputtered into motion; the cane thudding softly into the carpet with each agonizingly slow step. "Come to my library when you're done."

I watched him shuffle down the hallway.

The words of defiance died on my lips. I swallowed them back, grimaced at the taste of my self-made bile, and screamed, the sound bouncing off the walls and skipping down the empty hall after him, dying a quick and agonizing death in the silence.

He didn't react, simply turned the corner and vanished, leaving me alone with my ghosts and my demons.

"Bastard," I muttered, as I snagged the aviator glasses and leather bomber jacket from the floor, and traced his path, trepidation thudding against my chest like an orchestra of bass drums.

At the intersection where he'd turned right, I spun left, stopped at the door that opened onto the path that supposedly led to my redemption. A path that for twenty years, even at Father Mike's solemn urging, I'd been unable to take.

But even as he was dying, Father Mike kept his faith that one day, I'd take that path and complete the journey. His faith was the only thing I'd ever hated him for.

I wrapped my hand around the brass knob, felt its passionless kiss on my fingers. Sweat rose on the inside of my palm, made the doorknob slick against my touch. My heart hammered my chest, its psychotic beat sucking my mouth dry, twisting my already knotted gut into a snarled ball of leaden string.

I turned the knob. Felt the latch click open.

Hesitation glued me to the floor at the threshold, my hand trembling on the knob as a voice whispered to me from the darkness of my soul, encouraging me to take that step and cross the line from darkness to light. I closed my eyes, tried to swallow past the sand coating my throat.

Without knowing I had stepped through, I found myself on the other side.

The rapping thud of my boots echoed from the tiled marble floor, reverberated off the vaulted ceiling and paneled walls. A few heads turned at my intrusion. Eyes stared. Curious. Hopeful. Fearful. After what seemed a lifetime, they turned away. Heads lowered. Whispered prayers resumed.

I glanced down at my boots, felt the heat rise to my cheeks. I should have known better. But maybe that's what Father Mike had wanted; The weight of strangers staring to force me forward past the boundary I never seemed able to cross. I thought of turning around and slinking back into the darkness that had belched me out.

But when I looked up, the innocent eyes of a small boy caught mine. He clung to the arm of a woman not yet in her twenties, whose crimped face bore the creases, lines, and years of a woman twice her age.

He was four. Maybe five, with thick wind-tossed dark hair that hung in random spurts around his small head over dark, grandpa-wise eyes. He let go of the woman's arm, brushed the errant strands from his face, snagged her arm again. His stare intensified, flicking to the crucified Christ hung on the wall behind the altar and back to me before I could suck a second breath.

I expected him to leer back. Shake his head. Tell me I was too late.

Instead, his eyes brightened. His shy smile grew. He nodded encouragement and invitation, holding my gaze captive for a second longer before turning back to the woman and leaning his head against her shoulder.

The spell shattered like fine spun glass.

I remembered to breathe, shook my head and blinked. When I looked back, the boy and the woman were walking slowly to the back of the nave. Her hand rested on his head. He clutched the side of her coat.

I shoved trembling fingers through my tangled hair, collapsed onto the wooden bench leaning against the wall beside the door that had somehow cut off my retreat. I clenched my fists into my lap, curled over and squeezed my eyes closed, trying to remember how to breathe.

When I looked up, the faithful few littering the nave had changed, didn't seem to know or care I was there. I reluctantly swung my gaze back to the crucified Christ. He continued to hang nailed to His cross from the wall behind the altar. Silent. Patient. Inviting.

Me.

I pulled off my boots and set them on the bench, stood, shed my wool coat, and shoved shaking hands into my jeans pockets. I sucked back the lump in my throat and strode quietly past bowed heads and mumbled prayers. Stopping at the bottom of the altar steps, I stared into the eyes of the crucified Christ, tried to kneel, but my knees had forgotten how to bend.

He stared back, his sorrowful gaze dripping with agony, but still overflowing with love. Compassion. Grace. Forgiveness.

A whispered voice sang through my thoughts. 'Forgive them Father. They do not know what they do. I will forgive you. Will you forgive yourself?'

I shuddered, shut my eyes against the tears welling up and out, hot and bitter.

The whisper in my mind continued. Soft. Compelling. Urging. *'Come to me. Allow me to forgive you and carry your burden.'*

"No," I whispered back. "I can't."

My eyes flew open. I stared up into His face, daring Him to offer forgiveness again. This time, I heard only silence.

I managed a small, guilty smile. "Thanks," I said. "But no thanks. Maybe next time." I shoved back the tears, swiped my eyes dry as I sucked the snot back up, smeared away what refused to go.

I turned on my heel, snagged my boots, coat, and what Tansy had shed from the bench beside the wall, and let myself out, the soft click of the door closing behind me tapping the bell of my soul with an empty and dead finality.

CHAPTER 7
FINAL WISHES

WITHOUT KNOWING HOW I ARRIVED, I stood in front of the door to my old rectory apartment. I stepped through the unlocked door into a comfortable darkness that carried the subtle scents of sage and rose, my two favorite aromas in my late teens.

I pushed the door closed behind me, dropped boots, coat, and bomber jacket, set the aviator glasses down on a burnished cherry nightstand guarding the doorway. I glanced down at the dark, mirrored surface, running my fingers over the scars from my name that I'd carved into the wood the first night I'd spent here.

A small blue-green ceramic bowl filled with sour apple candies glinted in the shadows from the center of the stand. Another favorite of mine. I popped one into my mouth.

Cobwebbed memories crawled out from the corners of the front room. Some good, most not so good, the rest hovering in that space between blessed forgetfulness and nightmare flashbacks. The good ones belonged to Father Mike. The not-so-good ones... I shoved those back into the corners with the tweeners, covered them with a fresh coat of paint and tried to forget they were there.

My old Go Bag sat in the back of my bedroom closet, stuffed

with fresh, clean clothes scented with the sage and rose I noticed when I stepped into my past, and my favorite pair of boots; the ones you always wear because they feel just right all the time, no matter how worn out they become. I smiled, thought of Sister Abigail and her tut-tuts that followed me through the rectory hallways the moment I stepped inside the parish. Ten years after my departure, she kept my apartment clean, fresh, and ready as if I'd never left. Or might be back.

I hoped the boots still fit.

The sixteenth-century Italian ear dagger, a double-edged blade inlaid with silver, that Father Mike gave me for my eighteenth birthday was sitting on top of my Go Bag. It was my companion on my first recovery, Emily Moreau. I'd bloodied it on our return from the Nether Realm when I'd used it to skewer the Juzarine witch trying to rip my throat out. That witch was the former owner of my bone dagger souvenir.

I found fresh towels, soap, and shampoo in the bathroom. I stripped, took a quick shower, dressed in the clothes from the Go Bag. After donning my black tactical pants and my old waterproofed leather combat boots, and a black, light woolen long-sleeved tee shirt, I admired myself in the mirror, managed a lopsided smile. Very Goth and filled with teen girl angst. I fingered the Italian ear dagger for a moment. Attached it to my belt.

I grabbed my wool overcoat and snatched the aviator glasses on my way out.

I found Father Mike in his library surrounded by floor-to-ceiling shelves cluttered with books and manuscripts of every conceivable type and subject. Grayish sunlight filtered in through the large picture window that dominated the wall behind him, haloing his head with a pale, almost cadaverous cast.

He sat in a comfortably worn dark blue cloth-covered easy chair I suspected had been around since the Stone Age, its wooden and metal frame woven together with duct tape and bailing wire. At least that's what Tansy and I told him when we tried to convince him to torch it and buy a new one. He'd balked, threw us out, and threatened to send us into foster care if we touched his chair again.

I smiled at the memory, wishing for a second I could turn back the clock and begin again. Just the three of us in our own Disney-inspired world where our dreams always came true.

Cocooned in a woolen blanket, he held a steaming mug between shaking hands. I detected the faint odor of Oolong White, likely flavored with a teaspoon of mint and honey.

He looked up when I came in, took a careful sip from the mug, just managed to set it down on the lamp stand beside his chair. I stood just within the threshold, arms crossed, my lips pursed into a grim line. "How long?" I said, my tone firm and unyielding.

He met my stare. A trembling hand hovered near the mug, decided not to attempt it and slunk back to his lap. "Until what?"

"Cut the crap." I strode into the room and collapsed into the chair on the other side of the lampstand; a smaller, newer version of the antique Father Mike sagged into. "*Please.*"

He pressed a linen handkerchief to his mouth, sputtered a cough. It came back smudged crimson. "Hours. Days. Weeks." He shrugged. "Doctors are worse than bookies. Makes it hard to plan dinner."

I nodded, biting my lower lip. The way his breath rattled in his chest and the lack of color in his complexion, I estimated *weeks*. At most.

I bit back the tears. "Who else knows?"

"Navarro seemed to know before I did." He shifted his gaze to his teacup. "I don't know if he's told Rouanet."

"That's why Commandery Coursers have been sniffing around," I said.

He lifted a shoulder in a half shrug. It seemed all he was capable of. Embarrassment sat fat and desolate across his blanched face. He reached for his tea.

I beat him to it, made him settle back into his chair before I handed him the mug, hovered until I was sure he wouldn't drop it, sat restlessly. "And Tansy?"

"She knows I'm sick."

"And?" I prompted.

Silence.

I shot from the chair, crossed to the door, fists at my sides, came back and stared down at him, wanting nothing more in that moment than to throttle him for his cowardice, even if he was dying. "Damn it! Why not?"

He stared at me like a puppy that had been scolded for crapping on the carpet but didn't know why. "I can't," he said, his voice barely above a whisper.

I fell back into my chair. "She needs to know," I said. "She deserves to know."

He ignored me. "What happened last night?"

Damn him for changing the subject.

I almost came out of my chair again, wanted to scream and shout and rail at him, but the shattered look behind his eyes made me pause. I sucked in a deep breath, used it to shove my self-righteous rage down into the abyss.

I considered lying to him, but he'd know. And he'd call me out for it, something neither of us needed in the moment.

"The Shining Man owns me."

He raised a brow, opened his mouth. A hacking cough came out instead of words.

I rescued the tea and set it on the table, waited until his fit ended, and he hid the handkerchief in his lap again.

"Tansy ended up at Jonnie's."

He crooked a worried brow, creased his lips into a paper-thin line, his eyes telling me that he already knew.

I paused and waited for his confession, shook my head in frustration from his silence, said, "Probably looking to score more Chaos or maybe Ebony. I don't know. I guess Jonnie saw an opportunity and tried to make her pay coin she wasn't willing to give, beat the crap out of her, instead. At least until Cleary showed up." I waited for a response, a reaction, hell, anything, but got nothing back for my hopefulness. "He took her to the Shining Man."

"Shit."

"Words," I said.

He had the decency to blush, which brought a little false color back to his face for a few labored breaths.

"It gets better," I said.

He frowned, reached for his tea, almost dumped it in his lap. I tried to intervene and received a scathing glare for my trouble, decided an honorable retreat would be best.

"A rogue operative from Navarro's Commandery created a Daemonrie Chimera and turned it loose. I have forty-eight hours to eliminate it and bring the head of the rogue to the Shining Man."

The way he stared at me brought back some nostalgic memories of when I'd tried to con him during my early Manifestation years. But he'd always been able to read me and call my bluff. I realized I was going to miss that.

He blew out a ragged, uncertain breath, touched the handkerchief to the goo-stained corners of his mouth. "We need to—"

"No... No way in hell," I said, leaning forward, pinning him to the back of his chair with a warning glare. "If Navarro gets wind of this, he'll bury it so deep no one will ever find out who or how. And if that happens, we'll never get Tansy or me back from the Shining Man." I shook my head. "It's what it wants. Me and Tansy on a platter, our souls wrapped with ribbon and ready to serve with a nice Bordeaux. I won't give it the satisfaction."

It was his turn to pin me to the back of my chair with his gaze. He may have been dying, but Father Mike still had enough strength behind his eyes to make me feel like that terrified ten-year-old girl again. "You're going to do something incredibly stupid, aren't you?"

I smiled and looked down.

He blew out a trembling breath. "You need to talk to Cleary."

I laughed at him. "And in what universe is that a good idea?"

"He'll protect her."

I snorted. "Like he protected me?"

He met my gaze. The silence stretched.

"I'll find someone else," I said.

He balked. "There is no one else" he said before another coughing fit filled the space between us. He managed to spit out, "If the Denver Commandery is compromised—"

He didn't need to finish his thought. He knew about my alternate. Still, even that chance had to be better than Alastair Cleary, onetime Noble Knight of the Four. Mentor. Lover. Mercenary. And now fixer for the Shining Man.

How the mighty had fallen. Or risen, depending on your point of view.

"I can't protect her. Not anymore," he said. "I don't—" Another round of coughing percussed through the room. His handkerchief came away from his mouth more red than white.

I tried not to grimace.

Embarrassment again flashed across his sunken cheeks as he shoved it between his leg and the chair arm, motioned behind me.

"There are more in the desk drawer. Abbie stocked them."

I pulled the drawer open. The well-oiled wood slid silent and smooth out from its hole. A stack of neatly folded, shimmering white linen handkerchiefs greeted me. I grabbed a few, found something else buried beneath the stack I hadn't seen in forever.

A photo of Father Mike, his wife Victoria, and their two daughters, Camila and Zoey. From his life before he became a priest and was indoctrinated into the Order of the Four. Victoria dead. Camila and Zoey abducted by the Otherkind a year before Audrey and I were born. They were never rescued.

I looked up, the handkerchiefs clutched in my fist, and turned, stared at the blank spaces on the wall above his desk, gaping. I pulled the photo from the drawer, shoved it at him.

"Why did you take them down?" I asked.

Chagrin flashed for an instant, followed by a deep-rooted sadness and guilt. He shook his head, refused to meet my accusation. "I couldn't let them watch me die."

I wanted to yell at him for his cowardice, decided on compassion instead. I dropped the photo back into the drawer, slammed it closed, and set the stack of handkerchiefs on the stand beside his tea, now cold and lifeless. Like he would be in a few weeks.

Kneeling beside his chair, I dabbed more crimson from the corners of his mouth, handed him the bloodied handkerchief.

He clutched it, smiled gratitude at me as I stood.

I slicked back my unruly jet-black curls, wished I'd tied my hair back before coming to say goodbye, stared into his once bright, powerful eyes now grown dull and cold, my mouth stretched into a tight line that was ready to snap.

"Gotta go," I said. "Got people to do and not much time to do them." Before he could respond, I strode to the door, put my hand on the door handle.

"What are you going to do to Jonnie?"

I hadn't expected that. "What he deserves. But not before I rip every shred of information I can from his insipid little brain." I winked at him.

Father Mike's gaze hit me, clear and calculating. He twitched a nod. "Be careful," he said. "Don't do anything more stupid than usual."

"Yes, Dad."

I yanked the door open. Stepped into the hall.

"Talk to Cleary," he said.

I closed the door, leaned my forehead against the wall, and allowed the tears to flood out. The sobs followed, wracking my body in their vise-like grip like a bottle of salad dressing; shake well before using. I slammed my fists against colorless drywall, screamed until my voice gave out and didn't care if he or anyone else heard.

When the hurricane passed, I shoved myself off the wall, wiped the tears and snot from my face, and sucked in a quavering breath. I peered down the hall toward Tansy's rectory apartment, thought about trying to talk to her again, before the excrement and worse blew through the fan, but I decided against it. She'd just tell me to go to hell. Standard Operating Procedure.

Instead, I pressed my palm against the library door, and whispered, "Don't die on me, old man. Not yet. Not until this shit storm is done and I have Tansy back. So we both can say a proper goodbye."

Another pause before I turned and walked out into my approaching apocalypse.

CHAPTER 8
SOUL SISTERS

TANSY STEPPED FROM THE SHOWER.

She stood with her eyes closed, breathing in the steam that hung in the air and clung to her as the water dripped off her, pooling on the slicked tiles beside her feet. She winced at the jabbing pain from the broken ribs and watched the fading Ebony sparks swirl past the inside of her eyelids. She reached for the relief and deliverance they promised, but she grasped only emptiness, anguish, and despair.

A quiet sob made her breath catch. She caught herself against the edge of the sink counter, the steamed marble slimy and clammy against her skin. The sparks dancing behind her eyes flared for an instant and died, evaporating into cold, dead ash. The power they had promised melted away, leaving behind the broken shell of her soul and the lie of release.

Tansy tried to remember what had happened, how she'd ended up at Jonnie's penthouse. A hazy memory of her phone call to St. Michael's, the eager voice on the line telling her that the Order would bring her in, keep her safe, and help her Manifest. That she had nothing to worry about.

Another memory flashed, misted with gauze, of her at Three Bears Bar and Grill, waiting, and on edge because the promised escort never showed. An Ebony addict approaching her, a Wannabe, asking for some scratch to help him through his slump. The front doors opening, spewing late afternoon sunlight into the bar. A face she recognized wearing a smile and a promise.

After that. Nothing.

A whispered voice wrapped in ice slithered through her thoughts, made her shiver, despite the heat and humidity still hanging in the air.

The dim, hazy image of her floating in a pool of Ebony, her mind whole and untouched, her life restored. The dead touch of chaos ebbing and flowing through her, and broken, ice-grimed concrete jabbing into her flesh, the burn of sudden, slicing pain. Blood and shattered glass. Scarlet-tinged coal-black, fathomless eyes staring at her from nothingness.

Another mind and essence that swarmed into her, taking and obliterating who and what she was, until only nonexistence remained.

A whispered name. *Adria.*

Corrupting acid that dripped from cracked and bloodless lips, burning through her soul.

And then... nothing.

No, not nothing.

Jonnie Hallows.

The prick.

She opened her eyes, slammed her fists against steam-slicked marble. Acid-laced tears ran down her cheeks, gathering at her chin before dropping and splattering against the countertop. She stared into the fogged mirror and gasped at the bottomless eyes dripping with an insatiable hunger that gazed back at her.

Blinking, Tansy wiped the mist from the glass and looked at

her reflection. Puffy, bloodshot, and blackened eyes, swollen, yellowing cheeks, and bloodied lips glowered back. She touched the split cleaving her upper lip, cringing from the sting slicing through it. That would scar, but hopefully in a small and sexy way when she smiled. She tried the smile, imagining. Another mistake. One more debt added to Jonnie's tab.

Her eyes slid from the ruin of her face to the bruises mottling her chest and sides. It hurt to breathe. Reaching behind her head, she brushed the gash in the back buried beneath tangled wet hair and grimaced, thankful that Cassie hadn't seen that one. If she had...

Tansy closed her eyes, and drew in a slow, shallow breath, imagining Cassie eviscerating Jonnie, feeding his guts to him before throwing him over his balcony railing.

She shuddered as images of Jonnie and the feral hunger in his eyes as he'd slammed her head against the wall flashed across her mind. She let the tears roll down her cheeks. The memories flooded through her thoughts, the weight of his body pinning her to the wall, his fist curled into her T-shirt, trying to yank it up. She fought him, screamed, felt the jarring impact of his hand against her face. His palm pushed up under her bra, his tongue as he forced it past her clenched teeth.

He screamed—unexpected, explosive—when she bit down and drove her knee into his crotch. Blood spurted into her mouth. A sudden excitement bubbled within her, igniting a small, fiery flame. She'd never tasted blood that wasn't hers before.

A swift, sadistic satisfaction boiled through her as he stumbled back, one hand clutching his crotch, the other hand clamped across his bleeding mouth.

She stood entranced; she had never seen so much blood before. She reached out, hand stretching toward the crimson streaming down through his fingers, rolling down his chin and staining the wood floor beneath him.

If she'd run, she might have made it out whole, but she didn't. Couldn't. The blood wouldn't let her. And it had been her undoing.

Jonnie's eyes had lit up, burning like a firestorm.

She'd never seen rage like that.

Had never felt pain like that.

Hoped to never feel it again as she collapsed into a ball on the floor against the wall as Jonnie's feet and fists pummeled her into mush.

If Cleary hadn't shown up...

He'd pried Jonnie from her and thrown him across the room. And when he smashed into the wall, he shattered like spun glass, falling to the floor in pieces. Cleary followed, stood over him for what seemed a lifetime, punching his boot into Jonnie's stomach, chest, and face until he screamed and cried and curled into a small tight ball that shivered and shook in a growing puddle of blood and vomit.

Or had that been the Ebony?

Cleary dragged her from the floor, dropped her into a chair, swearing as he glared into her eyes.

She blinked, stared at her reflection in the mirror, tasting Jonnie's blood on her tongue one more time, grinning as an exhilaration she'd never felt before lit her nerves with magma. She wanted to taste Jonnie's blood again, feel its warmth on her lips. She wanted him to feel what he'd done to her.

The pain.

The agony.

The humiliation.

Before she cut off his balls and fed them to him.

Her sides and chest burned.

Jonnie would pay dearly for what he'd done to her. And it wouldn't be Cassie who made him pay. Despite what she may have thought.

Tansy narrowed her eyes and stoked the fire of her burning rage.

The mirror shattered.

She stumbled back, a surprised breath caught in her throat.

An unfamiliar power danced across her skin, caressed her nerves, and enticed her mind.

She stared at the closed bathroom door, felt the hunger inside her grow.

Snagging her bathrobe, Tansy gingerly slipped it over her battered and bruised shoulders, wincing as she cinched it closed. She paused at the door, pressed her ear against the wood. Fae-daemon power continued to pulse through the air, inviting her to come out and play, its whispered call seductive and bewitching, its caress scratching chills across her nerves.

Tansy opened the door and stepped into the unnatural darkness.

Hadn't she left the lights on when she went into the bathroom? Were they still on? She thought she saw light squeezing through the darkness but couldn't see past the shadows clinging to her.

More whispers slid past; they brushed her thoughts, leaving goose pimples skipping in their wake.

A faint sound rustled from the corner against the far wall. Hushed voices called to her, inviting her to come and play, pulling her with their insistence. She barely caught herself as she stepped toward the noises, stopped despite the yearning twisting her into knots.

Tansy staggered to her desk. She knocked off the tray of food Abbie had left. It slammed into the floor, splattering eggs, bacon, hash browns, toast with orange marmalade, and orange juice across the carpet at her feet.

She wrapped trembling fists around the back of the chair next to the desk and squeezed.

"Who's there?" She asked in a quivering voice.

A contented purr crept from the darkness.

Had the sound come from her mind or from the other side of the room?

"Who's there?"

"Adria. A friend. Your friend." A young girl's lilting, high-pitched voice wrapped in a teasing giggle.

Tansy closed her eyes, swallowed past the growing lump crawling up the back of her throat. "Please God. No," she whispered.

A low hiss slapped her from the shadows.

"Why do you talk to *him* instead of *me?*"

Tansy suppressed a shudder. "Because you're not—"

"I am," the voice shoved back. "*I* am here. *He*... is not."

"Leave me alone."

"No," Adria said. "I want you to come out and play."

"No." Tansy marshaled her flagging strength and pushed back at the power caressing her soul. "Why are you here?"

"I told you, silly. To be your friend."

Tansy began to shake. She twisted her fists around the back of the chair, squeezed. Wood shattered and splintered, slicing through her palms.

She grimaced from the sudden sting. Blood, wet and sticky, oozed from between her fingers. She pried her hands free, stumbled back, bumping against the wall, memories of Jonnie's fists smashing her into pulp smacking into her mind. She began to cry and slid down the wall, thumping against the floor. Pulling her knees to her chest, she buried her face into her arms, sobbing.

"I don't need a friend," she said. "I need—"

"Vengeance."

Tansy blinked, sucked in a surprised breath, and grimaced. "What?"

"Vengeance," Adria's lilting voice said. "I can give you vengeance."

She wiped the tears away, squinting into the shadows, trying to make out a shape that might have been crouching in the corner across the room.

"I—"

"That is what you desire, is it not?"

The denial dribbled from her lips, ready for her to spew into the air.

Jonnie's face rose from the blackness. He huddled on the floor at her feet, crying, begging her not to kill him, to let him live. Let him go. He was sorry. He hadn't meant to hurt her. He couldn't help himself. He needed help. One shaking hand shimmied up, bloody fingers snatching at her. It wouldn't happen again. He'd give her anything she wanted if she'd just let him live.

Tansy watched her arm rise, a burnished bone dagger glittering in the darkness. Her arm swept downward, the blade slicing effortlessly through his throat.

His eyes went wide with astonishment, his life draining out onto the floor. He crumpled into a heap, his face buried in the bloody ocean growing at her feet.

She began to shiver with an ecstasy she'd never felt before, never knew existed. Fae-daemon power coursed through her, making her twist with desire. It felt almost like... Ebony. Only this made her feel alive and in control as her mind grew beyond the confines of her physical self and expanded to encompass the universe and beyond.

She cried out.

Could it be real?

"Yes," Adria hissed. "It can be. It is."

Tansy shuddered, shaking the last of the vision's webs clinging to her thoughts free. "You can make it happen?" she asked. "You can free me from this prison, and I can keep my mind?"

"We can," Adria breathed. "We can be free of the chains holding us to this existence We can create our own reality where we will be free of the pain and suffering others have caused us. We can have our vengeance... and more. So much more."

Tansy swallowed, the excitement twisting her consciousness into knots that made her squirm for more. "Yes," she said into the dark. "It's what I want, more than life itself." She licked her lips, winced as her tongue dragged itself over the ragged edges of her split lip.

She sucked in a trembling breath and opened her eyes.

The corrupted, scarlet-tinged coal-black, and fathomless eyes that had peered at her from the bathroom mirror glowed from the murky shadows. They swirled with madness, drew Tansy toward them, pulling her into their delirium, promising her power, vengeance, and finally release.

And... something else that made her tremble with anticipation.

Acceptance.

She blew out a breath. "Tell me how."

"No."

She tensed. "But you—"

Crazed laughter answered her, pinned her against the wall, winding eager fingers through her thoughts and desires and teasing them out. One. By. One.

Confusion grappled with her desire. She wanted Jonnie to suffer. She wanted release from the prison of her disintegrating mind, freedom from the pain slowly destroying her, and...

Images of Cassie flashed through her thoughts, and someone...

else. Agony flared, tore through her, burning her physical body to ash, leaving only her Essence, trapped, and imprisoned in glass. Forever.

Tears streamed down her cheeks. She shook her head, tried to free herself from the vision and the webs clinging to her mind that dragged her into the blackness. She cried out, tried to slam the door closed on the darkness, and what it had shown her. But the door stayed open, allowing the nothingness to crawl through.

"Who are you?"

"I told you who I am."

Tansy tried to crawl back inside herself. "I don't—"

"You do."

The image of a face flitted past her mind. She grasped at it. Missed.

Adria giggled. "Not yet. Not until you are ready."

Tansy banged her head against the wall, tried to use the jolting pain from the gash in her scalp to jar herself free. But she had sunk too deep. The hands grasping her from the abyss were too strong.

"Why are you here?"

"You know why I am here."

Her chest lurched, twisted into a knot. More tears leaked from her eyes, rolled down her cheeks. She slammed her head against the wall again. Jonnie had promised release and freedom, too. He'd lied. She tried to use the pain of that lie, but it slipped through her grasping thoughts.

"I can't."

"You can," Adria answered, caressing, comforting as it drew her in. "I know who you are. What you are. Our souls are—"

An image of the Shining Man slid past Tansy's thoughts. She gasped. "You belong to the Shining Man."

A slight pause. Something else.

Hatred?

"I am not from the Shining Man."

Confusion and doubt. Uncertainty and fear.

She stared into the chasm. The glowing feral eyes stared back, dripping hunger. Slender, almost bloodless lips slid into a slow, deranged smile, showing gleaming ivory teeth.

"What do you want?"

"To show you the way."

A different door cracked open in the back of her mind and let through a razor's edge of scintillating coal-black and sooty light. She strained toward it, but as she brushed the light, the door slammed closed. Tansy sat in darkness again, the torn edges of her soul rotting a little more.

An image of Cassie and the Shining Man bargaining for her soul faded into view. Rage flared. They had no right to bargain for what was hers. The licking flames burst into a firestorm.

"But I don't know how," Tansy said.

"That is because you search for heaven amid hell."

Another gentle caress of power stroked the edges of Tansy's shattered soul. Her shudder grew, made her ache in every corner and crevice of her being. The door cracked open again, gave her a fleeting glimpse of what lay beyond.

Salvation.

Tansy reached for it, pulled back at the last instant. The door slammed closed. Her mind went dark.

She crumpled to the floor, sobbing with anguish. She shook her head, blew out a hushed, twisted sigh. "Please stop," she said. "I can't."

"Then you are lost," Adria hissed. "They will crush your mind. Your spirit. Your soul." A deafening silence. "You will be their creature for eternity, your mind shattered, and your will trampled into dust."

Darkness enveloped her, weighed down on her, ground her into oblivion.

She tried to move. To breathe. To stand. But she couldn't find her body.

"Am I dead?"

"You are not yet dead. But if you do not come with me, they will turn you into something worse than dead."

Tansy managed to shake her head, a slow, drawn-out movement. "What you want... I can't."

An impatient sigh caressed her cheek, grasped at her stumbling thoughts.

"I grow weary of this game," Adria said. "I do not think I want to play anymore."

The power slid back, tore itself free from Tansy's desperate, grasping soul, and took the light with it. Utter blackness rushed in, filling the vacuum. Thunderous silence followed, buried her in absolute nothingness.

Tansy screamed, "Wait!"

Hesitation. Hunger, pure and ravenous. Eager to be satiated.

"You won't... betray me?" Tansy asked.

Quiet laughter. "How could I betray the other half of my soul?"

The door in the back of her mind opened. The gleaming darkness flooded through, inviting and welcoming.

"You have but to grasp hold of it," Adria cooed. "And I will lift us both to heaven and our salvation."

Tansy strained forward, stretching eager fingers into the sooty light. They brushed the feather tip of power and ecstasy. She jerked back, her fingertips burning with unfulfilled desire.

"Look at us."

Tansy lifted her eyes. A body slid from the darkness, kneeled in front of her. Gentle fingers that breathed winter's embrace touched her chin, forced it up. A girl about her age stared back at her from within the bright fire-lit depths of madness.

A hand grasped hers, pulled her to her feet as slender, bony arms wrapped her in a loving embrace.

The pain dissolved from Tansy's body and her mind, replaced by warmth and acceptance.

And love.

Lips pressed against her ear, "Welcome, my sister."

Tansy melted into the embrace. Light and dark. Something more that slid past and into her soul where it took root and blossomed. She shivered, nestled against a soft, caressing touch.

And then... nothing.

CHAPTER 9
CONUNDRUMS

I LINGERED at Gracie Dryden's kitchen table, my hands wrapped around a lukewarm mug of her latest herbal tea concoction. Beside my elbow squatted a short stack of new vintage film DVDs that Gracie had scrounged for me during her monthly thrift store road trip. "The Wrath of Khan," one of my favorites, sat on top, gazing longingly at me. I ignored it, concentrating instead on the apocalyptic thoughts racing through my mind.

Pushing ninety-nine, weighing one-hundred pounds soaking wet, with iron-gray hair, a dour, 'don't screw with me' expression and more wrinkles than a California Raisin, Gracie was the oldest living Touched I'd ever known. And I'd come across a few that had survived semi-sane into their early Golden years before turning maximum overdrive Looney Tunes.

I'd taken a couple of sips of her herbal poison to humor her, managed a fleeting sour smile before mumbling an insipid pleasantry. I hadn't lifted the mug from the surface of her ancient and marred hackberry table since.

Instead, I focused on the lingering rapturous smell of freshly baked pumpkin spice bread, Audrey's favorite; strange that I remembered that. I tried to allow the heady scents and memories to wrap me in a comforting blanket that reminded me of home.

Before Audrey never came back from the Nether Realm. Before my dad blew his brains out. Before my mom dumped me on the steps of St. Jude's Parish.

Gracie offered me a slice when she poured me the cup of tea. I graciously accepted it, politely nibbled a corner, not having the heart to tell her that I'd loathed everything squash since my twin's abduction. Loved the smell. Hated the taste and texture.

Her small-kitchen was stuffed with an eclectic collection of antique kitchen utensils, glass canning jars, and assorted incomplete China sets that always made me feel at home in a busy, cozy, homey, inviting, and accepting sort of way. Feelings from another era in my life that had faded to the point of cliché.

We sat together at the table in silence for what seemed more than a lifetime, though the slightly odd Bavarian cuckoo clock on the wall behind the table irritatingly continued to remind me that barely thirty minutes had passed since I'd blessed her doorstep. The sunlight peeking through the small picture-framed window above the sink had fled not long after I arrived, choked back behind a thick wall of dark menacing clouds.

More snow on the way.

I shifted in my chair, lifted my gaze to the clock for what seemed the hundredth time, then turned my eyes back to my cold mug of tea. I felt Gracie's stare, probing, silently asking the questions that I needed to answer. If not for her, then for myself.

I was burning precious daylight. I had forty-four hours to eliminate the chimera and bring the head of the rogue Denver Commandery operative to the Shining Man. I knew the consequences for failure, felt its hand slowly crushing my chest, squeezing the life from my soul. It's what the Shining Man wanted and hoped for. That failure. It began to feel like I was going to grant him his wish, no matter what I did.

Gracie cleared her throat, the sound like gravel crunching under a truck tire. She shifted restlessly in her chair, ancient joints cracking and popping through the silence.

She'd been patient with my maudlin silence, which had been very un-Gracie like. Now it was time to put up, shut up or go home.

I lifted my gaze. She threw it back at me, growing irritation plastered across her grizzled face. She absently reached down and scratched Beegle, my Touched and unhinged beagle I'd rescued from the Nether Realm, behind his ears. He panted doggy ecstasy as he leaned into her scratching fingers.

"You going to tell me what's is going on? Or we going to play twenty questions with the Louisville Slugger?"

I snorted and flashed a smile, leaned back in my chair, the ancient wood creaking beneath my weight as I pinched the bridge of my nose with trembling fingers. "Father Mike's dying."

"Bout time."

Not the answer I'd expected, but it was Gracie. Always Pandora's Box.

She reached across the table, rescued one of my hands from my clammy mug of tea. "He's been struggling with cancer since before you came along. Off and on. You just never saw it till now."

If she'd meant that to make me feel better, she failed miserably. It just made me wonder what else Father Mike had hidden from me over the past twenty years. I thought about asking, decided maybe it wasn't the best time, or any of my damned business. Sometimes ignorance really was bliss.

I grimaced and took my hand back.

Gracie continued to stare, continued to offer her hand a

moment longer before she sighed and reclaimed it. "How long he's got?"

I shrugged. "A few weeks. Maybe. He won't tell Tansy."

Her turn to grimace. "A lot of pain still buried under that hood. He's trying to protect her."

"From what? More loss? Pain? She's already an expert at that. We all are. She knows he's sick."

Gracie arched a pencil thin silvered brow, shrugged and spread her hands out. "Probably already knows he's dying. Maybe she doesn't want to know *the* when. Maybe she's content knowing that *it is*."

"Bullshit." I shot out of my chair, managed to startle Beegle, something that rarely occurred.

Gracie snagged Beegle's collar, smacked me with a *you better mind your manners, girl* glare. Beegle woofed at me for emphasis.

I tried to stare them both down, managed only to collapse back into my chair, my wind gone. I buried my face in my hands, stomped down hard on the grief knotted up in my chest. I felt Gracie lean forward, feared she was going to snag one of my hands again.

"What's got you all tied up in knots, girl?"

I shook my head and cleared my throat, sat back in my chair. "It's nothing," I said. "I'll take care—"

Gracie stared me down through narrowed eyes. "What's Tansy got herself into now?"

I started to lie, felt the words drip from my lips and caught myself. I was a consummate bullshitter, except with two people. Father Mike was one. The other glowered at me from across her kitchen table.

I blew out a harsh breath. "Jonnie Hallows," I said. "He tried to rape her. Beat her up pretty good instead. Cleary showed up. Took her to the Shining Man. She owes him a life debt."

Gracie blew out an arid breath scented with cloves and cinnamon. "What's it got you doing to work off that debt?"

Another lie tagged my tongue, but the look Gracie slapped me with warned me explicitly about giving voice to that fabrication.

"One of our own went rogue," I said. "Created a Daemonrie Chimera and set it loose in our world."

Deathlike calm settled between us. I didn't know what I'd expected from her, but that wasn't it.

She leaned back, hissed a slow whistle between her teeth. "How long you got?"

I glanced up at the cuckoo. "Forty-four hours. More or less."

"What do you need from me?"

I began to ask her to watch Tansy. Protect her after Father Mike died if I didn't make it back. I knew she'd say yes. I also knew she didn't have it in her. Not anymore, not for a long time. She'd try, might even give Cleary something to worry about for a few heart beats when he came for Tansy. But not the Shining Man or Navarro. They'd eat her alive. Then tear Tansy to pieces using her against each other.

Instead, I said, "If I don't make it back, make sure Father Mike is taken care of."

"And Tansy?"

I shrugged. "If I don't make it back, that won't matter."

I shoved myself from my chair, grabbed the stack of DVDs. I wished I had time to watch a couple of them before my world ended. "Thanks for the tea. I'll see myself out." I walked from the kitchen, paused and turned when I realized Beegle hadn't followed me. I quirked a brow at him. "Seriously?" He looked back, tongue lolling, that damned beagle smirk on his face. I looked at Gracie. "Please give him whatever you promised him so we can get going?"

Gracie smiled, leaned over, whispered something into Beegle's ear. He whisper woofed in response. Gracie chuckled, and reached into her apron pocket, fed him a couple of homemade dog biscuits. I don't think I saw him chew.

"Can we go now?"

Blissful once more, Beegle scrabbled toward me, threw me a *why are we still here* look as he trotted to the front door and sat, panting, his tongue lolling from between his teeth.

I shot one last look at Gracie. "You spoil him too much."

She grimaced, dug herself from her chair. "I think I've earned the privilege. Watch your back."

I snorted. "Always do."

Gracie's sarcastic words, "Yeah, right," followed me out the door.

I fired up the Bronco and blasted the heat for Beegle.

He sat in the passenger seat and grinned beagle-like as he stared out the unfogging windshield.

I sighed, my brain juggling spinning plates on glinting bone spear tips as I tried to figure out how to protect Tansy from herself until I finished the Shining Man's grizzly business. After that...

Father Mike's words snuck up on me through the noise of my thoughts. *Call Cleary.* Bad mojo, that. Especially after he'd taken Tansy to the Shining Man instead of bringing her back to Father Mike. How did you trust someone who'd betrayed you every which way but loose? Forget about the crap from ten years ago.

I stared at the second number I should have deleted from my contacts list. My thumb hovered again, Father Mike's warning words pin-balling through my skull. *Navarro's Commandery had been compromised. I didn't know who I could trust.* Still...

It had been six months since I'd burned Peter Oliver and his bridges to ash in a firestorm that made Shock and Awe from Desert Storm look like a quiet Saturday night family backyard campfire. Six months? Felt like six minutes. I shoved that agony down and wiped away a stray tear. I hoped he'd come out the other side of our mess a little less crispy than I had.

I swept my hair out of my eyes.

My thumb pressed *Call.*

Peter answered before the echo of the first ring died. I hadn't expected that. I thought my call would go straight to voicemail, be blocked, or that my phone would explode in my face.

"Are you insane?"

I hesitated. "Hello to you, too."

"What do you want?"

"Can't a girl just call to chat?" I asked, hoping I didn't sound as disingenuous as I felt.

"You blew those bridges all to hell six months ago," he said. "Jessie is probably listening. And you know what she'll do if she is."

I sighed and closed my eyes for a moment, trying to settle my jittery nerves. "I need a favor," I said, my voice trembling.

"No. Don't call this number again. Ever." He hung up.

I dropped my phone as if it had burned my hand. I hadn't known what to expect when I'd called, but I hadn't expected that. An image of Father Mike flashed into my mind's eye. His cadaverous face wearing an *I told you so* smirk.

I sucked back my shattered hopes, threw the lid down on my grief and pain. Life moved forward, whether we wanted it to or not. I had thought Peter would be part of that. Spoiler alert, no Hallmark movie ending there. My bad. But what had I expected? Especially after the fallout involving Ellis Wynn's assassination and the scrutiny it created from the Office of the Grand Master.

Navarro and his political machinations were bad enough. But the continued microscopic surveillance from Sébastien Rouanet and his Grand Inquisitor, Marshall Stimson, took its toll.

The Order discouraged romantic relationships within the

Commanderies. It forbade liaisons with outsiders, though discreet dalliances were tolerated. But Jessie couldn't resist flaunting the rules, making her affair with Wynn as public as possible. Which still might have been overlooked, if Ellis Wynn hadn't been a detective with the Colorado Bureau of Investigation, and secretly investigating the existence of the Order of the Four and its involvement in several unsolved homicides throughout the decades.

Navarro warned Jessie to end her relationship with the detective and of the consequences if she did not.

She did not.

Navarro gave the command, ordering me to carry out the deed, knowing it would destroy my friendship with Jessie.

I disobeyed that order, choosing instead to walk away, but not until after confronting Wynn and walking out of his apartment following a tense and physical altercation that left me bloodied and bruised. But Jessie refused to believe that I hadn't killed her lover, and ended our friendship, vowing that she'd get even one day.

I knew Peter Oliver had been there, observing to make sure Navarro's orders were carried out. I didn't know if Peter had killed Wynn after I left. All I knew was that CBI detective Ellis Wynn had later been discovered shot to death inside his apartment and that the CBI and the Denver Police were searching for a dark-haired woman seen leaving his residence near the time of his death.

Disobeying Navarro had been my fatal mistake.

Recovering Stephanie Brandt from her Juzarine abductors was supposed to be my way back into the bishop's good graces. Only, the mission had been a setup intended to make sure I didn't come back, giving Navarro his pound of flesh for my recalcitrance. I did manage to return, though, barely alive, but without Stephanie Brandt, who was declared lost because of my negligence.

So Navarro had his vengeance.

I was excommunicated, stripped of my rank as a Noble Knight of the Four, and banished from the Order in perpetuity.

Throughout our affair, Peter stayed with me through the worst of my nightmare, until I discovered Navarro had sent him to ensure I completed my mission with Wynn.

The fight we had when I confronted him was epic and apocalyptic.

The conflagration we unleashed on each other that night six months ago, still burned.

Beegle stared at me. I managed a wan smile, leaned over and hugged him, Whispered, "Thanks buddy," into his neck. He tolerated it, whining and licking my ear. I drew back and wiped beagle spit from the side of my face.

Snagging my phone, I opened my contacts list to the first number I should have deleted from my phone ten years ago. Alastair Cleary's face and number stared back at me. Even now, ten years after that Disney fairytale had been extra crispy fried into oblivion, looking at Cleary's picture made my gut twist. I didn't know if I still wanted to bed him or gut him. Probably the former. Followed by the latter.

Get a grip, girl.

My thumb hovered. Indecision roiled.

Crap.

I dropped my phone onto the seat.

As much as I loathed it, this one needed to happen face to face. I needed to look into his eyes when I asked so I could see his reaction, know if it was genuine or not. And why he took Tansy to the Shining Man instead of bringing her back to Father Mike.

There was a lot of history there.

Father Mike and Cleary had been best friends, closer than brothers. If you could believe Commandery gossip.

Jessie and I had just hit eighteen, but we were going on thirty, completely Manifested and still mildly sane. We'd become erratic and uncontrollable. A deadly combination. Too hot for Father Mike to handle, or so we thought.

Our antics had gained Navarro's attention, the one thing above everything else Father Mike had wanted to avoid. Jessie and I didn't give a shit, because we were kicking Otherkind ass.

We had no clue.

Jessie and I blew the lid off that box when we mistook Cleary for an Otherkind. We found him in an alley off the Sixteenth Street Mall, after the bars had vomited out the last of their regulars, talking up a working girl. He had her pinned against a filth-grimed brick wall, Otherkind power washing off him like a tsunami-driven tide.

So we thought, but turned out we were wrong.

We tried to take him out. Cleary handed our asses back to us without breaking a sweat.

It turned out the girl was the Otherkind and Cleary a Noble Knight of the Four, connected with the Denver Commandery. He'd been on a Recovery. But thanks to us, his lead had escaped before he could get what he needed from her.

Jessie and I barely managed to crawl out of that alley alive, an angry Cleary driving us like we were the stragglers at the back of a herd of cattle.

I remembered looking into glinting violet eyes as he kneeled beside me, his smile mocking me as he brushed tangled strands of hair from my face. His gaze had flicked back and forth between Jessie and me then he sighed and shook his head.

I thought we were dead.

"You two miscreants belong to Michael Howe. I smell him all over you." He stood after that, buttoned his suit coat. "Tell Michael I'll be by in a few days to collect what he owes."

I hadn't expected the British accent. Or the way it made my breath catch in my chest.

Without another word, he turned and sauntered back into the alley, whistling a boisterous ditty as he disappeared into the dark.

Father Mike had been livid. He forbade us from going out again until we were sixty. It didn't matter that we were legal adults. Not that we could have done much except hobble around the grounds of St. Jude's. We could barely dress ourselves after the beat-down Cleary put on us.

True to his word, Cleary showed up a few days later.

He and Father Mike closeted themselves in the library, but I'd never heard Father Mike yell so much or so loudly in the eight years I'd been with him. I wasn't sure about Jessie, but I was terrified. Especially since I didn't know what they were yelling at each other about.

Father Mike burst through the library door a few minutes later, his face red and puffy, his eyes livid, his mouth pulled into a tight line. He glanced at Jessie then threw his gaze at me, shook his head, and stalked off without a word.

The library spit Cleary out a few seconds later.

He backed Jessie to the wall with his gaze. "Pack. Bishop Francisco Navarro has requested your personal attendance. You won't be coming back."

She balked, defiance bubbling on her lips. Before her next breath, Cleary rammed her against the wall, the razor edge of an enchanted switchblade creasing her throat, a thin line of blood oozing from beneath the blade's edge. Cleary leaned in, whispered into Jessie's ear. She blanched, her eyes going wide. She gulped and nodded.

Cleary released her, watched her scurry down the hall in silence. A moment later, it was as if she'd never existed.

I'd never seen Jessie terrified before of anything. It made me go cold.

The knife vanished beneath Cleary's coat. He glanced over his shoulder at me, his eyes narrowed and calculating. My heart stuttered under that look. He smiled the same mocking smile he'd caressed me with in the alley.

"You have three days to say your goodbyes. Make good use of them. Then you're mine." He winked, buttoned his coat, and disappeared down the hallway in the same direction Father Mike had fled.

Two years later, I was back at St. Jude's, licking my wounds as one of Alastair Cleary's cast offs and trying to live the heroic the *world is against me* fantasy.

Father Mike had tried to warn me, told me to keep Cleary at arm's length, not to let my guard down. Allow him to train me, nothing more.

I'd ignored him, thought I could handle the British bastard.

It turned out every girl before me had thought the same. We'd all been wrong.

During those two years, I'd never seen Jessie. I asked Cleary. He never answered. It turned out Navarro and his Commandery had other plans for her.

A few months after I'd crawled back to him with my tail between my legs, Father Mike, tired of my Vegas show pity party, sat me down, and told me, *Life's a bitch. Get over yourself. You don't have to forgive him. Or me. But forgive yourself. Learn from this. And when the time comes, use him for your benefit.*

I'd listened. Mostly. It wasn't the apology I'd expected, or wanted, but it was all I was going to get. I took it and kept it close.

Not long after my unceremonious return to St. Jude's, Jessie resurfaced as Navarro's lieutenant. She and I tried to reconnect, tried to become what we'd been. But we'd both changed, neither of us for the better. We each yearned for who we had been, before, tried to rebuild that shattered fence.

Five years slid by.

Cleary fell from grace, his excommunication shaking the Commandery to its foundation.

And then Ellis Wynn happened.

Turned out the old saying was true. *You can't go home again.*

I hated to admit it, but with my other slim-to-none option shot to hell, Father Mike's pragmatic words smacked me upside the head. I had to smile, though. Father Mike hated Cleary almost as much as I did. Like Gracie had said, *lots of pain still under that hood.*

Another sigh and another quick Beegle hug.

If Cleary was all I had left, so be it. I'd use him the way he'd used me, which brought the flash of a venomous smile.

He'd want cash. I had five large at my house, the last of my apocalypse reserves. I knew it wouldn't be enough, but it was all I had or could get my hands on at the moment.

I'd deal with it.

I threw the Bronco into gear, spewing snow and ice into the air. As I pulled away from the curb, I caught Gracie's reflection in the side view, watching me through her front window.

An icy hand squeezed my heart as if it would be the last time we saw each other this side of the grass.

CHAPTER 10
A TEA PARTY

RAW-BONED SLEET METEORED FROM A DOUR, gray cloud-choked morning sky as my Bronco crawled down the unplowed street toward my house. The wind-flung snow and ice camouflaged the surrounding open spaces and far-flung gentrified suburban farm homes, cocooning me in a blistering, frozen world empty of life.

Beegle sat quietly and comfortably beside me, panting as he stared critically through the ice-crusted windshield. The heater blasted volcanic-hot air, accompanied by the frenetic slap of the wipers as they desperately tried to keep pace with the blowing snow and ice clutching at the blades.

As I pulled even with my house, Beegle tensed and began to dance in his seat. He woofed worry at me as I grimaced and slowed the Bronco to a snail-crawl and rolled down the passenger window. Blowing snow boiled in through the sudden cavernous opening, filling the air with a chaotic, cocaine-fueled white whirlwind. Beegle whined and barked as he scrabbled up to look into the roiling tumult. I leaned across the seat, scratched him behind his ear to try and calm him down. "I see it," I said. "I'm not blind, you know."

He looked at me as if my brain were a warped pine two-by-four.

I snorted. "Chill and give me a moment between breaths to check it out."

He gave me another look that told me I was the one that needed to chill.

That dog wasn't right in the head. Guess that's why we got along so well.

A pitch-black, official-looking Suburban with blacked-out windows loitered beside the snow-packed curb in front of my house. Melting snow dribbled off the windows and down the side but had piled up at the base of the windshield in heavy, uneven layers. The last, dying wisps of steam clawed up from the hood into the raging snow, their frayed and decaying fingers beaten into extinction.

Order of the Four.

The taste in my mouth turned moldy-bread tangy. I couldn't see through the tinted windows into the redacted interior, but I assumed no one had chosen to sit inside and freeze their butts off. The Suburban felt too crypt-like. Which meant they were inside my house, cozy and comfortable, watching my cable and drinking my tequila while they waited for me to stumble in on their little party, like the unpopular girl who hadn't been invited.

But the itch crawling beneath my skin at the nape of my neck told me that I was the guest of honor; they just hadn't bothered to mail my invitation.

I hated surprises more than I hated blind dates.

Damn. I hoped they hadn't drunk all the tequila. The liquor stores were still closed, and the itch creeping below my skin told me I was going to need some shots. A boatload of them.

I managed a tight smile and blew out a loud, stupid, and heavy sigh. Guess it was time to get the party started.

Swearing under my breath as I endured Beegle's disapproving glare, I fishtailed the Bronco into the driveway, slid it to an abrupt, jaw-snapping stop a foot from the garage door, my hands white-knuckling the steering wheel as my scrambled mind tried to form a semi-sane plan. I stared at the garage door, decided to stay out in the storm. Not that whoever was inside my house didn't already know I was here, like I knew they were here. Sometimes, though holding onto the illusion of the surprise kept you crispy.

A girl had to have her hobbies.

"Got any ideas?" I looked at Beegle. He glowered back with stoic and disgruntled doggie silence. No help there. "Fine," I said as I cracked the driver door open on squealing hinges and slid from the Bronco into the teeth of the December wind, ducking my head to protect my face from the stinging sleet. Fingers colder than death snatched at my hair, teased a few split ends out from under my fedora, slapped them back into my eyes.

I pulled my Walther from its home, held it down at my side. I glanced back at my stupid dog. "You coming?"

Beegle gave me an unsubtle look that told me I was the stupid one before scrambling out into the piled snow.

Slamming the door closed, I crunched through the wild blanket of frozen cotton, embracing myself, chin tucked against my chest. I rarely felt the cold. But something not quite natural skipped teasingly just below the surface of this storm and its five-fingered wind.

Three quick steps brought me to the ice-slick red wood deck where we huddled for a moment, basking in the fantasy of protection beneath the roof.

I blew my breath out in dim white swirling clouds, opened the front door. Unearthly power caressed my fingers as they slid over the brass handle, sent giddy shivers racing down my spine. I cringed them back, nodded to Beegle. He slid through the narrow opening into my entry way and stood, nose sniffing the air, his low, rumbling growl grinding through the silence.

I closed the door behind us, ignored the wind as it died at my feet. I raised the Walther, and flicked on the laser sight, unease twisting my gut.

A huff of warm, inviting air brushed past me as I stared into the murky light clinging to the hall.

Silence wrapped cold, cloying hands around me, its empty promises tugging at my anxiousness.

Except for the rhythmic ticking of my dad's grandfather clock from my dining room, I heard nothing. Dim, subdued light pooled at the end of the hallway, giggling its invitation.

Power licked the edges of my mind. Not fae-daemon. Human. Touched and Manifested. But not wild. This was trained, skilled, talented, and potent.

I knew that power, had endured its blunt, unapologetic punch a year earlier, during the sentencing that led to my excommunication instead of death. I guess I should have felt grateful instead of resentful. But bitterness and rage over my betrayal by Navarro and the Denver Commandery because of my decision to leave Stephanie Brandt in the Nether Realm stripped away any possibility of gratitude.

A more covert power wound subtle spider-webbed legs around my thoughts and tried to fill my mind with distractions. I knew that touch as well, and it didn't bode well.

Swallowing down my growing agitation, I re-established my grip on my gun, glanced at Beegle, and winked. He padded silently down the hall toward our approaching destiny. I followed, hugging the inside wall, carefully sweeping the gloom with my eyes.

Darkness cradled the living room a hop and a skip to my right where Beegle usually reigned from his tiny island kingdom beside a tan, suede covered Star Trek-era La-Z-Boy rocker recliner Gracie had forced me to buy for her. Its heated seat and back with massaging technology had been damned expensive and way overkill but a non-negotiable requirement for Gracie's time watching my *little shit dog*. Her words, not mine.

A moment of indecision gripped my chest before I swept around the corner and scrutinized the living room's inky darkness. Gracie's La-Z-Boy huddled empty in the opposite corner.

I backpedaled a step. Swept left. Paused.

Still no movement. No sound.

I swallowed down my growing anxiety, continuing to cling to the inside hallway wall, my Walther pulling me out from the deeper shadows. I stopped just outside the light pooling from the kitchen. Waited and listened.

Beegle's warning growl alerted me a breath too late.

The muzzle of a suppressor pressed into the base of my skull. Wandering a heartbeat behind strolled a soft, artful, woodsy scent mingled with hints of rose, raspberry, and cinnamon, what we girls liked to call cool girl energy.

"Kain."

Harmonie Bonnet's gentle, melodic, and genial French accent flowed through the surrounding air.

I huffed out an exasperated breath, glanced down at Beegle. He sat at my feet, looking up at her. "Traitor," I hissed.

Beegle ignored me.

A soft mocking chuckle danced through the shadows.

"He likes me better than he likes you."

I felt the soft, insistent tap of a gloved hand against my shoulder.

"The Walther, if you please."

I handed her my pistol.

"And the dagger."

Blowing out another irritated breath, I unsheathed the Italian ear dagger, handed it hilt first, glowering down at Beegle. "Did you tell her everything?"

In response, he stood, tail whipping the air above his butt, ignoring me as if I'd never existed.

"Stupid dog," I muttered.

The suppressor urged me forward.

As I stepped into the kitchen, I heard Harmonie kneel behind me, cooing softly to my Benedict Arnold dog, complimenting him on being such a 'good little doggy'. I wanted to spit nails.

Marshall Stimson, Master Inquisitor of the Four and Bishop Sébastien Rouanet's right-hand man, lounged in one of my better black cherry dining chairs next to my matching kitchen table. Beside him sat a mug of spiced chai, cinnamon-laced steam rolling off the top. Behind him, skulking in the corner, stood a Chasseur, Stimson's personal sentinel, hands clasped at his waist, discomfort worming over his face.

Stimson took a sip of tea, turned his severe Doctor Strange faded blue jeans eyes toward me. He smiled, not an unfriendly expression, but nerve-wracking because he rarely smiled, and when he did, death usually followed.

Motioning me to an empty chair, he said, "Join me." He indicated his cup. "And perhaps some Chai as well?" He gestured casually to the Chasseur standing stoically behind him. "Erick is an absolute wizard with Chai." Without waiting for my response, he continued. "Erick, a cup of Chai for our guest. And perhaps a little something extra as well." He flashed me a conspiratorial grin and winked.

Erick began concocting my Chai as I sat.

Harmonie squatted in the kitchen entrance, playfully hugging

Beegle, scratching his ears, and making him look the part of a foolish, undisciplined puppy. She looked up at me, a saccharine sweet smile on her slender lips. "I never understood why he attached himself to you," she said. "You clearly don't deserve him."

I mocked her with a vindictive smile.

Harmonie was in her late thirties. She was tall and slim, all sharp angles and lines, with long straight brown-blonde hair down to the middle of her back. With fierce brown eyes and a long narrow nose, Harmonie was not what men would call a stunning beauty. But what she lacked in double-take good looks, the inquisitor assassin for Sébastien Rouanet, made up for in elegant and deadly skills.

Something you would never suspect watching her play with my duplicitous dog.

"Harmonie," Stimson said. "Would you mind spending some time with Beegle while Cassidy and I talk?"

She paused, glancing between Stimson and me before nodding. Setting my Walther and dagger down on the table beside him, she called to Beegle and led him baying and dancing excitedly from the kitchen.

Erick placed a steaming mug down in front of me. Beside it, he placed a shot of my best tequila, stepped back, and waited.

Stimson studied me for a moment and nodded. Erick turned on his heel, silently followed Harmonie and Beegle out of the kitchen.

"Try the tea. It's marvelous."

I threw back the shot, wished Erick had left me the bottle. "What the hell do you want?"

"Same old Cassidy," he said. "All brimstone and brambles." He sipped his tea. "You might want to try roses and sugar sometime."

"Roses have thorns," I said.

He smiled, the expression almost weary. "So they do. "How have you been?"

I thought about throwing my tea at him but decided I wanted to keep the mug. It was kind of cute in a kitschy sort of way. Just my style. Without waiting for permission, I wandered to my liquor cabinet, brought back my last bottle of AsomBroso Añejo. The tequila was expensive as hell. I slopped some into my glass, threw it back.

"You should know, shouldn't you?" I said. "Your spies have been watching me this past year." I sucked down a third shot, corked the bottle. "Why are you here?"

Blowing out a fatigued sigh, he reached into his suit coat pocket, slid a photo across the table at me.

I looked down. Howard Brandt. My stomach flip-flopped then turned inside out. I stared at him through narrowed eyes. "I haven't seen or heard from him since my ceremonial execution," I said.

"I haven't asked yet."

"Thought I'd save you some time. You can leave now."

He retrieved the photo, glanced at his tea, reached for my tequila and glass instead. "He's been missing for three days."

I threw him an 'I don't give a crap shrug'. "And you're telling me this because—?"

"When was the last time you visited the Warrens?"

Coy as usual and very lawyer-like: only ask the question you already know the answer to.

I kept my face impassive, leaned forward. "I haven't seen, heard from, or contacted Howard Brandt since my trial. Please leave."

That damned, shrewd smile slid across his lips. "You didn't answer the question," he said.

And I wasn't about to either. I knew he'd been watching me

since my expulsion from the Order. He knew how often I'd visited the Warrens since then, and he knew when I'd last been there. Indecision boiled through my thoughts. Truth or lie? Truth would send me to the proverbial gallows. Lie would more than likely lead me to more realistic gallows.

If it were anyone besides Marshall Stimson, I'd think he was trying to trap me into confessing my sin. But despite our mutual and respectful dislike, I knew that the Grand Master's Chief Inquisitor cared only about the truth, politics and inconvenience be damned. He was fishing for something else.

"You know I don't need the Nexus at the Warrens to cross into the Nether Realm."

He sighed, helped himself to another shot of my tequila. "Yes, your Cheval mirror. But you haven't used it to do what you're not doing, have you?"

My hand twitched at the tequila. I forced it toward my mug of chai, took a careful sip. I didn't know squat about Erick, but now I knew he made a magnificent chai tea.

"Why not?"

"Why are you looking for Howard Brandt?" I asked.

Stimson frowned, his faded blue eyes thoughtful. "He missed our tee time," he said and stood, buttoned his coat. "And he owes me money from a bet he lost from our last round."

I watched him cross to the kitchen entry.

He turned, the same thoughtful expression creasing his brow that he'd worn at the table. Silence stretched between us. And though he tried to mask it, I saw the struggle behind his eyes and in the set of his mouth. He wanted to tell me something.

In the end, he decided against it. "A word of advice, Cassidy. I know you won't take it, but I'll offer it."

I arched my brow in question.

"Be careful," he said. "I know you're in the middle of something messy. You always are, despite the Order's decree prohibiting you from doing what you're... not doing. The Stephanie Brandt you abandoned isn't coming home."

My gut clenched with guilt and anger.

"Where was the last place you saw Howard Brandt?" I knew I shouldn't have asked the question, but I couldn't help myself. Just like a moth couldn't help but fly toward the flame and its death.

"We tracked him to the Warrens." He shrugged. "After that, nothing."

Another twisting corkscrew drilled into my gut, impaled my bowels along the way and drove them through the other side.

He stepped through the doorway then turned back. "Despite what you believe, I do like you and I don't want to see you get destroyed by whatever mess you're *not* in the middle of." He paused, pursing his lips. "You've been a breath of fresh air for me, something the Order has needed for quite some time." He tipped his hat. "Thank you for the tea and the tequila. I know you won't, but please be careful."

He left me alone with our cooling tea and the rest of my tequila, which wasn't much. I'd hoped he would offer to pay for another bottle.

Cheap bastard.

A moment later, Beegle wandered into the kitchen, a storm of snow and ice tangled through his short hair. He looked at me, a devilish grin pasted across his snout, clearly pleased with himself.

I shook my head. "You're grounded for the rest of my life," I said, rising from my chair. "Come on you little bastard, we've got things to see and people to do."

Beegle bayed enthusiastically, shook the melting snow and ice from his coat, plastering it across the floor and walls before trotting down the hallway in front of me.

CHAPTER 11
WHO'S THE SKANK?

I FOLLOWED a Jefferson County snowplow west down Morrison Road past the C-470 overpass until it turned into Bear Creek Avenue. I split right from the plow onto Mt. Vernon Avenue, a backstreet that hugged the edge of a marathon-long red sandstone saddleback on the right. It was snowing again. The slow, heavy flakes were clinging possessively to everything they grasped.

Mt. Vernon hadn't been plowed yet.

I kicked the Bronco into four-wheel drive and crunched a short four blocks through iced snow-laden chaos, before jerking it left into an empty, pothole-filled, frozen over gravel, stingily shared parking lot. Cleary's saloon, affectionately named Outcast Bar and Grill, a narrow, unassuming two-story building sandwiched between a dilapidated mom and pop motorcycle repair shop and a sleepy New Age tourist trap, squatted in front of me.

Cleary operated under the radar from his business as an independent facilitator, but mostly, he ran interference for the Numen Galére against the organization he'd betrayed and been banished from.

The saloon served the disaffected, disenfranchised, and exiled. Mostly Otherkind Solitaries. Sometimes human. It gave them a place to gather and gripe, plan or hope, though not much more. Cleary allowed no activity in his establishment that would attract unwanted attention. From the Shining Man or the Order of the Four.

The Shining Man ran a tight ship as well, dealing swiftly and severely with anything that went off his script.

Enter me.

I bucked the Bronco into an unsettled stop.

Steamy exhaust belched from the tailpipe, rising turbulently into the frigid late morning air. Beegle threw me a disgruntled look but forgot his displeasure when he looked out his window, woofed, and began dancing an impatient jig. He looked back at me, his eyes sparkling with a 'why are we still in the car?' beagle stare.

I had to smile despite the hurricane of emotion roiling through my gut at the prospect of seeing Cleary. His was the wound that never quite healed or scarred over enough to prevent profuse bleeding when pricked. And then there was Beegle in this moment. I wasn't sure, but I thought he might enjoy romping through the snow with total abandon more than hunting Otherkind. I frowned, tossed back a hurt expression. He responded with a beagle version of rolling his eyes, turned and scratched at the window. I shook my head.

Stupid dog.

I completed one last obsessive compulsive pass to make sure I was well armed with the Walther, a couple of extra magazines, Dad's fully loaded .38-Special, and Father Mike's dagger just for grins and giggles.

A girl couldn't be too prepared.

Especially when dealing with a sociopath like Alastair Cleary.

I shoved my door open, slid from the Bronco, and planted my

boots firmly into the snow. Beegle's hot doggy breath blew across the back of my neck. I offered to lower him down; he shoved past me, launching himself like a missile from the Bronco, and landed with beagle-like grace into a pile of fresh powder. He shook himself, glanced back at me then bounded through the snow toward the saloon.

I shook my hair out and settled my leather bushman outback hat on my head. I hadn't worn it since the Stephanie Brandt job. This seemed an appropriate occasion.

I followed Beegle through the snow, hoping he would remember his manners when it counted.

A few feet from the bar's covered stoop, Beegle stopped and went stiff, his nose lifting to test the air. He curled his lips and pushed out a low, throaty growl.

I stopped beside him, shook myself with an uncomfortable double-take as the image in front of me shivered. Fae-daemon power caressed my mind, demanding that I turn around, get back in my car and drive away.

Subtle. Strong. And very Cleary.

When I first knew him, I would have obeyed that glamour without a second thought.

He was an enigma. Touched and Manifested, but with the ability to cast fae-daemon glamours. Something a manifested Touched shouldn't be able to do. Except, Cleary wasn't simply Manifested or Touched. He was also partially Changed. Turned out he'd used a Medusa Mirror on himself to suck in and trap an Otherkind essence. I never discovered how he'd managed to come out the other side of that stupidity still mentally intact or how he'd managed to keep a loose grip on his sanity and keep his Soul.

Well. Sort of.

He'd never said. Or evaded the question when asked.

It was that action that saw him excommunicated and disavowed by the Order.

I curled my lip in distaste, shrugged the compulsion aside long enough to peer through the misty illusion, before sliding through it, Beegle at my side, his earlier playful abandon forgotten. Like me, he was all business now. I grudged him a quick smile as we stepped onto the stoop and shook the last clinging tendrils of magic and snow from our coats.

Leaning against the door, I squinted through the chiseled and flowing glass into the cave-like tavern. Several distorted figures wavered behind the glass. Two seemed to be seated at the bar. Another stood behind it. What looked like a couple of waitresses stood at the far end of the bar. I couldn't see anything or anyone else from where I stood staring through the glass in the door, hoped that I wasn't walking into a hornets' nest.

Yanking in a shaky breath, I pulled the door open.

Beegle shot across the threshold, scrabbled to a sliding stop on the worn and polished toasted almond hardwood flooring. I followed, stopping just inside as the door swung silently closed behind me, allowing my eyes to adjust to the sulking smoky darkness. Sixties hard rock blared through tinny speakers. A glowing emerald haze hung just below the ceiling, that seemed to quiver in time to the banging beat of the music. The stench of something dead too long dangled in the stagnant air causing my gut to rumble in angry rebellion. I shoved it back, clamped down hard until it settled.

The waitresses I'd spied through the door lounging at the far end of the bar were Wannabes. They wore black leather micro-minis, knee high black leather stiletto-heeled boots and might as well not have been there low-cut form fitting blouses and were doing shots of dust-laced whiskey.

Otherkind Solitaries from five of the six fae-daemon clans sat

scattered across the room, entrenched in their quiet conversations or concentrating on what they were drinking. A few
glanced in my direction, curled their lips in disgust, decided
Beegle and I weren't an immediate threat, and went back to their
business.

I swept my gaze back to the bar, where three sets of hostile
eyes glared at me. I glowered back, then slid my left hand meaningfully beneath my coat, and let it rest on the back of my hip.

Two of the owners of those eyes were from clan Raekorah,
their bulging buggy eyes flaring for an instant behind their world-
weary beguilement before returning their attention to their plates
and the origin of the rotting stench raping the air on the bar
between them.

I recognized the bartender, Frankie, a barely there Touched
who had hooked his wagon to Cleary back in the day when I'd
been glued to his hip, and who'd hoped to use him as a ticket into
the Order of the Four. Looked like that hadn't worked out.

He stomped to the edge of the bar, stabbed a shaking finger at
Beegle, and lashed me with sunflower-yellow flecked dull brown
eyes. "Get that damned dog..." he began then stopped, his mouth
hanging open. His eyes widened with surprise, indignant rage
melting in a breathless heartbeat that turned to dread, followed by
shocked horror.

Frankie had been the one to dump me at St. Jude's after
Cleary discarded me. And in my distress and vengeful rage, I had
sworn the next time I saw him I'd rip him open stem to sternum
and feed his guts to the rats. He'd scoffed at my threat, laughing
when he tossed me and my crap from his F-150, and gave me the
finger as he drove off.

Apparently, my reputation had gained some muscle over the
last ten years.

I threw him a smirk and sauntered over. I pulled the Walther, laid it gently on the bar, muzzle pointed at his scrawny scarecrow chest, my finger twitching dangerously close to the trigger.

Frankie stiffened, his eyes wild and wide. Kind of reminded me of a deer in the headlights, or maybe a rabbit. I scrutinized him a little more. Yeah, definitely a rabbit.

"Hey Frankie," I said in a sultry tone. "Been a minute and a half." I leaned forward. "How's it been hanging?" I asked as I glanced meaningfully down over the bar at his crotch, frowning with disappointment, before looking up and hooking my finger over the Walther's trigger. I winked. "Remember my parting words?"

His face paled, his hands shooting up over his head. "I was just doing what I was told, Kain. It was business. Nothing personal."

The quiet droning conversation buzzing around the bar faded into an uneasy silence.

"It felt personal to me." I shrugged. "But today is your lucky day." In one swift motion, I holstered the Walther, leaned over the bar, and snagged Frankie's shirt lapel, dragging him up over the top. I slapped him with a 'your dead meat the next time I see you' glare. Then let him loose.

He stumbled back, nearly tripped as he slapped against the liquor cabinets.

"Cleary," I said.

Frankie managed to swallow down the ball he'd sucked up into his throat. He flicked his head toward the rear of the saloon. My eyes followed his motion, took a moment to recognize the back of Cleary's head, the once rich reddish auburn curls now faded and streaked with silver. He sat in a booth, his back to the front and exposed, hunched slightly forward, probably over a bourbon, a gangly strawberry blonde with long curls sprouting from his side.

Arrogance or ultimate confidence. I wasn't sure. Didn't care.

I threw Frankie a look, blew him a kiss as I sashayed toward

Cleary and his female ventriloquist dummy. Beegle trotted at my side, the click of his nails on the hardwood echoing against the walls and through the quivering sunflower-tinted Dust haze above.

As I drew closer, a dark awareness titillated my senses. I shuddered; felt my body twist with an excitement I'd only experienced in the Nether Realm. Feral. Deadly.

An instant later, fae-daemon power coiled around my mind, arousing my thoughts, and making my skin tingle with its seductive touch as it tugged my reality into a world that only existed in porno flicks.

Unprepared for the assault, I stumbled a step, staggered against the side of a table, uncertain of my balance. My world wavered; my body tensed in anticipation.

A low, distant baying woof slid through the darkening mist clouding my thoughts, followed by a clawed foot scratching my leg, and a gentle nudge and a nip.

I shook myself. Drove the web of lies from my mind and shoved myself from the table, sweat gathering beneath my hat.

The assault pushed against me for another moment, but I was aware now. And prepared, something I should have been before I walked into the gaping jaws of the ravening lion. The power slunk back into the dark, where it waited. Hungry. But patient.

I managed a weak smile down at Beegle. He stared up at me unblinking. "C'mon boy," I muttered. "Let's get this over with."

I could now see the back of the woman seated in the booth beside Cleary more easily, her strawberry blonde curls strewn haphazardly across bare, silky, milky-white shoulders. She leaned against him, cherry red lips nibbling his earlobe, whispering into his ear. He stiffened and chuckled, shook his head. He straightened in his seat. The woman leaned away from him, but kept a possessive arm draped seductively over his shoulders.

Fear seized me that he'd been Enthralled.

My hand crept beneath my coat toward the Walther. I didn't want to shoot my way out. But if things went to hell...

"Stop skulking behind us in the shadows," Cleary said, his voice still strong, clear, unaffected. And very much British. "Have a seat."

I hesitated.

"Now you're just being rude."

I blushed, dropped my gaze as I curled my hands into fists at my sides.

Ten damned years since he'd thrown me to the curb. Twelve if you counted the two years I'd been enthralled by his charm.

How could the sound of his voice still turn me into that naïve eighteen-year-old girl who'd been so full of herself. And yet so eager to please, entranced and trapped by his carefully spun and powerful web of lies.

The woman giggled, the pitch like fingernails scraped across a chalkboard or a vacuous twenty-something California Valley Girl.

I threw off the scraping fingernails, settled for the vacuous twenty-something California Valley Girl.

The spell evaporated.

I shook myself, glanced down at Beegle, and arched a brow at him. He stared back up at me, his eyes sparkling, tongue lolling, and panting slow and relaxed. Like he'd been born for this. I smiled. Not born but made. Like me.

I swept around the table. Slid into the opposite seat.

Beegle sat a few feet away, his eyes intent on the woman.

Not human. At least not on the inside. Otherkind. But not her body.

An Otherkind Mimic.

She scowled, flicked her crimson eyes at me. I shuddered, the memory of that burning gaze staring out at me from behind Cleary's eyes smacked me upside the head.

I took a deep breath, uncoiled my body, and did my best to ignore her for the moment. Focused on Cleary instead.

He'd aged. But in a dashing Errol Flynn sort of way.

Leaner. Not as muscular. His hair thinner, the rich color faded, now streaked with silver and an attractive shade of gold that still framed a clean-shaven face, chiseled from faintly blushed marble creased, and marked by laugh lines and a few well-placed wrinkles. His violet eyes glinted bright, clear, and strong. Full of intelligence and deadly purpose, and something else that made me want to squirm.

I flicked my eyes to the Mimic, noted the insolence glinting from her burning gaze, the scornful lift at the corners of her full lips. I looked back at Cleary. The hint of a mocking smile brushed the corners of his number two pencil thin lips.

I glanced once more at the Mimic. The insolence behind her eyes had faded, along with the scorn curling her lips; her expression faded to blank. She shivered for an instant as a shadow passed across her vacuous Valley Girl face.

Feeding time. An Otherkind succubus and her human cattle.

My eighteen-year-old girl desire for Cleary died, replaced with disgust.

I leaned forward, planted my elbows on the table, and propped my chin on my folded hands. I flashed him my own vacuous Valley Girl smile. "Hey babe," I said. "Been a few."

Cleary stared back, eyes narrowed slightly, waiting for the punchline.

I tossed a look at the Mimic. "Who's the skank?"

She hissed at me.

I wrinkled my nose in distaste. "Likewise."

"Same old Cass," he said. "Still a killjoy bitch."

I shrugged. "You would know," I said. "You made me."

"What do you want?"

"Not in front of... that."

The Mimic glowered, her power crawling back from the darkness, coalescing, building into towering thunderheads. The air between us throbbed, grew shadowed. I shot her a bland look and shrugged. Reaching behind my back, I drew the Italian ear dagger, stabbed it into the tabletop.

Cleary scowled.

The Mimic went taut.

I leaned forward. "Good. You know who I am. Why are you still here?"

Cleary sighed, the sound tired and used up. He yanked the dagger from the table, shoved it back toward me. "Be a dear, Natasha," he said, his gaze pinned to my face. "Go help Frankie with the inventory. Cass doesn't like you. And I don't have another host for you at the moment."

Natasha didn't move.

Cleary snapped a sideways look at her. "Please."

Rage fire storming behind her eyes, she slid from the booth and stomped to the front of the saloon. She leaned against the bar, glaring back at me, her crimson eyes pulsing with power.

I turned back to Cleary. Arched a brow.

Another weary sigh slid from him. "So now you know my secret."

"I've known since that night at the Brown Palace," I said. "I've just never understood the how... or the why." I nodded toward the bar. "What about the host?"

He shrugged. "Like consensual sex between two adults."

"More like human trafficking," I said. "Or rape." I shifted in my seat, shoved down the burning rage bubbling up from the depths of my self-righteous soul. "What happens to the host when... Natasha uses her up?"

An uncaring shrug. "A trip across the Veil—"

"And dumped into the Nether Realm where her soulless body will rot for an eternity—" I said.

"... until another fae-daemon Essence inhabits her," he finished. "It's what she signed up for... voluntarily."

I snorted. "Voluntary my ass. More like slavery."

Disinterest flashed across his lean face. "Tomayto-tomahto." He lifted his hand above his head. "Drink?"

Frankie shoved a tray at one of the Wannabe waitresses who shambled toward our table and deposited her load: Cheap tequila and two shot glasses. She shuffled off without a word.

The shot glasses gleamed with rainbow colors in the uncertain light. Enchanted.

I arched a brow.

He snorted. "Good help is so hard to find, but I make do with what drags in through the doors." He poured us a drink. Slid one glass toward me.

"You know that won't work on me."

He smiled. "Not meant for you. But I guess Frankie might be behind on the local gossip."

I snagged the glass. Threw back the shot, grimacing from the kerosene burn rolling down the back of my throat, chased by the restless illusion.

I slapped the glass upside down on the table. Frankie glared at me, his mouth agape, his eyes eager. I twitched a smirk at him.

He scowled and joined Natasha at the far end of the bar for a private pout fest.

Cleary turned my glass back over, slopped more tequila into it, and raised his glass in a mocking toast. "To old times?"

"Go screw yourself."

He chuckled, tipped his glass back, and smacked it down upright on the table. I watched but didn't see the kerosene burn grimace. Or the bewitchment. Not that I'd expected it. Much.

I noticed Natasha watching us surreptitiously from the corner of her eye. She leaned against the bar, pretending to help Frankie. I figured one more taunt wouldn't hurt. I stared at her, raised my glass in mock salute and threw back the second shot, managing to crush the kerosene burn grimace this time, shrugging the bewitchment aside without a thought while Cleary studied me.

I turned the glass upside down in my hand; studied the slowly undulating kaleidoscope of colors and pursed my lips. Sloppy magic. I set it on the table, slid it toward Cleary.

He tossed another disinterested shrug. "The local expats like it. Seem to expect it. Like doing non-clan Dust for the high." His gaze tried to draw me in. "Without doing Dust."

I ignored the bait. "And the humans?"

He sighed, poured himself another drink, threw it back, and leaned back in his seat, arms crossed. "Makes them believe they have some power and purpose while they're here before they go back to their crappy little unimportant lives."

I snorted. "And I thought I'd hit bottom."

"Judge not, unless ye be judged."

"I don't think paraphrasing scripture out of context is an appropriate defense."

A well-remembered condescending expression slid across his marble-chiseled face. "And how does that self-righteous crown you're still wearing fit?" He flicked his eyes up, frowning as if he were examining something unusual. "From here it looks like it's grown a little small for your head. A little tarnished and tainted."

That stung.

The humor behind his eyes faded, replaced with boredom. Apparently, I was still an easy mark for him. Too easy.

"What do you want?"

I reached into my coat, pulled out the envelope with the last of my cash, and slid it through the cheap tequila puddles across the table. "I need a favor," I said, my voice even and unemotional. At least that's what I hoped I sounded like.

Interest flashed across Cleary's face. He peered down at the envelope, his arms still crossed. Raising his eyes, he shook his head slightly after a few seconds. "Even my balls aren't that big." He pushed the envelope back across the table with the tips of his fingers. "I don't know whether to be flattered that you thought I could do it. Or insulted that you thought I'd be stupid enough to try it." His gaze held mine a moment longer. "I wish you luck, though."

He started to slide from his seat.

"It's for Tansy."

He paused. "That deal is done. Nothing I can do to change it."

My temper flared. "Because of you," I said. "You could have brought her back to Father Mike."

He scoffed. "Really? And in which universe would I have survived that stupidity?"

My answer fell from my lips before I wanted to think about it. "It would have been the right thing to do."

His gaze rose to the top of my head. "Crowns and glass houses," he said. He looked at his watch. "You're burning daylight." He smacked me with a mocking stare. "And tell Michael to mind his own house from now on. Unless he wants it burned down around him." He stood.

"He's dying."

Another pause and a quick glance to the front of the bar. Natasha pursed her lips, shook her head in warning, her eyes glimmering intently. He slid back into his seat, looked at his watch. "You have thirty seconds."

"I need someone to babysit Tansy so I can finish this shit show you pulled me into."

The corner of his mouth twitched. "You have twenty seconds."

I sighed. "Father Mike isn't..." I choked on my next words, tried to grind the pain clenching my chest into the dirt. "Up to it." I shoved the envelope toward him. "It's all I've got left."

No reaction.

I heard the last of my thirty seconds tick off.

Cleary looked up at me; expression masked. His hand snuck out, grasped the envelope and pulled it back. "It's light," he said.

"You know I'm good for the rest."

He flashed that damned mocking smile at me and began to stand.

I slammed my hand down on his, pinned it against the envelope and the table. "I need a ghost."

His eyes twinkled. "When am I not?" He pulled his hand from beneath, shoved the envelope into his tweed jacket pocket. He twitched his head at Natasha.

I stood. Beegle came to attention, his hackles raised, head lowered slightly.

Cleary stared at him and snorted. He flicked a glance at me. "You have me until you don't. Make sure you use what time you have left wisely."

Natasha   sauntered   up,   her   crimson   eyes   sparkling humorlessly.

"My business with Cass is finished, please see her out."

Natasha scowled.

Cleary's hand shot out, gripped her arm. She winced as he leaned toward her ear. "No harm until my business with her is concluded." He lifted his brows for emphasis.

She tore her arm from his grasp, a feral growl curling her upper lip, and dragged a suggestive finger across his jaw as she walked away. Cleary leered.

He slapped me with one last mocking stare. "I'll call if there's news. Don't do anything more stupid than you usually do."

He walked away.

I watched him until he disappeared through a hidden door behind the bar, glanced down at Beegle. "Ready to go kick some Wannabe ass?"

He woofed, wagged his tail, and followed me from the saloon, making me smile when he nipped at Natasha's shins as we walked out into the howling teeth of the snow.

CHAPTER 12
KARMA'S A BITCH

TANSY STOOD inside the entry to Jonnie's penthouse apartment, cloaked within her own darkness; her bare feet slimed in a sticky pool of coagulating blood, chest rising and falling to the slow staccato beat of her heart. The tip of the Juzarine dagger's bone blade she clutched dripped obsidian onto the glassed tiles at her feet. To her left, the front door stood open, the gaping doorway shimmering in shadow, the hall beyond glowing brightly with virgin white mingled with red, green, blue and yellow Christmas lights promising peace, joy, hope.

Lies.

Starless night caressed her soul, power singing through her blood that whispered seduction into her thoughts. A lover's gentle and eager touch. She quivered, tasting the promised fulfillment of desire.

She hugged herself, lowered her gaze to the floor, where the dead Chasseur lay in a gelatinized pool of his own blood, his throat cut, a beatific grin carved in pallid cadaverous stone etched across his face.

Her work. Quick. Silent. Efficient.

Her motions dancer graceful and fluid as she first glamoured then slit his throat between two languid heartbeats.

Tansy's mind strayed to Cassie, wondered if she were as lethal, as graceful, realized that she never thought to ask. Not that Cassie would have told. Cassie only told what benefited Cassie.

Adria's stealthy whispers wound through her thoughts, soothing and calming, pulling Tansy away from her introspection and back to the shadowy-filled room gawking at her in terrified silence.

A muted whimper slid from beneath Jonnie's bedroom door; slammed closed and locked before she killed the man lying at her feet. Rage flashed, firestorm intense, and almost destroyed everything before the power calmed her, slowed her down, and allowed her to first taste, then savor her approaching triumph.

She closed her eyes, licking dry, cracked, and swollen lips, touched the cut that split her upper lip with the tip of her tongue. She tasted the coppery flecks clinging to her lips, caught the growing stench leaking out the man's bowels buried beneath his stiffening body.

She smiled, and closed her eyes, swayed to the beat of her own thoughts and the whispers winding through her splintered mind. She conjured an image of Jonnie kneeling at her feet, slimed in his own blood and filth, begging for his life. A shrill giggle echoed off the narrow entry walls.

Tansy opened her eyes, wondering whose giggles were bouncing through the air, grinned when she realized they were hers.

Muffled cries and sobs slithered from beneath the closed and locked bedroom door she faced; Jonnie's, begging for his life, his shrill, little girl timbre sending thrills racing down her back and arms.

A stray memory flitted through her thoughts.

The surprised shock on Father Mike's withered face after her second stroke. A dark stain spreading across his white linen shirt. His chest stuttering. The Juzarine dagger she wielded in her trembling hand, blood dripping from the blade tip to join the stain growing across his chest. His eyes wide, mouth agape before collapsing at her feet, motionless, but still breathing. A dark wet pool spreading beneath his crumpled body.

She stared down at him, grief and regret blossoming behind the savage excitement cascading through her blood and bones. Adria appeared in her thoughts, gently guided her back from the abyss, pulled her across Father Mike's shuddering body, through the open doorway, and down the hall. Dragged her around a corner.

Tansy stopped, resisted Adria's pull long enough to turn, her thoughts clearing for an instant as she mouthed, "I'm sorry," into the emptiness.

As the silent words fell from her lips, the clarity embracing her mind faltered, and died, replaced by the acid drip of darkness and nihility.

The memories stumbled, fell and shattered at the bottom of the abyss, yanking Tansy back to the present. She thought of Jonnie, whimpering behind his bedroom door, and the rage built to a volcanic boil. Another sin to add to his tab.

She glared at the bedroom door, the glossy white finish splattered with blood, her mouth set into a razor-thin line. Gripping the dagger tighter, she stepped over the man's body, and touched the door, felt power rise and coil around her will. An instant later, the door blew inward off its hinges, spraying the bedroom with crimson flecked splinters.

Jonnie shrieked.

She found him cowering in the farthest corner from the shattered door, wedged between his nightstand and closet door, babbling and begging. Tansy tore him from his hole, dislocating his shoulder as she dragged him from the room by that arm, the arm he'd used to beat her, across blood-slicked mirrored ebony floor tiles, and past the man lying dead in the entry.

Jonnie howled, tried to pry her crushing fist from his wrist as she dragged him through the entryway, smearing ceramic tiles and wood with blood, urine and his own filth.

At the end of the entry, Tansy stopped, twisted Jonnie's dislocated arm until he squealed and fell back, quivering and limp.

She yanked Jonnie back into motion, dragged him into the living room, his scrabbling bare feet squeaking against the polished cherry parquet floor, dumped him in the center of the living room, stomped his ankle when he tried to crawl away. He screamed, curled into a fetal ball, his broken ankle clutched between shaking hands.

Tansy stood over him, fists clenched, breath hissing from between clenched teeth, rage churning through her fragmented thoughts. She shook with it, the memory of what he'd done to her feeding the building firestorms.

Kneeling, Tansy wrapped a shaking fist into the collar of Jonnie's bloodied silk pajama top, yanked him to his feet, shaking him until his teeth rattled in his skull. "Shut. Up. Or I'll gut you now and let you bleed out in your own filth." She slapped him, dropped him. He crumpled as he slammed into the floor, curling back into his fetal ball, and continued to cry, his sobs more garbled and intense.

Adria's soft, hissing words breathed fire through her thoughts, coiling oily fingers around her mind, stroking and teasing.

Tansy shuddered, closed her eyes and bit her lip. Quiet laughter followed, tormenting and mocking. The image of Jonnie with his hands under her T-shirt exploded, shaking Tansy to the foundation of her soul. Screaming, she yanked the dagger from her belt, pried Jonnie from his terrified cocoon, pricked the flesh of his neck beneath his chin with the tip of the blade.

Blood oozed and dribbled down his throat.

He flinched, went suddenly motionless, his sibilant sobs fading, their scrabbling run through his body dying as he managed to gulp past the dagger blade's tip.

Grinning, Tansy dragged the point of the blade down Jonnie's throat to his sternum. She sliced off the crimson-stained ivory buttons, flicked his pajama top open. She pressed the blade's tip into the hard flesh of his chest, over his heart, leaned in with her weight, slowly shoved it through to the bone.

"We are your Angel of Death," she said, her voice a quiet hissing whisper.

Jonnie's eyes went wide. He tried to control his breathing, slow the slapping of his breastbone against the dagger tip.

"We're here to judge you for your sins."

He heaved out a stammered cry and shook his head, his eyes round and wild, body shaking as he tried to wrench himself from her grip.

Tansy rattled him against the floor. She lifted him up by his hair, and peered into his eyes, breathing in the wave of satisfaction washing across her soul. The promised power and peace. She closed her eyes, reveling in the deep calm.

Dropping Jonnie, she walked over him carelessly, kicked him recklessly in the side of his head.

She stopped beside his settee, framed shadow-like in front of the sunlight leaking past the tailored edges of the pastel curtains hiding the balcony windows.

She rubbed her fingers against the fabric along the arm, lingered in the memory of the sheer linen as it moved against her fingertips, smiling as she contemplated Jonnie's promises when they had been...

The scratch of a body dragging itself across the parquet flooring tore Tansy from her memories. She turned, watched Jonnie snail himself across the gore-smeared cherry planks. His dislocated arm hung useless from his shoulder, hindered his speed. The ankle she'd stomped followed behind, couldn't seem to keep up.

She watched him with detached fascination, wondered if he would shrivel up and die if she doused him in salt. Agonizing, but too quick. He deserved more.

Much more.

Tansy began to hum a dissonant and shapeless melody she'd heard during her captivity in the Nether Realm, wondered why she remembered it now, eleven years away from the Juzarine. She smiled at the inharmonious sound as she found the automatic curtain controls and looked over her shoulder through the murky light at Jonnie, thought about sitting on the settee and watch him drag himself across the floor toward whatever safety or rescue he thought he might find.

But no, she did not have time. The voice inside her mind murmured for her to be quick and efficient. Toy with him. Build his terror. Savor the taste. But don't drag it out. Too much would taint him, ruin the flavor of his dread.

No false promises or lies. Only the sweet flavor of truth and freedom.

She pressed the button.

The curtains shuddered, rolled back from the balcony windows with a quiet whir that reminded her of a cast-off kitten she had adopted before she'd fallen into eternal nightmare. The kitten had offered her a little solace and peace during her early Manifestation rages. One day, though, the kitten disappeared. Tansy spent almost a week looking for it but couldn't find it.

Heart-broken, she asked Cassie about it, received a hard, quiet stare in answer. She stopped looking after that.

Faded gray late morning sunlight crawled through the muddied shadows, rolled them back into the corners. Tansy unlocked the balcony doors and slid them open. The winter wind marched through the opening, stinging her cheeks and chest with an icy slap that calmed her mind.

She strolled back to collect Jonnie, continuing to hum the droning Otherkind melody. She caught him at the edge of the kitchen floor. He fell onto his back, reminding her of a struggling turtle as he tried to slap her hands away with his good arm. She scowled, stomped his left ankle again, and grinned as bone snapped beneath the leveraged drive of her heel, laughed when he screamed. Grasping him by his untied greasy hair, she dragged him through the living room and onto the balcony, into the teeth of the driving wind and snow. Tossing him down, she stepped back inside and retrieved the cordless nail gun he stored in his coat closet. A nicknack snagged from a former customer who couldn't pay their bill. Jonnie had paraded it during one of her past visits for Chaos, taunting her until she paid him with the coin he preferred to extort from her.

Outside, she found him huddled against the wall, snow and ice clinging to his eyelashes and tousled hair and tinting his face and chest with a frosted blue. He clutched his dislocated arm over his chest and shivered, teeth chattering. Tansy stood over him, the nail gun clutched in one hand, the Juzarine dagger in the other.

He looked up. Squinted into the wind and light glinting off the snow. "Who are you?"

Tansy chortled, the sound stolen from her lips by the wind. She kneeled in front of him, set the nail gun and dagger into the snow beside her. "Seriously? You don't recognize us? After what you tried to take from us last night?"

His eyes widened.

He whipped his head to the side, toward the open balcony doors. "She promised to protect me. She…"

Tansy backhanded him, slid her finger through the trail of blood leaking from his split lip, sucked it clean. She leaned in close, watching his growing horror with macabre fascination. "Are you ready to die?"

He flinched away from her face, closed his eyes, began to whimper again. She backhanded him a second time, then wrapped her hand around his neck, and lifting him from the snow, dragged him up against the wall until his eyes were even with hers.

He began to choke, fighting for breath as he struggled against her grip.

Tansy watched him with growing malevolent fascination, the way his face slowly turned red and his eyes bulge as they grew red as well. He reached up with his good arm, tried to shove her away from him, shifted his grasp to her hands. His struggling began to wane, and the hand grasping her fist slid away and dropped to his side. His eyes began to fade with the dying fire struggling in his chest.

A slow, malignant grin grew across her face. She let go of his neck and watched him slide down the wall into the snow-crusted concrete. He cried out, tried to cradle his dangling arm as Tansy squatted down between his legs, entranced by the pain and the knowledge that he was about to die.

"Please," he said, his voice hoarse and scratchy, tinged with growing hysteria. "Let me go. I'll make it up to you." His voice cracked, shot its way up a couple of octaves, the sound scraping claws down Tansy's spine. She cringed for an instant, tilted her head, infatuated by his growing desperation.

Jonnie licked ice from his lips, wiped the snow from his eyes. "Please," he whined. "I'll do whatever you want me to do. Get you what you want me to get you." He paused as a quivering breath strangled its way from his chest. "Do you want more Chaos? I can get it for you. All that you want. I can even get you Ebony. The genuine stuff. Pure. And from the source. Just, please—" he began to cry, his body shuddering with the sobs, half-frozen tears crawling down his icy cheeks. "D... don't kill me."

"Really?" She asked, her voice shrill with little girl excitement. "Ebony? All that we want?"

Jonnie nodded vigorously, a faint spark of hope igniting behind his eyes.

"And if we want something else, you'll give it to us, no matter what it is?"

His head bobbed up and down with manic precision, the light of hope burning brighter. "Yes," he said in his weaselly little voice. "Anything you want. It's yours. Just ask and I'll make it happen."

Tansy giggled with sudden delight, pretending to consider his offer. After a few seconds, she leaned close to him, blocking the howling wind from his face. "We want you dead."

Before he could react, she snatched the nail gun from the piling snow and yanked Jonnie up again by his neck, sliding him against the frost-slick wall until his eyes were even with hers.

She grinned as she shoved the nail gun into his dislocated shoulder. "This is going to hurt a lot," she said.

Jonnie screamed, his shrill cries drowned out by the buffeting wind.

CHAPTER 13
PUZZLES AND ENIGMAS

I SAT and stared out the Bronco's windshield into the blowing snow. Natasha stood under the shadowed cover of the stoop, glaring back at me, her luminous eyes swirling with blood-red storms that glinted off the volcanic ash snowflakes like fire. She shot me a wicked sneer and vanished back into the bar.

I sighed and shoved my hat onto my head. Beegle woofed from his seat, his tail thumping out a beat against the leather and door. I reached over, scratched him behind his ears. "What do you think, Beegle. Are we screwed, or what?"

He stared at me, his soft brown eyes glinting with ecstasy as he leaned into my hand.

Shaking my head, I leaned over and hugged him. He hugged me back in his own beagle way, his hot doggy breath washing across the side of my face. I leaned back and continued to rub the bottom of his chin and throat. He smiled back at me.

"You're my rock, you know. My foundation. Now that Father Mike is dying."

The words flatlined at the back of my throat, their remains misting away like the morning fog. I wiped a stray tear from my cheek, then dug out an unused tissue from the bottom of the center console, hidden beneath a few rags—grimy, but not completely grease-soaked. I used it to blow my nose, thought of how Father Mike would pretend to be so proud that I hadn't just used the back of my hand or my sleeve. When I was finished, I shoved the sodden tissue back into the center console for another such emergency

My tattered thoughts strayed to Alastair Cleary.

I had him for as long as my five large lasted, which might be a tad past my fifteen seconds of fame. But that's what you got when dealing with a narcissistic sociopath. Still, as much as I hated to admit it, he was that good.

Not that I had a choice.

I fired up the Bronco and glanced at the clock on the console. One p.m. Burning daylight all right. Only I had no clue where to start.

A first for me.

Jonnie Hallows?

My chest tightened into a clenched fist.

The bastard needed to pay for what he'd done to Tansy. And he needed to pay dearly. But he was protected. By both sides.

Like Cleary, he played both sides of the street, but he was more of an alley cat, slinking through the shadows where he thought no one could see him. Or, if they did, they ignored him, as long as what he stuck his greedy little paws into didn't interfere with the bigger picture.

It was a frustrating conundrum, one that always made my brain hurt when I dwelled on it too much.

Corruption and avarice thrived when ambition picked at the line between good and evil, and ambition had been fraying that line, at least in Denver, for a very long time. At the moment, the line felt like it was ready to unravel.

I shook my head, trying to cleanse the muck and mire clogging my mind.

Touched and Manifested in his late teens, Jonnie Hallows, one of Jessie's recoveries, chose to embrace the darkness instead of trying to learn how to control it, which attracted the attention of the Numen Galére and later, Navarro and the Denver Commandery.

A gifted and brilliant alchemist, Jonnie, following his indoctrination into the Shining Man's cabal, quickly unlocked the secret to synthesizing fae-daemon Nether Dust, what we humans called Ebony. Now in his early twenties, Jonnie not only controlled the export of the seven natural fae-daemon Dusts from the Nether Realm for the Numen Galére and their illegal Dust trade in the human world, he also manufactured, distributed, and sold synthetic Ebony, the most potent, addictive, and lethal fae-daemon dust in the human realm, from which the Shining Man took a substantial commission.

To keep from running afoul of the Order of the Four, Jonnie also fed information to the Denver Commandery regarding small-time Otherkind human child trafficking activities across Colorado.

It was a thin line and sometimes inconvenient for both sides, considering Jonnie's sexual predilections and less savory vices. But despite being the occasional and biblical thorn in their sides, both the Numen Galére and the Order of the Four considered Jonnie more of an asset than a liability.

If the Shining Man was expanding the distribution and sale of Chaos beyond negotiated boundaries, it could mean a bloody civil war between the Otherkind clan factions of the Numen Galére and an even bloodier street war between the Numen Galére and the Order of the Four with the Denver Commandery on the front line.

Was that what the Shining Man wanted, a civil war within its cabal and a street war with the Order?

Both it and Cleary had to have known Tansy was high on Ebony. They also both had to have known Jonnie was her source. And yet, neither had mentioned it. Which meant... what, exactly?

I worried my bottom lip as I pondered the enigma.

Apocalyptic times.

Jonnie and his Chaos and Ebony were part of this mess, but not the center. That honor belonged to the Daemonrie Chimera the Shining Man had so kindly forced me to eliminate. And its creator, a rogue Noble Knight of the Four, probably connected to the Denver Commandery.

Another rotted thread unravelling Francisco Navarro's tapestry.

Although it seemed pertinent, Jonnie's Ebony was not my immediate concern. The Daemonrie Chimera was. Tracking and finding the chimera before it could lose a firestorm had to be my priority, which would lead me to the Ebony and hopefully Jonnie's balls stuffed into his mouth.

I needed to find the chimera's source, where the Medusa Mirror had been brought into the human world.

Marshall Stimson had mentioned the Warrens, subtly alluding to my illicit nocturnal visits and my unsanctioned crossings into the Nether Realm through the Nexus located in the basement of the abandoned house.

Was that where the Daemonrie Chimera had originated from? Had the rogue Noble Knight managed to open the Nexus at the Warrens into the Nether Realm without Navarro of the Denver Commandery noticing? The possibility jarred me. But there was only one way to find out. I needed to go to the Warrens.

CHAPTER 14
IT'S ALL YOUR FAULT

MY PHONE RANG. Rachel Moreau's name scrolled across the screen. I shivered, thought back to the call I'd received from her three days ago, before all this mess started. I didn't answer. She didn't leave a voicemail, and I hadn't thought about it again until now as I stared at her name and phone number scrolling across the screen.

Her daughter, Emily had been my first successful recovery as a newly minted Noble Knight of the Four. She'd be seventeen now. And Emily's baby sister, Rose, would be twelve.

I hadn't spoken or been in contact with Rachel or her family for five years, though for the five years before I'd remained close to Emily to help prepare her for her Manifestation. I'd heard through the Commandery grapevine that her husband, Kincaid, had left them unexpectedly and divorced Rachel about four years ago. I didn't know why. Rachel didn't reach out to me about it, and I didn't bother to find out, something that now made me cringe with guilt and regret as my thumb hovered over the talk button.

Why would she call me now, after five years of silence?

Only one way to find out.

I answered the call.

An eerie static greeted me. Electricity crackled down my back, chased by Mount Everest sized goose bumps.

"Rachel?"

A shrill sing song voice skipped out of the static, set my teeth on edge as I tried to hear what it said.

Then, "You need to come. Now."

Rachel's voice. Edged with... terror.

"Rachel?" Apprehension bubbled in the pit of my gut.

A choked sob cut through the static. Died.

Scratchy silence. Then, "Do you know what it feels like to die over and over?"

Not Rachel's voice, but similar. My mind tugged at the loose ends of a dim memory. "Who is this?"

"You should have made sure... before you left."

A slow, frigid chill crawled down my back. I tried to force down the rising dread. "Who is this?"

"You do not have much time."

My mouth went dry. Cold shivers played tag up and down my arms.

"Rachel? Who the hell is this?"

The voice snickered. "Everything that happens is your fault. Remember that."

The line died.

I stared at my phone. Rachel's name vanished.

My mind tugged on too many loose threads. The memory unraveled. I reached for it, watched helplessly as it disintegrated and vanished. Clenching my fists to stop their shaking, I glanced at Beegle. He'd felt it, too, whatever the hell it was.

Images of decaying sugarplum faeries high on Ebony danced through my jittery thoughts. Something was wrong, but what?

Dread sat on my heart and squeezed the air from my chest like an accordion.

I thought of Tansy sitting on the floor in front of the Shining Man's gray battleship desk, the accusation bubbling in her eyes. 'We're not sisters.'

I slammed the steering wheel with my fists.

'Do you know what it feels like to die over and over?'

The high-pitched sing-song little girl's voice raked blackboard fingernails down my back.

What the hell was I supposed to do?

Beegle placed a calming paw on my arm. I looked into his wise beagle brown eyes, saw grace and compassion. And understanding, like the boy at St. Jude's Parish.

Cursing, I slammed the Bronco into gear and crushed the gas pedal. The tires spun, throwing icy gravel into the snow-laced air before the studs bit down and heaved us into the street.

Sixty minutes later, I turned down the street leading to the Moreau's compound.

I peered through the icy fog as I crawled the Bronco to the privacy gate and braked beside the intercom, gazing through the gloom curtaining the grounds past the ornate iron gates. I couldn't see shit.

I rolled down my window, hesitated, wondered if I should be more discrete, considering Rachel's phone call, but ditched the idea. Subtle wasn't part of my repertoire.

I pressed the call button.

No one answered, but a moment later, the gates shuddered open, the squeal of frozen gears muted in the clinging fog. I nudged the Bronco through the opening, knew immediately this was a bad idea as soon as the gates moaned closed behind me, shoving me deeper into the waiting abyss and cutting off any hope of escape.

I drove slowly up the winding drive, hunched over the steering wheel, my nose pressed toward the windshield, as if that would magically allow me to see past the clinging mist and know what waited for me at the end of the drive.

I glanced at the console clock and pursed my lips at the hour it took me to drive here.

The Bronco's brakes protested as I slowed to an uncertain stop at the bottom of the steps leading to the covered porch entrance. Dual porch lights clothed behind sullied glass stood guard to either side of the doors, squinting through the fog, their leprous light scratching its way down the ice-slicked steps.

I killed the engine, stared out Beegle's window into the gloom clinging to the house. The faint prickle of an unfamiliar fae-daemon power itched the underside of my skin. The kind you needed to scratch, but couldn't, no matter how hard you tried.

I glanced at Beegle. The way his fur trembled. The curl of his lip showing teeth. And the low growl in the back of his throat.

I pulled the Walther from its door holster and ejected the magazine. I selected a different one loaded with brimstone-coated rounds, checked the first round, just to make sure. I didn't want this going south on me if things got... a little tense, like it had at the cemetery. I slammed the magazine home and racked the slide, grabbed two more of the same.

I took a calming breath. "You ready?"

Beegle looked at me and stood, taut and tense.

I stepped out, creepy crawlies skittering up and down my body. Beegle scrabbled out and stood shivering beside me.

I paused at the edge of the front fender, gazed up into the fog, reined in my romping imagination.

Nothing moved. Not even the fog.

Fae-daemon power throbbed through the air, just below the surface, enough to suck the spit from my mouth, and make my hands clammy and slick. I swallowed back my apprehension and wiped my hands on my pants then reacquired my grip as I circled the front of the Bronco, pausing at the bottom of the portico steps.

I brought the Walther and woke the targeting laser as I peered into the misty gloom to either side of the front doors as far as I could see, which wasn't much, certainly not to the corners of the house, where the porch vanished past each turn. But I didn't sense any presence, physical or supernatural, waiting for us outside, and Beegle remained focused on the front doors, a coarse growl scraping up from the back of his throat. Whatever waited for us, waited inside. Alone, hungry, and eager. Impatient to spring its trap.

I walked carefully up the steps, planted each foot firmly against the ice greasing the treads, Beegle at my side. At the entry, I used my coat sleeve to swipe away some of the frost from the window glass and peeked through. Emptiness glared back at me from the clustered shadows, the itch below my skin growing into a faint electric hum like an army of ants crawling through my veins.

As I pressed down on the door latch and pushed the door open, I wondered why the damned doors in horror movies were always unlocked.

It swung inward silently on well-oiled hinges, bumped against the inside wall.

Beegle trotted over the threshold, his nails clicking on polished granite tile, and stopped in the dead center of the parlor. He stood at attention; nose pointed left toward the hall leading to the library as fog roiled across the doorstep and hugged my boots.

I brought the Walther back up from high ready. A javelin of red light shot through the air, disappeared down the hallway.

The faint hiss of the maniacal giggle I'd heard on my phone rode the light back from the library, setting my teeth on edge.

I swept the targeting laser across and down the hall, made sure it was empty before I took my first step toward the monster waiting for me.

Keeping to the center, I crept toward the entrance standing open and slasher movie inviting on my left, my boots creaking softly against the glassed floor tiles. Beegle walked in step beside me, hugging my right leg, his clicking toenails a staccato counterpoint to my squeaking boots.

We stopped just beyond the doorframe, hidden from what waited inside. Wavering light spilled from the yawning opening across the hall floor, teased the fog following us from the parlor. Otherworldly power, not so subtle now, vibrated against the back of my teeth, skinned my nerves with its keen edge. I glanced down at Beegle. He stood at my leg, quivering, his lips pulled back into a silent snarl.

I caught the whisper of movement from inside, chased by a desperate whimper and a choked sob.

Swallowing back my dread, I nodded down at Beegle, whispered, "Go."

He shot through the doorway, his sudden explosive baying reverberating through the emptiness. I followed an instant later, stepping around the corner, and swept the room with my eyes and targeting laser.

I slammed to a sudden stop.

Heavy ornate curtains embraced the floor to ceiling picture framed windows dominating the back wall, shutting out the gray, snowy daylight. Elaborate and elegantly designed lights glimmered uncertainly from the vaulted ceiling, casting an eerie glow against the books lining the walls.

Emily Moreau, sporting the whip-thin body of a long-distance runner and taller than the seven-year-old I remembered stood behind two finely carved, burnished elm dining table chairs in the center of the room, her dark, brunette hair hanging in limp and tangled ropy strands over her eyes and down past her shoulders.

She clutched what looked like a Juzarine dagger. Blood, bright and fresh, coated her hand, ran down past the guard, and painted the burnished, flat, razor-sharp edge. The dagger quivered in her hand, dripping blood from the tip in a slow, insane staccato rhythm.

I looked into her once bright, full of life eyes and swallowed back my rising panic. My skin went cold and clammy.

Ebony swirled through those eyes, glinting with the madness hovering beneath.

Nightmare memories of Stephanie Brandt and the reason I had abandoned her in the Nether Realm scratched through my mind, gouging ragged furrows through my thoughts. Stephanie had glowered at me through the same demented mania that frolicked behind Emily Moreau's Ebony saturated eyes.

She'd been Changed.

I flicked my gaze down to the chairs, licked lips gone dry.

Kincaid Moreau's severed head squatted in the chair to my left; the seat rouged in a lake of crimson. Blood shone dully off the oak floor tiles beneath. Tangled forest deadfall hair matted the sides of his head, and dead, empty eyes stared accusingly from a sunken colorless gray face. His lower jaw was missing.

I swallowed back bile, stomped down on the boiling in my gut, and slid my gaze to the right.

Rachel Moreau stared back at me, shaking, bound with gossamer to the other chair, eyes wide that glistened with tears and flashing terror. Blood flocked hair hung limp and loose in sleep tangled curls over her right shoulder, soaking the side of her sweatshirt. Her mouth worked in twisted, painful movements, trying to scream, but managed only strangled silence.

Rose lay in repose at the base of the two chairs. Her dead eyes stared blankly up at the flickering ceiling lights, her slender hands lovingly crossed over her chest, the light glowing dully off her grayish white pallor.

Terror clenched my heart, which did a triple somersault into the pit of my stomach.

I looked up, took a slow, steady breath, surprised that my targeting laser still quivered over the center of Emily's blood-smeared forehead. I remembered Beegle, found him hovering to my right, standing stiff and alert. Waiting.

Emily's eyes followed my glance, found Beegle. She frowned as if confused.

Beegle bared his teeth and growled.

Emily leered, suddenly unconcerned by his presence or his menace.

She turned her eyes back on me, stared with wide-eyed madness, twitching and muttering as if arguing with someone.

"Hey Ems," I said. "Remember me? It's been a few, hasn't it?"

She snarled, revealing crimson-stained teeth. Bloodied saliva dripped from her mouth. She wiped it from her lips with the back of the hand clutching the dagger. "We wondered if you would come."

I tried a nonchalant shrug. "Traffic's a bitch this time of day. Especially in this weather. I'm here now, though."

She squealed a high-pitched little girl giggle.

The memory of Stephanie and the madness spiraling across her twisted expression kicked me in the gut.

Her eyes lost focus, meandered around the room behind me, and came back. Sharp. And full of deadly intent.

"You should have been here," she said. "We invited you. Why did you not come?"

I glanced at Rachel.

She sat stone still, her eyes wider than before, mouth clamped shut. Sweat dribbled down the sides of her face, mingling with the blood splattering her tangled hair.

"I'm here now."

"Daddy said he didn't like us anymore, that he was afraid of us." She gestured toward Rose. "He said he was going to take Rose away from us. From mommy."

I froze.

She stared at me, her eyes narrowed, slid her gaze over the back of the chair holding Kincaid's head. "Why would Daddy be afraid of us?"

I glanced at Rachel.

She stared back at me, eyes grown wider and wilder. She worked her mouth, but still only managed to spit silence. She finally twitched her head in a desperate shake.

I caught Emily eyeing me; a shrewd expression slapped across her bloodied face. The dagger trembled in her grasp, the flat of the blade tapping out a chaotic beat against the top of the back of Kincaid's chair.

Beegle inched toward her.

She glanced at him and snarled, crept the point of the dagger toward Rachel's head.

"We don't like your demon," she said, her voice edged with hysteria. "He is... in my head." Her eyes came back to mine. "Make him stop." She inched the point of the dagger against the back of Rachel's neck.

I held out my support hand.

"Okay," I said, tried to sound soothing and calm, the exact opposite of what I felt. "He can be annoying sometimes." I twitched my eyes at him. "Beegle. Down."

He hesitated.

For a heart twisting moment, I thought he might choose to ignore me. He did that sometimes. With unpredictable consequences. I didn't want this to be one of those moments. But after what seemed a lifetime, Beegle looked up at me, held my gaze for an instant before backing up a couple of steps. He sat; his concentration still focused on Emily.

I breathed a sigh, turned my eyes back to Emily, and tried a reassuring smile. "Hey Ems, how about you put down the dagger, okay?" I chanced a quick glance at Rachel. Tears from silent sobs squeezed from the corners of her eyes. "The three of us... we can get some Rocky Road... you still like Rocky Road, don't you? We'll talk about what's bothering you. You, me, and your mom."

Emily hissed, turned her gaze toward Rachel, stroked the top of her mother's head with a shaking hand. She looked up at me, her eyes grown more hysterical.

"She knew," Emily said. "What Daddy wanted to do. What he planned to do—" Her gaze roamed the room for a moment, settled on Rose. "To both of us."

When her gaze came back to mine, she grinned, peered at me from beneath her brows.

"Why did you kill us?"

I gaped at her.

She sighed and nodded, slid the dagger down, touching the blade's edge to the side of Rachel's throat.

Rachel tensed, held her breath.

Emily's eyes never left mine. "It is too late for her," she said. "It is too late for you."

The edge of the dagger trembled against Rachel's throat.

I didn't dare take the shot. The reflex from the impact might cause her to cut her mother's throat.

I held my right hand out, slowly lowered the Walther to my side. A bad decision, but I didn't know what else to do. I needed to talk Emily off her ledge. Maybe becoming less of a perceived threat might work. More than likely, it wouldn't. Hysterical insanity born from fae-daemon Changing magic made people unpredictable. But it was all I had.

Ebony-fueled power throbbed through the air, building to a slow and inevitable crescendo.

My vision suddenly blurred. My body swayed. I forgot to breathe, aching for what caressed my soul. My spirit stretched toward what that power promised, screeched when it vanished. I stumbled, nearly collapsing to my knees before regaining my balance.

For a panicked moment, I thought I'd lost the Walther, found it still pressed into my cold, sweaty hand.

Emily smirked, her gaze knowing and eager. "You felt it. Did you not? The Call?"

I managed to swallow past the sand clinging to the back of my throat. Nodded. "Yes, Ems, I felt it."

The smirk faded as loss slipped across her face. She hummed an inharmonious and chaotic melody. Sang, "Too late, too late. Always too late for you."

Her eyes came back, their focus still distant, but filled with something... else.

"Why did you kill us?" she asked again.

I frowned. "I didn't—"

"But you did, when you left us behind. You promised to take us home. But you didn't. Lies and broken promises." She dragged the dagger against Rachel's throat, drawing a thin crimson line.

Rachel tensed. Squeezed her eyes closed.

Panic tried to steal my resolve.

I brought the Walther back up, trained the laser at the center of Emily's forehead. A lousy shot. But the only one I had. I swallowed, tried to wet my lips. "You're here now, though," I managed. "With your mom. Me." I glanced down. Nodded toward Rose. "And Rose."

Manic amusement swept across Emily's face. She lifted the dagger from Rachel's throat, turned it in the air in front of her glittering eyes. Ebony reflected off bone and blood.

Her eyes came back to mine, still distant, but now filled with a malevolence that made my blood run cold.

Emily leaned forward slightly, rested the flat of the blade on the back of the chair beside Rachel's neck. "Answer us truly," she said, flicking her eyes toward her mother. "And we will spare her."

I swallowed down the trepidation clogging my throat. "Okay."

Emily giggled. "I lied."

With inhuman speed, she sliced the edge of the bone blade across Rachel's throat.

Beegle snarled, launched himself at her

I squeezed the Walther's trigger

Blood sprayed from Rachel's throat, streamed down her neck, soaking her sweatshirt.

Emily's head snapped back.

Beegle wrapped his jaws around her left wrist, used his weight to drag her down and back from the chairs.

She dropped the dagger, ripped Beegle from her wrist, leaving torn flesh and muscle clinging to his teeth, and flung him away from her.

He landed cat-awkward a few feet away and slid across the floor into a bookcase.

The light fled from Rachel's eyes. She slumped forward in the chair, twitched, and went still.

Emily swayed on her feet.

Blood dribbled from the hole in the center of her forehead. She focused her eyes on me, managed a maniacal grin. "Everything that happens is your fault," she slurred, collapsing to her knees, body twitching before going still. Her eyes stayed open. Blank and accusing.

CHAPTER 15
UNINVITED GUESTS

I KNEELED beside Emily's body.

She slumped down on her knees, sunken into herself, chin resting on her chest, eyes open, and staring blankly at the bloody floor. Her hands lay open and empty at her sides, her expression twisted and agonized, even in death.

A few ghostly flecks of Ebony swirled weakly through her empty eyes, fading slowly and vanishing. Fae-daemon power tickled the underside of my skin, scraping my anger and grief raw and red, before dissolving into memory with the Ebony.

The ceiling lights flickered with ambivalence for a few heart-beats before skipping town, plunging the library into shadowed darkness hemmed by the dingy light leaking in around the curtain edges. A dull glow stood in the open doorway, reflected off the buffed hallway floor tiles, refusing to cross the threshold.

I heard Beegle scrabble to his feet behind me and glanced over my shoulder at him. He shook himself and stared at me then began to clean the blood from his snout. I twitched a smile at him, turned my gaze to the back of the blood-stained dining room chairs.

I stared at the top of Rachel's head, how it slumped forward, chin resting against her chest. Blood dripped from the edges of her seat, pooling around the chair's legs.

I spied the back of Kincaid's head through the chair's carved wood lattice, the way his matted and tangled curls lay plastered against the back of his skull.

Finally, I peered through the gap between the chairs at Rose, noted her pallid skin and sunken cheeks, resting my gaze on the crimson ocean staining her nightgown over her chest.

I wiped away a tear and closed my eyes.

An image of Audrey blossomed into view.

Our fifth birthday. We were playing outside behind the house in the woods we weren't supposed to be in, relishing the exhilaration of our disobedience. It had been a thrill followed by our terror when the monsters snatched us from our world into theirs. The image wavered, refocused on Audrey's empty grave and my lost hope of ever finding her and bringing her home.

Guilt and regret strangled my chest as a sob escaped its prison and shook my body.

Stephanie Brandt appeared next, her eyes swirling with coal that drowned out the hazel light of her eyes. Changed into a fae-daemon human hybrid meant to sow havoc and chaos in the human world, her body stripped of its essence and replaced by a fae-daemon consciousness. A savage and brutal Juzarine that stared at me from where I had pinned it into the mud after putting two rounds into Stephanie Brandt's chest.

I straddled the Stephanie Brandt Changeling, blood flowing from the two holes I'd put into its chest, pinned its thin, gangly arms beneath my knees, kept its legs pried open with my feet to keep it from bucking and kicking so I could deliver the punchline; the bone blade of the Juzarine dagger through its heart. The same dagger confiscated by the Shining Man.

Pain, guilt, and regret separated by decades, but still raw and bleeding as fresh as on the day the wounds were inflicted.

I blinked my eyes open, blew out a heavy breath, and waited for the images to melt back into the abyss.

I holstered the Walther and stood, wondered all the 'what if's' as I scanned the murkiness, and turned my gaze to the top of Emily's head.

She'd been Changed.

I shuddered, kneeled back down before her, peering again into her dead eyes. They were dark. Empty. Powerless. But the memory of those coal-black flecks swirling through her eyes remained. I saw them again, the way they glinted when she stared at me.

Where had she gotten the Ebony?

Jonnie?

Why?

I'd witnessed Emily's Manifestation, helped to guide her through it the best I could. And despite my awkward and often clumsy guidance, she'd come through to the other side better than most. At least better than me.

Beegle's warning growl brought me up short.

I rose, turned toward the library doors, hand grasping the Walther as targeting lasers tattooed my chest. Two heavily armed and armored figures in tactical gear, riot helmets, and face masks, stood just inside the threshold to either side of the gaping doorway, the assault rifles they aimed at me spewing red hot light beams.

A third murky figure stood in the center of the doorway, slender face hidden in shadow, framed by slightly wavy fiery red hair stuffed up into a commander's cap and pulled back into a tight ponytail. Lithe body, slim waist. Gloved hands crossed in front of a narrow waist. The top hand grasping a semiautomatic pistol.

Her eyes were hidden beneath the bill. But I knew they were green in the moment. Angry. And ready for violence.

Beegle continued to growl.

I heard him stand, nails clicking on the hard wood behind me.

Jessie gestured with an impatient nod. "Shut that damned dog up."

Before I could react, a fourth figure emerged from the hallway and raised a rifle.

A loud puff reverberated through the library.

Beegle yelped.

I heard his nails scrabble against the floor, turned in time to see him flop down onto his side.

I swung back, drew the Walther, rage gurgling in the back of my throat, saw a third red dot materialize over my chest. I froze, picturing the smirk Jessie threw at me from the shadows.

"Same old Cass," she said. "Always shooting first and never asking the questions after."

"Only my friends call me Cass," I said, my voice dripping acid. "And you ain't one of them. Jess."

"Back at you, babe."

"Bitch."

"Whore."

Ouch.

I thought I carried a grudge. But I guess for her, Ellis Wynn had been worth it. Too bad for him she didn't end their relationship in time.

She gestured toward me with her chin. "Hands."

I weighed my options.

"Extreme prejudice," she said. "Hands. Where we can see them."

I heard Beegle's lethargic whimper, shoved the Walther back into the holster, and raised my hands.

Jessie raised her pistol and centered the laser on my chest.

I felt her finger find the trigger and begin to squeeze it back, tensed for the shot, heard her mutter something under her breath. She lowered the pistol.

"Not dead," she said. "Just tranqued. Him I still like. Sort of." A gesture with the gun. "Knees. Hands behind your head. Fingers interlaced."

I didn't move.

She raised her pistol again, centered the laser on my chest. "Extreme prejudice. Remember?"

I swept the three figures around her with narrowed eyes, as if that might give me X-ray vision, felt Jessie's wintry smile.

"Peter's not here," she said. "Not enough water left under those torched and scorched bridges." She shrugged. "And I need him focused on other things at the moment."

I sighed, dropping to my knees beside Emily, feeling the blood soak through my tactical pants. I placed my hands behind my head, interlaced my fingers.

"Maybe you *can* teach an old dog new tricks." She nodded toward me with her chin. "Go."

The Chasseur standing beside her with the tranquilizer rifle side-stepped to their right, came around the chairs, positioning themself for a clean shot behind my side. I imagined I could feel the spear tip of the targeting laser pricking the side of my neck.

The two Chasseurs standing to either side of the doorway slung their rifles and drew their sidearms. They approached me from opposite sides. I didn't move, held Jessie's probing glare.

The Chasseur to my left stepped into the lake of blood surrounding the Moreaux hesitated. I imagined the grimace and the revulsion; the sudden turn of thoughts that said I had done this. I had. But only the last part. In the end, it wouldn't matter. Jessie would make sure of it.

I saw the glare of the targeting laser from the corner of my eye, wondered which way they'd take me if I chose to resist.

The third Chasseur came behind me, but not close enough for me to engage hand-to-hand, just in case. I had to smile, though I was on the wrong end of this party.

Jessie stepped toward me, her gaze drawn down to the floor where Rose lay, puffed a soft gasp. A reaction I hadn't heard from her since our first kill.

Before Cleary.

Before Navarro and the Order of the Four.

Before our lives had gone to shit.

She swept the chairs with her eyes. Kincaid's head. Rachel slumped forward, still bound in place by the slowly dissolving gossamer. She looked up, glanced at Emily, her mouth set into a tight line, then looked at me, her expression edged with flint and something else behind her eyes.

Satisfaction. And my death.

I welcomed it until an image of Tansy under Jessie's control flashed through my thoughts. I shifted. The whisper of a movement, but it was enough.

Jessie brought up her pistol, tagged my forehead with the laser. "What the hell have you done?"

I met her indignant glare. "Why ma'am," I said in the worst imitation of Scarlett O'Hara I could manage. "Whatever do you mean?" I couldn't help myself, despite the venom glittering from Jessie's eyes, and the promise of a great deal of agony coming my way, followed by a slow, and agonizing death.

Jessie flashed a smile.

I guess great minds thought alike.

"Down," she commanded.

I glanced at the blood pooled around me, looked up. "I'd rather not."

A boot slammed into my back, shoved me face forward into the gore, barely managing to break my fall as my face slammed into the gooey mess I'd knelt in.

A knee ground into the small of my back, followed by the muzzle of a suppressed pistol into the back of my skull.

I spit blood, didn't know who it belonged to.

"Try anything, and your brains will become part of the casserole."

A woman's voice, early twenties, hopped up on adrenaline and fear. She radiated unstable power. Touched, but beginning to Manifest. Late. Something new for Jessie. And worrisome.

I wondered if Jessie's other Chasseurs were girls as well.

The muzzle in the back of my skull vanished.

Hands, stronger than I expected wrenched my arms behind my back, made my still healing shoulder scream. They bound my hands with ensorcelled zip ties made for people like us. I tried to peer up at the Chasseur but only managed to ogle the top her boots. The hands yanked me to my feet, turned me to face my former bestie.

Jessie snatched my Walther from its holster, ejected the magazine, and chambered round, handed them to one of her girls. She tugged the .38 from its home, dangled it in front of me, arched a mocking brow. "Still carrying daddy's guilt gun? Don't know why I'm surprised." She snapped the cylinder open, dropped the rounds into her palm, handed both to the same Chasseur. "Does Father Mike know?" She peered into my eyes and smirked. "Guess not. Not that it matters... anymore." Her smile grew cold and vengeful. "Can't say that I'll miss him."

I spit blood in her face.

She backhanded me.

I wished people would stop doing that. Healing abilities or not, the cuts and bruises felt like crap and would for a long time.

Jessie fished a small vial from her pocket. Held it close to my face.

Sleoneaxar Clan Dust. Nasty crap.

For normal humans, the Dust produced deeply profound hallucinations. For Manifested Touched, the effects were closer to a really bad acid trip.

I tensed, tried to wrench myself free.

Jessie slammed a fist into my gut.

I lost my feet.

Those same stronger-than-expected hands twisted into my hair, yanked my head back.

Jessie brought the vial close to my face, her eyes touched with enraged madness. She grinned, an expression I hadn't seen since she swore to put a bullet through my head for Wynn.

"I know how much you love the stuff," she said, mock concern on her face as she slammed another fist into my gut, snapped the cap off the vial, as the hands twisted through my hair wrenched my head back. Jessie dumped the Dust into my gaping mouth and pinched my nose closed, forcing me to swallow.

Electricity jolted my brain, scrambled my thoughts, shattering my mind into a million pieces. I went limp, slumping into the hands holding me, my feet no longer my own.

Jessie snorted, "We're burning daylight." And walked from the library.

I followed, dragged between two of Jessie's Chasseurs, my feet trailing through blood and gore as they walked me around the chairs holding Kincaid and Rachel Moreau.

Past Rose.

She continued to stare with dead eyes up at the darkened ceiling.

As they wormed me from the library and down the hallway, I

felt Emily's dead stare against my back, and a salacious grin plastered across her cadaverous face as she whispered, "Why did you
kill us?"

CHAPTER 16
REVENGE OF THE PRODIGAL

JESSIE STOOD in the center of the anteroom that led to Navarro's palatial office, her hands bound with fae-daemon gossamer threads. A precautionary stipulation from Navarro before he agreed to allow her to surrender herself in exchange for the lives of Peter Oliver and the other disaffected and disavowed Commandery agents she'd recruited. Two stoic-faced Chasseurs flanked her, hands clasped at their waists, eyes hidden behind mirrored sunglasses. They belonged to her, had infiltrated Navarro's sanctum months earlier. The Claro walnut desk near the wall to her left stood empty, Navarro's administrative assistant having been dismissed before her arrival.

A light brown, creased leather attaché case lounged on the floor beside her. Next to it sat a ceramic-lined cold storage container, the kind used to transport perishable medicines, organs designated for transplant, and other biodegradable materials.

Sullen sunlight waded cautiously in through the windows, casting away the dull-eyed yellow light falling from the crystal-jeweled chandelier hanging above three matching vermillion-cushioned Claro walnut chairs placed against the wall, beautiful and out of the way; just the way Navarro preferred his enemies.

The dulcet aromas of myrrh, black pepper, sandalwood, and frankincense mingled through the invitingly warm air, reminding Jessie of the soft and silent lull following a gentle snowfall. She closed her eyes, allowing her thoughts to pull her through the moment for a few seconds as she stretched her hands.

The men behind her shifted their weight, yanking Jessie back from her musings and into the reality of her immediate peril. Despite her intricate and immaculate planning, she frothed with apprehension and a gut twisting sense of foreboding, something she hadn't experienced since Cleary had brought her before Navarro twelve years ago, all hard, candy-coated shell with an ooey-gooey chocolate center. Navarro may have been declining physically and intellectually, but he still kept a strangle hold on the Denver Commandery and its assets and could still teach the serpent from the Garden of Eden a few things. The tiniest misstep in this moment would see her exiled to the Nether Realm as a permanent plaything for the Juzarine.

She glanced at the French Empire Ormolu Bronze and Green Marble Three-piece Clock squatting on the table standing between the windows, looked back to the closed doors leading into Navarro's office. Peter Oliver had been closeted with Navarro for over an hour. Longer than she'd expected or planned for. A tendril of worry wormed through her thoughts. Had Navarro seen through her subterfuge? Or worse, had Peter betrayed her to Navarro?

A tendril of worry wormed through her thoughts.

Coming home, asking for forgiveness, and a chance to be welcomed back into the family had been a calculated risk. Especially considering Peter's sudden and unexpected moral quandaries. But being brought back into the fold was an essential piece of her plan. She needed Navarro's acceptance and forgiveness, no matter how suspicious or cautious he might be at this moment. It was the only way she could gain control and unfettered access to the internal organs of the Commandery, where she could spread through Navarro's organism like an undiagnosed cancer, accelerating its degradation and corruption until she tore its beating heart from its chest.

Jessie shifted her weight to relieve the stress and cramps beginning to twist her arms and legs into knots.

Peter, despite his recent moral recalcitrance, wouldn't betray her to Navarro. His sister and her children were too dear to him, too precious. He wouldn't gamble their immediate safety or their future on any promises from Navarro to protect them. Like her, Peter had learned from hard experience that Navarro couldn't be trusted and that his word meant nothing.

Strange how family, no matter how tenuous the connection binding them together might be, unfailingly made people prisoners of their own emotions and choices.

She thought of Cassidy and Tansy and their unorthodox and uniquely untraditional relationship. Cassidy regarded Tansy as her baby sister while Tansy chafed beneath what she believed to be an artificial construct. In Tansy's mind, everything Cassidy and Father Mike did was an illusion, a contrivance built on a house of lies and delusions.

Which had made Tansy the perfect target, Cassidy's greatest blind spot and vulnerability. And it would be her undoing.

Misted tendrils of human tainted fae-daemon power slid through the air from behind Navarro's closed office doors. They slithered toward her, the undulating, snake-like fingers stroking Jessie's mind, pressing and probing, searching for a hole, a crack in the armor surrounding her thoughts and the lies behind the truth she'd built for the story Peter was spinning for Navarro.

She tensed, grit her teeth against the unwelcome and familiar corruption dripping acid from Navarro's touch. Carefully concealed memories clawed up through the detritus she'd buried them under, stumbled zombie-like from that blasted and broken terrain, its beauty shattered long ago by the depraved mind fondling her spirit and soul.

Sweat beaded across her forehead, rolled through the creased landscape of her deepening scowl, dripping into her eyes. She blinked the stinging sweat away, snapped her head, flinging the befouled remnants from her hair.

Navarro's power clung to her soul for a moment longer, stealthy and predator patient, waiting and watching.

Jessie gathered her strength, anchored her will into her purpose. She met Navarro's probing inquisition with finely honed resoluteness, dangled her last carrot before his ravenous mind, the one she knew he could not resist, 'Take me back or not, old man,' she flung back at him. 'I don't care. But know that the folly of your hubris will be your downfall and destruction.'

Silence.

One last slimy thrust speared into her mind.

Jessie bit back a soundless scream.

The power vanished.

She staggered a step to reclaim her balance.

Hands gripped her arms, hauled her upright—then vanished as the iron-bound dark elm doors swung open, their burnish long since faded, dull as Navarro's failing body.

The air surrounding Jessie shuddered, slunk through the sudden gaping breach, sucking her across the threshold and into Navarro's ravenous and waiting maw. He lounged in his favorite seat, a mid-eighteenth-century French fauteuil à la reine armchair, sipping Earl Grey from an Old Paris Porcelain teacup, one of a set of eighteen he used for various functions and activities. Grandiose and pretentious affectations he flaunted to humiliate and belittle those he deemed unworthy of his attention or stature; innumerable indignities she'd endured during the twelve years he'd used her for his purposes. In contradiction to his lavish furnishings, he was dressed in an unadorned royal purple vestment and matching slippers. A carefully constructed charade meant to convolute and muddle, keeping him on control of every situation and conversation.

Snow-misted sunlight executed a volte-face from the naked floor to ceiling picture-framed windows behind his desk, dragging the advancing shadows behind it, staining the elm-paneled walls a depthless shade of charcoal black.

A Brahms concerto sighed contentedly in the background, wrapping the sumptuous space in a calm and inviting embrace.

Jessie swayed unsteadily where she stood for an instant, stumbled forward a precise step to the edge of a mid-century Turkish Hereke rug, regained her balance as the leather briefcase and white-marbled ceramic box were discreetly set down beside her, followed by the muted click of retreating steps across the polished antique Calacatta marble and the whispered clack of closing doors behind her. More myrrh, black pepper, sandalwood, and frankincense glided through the cool air, their flirtatious fragrances beguiling as they mingled through the office spaces, breathlessly coaxing Jessie to relax and let down her guards.

She ignored the smoky wisps tickling her thoughts, focusing her attention on the bishop.

Navarro sipped his tea, his narrow skull-like face nearly transparent in the subdued lighting. He looked at her over the rim of his cup, his dead eyes glinting, the promise of a cold-blooded smile touching his cheeks. Peter stood to the side, hands clasped at his waist, face masked and emotionless.

Threat and calculated risk wafted through the air, tangled

with the soothing rhythms of the Brahms concerto, twisting the melodies until they began to choke and gasp for breath.

Navarro set his cup down, clasped his spider web-thin hands in his lap. "And so, the prodigal returns," he said, his voice scraping a dull knife blade down her spine. His vampiric grin widened for an instant before dying on nearly bloodless lips. "Peter has told me an interesting tale. A story spun with great skill and finesse, one worthy of the greatest storytellers from history." He leaned forward, his dead expression twisting suddenly into a feral nightmare. "Why should I believe him?"

A sudden darkness made the room contract, become claustrophobic. It pulled the walls toward her, sucking the air from the surrounding space until it seemed as if she couldn't breathe.

Jessie remained still, sweat dripping into her eyes and running down the sides of her face. She kept her expression as dead as the mask Navarro wore. "Take me back or not, old man. I couldn't care less." She paused, drew in a careful breath as she glanced at Peter. He stood tense, stretched to the snapping point, war raging behind his eyes. Navarro had to know. There was little he didn't know. One confessed word and she would be dead where she stood, her essence ripped from her before her body crumpled to the floor. "Either way, your hubris will be your undoing."

The otherworldly tendrils twisting and coiling through her mind paused and stared, considering and evaluating. It saw through the cracks in her deceptions and carefully constructed lies into the heart of what it thought was her truth. For an eye blink, an all-consuming blackness shrouded her mind, severing her link with reality and life. A crushing weight slammed down against her, incinerating her essence.

Jessie felt herself begin to buckle as her essence burned to ash. She screamed.

The illusion vanished, evaporating as quickly with the wispy threads of a morning fog.

Jessie collapsed her knees, panting, sweat dripping like blood from her face, splatting unceremoniously into the rug she leaned over. She looked up, caught Navarro's smile as it faded from his lips, the glint of satisfaction hovering behind his eyes.

An uncomfortable silence filled the room as Navarro continued to stare, eyes narrowed, expression contemplative. An instant before the stretching silence snapped, he nodded. The movement curt. Almost imperceptible.

Peter strode to Jessie, hauled her to her feet. The metallic snap of a knife opening stung the air, followed an instant later by the whispered tug of the blade against her bonds.

Her hands came free, dropped sullen and numb to her sides. She met Navarro's icy stare, a silent battle of wills, one she gladly relinquished as she fell clumsily back to her knees in obeisance, head bowed, tingling hands planted firmly against the coarse weave of the Turkish rug.

A low, hollow chuckle rumbled through the space between them. "Cassidy may have been the better player, but you were ever the better actress," Navarro said. "And I have missed our games."

She looked up. Navarro continued to lounge, but had extended his hand toward her, offering her the acceptance she had come to reclaim. The amethyst in his ring watched her, leering with eager expectation.

She wouldn't die today.

Smiling inwardly, Jessie allowed Peter to pull her to her feet again, her balance before crossing the abyss separating her from the next phase of her vengeance, her boots murmuring against the rug. She noted the simple writing desk fashioned from lightly stained oak, Navarro's armchair resting against it. Beside them loomed the small oval lamp table, its finish twin to the desk. The

Buccellati sterling silver Piemontese tea service preened from the tabletop. An Old Paris Porcelain teacup filled with Earl Grey lounged near the tea service, steamy wisps crawling from the cup into the air.

For an instant, she allowed the anger to boil behind a carefully woven mask at the way he treated her like a misbehaving acolyte, made her feel like that eighteen-year-old girl again, so full of herself, but ignorant of his world and how it truly worked. She endured his lingering asexual leer, tried to ignore how it made her feel exposed and vulnerable. Under his control.

All of that was about to change.

Jessie kneeled carefully at his feet, still uncertain of her balance, and bowed her head. She took his right hand, laid a gentle, if not quite reverent kiss against the ring on the index finger.

Navarro smiled, pulled his trembling hand back into his lap.

She looked up at him through her brows, waiting for his permission to rise.

Navarro's health was rapidly declining, leeching away with each passing day, his death quickly approaching, though she couldn't guess how much time he had left. Days. Weeks. Months. Years. And despite his frail appearance, Navarro displayed a robust heartiness at ninety that men in their twenties would envy. Which meant that as much as she might wish it, she couldn't wait for nature to take its course. She wanted his world burn to cinders around him. And she wanted him to know she was the one responsible for it.

"You've brought gifts," Navarro said.

Jessie heard the rustle of leather and ceramic lifted from the floor, she soft murmur of approaching steps. Navarro motioned to the table beside his chair. Peter set them down carefully, stepped back.

"Leave us."

Jessie felt Peter's gaze on the back of her head for an instant, his continued struggle behind his piercing stare.

"I'll be outside," Peter said. "If you need me."

A light, condescending chuckle wafted past her. "Will we?" he asked. "Need him?"

Jessie bit her bottom lip, shook her head.

"Thank you, but no. I think Miss Colemann and I shall be quite comfortable alone for the remainder of our... conversation."

Another whisper, followed by the caressing brush of air against the back her neck. The faint, jarring metallic clack of the door opening and closing.

Navarro sipped his tea. "You've been busy," he said as he set down his cup and laid a shaking hand on the ceramic case. "But before we discuss Jonnie Hallows and his untimely demise at the hands of Tansy Harper, tell me about the Moreaus."

Jessie paused, wondering how much Navarro had known, had guessed, and had pried from Peter. She'd expected this. Still, knowing that Navarro was this well informed made her gut twist for an instant. She considered lying, which had been an option. But Navarro had spies everywhere, including within her small group of disaffected rogues, including Peter, who was an effective if somewhat unstable and chaotic playing piece on her game board. Fortunately, she knew the identities of Navarro's spies and would eliminate them at the appropriate time.

She decided on the truth, or at least as much of the truth that she wanted to divulge until she knew the extent of Navarro's knowledge.

"Unfortunate, but necessary," Jessie said.

Navarro studied her from his height above her, once an impossibly high distance that had slowly eroded and diminished until now, it was nothing more than what it was; an old man who had outlived his usefulness and life attempting to keep his disintegrating control over people that abhorred and hated him.

He continued to stare, his expression inscrutable.

"Dangerous," he said into the strained silence. "And wasteful." He took another trembling sip of tea and frowned. He slapped the cup back onto its saucer and shoved the service away.

Jessie suppressed a smile. His tea had grown cold. Like him.

"Why the entire family," he asked.

"To open the final door," she said.

He arched a brow, the curiosity and sudden wariness skipping across his face vanishing almost as quickly as it had appeared.

Jessie nodded toward the briefcase. "What's inside that will explain everything," she said.

Navarro hesitated; the first instance of uncertainty Jessie had ever witnessed during the twelve hellish years she'd been caught beneath his grungy and greedy thumb.

He leaned over, carefully lifting the bag from the table, his thin, stick-like arms straining with the effort, his expression clenched within a tightening vice that looked as if it might crush his skull between its jaws. He dropped it into his lap, stabbed her with a glance before opening it and peering into its depths. He hissed suddenly, fear exploding into a raging fire across his face as he glared down at her, trembling, his hands clenching the sides of the attaché.

"What have you done?"

Jessie allowed herself to smile as she stood, towering over him. She reached down, carefully retrieving the Medusa Mirror from the oily depths of the bag. She studied it for a moment before lifting the case from his lap and dropping it at his feet. Leaning over him, she reverently set the mirror in his bony lap, grinned when he squirmed at its touch.

Even now, empty, the mirror radiated unhallowed fae-daemon magic; thin, misty tendrils from Stephanie Brandt's Essence.

She straightened, stared down at him, wondering why or how she had ever considered him to be a great man, someone that would lead her toward the destiny she knew was hers to take.

Navarro lifted his gaze from the mirror, sudden rage attempting to strangle the terror coursing behind his eyes. "What did you promise the Juzarine in exchange for this monstrosity?"

Jessie snorted. "You." She knelt and drew a small syringe filled with an oily, charcoal black liquid, glinting darkness and death from her boot.

The Brahms playing in the background suddenly shrank back and stuttered, shattering the serenity flowing from its quiet harmonies. The relaxing smells wafting through the office shuddered an instant later, falling to the floor where they lay writhing in agony.

Navarro's eyes went wide, his hands gripping the arms of his chair. He shrank back, opening his mouth, his voice hoarse, the words stumbling from his lips as Jessie leaned over and pressed the tip of the needle to his neck.

She felt his power rise like a sudden tidal wave, rolling toward her, ready to crush her into pulp. She brushed his illusion aside, drenched it in gasoline, and lit the match. Pressing her lips to the side of his ear, she whispered, "You know what this is old man, and what it will do to you."

He swallowed and nodded. "Why," he asked, his voice weak and trembling. "I gave you everything."

She blew out a hot ragged breath, plunged the needle into his neck, shoved down the plunger. "And you took everything from me," she said, capping the syringe and shoving it back into her boot.

She stepped back and watched as Navarro's face paled, his

dead eyes shrinking back into his skull, their fiery glint beginning to grow cold and cadaverous. "Your mind won't be stripped from you immediately," she said. "You'll have more than enough time to contemplate the agonies the Juzarine will inflict on you before stripping your essence from your body and sealing it into its own mirror." She paused and leaned over him. "And I want you to watch what happens next, knowing it will be your last time."

She turned, strode to the door, placed her hand on the handle, felt a subtle shift behind her.

"And does Marshall Stimson play a part in our quiet melodrama?" Navarro croaked out, his words beginning to slump and slur.

Jessie paused, surprised she hadn't known that Rouanet's pet inquisitor had been thrown into her stew pot. Without turning, she flung a nonchalant shrug back at him. "I welcome the plot twist," she said, opening and closing the door quietly behind her.

Peter detached himself from the opposite wall, watching dispassionately as she approached.

"Stimson is here," she said, watching him pale for an instant before recovering his composure. "Find out why."

"Bonnet will be attached to his hip."

Jessie flinched a smile. "Then don't get caught." She left him staring after her, the click-clack of her heeled boots against the marbled floor bouncing off the walls trailing her down the hallway.

CHAPTER 17
TRUTH AND CONSEQUENCES

AN OCEAN of ice thrown into my face tore me from unconsciousness.

I spewed water from my mouth, shook it from my face and tangled hair, blinked the fog from my eyes. I tried to focus through the gloom clinging to the spaces embracing me. Sun-intense light blazed from the low ceiling, making me squint.

A Dust hangover pounded a silent beat against the back of my head.

I tried to move. Enchanted cable ties sliced through the flesh of my wrists and ankles, binding me to a metal chair. A cord of gossamer hung looped around the base of my neck, slowly tightening the noose as I struggled against the chair. I leaned back, felt the constrictor knot at the base of my skull.

I'd been stripped to my skivvies; bare feet planted firmly against the frigid concrete floor in a puddle of water fed by a drip line.

That's when I felt the electrodes gripping the ends of my fingers on each hand. Wires ran from each electrode, snaking into the darkness just beyond my feet, reappearing a few feet away where they slithered into an electric generator humming with quiet eagerness.

Dread gripped my heart and squeezed. I tried to remember to breathe, watched the vulture-like dread sitting on my shoulder leering at me and shaking its head with thirsty anticipation.

I sat in the sub-basement of St. Michael's Parish, fondly named the Extermination Room by my former Commandery besties and Navarro's favorite three ring circus.

I'd been in this room more times than I cared to remember. At first, as an ardent participant for training to learn how not to kill Otherkind I was torturing. In the end, after Stephanie Brandt, briefly as a side attraction, but never in the center ring.

Despite knowing that struggling was useless, my panicked mind told me I had a chance. If I tried hard enough, I could snap the tethers slicing through my wrists and ankles and rip the gossamer cord from around my neck before it strangled me to death.

And get the hell out of Dodge.

Yeah. Right. And unicorns were real. Did rainbows count?

A restless body moved from within the blackness surrounding my tiny about-to-be agony filled world. A quiet cough scratched the air from another direction. I craned my neck to get a view, remembered too late the gossamer cord looped around my neck.

Clenching my jaw, I forced myself to relax. I wasn't looking forward to the coming slow electrocution. But I also didn't want to strangle myself to death, either.

I caught the scent of lavender and roses. Jessie's favorite fragrance combination during the Year of Wynn. A scent she hadn't worn since.

Unpleasant memories sidled next to my trembling thoughts, sadistic eagerness gleaming from their feral eyes.

I sucked down an anxious breath, stared past the blinding

lights. "Hey Jess," I croaked, my voice a little shakier than I liked. "You should change your scent. I can smell your stench a day before you arrive and two days after you leave. It's worse than old lady perfume."

She melted into the light, wearing black tactical pants, boots and a matching black clingy tee that emphasized her tall, lanky figure and feral beauty. The jagged scar running down the right side of her face from her hairline to the edge of her jaw helped. I'd given her that scar. Not quite three years ago, after she confronted me about Ellis Wynn's murder, the hit ordered and sanctioned by Navarro.

It hadn't mattered that I'd left Wynn's place before my backup snuck into his apartment and assassinated him. Wynn and I had had some pretty heated words, and I'd roughed him up pretty good, warned him to stay away from Jess or pay the ultimate price for his stubborn pride. He'd never had the chance to heed my warning.

Love really sucked in our business.

My eyes wandered to the combat knife on her belt. Aluminum handle. Engraved with the words, "You're my forever person. I'll be there for you, even when you don't know you need me." Words I thought would always be true. Double serrated nearly seven-inch blade. The one I'd given to her on her eighteenth birthday. When we were tighter than besties.

Her eyes followed my gaze. She drew the knife from its sheath. Held it up. Admired the way the light glinted off the oxide-coated blade. She looked at me, smiling as she sauntered over, and ran the tip of the blade across the right side of my face, from the edge of my chin toward my hairline, before she wandered around behind my chair. The tip of the blade flicked. Drew blood, making me flinch.

I heard an exaggerated sniff.

"At least I bathe regularly."

I shrugged, regretting the movement as the gossamer noose tightened. "At least I still believe," I said. "I had a friend once, who believed with me." I tried to look up at her over my shoulder. "She probably could have taught you a few things."

She snorted and leaned down, the side of her face almost touching mine. Her breath smelled of peppermint and malice.

"Is that what you call this?" She held up the .38 Special round I kept in my pocket as a personal party favor for my special moments when thoughts of my dad overpowered my will to live. "Belief?"

I stared at it, fascinated by the way the brass caught and reflected the light blinding me from the rest of the room and the eager figure hidden within the shadows beyond. Navarro.

The round vanished. "What? No pithy comeback? Or sarcastic remark?"

Jessie stepped in front of me, held my dad's Colt in one hand and the round I'd saved for myself in the other. She glanced from them to me, back.

"Here," she said. "Let me help you believe." She snapped the cylinder open, slid the round in. Spun the cylinder. Snapped it closed. She pressed the muzzle against my forehead and pulled the hammer back. "Give the word," she said. "And I'll help you truly believe."

I closed my eyes and tried to conjure memories of happier times, despite knowing the truth that there were no memories of happier times. Guess it sucked to be me in our moment of togetherness.

The pressure of the revolver's muzzle against my forehead vanished.

I opened my eyes.

Jessie had stepped back, lowered the revolver's hammer. She

set it down on a small table just beyond the edge of the island of light I'd been marooned on. Nodded.

I heard the faint click of a switch.

Electricity exploded from my fingertips into my arms, and through my body. I jumped and bucked against the chair, feeling the gossamer noose tighten around my throat, barely managing to avoid biting my tongue in half.

The electricity burning through my veins vanished as quickly as it materialized.

I slumped forward in the chair, tried to gulp air, jerked back suddenly when the gossamer noose scissored into my throat. My chest heaved as I fought to stay conscious. And alive.

Jessie reappeared in my blurred vision, her face uncomfortably close. She smiled a maliciously sweet smile that made her glow. I wanted nothing more than to rip her face off, but the gossamer noose strangling me had other plans. Instead, I sat upright and rigid, my back pressed against the chair as I glared back at her through tears and agony.

She straightened. Stared down at me from an impossible height, gestured toward the revolver. She arched a brow in question. "Say the word, and I'll help you end it now. Easy-peasy lemon squeezy. Just the way you like it."

I glowered at her, strained against the enchanted zip ties, ignoring the cutting pain slicing through my wrists and ankles.

A quiet, subtle power slithered into my mind, wound its way through my thoughts, my longings. It curled comfortably around my conscious yearnings, staring with loving expectation as it shoved a cold, wet nose at me. 'Give up,' it whispered. 'Tell her what she wants to know.'

Except, Jessie hadn't asked me any questions.

I licked blood from my lips, threw an angry glare at her.

She tossed a saccharine sweet grin back at me, malice glittering from her eyes. "Looks like there still is a little of the old Cassidy I knew in there." She bent down and grasped my chin. Forced my mouth open as she shoved a hard rubber mouth guard between my teeth.

I tried to spit it back out into her face as she straightened and flicked her finger.

Blinding hot lightning surged through me again.

My body bucked and jerked like a drunken marionette as torment seared my body.

The current died.

This time, I didn't care if I choked to death. I slumped forward. The gossamer noose tightened, sliced fire through my neck. I gagged, struggling for breath. I heard rustling behind me. Hands gripped my shoulders, pulled me back against the chair. The noose loosened. And suddenly, I could breathe again. I sucked air, coughed and winced.

A fist wrapped itself into my hair, jerked my head back. Jessie reappeared, mock concern splashed across her face. "You're not going to die yet. But probably sooner than you expect... or would want." She let go of my hair.

The hands holding me back against the chair kept my head from falling forward. I managed to shove the mouth guard out, spit blood. "Go to hell," I said.

She chuckled, snatched a wooden folding chair from the shadows, and planted it in front of me just beyond the edge of my tiny ocean. "I'm glad there's still some of that old Cassidy spunk inside," she said, narrowing her eyes as she studied me with clinical detachment. "I'd begun to wonder." She leaned back, crossed her arms. "Tell me about the Shining Man."

"Who?"

She blew out a disappointed sigh, flicked that damned finger.

Another surge of electric agony shot through me. My back

bowed, tried to snap, left me gasping and gagging when the surge ended.

I couldn't feel my legs. Didn't know if that was a good thing or not. What was the point of having fae-daemon abilities if the morally questionable, super-secret organization you used to work for could electrocute you at their leisure?

Jessie stared at me. "The Shining Man?"

"You're aware," I managed, "that torture is at best unreliable for extracting information."

"I've been told." She flicked that damned finger again.

I wished I could rip it off her hand and shove it down her throat.

Despite the warning, I failed to prepare for the next crushing shock that stampeded through me.

When it ended, Jessie leaned over, whispered into my ear, "It might matter if I cared. But I don't. The Shining Man?"

I didn't know how much more I could take. Jessie probably knew but couldn't care less. For her, it wasn't about the information. It was about the control and how much pain she could inflict. How much she could make me suffer.

I wondered if this was still about Wynn or if she'd manage to conjure another, more elaborate hatred for me based on something I didn't do but could have done more to prevent.

I sucked in a trembling breath, tried not to wince from the pain throbbing through my chest. Or the caustic sting slicing through my neck.

Jessie stared at me from across the abyss. Waiting.

I just managed to stare back.

"How long have you been working for the Shining Man?"

I didn't blink. At least I don't think I blinked. But she smiled, looked over her shoulder into the darkness. She turned back, wearing a smug, self-satisfied grin that illuminated the stone-cold hatred glinting from her eyes.

I'd forgotten how good she was at this. A lot better than I ever was or ever wanted to be. But I guess when you have a taste for something, you carefully grow a passion for it, becoming the best in the business. And she had.

Trapped. Shot. Gutted. Dressed. And hung up to cure like a Christmas goose. Was I the main course? Or the side dish?

I heard the slither of fabric from the darkness surrounding my little island paradise.

Jessie spared me a ravenous look, the secretive smile splayed across her face shoving ice water through my veins. She stood, flicking a gob of bloody spittle from her pants. "Bring her." She turned and dissolved into the shadows.

The gossamer noose around my neck dissolved.

I gasped, tried to ignore the burning sting still strangling my neck as the zip ties slicing flesh from my wrists and ankles were cut away.

Despite my resolve to maintain some sort of dignity, I began to slide down out of the chair. But I guess maintaining your dignity after being electrocuted in your bra and panties by your former bestie in front of a sadistic asshole wasn't part of the deal.

Hands snagged me from under my arms before I could completely slither down to the stained concrete floor and hauled me into a vaguely vertical position.

I tried to find my feet, worried for an instant that maybe they'd been sawed off during my teatime with Jessie. I glanced down. Nope. Still there. They glowered up at me, demanding a long hot bubble bath and a bottle of the best tequila money could buy. The rest of my body chimed in a moment later.

I tried to ignore the whole damned nagging mess.

Without knowing how or when, I discovered I was following

Jessie from my island of light and into the stormy darkness where the monsters lived. I still couldn't feel my body below my butt.

Maybe unicorns were real.

I passed through a space of oblivion, emerged into a small pool of vague illumination crammed with two burgundy-covered, uncomfortable looking armchairs that had been breathing since the French Revolution, and a small round end table hacked from a cherry tree. A sterling silver tea service squatted in the center of the table, a tendril of steam wafting from the spout of the teapot.

Brahms wheezed in the background, the melody wafting through the dingy air with sibilant and discordant sounds, like fingernails dragged slowly down a chalkboard.

Exiled from the tea service stood a glass bottle partially filled with a golden liquid that squinted weakly from behind its glass prison. Probably tequila. The cheap, crappy stuff. The kind that tasted like turpentine and burned like sulfuric acid on its way down... to remind me of the dive bars we used to inhabit during the golden years of our bestie friendship a lifetime ago. Just when I thought my day couldn't get any worse.

Bishop Francisco Navarro lounged board-like in one chair, dressed in a black cassock, stick legs crossed, age veined hands clasped nonchalantly in his lap. He stared up at me from his skull-like face, thin bloodless lips stretched into a tight line. A greasy black shadow watched from behind his dead eyes, prowling over my body, lingering for a long, tortuous moment with pure exquisite sadistic pleasure.

I shuddered, tried to match the leering glare, waiting for the silken gravel voice to weave its slimy spell.

His jaw strained and worked to form words but only spewed horrified mewling sounds that fell to the floor at his feet, squirming and writhing for a few seconds before dying an agonized death. He shuddered, his body twisting and warping, the brittle bones wandering beneath his aged skin cracking and popping from the effort.

He leaned forward, trying to tear himself from his own body. His eyes bulged from his skull, his jaw stretching open into a silent scream, his bony hands clasping the chair arms until his fingers snapped from the stress, the sounds wrapping against my mind with the head of a thumping hammer.

I flinched away from the snap, crackle, pop of Navarro's agony, long-buried memories scratching their way through the dirt to the blasted landscape of my first night spent in the bowels of St. Michael's Parish.

I was eighteen again. Standing for the first time in front of Bishop Francisco Navarro, his dead eyes raking me with sadistic ruthlessness. Evaluating. Judging.

Alastair Cleary stood beside me, but not in support. I was his sacrifice to the god of the Denver Commandery. No words were spoken. But more than enough had passed between them during the eternally long fifteen minutes I'd spent enduring Navarro's caustic glare scouring away my pride, dignity, and self-assurance. The offering had been accepted, if unenthusiastically.

I spent that night alone curled into a corner of a cold and barren stone-bricked cell in the bowels of St. Michael's, stripped down to my bra and panties, the tree thick wooden iron banded door locked. Its solid silence a wary warning that despite my best efforts, I wasn't going anywhere. They'd left me a moldy straw pallet for a bed, a battered steel bucket for a latrine, and stale, maggot-infested bread and brackish water for dinner.

Human tainted fae-daemon magic throbbed through the dank air, probing and pushing for weaknesses in my mental armor, a way into my inner most thoughts, where it could corrupt and dismantle my hard-won semi-sanity until nothing remained except for an empty and rotted shell that Navarro would put down at his leisure like a rabid dog.

Sounds like the ones popping from Navarro's contorting body, skipped out from an air vent set near the high ceiling, whirling and cavorting obscenely through my cell.

I crawled to the pallet, pressed my bare back against the frosty, sandpaper-rough bricked stone wall and hugged my knees to my chest. I slapped my hands against my ears, praying to a God I didn't know if I believed in or not, to make it stop. That if he allowed me to live through the night with my mind intact, that I would believe in him and that I would give myself to his service.

He had. And I did. Mostly.

Shame boiled up. Followed by anger.

I followed it to the deepest roots of my soul, found the smoldering spark from that eighteen-year-old, dragged it out of its grave, and fanned it into a flame. I fed it, grew it into the firestorm I'd used to keep Navarro from breaking me that night twelve years ago.

The snap, crackle, pop jumping from Navarro stopped. Silence rushed in to fill the vacuum.

I blew out an explosive breath, sagged back into my chair, shivering.

"Are you cold?"

The voice tickled my memory. Not Navarro's. A woman's.

"What?" I opened my eyes, hadn't realized I'd squeezed them closed, and dragged my gaze up, just managing to stare into Jessie's hazel eyes.

She stood behind Navarro, hands laid gently on the back of his chair on either side of his head.

Navarro sagged back, no longer board-stiff, jaw slack, his eyes empty except for the oily oblivion swirling behind them.

I shuddered. Ebony.

"You look cold," Jessie said as she shoved Navarro from his chair.

He fell over, a jumbled, overused bag filled with broken bones and rotted organs.

Two Chasseurs hauled him away, the rustle of his silk robes against the stone floor scraping down my spine.

I turned my gaze back to Jessie. "What do you want?"

She smiled as she sat in Navarro's chair, her eyes burning with a sadistic glee.

"You," she said, her voice honey smooth and sweet.

CHAPTER 18
KOBAYASHI MARU

I MUST HAVE GAPED.

Jessie shifted her weight. She stared at me, the vitriol behind her eyes compressing me, shivering, back into my chair. Her smile flitted playfully across her face for a moment, slid back beneath its rock. She glanced into the shadows where Navarro had been dragged. "No need to worry," she said. "The Ebony will heal his body, if not his mind." She turned her gaze back to me, the fire burning behind them bright, corrupt, almost demonic from the hatred fueling the raging flames. "The Juzarine will make sure of it."

"What did you do?" I said, my thoughts a jumbled mess, still trying to put themselves back together after our electrifying play date.

"I'd offer you some tea," she said, her tone innocuous and friendly. "But I know how much you despise the stuff." She paused, a sly smile spreading over her lips. "I hear, though, that Stimson's driver makes an awesome chai." She winked. "On the other hand, I never knew how you managed to choke down the sludge Gracie forced on us every time we found ourselves trapped in her kitchen."

I glanced at the teapot. Steam wafted invitingly from the spout. Earl Grey. It had been Navarro's drink of choice for as long as anyone could remember. I shifted my gaze to the bottle of caramel-colored turpentine. The shot glass embracing the bottle's neck. But at the moment, Jessie could not only lead this horse to water but could make her drink as well.

She chuckled, reaching for the bottle. "My apologies for serving you this crap, but Navarro was always a cheap bastard when it didn't suit his own narcissistic tastes."

We both noticed she didn't hand me the shot glass.

She watched with clinical curiosity as I snagged it with hands that shook like an addict in withdrawal, threw back the swill she'd poured. I bit back the burning sting sloshing down my throat, just managed to dump the glass back onto the table beside the bottle before my strength died.

Without asking, she dropped the glass over onto the bottle spout, shoved them toward me.

I reached for the bottle before I knew what I was doing, hesitated, wrapped a trembling hand around my throbbing ribs with a motherly embrace. Panic tore through me. I glared at the bottle, Jessie.

She watched me.

Had she laced the tequila with Dust? I hadn't detected anything. But I'd also been electrocuted more times than I could count in less than twenty-four hours.

Jessie shook her head. "No, the bastard didn't spike your tequila. And neither did I." She leaned forward. "I need you whole and hale for what's coming for you." She leaned back, grinning as she motioned with her hand.

The sparse whisper of boots against stone echoed through our intimate pool of light.

A moment later, two silent Chasseurs strode into my tiny, fun-filled world carrying a white ceramic box, its edges-stained crimson, and a battered and worn, tan leather attaché case. Without speaking, the first Chasseur deposited the case on the floor at my feet, the second handed Jessie the briefcase. She gestured toward the stained box sitting obediently at my feet, her gaze sparking with flint and steel. The Chasseurs stepped back into the shadows behind her chair.

I stared down at the box, glanced back at her, trepidation slowly squeezing my gut into knots. "What's this," I asked, dreading the possibilities swirling through the gulf separating us.

Jessie jerked up the corners of her mouth. "The beginning of your doom."

I continued to stare, didn't want to move. Not because everything in my body felt like it had been stuffed repeatedly through a wood chipper, because that's exactly how everything felt. But because opening that box meant Jessie would own me. Like the Shining Man owned me.

I glanced down again at the box. Hesitated. Looked up.

She gestured impatiently. "I'm afraid you don't have a lot of time to waste," she said, her expression blank, except for the hatred dripping acid behind her eyes.

With an effort, I pulled myself forward, snagged the box, hefted it into my lap, noticed a sloppy thump from inside as I shoved myself back into the chair, the box a dead weight in my lap.

I peered down at it. Disquiet whisking my gut as I chewed my bottom lip. With growing trepidation, I pried off the lid. A severed head glowered up at me from inside, planted in the center of a sea of crimson goo, eyes gouged from their sockets, shriveled, walnut sized testicles stuffed into the mouth.

Jonnie Hallows.

Alarm squirmed through my jumbled and panicked thoughts. "I didn't—"

"I know."

I stared at her.

She rifled through the attaché case, pulled out a manila folder, tossed it into my lap. It thudded against the top of Jonnie's new forever home, began to slide off the side. Against my better judgment, I pinned it against the case, my gaze trapped by Jessie's burning hatred. She nodded at the folder.

"She did."

The lump squatting in my chest grew three sizes larger, but unlike the Grinch's heart, it didn't give me super strength or the sudden understanding of the meaning of Christmas. I opened the folder. Tansy glowered up at me from a grainy security camera image, leering with insane glee, something vaguely familiar glaring out from behind her eyes. She held up Jonnie's severed head by its blood-matted hair. Only, it wasn't Tansy. Or it wasn't entirely Tansy. The thudding lump in my chest exploded.

I gasped, flung the folder away, shoved the case from my lap.

It slammed into the floor at my feet, fell over. Jonnie's head rolled out, sliming blood and goo across the stone.

I heard Jessie's chuckle, the satisfaction bouncing through the air, managed to tear my horrified gaze from Jonnie's head.

She leaned over, shoved an object into my hands. They grasped it without thinking, hugged it into my lap.

Warped, jagged, and splintered wood jabbed my hands. I stared down into a shattered mirror, my fractured reflection gawking back, dark eyes fragmented, face haggard. Vestiges of fae-daemon power hissed from the broken glass, winding teasing and subtle tendrils into my mind, coiling into my thoughts and nightmares. Vague and faded images fluttered into view.

A reed-thin girl, maybe ten. With sunburned skin, long, bramble and mud matted raven black hair, and piercing neon green eyes scowled at me through a shifting, simmering mist. Fury-fueled madness spit from her eyes. She smiled a Cheshire Cat grin dripping feral malice.

The image evaporated, dissolving in a frothing sea of smoldering acid, leaving the tattered remains of my own shattered reflection.

"What have you done?" I hissed from between clenched teeth.

"The last person that asked me that question is on his way to the Nether Realm, his mind shackled with Ebony, as a plaything for the Juzarine."

I managed to tear my blurring gaze from the mangled mirror.

Jessie returned my look. She lounged comfortably in Navarro's chair, legs crossed, hands folded neatly in her lap. The worn and beaten leather attaché case sat quietly and obediently at her feet. She smiled, the expression cold and empty like the vacuum of open space.

I sucked in a raspy breath, clenching my hands against the mirror, tried to use the searing pain of the glass splinters tearing through my hands to focus and center my building rage. "Why?"

Her empty smile vanished. "Wynn."

Revenge. Simple and tidy. I'd known, but I hadn't wanted to admit it. Funny how wearing mental blinders never really protected you from the killing stroke.

The old Klingon proverb about revenge skipped across my thoughts.

"I didn't kill Wynn." Second verse, same as the first.

"Maybe not," she said, her voice beginning to rattle with pent up fury. "But you made sure he'd be easy pickings for the second string."

Navarro.

In the back of my mind, I knew he'd have eyes on me, waiting for me to disregard his orders. I should have cared, but in that moment, I didn't. Ellis Wynn was stealing away the other half of myself, and I wanted her back. No matter the cost. Jealousy? Yeah, sure. The petty, self-serving kind that tossed everything out in the trash and burned it to ash.

Turned out the cost was higher than even I could pay. It also turned out that Ellis Wynn had already stolen the second half of myself, and so it didn't matter what I did. I would never get her back.

Guess I should have torn those blinders off a little sooner.

She recognized the thought flashing through my eyes. "As you saw, he's already gone."

"And Peter?" I cringed as his name slid past my lips. But I couldn't help myself. Like a serial arsonist, I had to watch every building I incinerated burn until nothing remained except a few glowing embers.

Jessie pushed herself from Navarro's chair, snagged her leather case. It yielded to her touch with quiet obedience, eager to please. The only thing missing was the puppy tail whipping the air at her side.

"Performing his one-hundred-billion Hail Mary's." She paused, introspection ambling through her eyes. "I haven't decided if they'll be enough. But probably not." She paused, her gaze blazing with apocalyptic ruin. "You took everything from me that I held dear in here," she said, touching her chest over her heart. "Just returning the favor, babe."

My memory sparked the fiery image of Emily Moreau and her family. Emily Changed. Her family dead by her hand. Jessie's doing?

Who was next?

Did it matter?

Probably.

Another thought sliced its way through my ragged mind.

Who'd been first?

Not Jonnie. His had been a revenge killing, driven by the combined rage of two teen girls.

Father Mike.

The realization smashed me into the wall, sucker punching me in the gut before throwing me against the floor and dropping a fifteen-thousand-pound elephant onto my back.

I looked at Jessie. Her smirk had grown to where it threatened to slice her bottom jaw from her face.

The only way to keep the rest of my world from burning to the ground was to save Tansy. But how?

Jessie possessed the Medusa Mirror that had imprisoned Stephanie Brandt's Essence. Like snowflakes, Medusa Mirrors were unique. No other Medusa Mirror could pull Stephanie's Essence from Tansy's body.

Without Stephanie Brandt's Medusa Mirror, the only way I could save Tansy from destruction was to kill her.

My thoughts clawed their way toward the Shining Man. I wondered if it had known Tansy was the Daemonrie Chimera when it had brought us together and extorted me into killing it and the rogue noble knight that had created it.

Double Kobayashi Maru.

Jessie paused at the knife's edge of our island of light and turned, her eyes gleaming with darkness and searingly bright starlight. "In case you're wondering, I am doing my best to play fairsies, giving you the same chance you gave me and Wynn." She paused for dramatic effect, making sure what she just told me sank in far enough that it would stick. "You'll find the only possessions left to you in your old cell. Your Bronco will be waiting in the parking lot. Don't dilly dally too long."

She snorted with amusement, turned and vanished into the darkness.

Solitude hugged me in its quiet crushing embrace, shoved the brunt of Jessie's blazing fury down my throat.

I stared down at the photo of Tansy, shuddering at the way Stephanie Brandt glowered back at me from behind Tansy's eyes with enough hatred and acidic vitriol to power a super nova. Jessie and Stephanie could form their own insane hater club.

I thought suddenly of Captain Kirk in 'The Wrath of Khan,' the impossible choices he faced and the decisions he ultimately made that saved his crew at the cost of one life, his best friend.

Would I be able to make that same hard choice? What lines would I willingly cross? How much of who I was would I be willing to sacrifice to save the girl I considered my sister?

The Shining Man's mocking voice rollicked through my memory as the surrounding walls threw their contempt at me from the murkiness, glaring and accusing.

Sticks and stones.

I heaved a weary, guilt-filled sigh.

Where was Cleary?

Dead?

If he weren't, he'd wish he were when I found him.

In the meantime, I was trapped in a conundrum, wrapped in a conundrum, and tied neatly in a bow with a conundrum. And I didn't know how I was going to get Tansy or me out of it.

Daemonrie Chimera.

The term seemed to have been whispered to me from the ether. But I didn't know what to do with it. Not yet. But it would come. And when it did, people would pay. I'd make sure of it.

I shoved myself from the chair, tried not to pass out as I used a trembling hand to steady myself before stepping into stormy seas, almost face-planted when I tripped over Jonnie's head.

Indiana Jones had nothing on me.

Regaining my precarious balance, I shuffled across the cold stone floor on wobbly legs and bare feet, stumbling against a thick, solidly built, iron-bound oak door. The only door. For an insane moment, I imagined it locked. Me trapped. But the door swung open on silent hinges.

A harsh, sterile light rushed into the opening, spilling across my bruised and battered body. I glanced down at my feet. They were still there, but they needed a ginormous pedicure and an infinite amount of tender loving care. I made a mental note.

Hey, a girl's gotta give herself a little self-serving tender loving care in between apocalypses. Otherwise, what was the point?

I staggered through the doorway into a narrow, dimly lit hall that stretched into obscurity. Naked, underpowered lightbulbs dotted the stark cement ceiling, blared nearsighted islands of garish light that hung limp and lifeless above my head. A raw air current snaked along the floor, wrapped wintry fangs around my ankles, sucking the heat from my legs as I turned left and shambled toward the acolyte cells buried deeper in the bowels below St. Michael's Parish, using the rough finished wall for support, the stippled surface snagging my skin with every stammered step.

After what seemed an eternity, I paused before an unvarnished, rough finished ash door.

Faded nightmares disguised as memories fluttered through my mind, dredged up images of a time I had done everything I could to purge. I reached up, touched the door's rough-hewn surface, brushed trembling fingers against the faded letters CMK+JEC=HOW carved into the wood.

I thought of the girl that had carved those initials. Her first nights locked away and alone. Guttering light. No heat. Flea infested bedding. A rusting steel bucket for a latrine. A moldy crust of bread and a cup of tepid water her only sustenance. Her only companion an ancient and desiccated rat that didn't have the strength or the guile to escape our prison. I'd thought of eating it, but neither of us could conjure the strength for the meal.

My hand found the ancient iron latch. I pushed the door inward, stood just outside the threshold as a breath of stale air riding the acrid odor of mothballs washed across me. Bedraggled candlelight danced just inside, casting uncertain shadows against the opposite wall. An unseen body moved, nails scratching against the bare floor, as it rattled a chain. I reached for my Walther, found only goose pimpled skin. Muscle memory was great until it wasn't.

I cursed under my breath, wondered if Jessie were still playing her sadistic game.

Probably. But only one way to find out.

I sucked in a breath, stepped into the room.

Beegle sat in the far corner of the cell, bound by an iron chain nailed into the wall behind him, his tail thumping the floor. My fear melted, replaced by sudden and overwhelming joy. I fell through the doorway, crawled over to him, and strangled him in a choke hold embrace. He wriggled in my arms, managed to slap my face with his tongue as I smothered him with kisses and tears, like two star-crossed lovers come together after an infinite separation.

I pulled out the pin binding the iron collar around his neck, tossed it into the corner.

After, I sat in the opposite corner, my bare back pressed against the frigid wall, my butt planted on the equally chilly floor. Beegle lay across my lap, his tail continuing to thump the concrete as I scratched behind his ears.

A pile of tactical gear and clothing lay neatly folded against the far wall. Beside the pile squatted a shallow and chipped ceramic-coated steel basin, the lip beginning to rust, the water inside long cold and dead.

I had no clue when I was, how long I'd been held in the bowels of St. Michael's, or how much time I had left to save Tansy, save myself, and rip out Jessie's throat.

Oh yeah, let's not forget the Shining Man.

Beegle complained suddenly, scrambled from my lap and sat beside me, glaring his irritation. I ignored him, shoved his snout from my face as I propelled myself to my feet, still unsteady, but no longer threatening to topple over at the faintest brush of breath.

Beegle whined.

I smiled down at him, stooped to scratch his ears before planting a wet kiss on his snout. He sneezed, followed me as I knelt beside the metal basin, splashed cold, dank water across my face, rubbed a couple of handfuls down my filth-smeared arms, dumped the rest over my head.

I dressed, wishing I could have indulged in more than a frigid water dowsing to wash away the sticky slime of Emily's blood still clinging to me like a needy lover. I'd probably feel her blood on me for the rest of my life. Like Stephanie Brandt's. No matter how much I scrubbed my skin raw.

Beegle nudged my leg, whining with expectation.

Time to go.

I shoved my unease and bubbling anger down, strode down the hall, Beegle's toenails clicking against the concrete floor behind me.

When this was done, either way, Jessie and I were going to have an accounting, regardless of the Shining Man's requirements.

The belly of St. Michael's remained deserted as I walked past the Execution Room door toward the stairs leading up to civilization and forgetfulness.

I paused at the ground floor landing, huffing breath I still hadn't reacquired, listening, and wondering if Jessie would have a mob to greet me when the stairs spit me out.

I elbowed the door open. Stepped out into... empty silence.

Surprise bitch-slapped me across the face. I didn't know why. Maybe I'd hoped Peter would be waiting, arms open in forgiveness, wanting to comfort and take me back, both of us riding into the sunset on the back of his sturdy virgin-white unicorn.

Yeah, right. And I'd win the lottery without buying the damned ticket.

The door crashed closed behind me.

After a brief pause to calm my jittery nerves, I crossed the foyer, slammed open the exterior, gothic-era doors, and stepped out into the face of a delicate sleet that waltzed chaotically through the gray afternoon daylight. I stopped, blinking against the dancing sleet, brushing the clingy ice from my frizzled and tangled hair.

My Bronco sat at the base of the steps, patiently belching steam from the exhaust, the engine rumbling with quiet content-ment. The windows wore an icy glaze that retreated unhurriedly from the steady onslaught of heat from the blasting defrost.

Jessie's orders. Like she'd said, she was playing fairsies.

I heaved a heavy sigh, glanced down at the steps. A narrow path haphazardly wound its way down to the bottom, ending in a glacial pool that stretched across the buried asphalt past the Bronco to cover most of the plowed lot. I peered into the miniature swirling spear tips, wondered if anyone was watching. Probably. If not Jessie, then Peter, to feed her sadistic vengeful lust.

Beegle shivered, shook a film of iced dust from his coat, threw me an impatient glare. I smiled back, started down the treacherous steps toward the Bronco.

After what seemed like weeks, I managed to place a shaking hand on the passenger side of the Bronco, caught my breath as I ushered Beegle into his seat before carefully plowing through more snow and ice to haul myself into the driver's seat. I leaned back, closed my eyes, my heart continuing to beat a sledgehammer staccato against my chest.

The blaring ring of a phone shot me from my moment of quiet paranoia.

My phone scowled at me from the dash, Cleary's name skipping across the screen.

I snatched it from the dash. "Tell me that Father Mike is still alive," I said, my voice quivering.

An instant of silence.

"It's nice to know that you're still alive. I'd hoped you were. Because we have a few things to catch up on." Marshall Stimson's velvet smooth baritone wound titillating fingers through my ears, teasing me with promises of hours of excruciating pain and pleasure. If you were into that sort of thing.

I caught the muffled sounds of Cleary's phone being handed off.

"Cassidy?" Cleary's voice, his accent thicker, like cooling molasses. Not as strong, some of the arrogance sucked out through a long, needle-sharp straw.

"Where are you," I said. "Father Mike," I stuttered. "Tell me that he's still alive."

Whispered threats in the background. Cleary's silent grimace groaning through the line. "I... don't know," he managed to grind out. Hesitation. Then, "Tansy—" He groaned, the sound quick and sharp. "His car is missing."

"Cassidy?" Stimson's voice, hopeful, but not too eager.

"I'm here," I said. "What do you want?"

"Same as before," he said. "But all three acts this time, not just the trailer." He paused, expectant silence wriggling its irritating finger at me. "Michael is in our custody at the moment. Alive. And we're doing everything in our power to keep him that way. Despite the cancer that has already ground him into hamburger. Tansy, however—"

Another pause, followed by Cleary's clenched grunts and groans in the background. "But I think in this moment, Alastair should be your immediate concern." He let that sink to the bottom. "He pissed Harmonie off, and you know how she gets when she's angry. Your choice. But don't take too long to make it. You know where to find us."

I stared at my phone, thought of Tansy, Stephanie Brandt glowering out from behind her lunatic eyes, the leering expression smeared across her face, Jonnie's head dangling from her fist. Emily Moreau wrangled into my thoughts a second later. She'd worn the same mad leer, had the same deranged look glowing from her Ebony-darkened eyes before she slashed her mother's throat.

I couldn't face the fact that Tansy could have attacked Father Mike. Why? She loved the doting fool, despite her words and her unthoughtful actions. Why would she attack him?

She didn't.

Stephanie Brandt circled back to my sputtering thoughts. The savagery blazing behind Tansy's eyes. And the malice.

For me. For abandoning her in the Nether Ream, tortured and driven insane at the slowly boiling pleasure of the Juzarine.

It didn't matter that I'd been set up to fail, that I was never intended to recover her. That abandoning her had been the goal from the recovery's inception.

But why leave Father Mike alive?

Saving him for the end. To ensure that I suffered for as long as possible before the coup de grâce.

I had to get to Father Mike before Tansy did the second time. I had to be there before she showed up for her finale.

It wasn't much, but it was all I had at the moment.

But I still had Cleary.

As much as I hated to admit it, Stimson was correct.

Cleary may have been a double-dog-dare asshat, but he was my double-dog-dare asshat. At least for this New York minute. I'd paid for his services, and though I was less than enthused by his crappy customer service, there were no returns and no refunds. And as much as I didn't want to admit it, I needed him as much as he needed me if I was going to clean up this shitstorm, save Tansy, put a round through Jessie's head, make nice with the Shining Man, and the Order of the Four, which meant I had no choice but to accept Stimson's party invitation.

I hated it when my scruples snuffed convenience and short-cuts into the dirt like a discarded cigarette.

The Bronco hiccupped.

I rifled through the go bag, retrieved my Walther and the Colt, loaded each with what I found at the bottom of the bag, slid them into their homes. I laid my dagger on the seat beside me, shoved the Bronco into gear and gunned the gas, doing a slip-slide from the parking lot into the snow-packed street.

CHAPTER 19

INVITATION TO THE PARTY

SILENCE SQUATTED HEAVILY as I turned onto the street leading to the rectory behind St. Jude's Parish. Creeping shadows hugged the edges of the road where the plows had piled snow and ice. The ghouls from my failures huddled in the darkness. Flat and dark, they glared balefully as I sped past, spraying ice varnished grime and gravel into their dead gray eyes. They leered back, unblinking, ready to devour the scraps Hell thought to toss at them.

Dark and foreboding in the failing afternoon light, the facade of St. Jude's rose to blot out the fire brushed horizon above the western foothills that had managed to sneak past the sloppy edges of snow clouds piling up into the darkening sky. Streetlights blotted the parking lot with tiny islands of shy, yellow light between blotchy dirty-white dunes.

As I drove past the parking lot, I slowed the Bronco to a creeping stop beside the glacier-choked curb. A sporadic line of skeletal ash trees, their scraggly branches weighted down by hoar-frost, marched in agonized silence next to me. Across the parking lot, a burnished black Mercedes Sprinter panel van, its fenders and sides spray painted with grayish snow grime, hugged the bottom of the steps leading to the rectory portico, its back doors flung open. A man and a woman dressed in dark-colored coveralls struggled to load a body bag-laden gurney into the back. Four dusky, characterless Chevy Suburbans with moonless night-tinted windows circled the Mercedes van, standing guard over what looked like a top-secret Presidential emergency. Several people hunkering in long, heavy winter overcoats stood within the protective circle, trying to look like they belonged at an emergency scene.

I knew better.

The portico doors squealed open, spewing a pool of garish yellow light onto the ice-slicked porch. Two murky figures enveloped in heavy winter coats and their heads obscured beneath fedoras, stepped from the doorway into the light. The taller figure bent its head toward cupped gloved hands. Fire erupted a moment later, illuminating a lean close-shaven face as he lit a cigarette. The flame snuffed out. Marshall Stimson looked up, his gaze fixating on mine across the snow-darkened abyss separating us. He took the cigarette from his mouth, leaned his head toward the second figure, who twitched a quick nod before disappearing into the rectory.

Stimson dropped his cigarette and snuffed it with the toe of his boot.

My heart hammered my chest. My pulse thrummed through my temples, the quiet throb beating thrashing waves against my brain, trepidation winding course knots through my thoughts. I flicked my gaze to the body bag, watched as the last of it was devoured by the panel van.

The body didn't belong to Father Mike. Stimson would have told me.

Then who?

Guilt-fueled rage erupted, fanned a spark with hurricane-strength winds until it burst into a hysterical firestorm that darted across the desiccated landscape of my mind, burning everything to ash in an instant.

I growled, the sound inhuman to my own ears as I gunned the Bronco and jerked the wheel over. It bucked wildly and jumped the curve, plowing through a mound of grimed snow between two of the decimated ash trees. Ice and frozen slush machine-gunned the air in front of us as I fishtailed through the parking lot toward the rectory entrance. I slammed down the brake pedal, side-skidded the Bronco to a lurching stop a few feet from the Suburban barricade. Beegle leaped up onto the front of the dash, baying at the milling circus, his frenzied tail whipping the air.

I killed the motor, shoved my door open.

Before I could move, Beegle scrambled down from his dash-board perch, clambered over my lap, and rocketed down into the slushy mess below, darted between two of the Suburbans toward the portico.

"Beegle, heel!" I scrambled from the Bronco, half sliding, half diving between the Suburbans in pursuit.

Beegle bayed into the night, doing his best 'I'm a beagle, so I'm going to ignore you' routine as he bounded up the portico steps, past Stimson, and vanished through the open doors. Two hulking bystanders standing near the portico steps watched Beegle fly past them, turned in pursuit, but stopped when Stimson held up his hand.

I found my footing a few steps inside the Suburban barricade, tried to gain some traction when a hand shot out from the shadows, snagging my arm. I spun from the grasp, confronted an NFL line-backer-sized body that could have also been the biggest damned bouncer in the world of giant, hulking bouncers.

I rammed my palm into the center of his chest, grimaced as the force from the impact reverberated up my arm and into my shoulder.

His beefy hand shot up, snagged my wrist and twisted. Pain lanced up my arm as I pirouetted into the move, shoved my free hand up at the base of his chin. He blocked my hand, continued to twist, the pressure from his grip forcing me to circle into him and down like a tightly wound spring.

I rammed the heel of my boot into his foot, felt the jolting impact from steel-toed shoes echo up my shin. He grunted, wrapped his free hand into the front of my coat, lifted me from my feet, and shoved me away as if I weighed less than a puff of breath.

I sailed through the air like a bag of potatoes, slammed into the frozen slush in front of my Bronco, tried to regain my feet, collapsed, unable to take a breath, wondering who the hell had stolen my air. I lay still for a moment, searching for my missing breath.

Darker shadows fell over me.

I heard shouts, the scramble of boots through the slush coming toward me.

Fish-flopping myself onto my stomach, I crawled away from the thickening shadows and voices, tried to slip beneath the front of the Bronco. I thought I'd made my escape when a hand suddenly grasped my ankle and pulled me back. I lashed out with my free foot, landed a solid blow, heard an accompanying grunt and a curse as I continued my sloshy scramble for the underside of the Bronco.

Grasping hands snagged both my ankles and feet the second time, began rope-pulling me back out. I scrabbled for purchase with my hands, kicking and wrenching my legs in a hurricane of movement against the grasping hands. Their grips remained unbreakable, though, as they hauled me out from underneath the Bronco and flopped me over onto my back like a landed fish.

Someone shoved the muzzle of a pistol into my face.

"Stop." A thickly accented woman's voice. Italian? The throb of Touched power thumped my mind.

I went limp, my eyes focused for an instant on the gun's muzzle, then past, found the tightly screwed up face of a light olive-skinned woman glaring down at me, sucking breath, the beginnings of a reddish bruise coloring her left cheek. I twitched the corner of my mouth upward. She growled at me, flicked her pistol from my personal space as unfriendly hands flipped me over onto my stomach, and shoved my face into the grimy snow.

An iron-hard knee slammed into my lower back, huffed my lungs clean of air again as my arms were wrenched behind my back, and my wrists cinched together. The knee in my back vanished. More unruly hands grabbed me under my arms, hauled me to my feet, and dragged me back inside the Suburban barricade. I shook gritty slush from my face, spit frozen gravel from my mouth a moment before they thrust me against the side of the nearest SUV.

NFL Linebacker Guy searched me, got a little too personal with his hands. I aimed a knee into his groin, thought I'd hit the bullseye when he grunted, but felt disappointment an instant later when nothing else came except for a twinkle in his eye and the flash of an evil grin as he yanked my Walther and the Colt from their holsters. He discovered my dagger a moment later, handed his new treasures to a tall lanky guy with long stringy sand-colored hair, an anemic five o'clock shadow, and a twitchy left eye.

As Tall Skinny Guy accepted his horde, he caught my gaze, stared for an instant before walking around the back of the Suburban, opened and closed the hatch. He came back around, smiling, and winked as he strode past and was swallowed by the deepening darkness.

Angry Olive-Skinned Italian Girl drew her pistol, shoved it back into my personal space, her dark eyes dripping rage.

Her power rolled off her, crawled over me like waves driven across the shoreline during an approaching tsunami tide. I glared back at her, huffing as I tried to reclaim my stolen breath.

I heard slamming doors, the start of a hoarse diesel motor, the crunch of tires through frozen slush and ice, and watched as the Sprinter Van faded into the clawing darkness. My gaze followed as it dissolved into oblivion, the red glow of its taillights melting behind a tsunami of slush spit out behind the back tires as the sudden crushing weight of dread drop into my already twisting gut.

I shook my head, heard approaching footsteps slogging through the slush, looked up from Angry Olive-Skinned Italian Girl toward the crunching footsteps, felt my already knotted stomach do an impossible gymnastics routine.

"Cassidy."

I managed a half-hearted smile. "Hey Marshall. Been a minute."

"Glad you could join us."

I twitched a nod toward the rectory. "Mind telling me what's going on?"

"Funny. I was going to ask you the same thing." He nodded at Angry Olive-Skinned Italian Girl. "Search her car. Bring what you find. You know where we'll be."

She looked at him, anger churning through her dark brown eyes, holstered her gun, and sucker punched me in the gut. A gloved fist twisted itself through my hair, yanked my head up. She leaned in close. "That is for the kick in the face." She let go, turned and walked away.

I stood doubled over, coughing up my guts, managed to fire back, "You're welcome."

"Same old Cassidy," Stimson said as he grabbed my arm and dragged me off the Suburban and marched me toward the Rectory portico. "Have you never heard the proverb about honey and vinegar?"

I snorted, tried to suck in a trembling breath. "Honey gives me hives."

He chuckled as he continued to drag me with him.

We reached the portico steps a few heaving breaths later. I managed to jump start my lungs, found the tattered remains of my dignity as he pulled me up to the porch and hauled me through the doors. They clicked closed behind us, leaving us in relative solitude, except for a scattering of forensics techs milling through the hallway. They paused, staring for a moment, before going back to their business without a word after a stern 'I'll rip your throats out if anyone asks' look from Stimson.

I tore my arm from his grasp, panic beginning to wrap icy fingers around my soul and squeeze. "What are you doing here? Where's Father Mike?"

He landed a solid punch in my gut. Not as good as Angry Olive-Skinned Italian Girl, but effective. Not bothering to allow me to regain my dignity or my breath, he reclaimed my arm in an iron grip and yanked me down the hallway past the milling techs. They cleared the center as we marched through, quickly averting their eyes when Stimson's gaze touched theirs.

He yanked me around the corner to the right, toward Father Mike's library. "We're going to have a conversation."

CHAPTER 20
BEST LAID PLANS

CHRISTMAS MUSIC WEAVED A LIGHTLY hypnotic and melodic tune below the surface of a raucous buzz of disjointed conversation and the obnoxious clink and clank of cheap flatware slapping against equally cheap porcelain plates and bowls.

Jessie sipped her Old Fashioned, smiling in appreciation as she returned the drink to its slowly growing puddle of chilled condensation sloughing from the glass. The out-of-date, out-of-fashion, scratched and scarred Formica tabletop sucked the bottom of her tumbler into a sloppy, wet kiss, the sound reminding her of her first time with a boy in the backseat of a car.

Inexpensive, equally beaten-up secondhand lighting fixtures blaring overpowered light hung precariously from the rough-hewn rafted ceiling. The subtle smells of cedar and pine snowed down from the beams, weaving their silken scents into the chaotic aromas from a sea of comfort foods spewing from the revolving kitchen doors.

Her smile growing wistful, Jessie leaned back into the corner of her booth, the worn, faded red vinyl grating against her jeans and flannel shirt, reminding her of Wynn's gentle touch, his finger-tips leisurely exploring her body after they'd made love.

The Hungry Cow had been their first actual date, what Wynn loved to call an 'acquired taste.' Like him. She'd fallen in love with the place at first sip and first taste, had fallen in love with Wynn not long after. An acquired taste indeed.

The restaurant, one of Denver's hidden in plain sight jewels, quickly became their favorite haunt and they one of its most favorite regular couples.

Blowing a disconsolate sigh, Jessie picked up her phone, began to casually leaf through the pictures of her and Wynn. She paused a moment here, a moment there, staring in melancholy longing, the fluttering memories pulling a wistful smile from her lips in between the darkness squeezing her heart,

She closed her eyes for a moment as she concentrated on the music, a classic from the late fifties or early sixties that she couldn't quite place. Cassidy would have known the song, including the lyrics, and would have joined in her own dissonant sing-along. She always did.

A sour taste crawled into Jessie's mouth up from her throat, throttling the last of the sweet burn of the sugared bourbon from her drink. She opened her eyes, caught a man staring at her from across the narrow aisle a few tables down. The faint lustful leer in his eyes shrank back and crept away like a scolded puppy. Jessie twitched a disgusted smile and gave him the finger.

The man tore his gaze away, his covert brazenness lying cold and dead at the feet of his secret desire as he turned his apathy back toward the woman seated across from him.

She snagged her drink, drained it, slapped the glass down into its tiny, chilled ocean.

"Want another?"

Vague recognition teased the corners of her mind. How long

since she'd been here? Three years at least. Not since Wynn's murder. The shadow of a dim memory picked at the edges of her mind. She narrowed her eyes as she reached for the name. "Gabe, is it?"

He smiled, the expression scraping at least ten years from his lean, biker's face, making him look more like a high school junior than the grad student she remembered. "Gary," he said.

"Sorry." She smiled shyly at him as she handed her empty glass up. "It's been a few years since I've been in. I'm surprised you remember me."

He nodded, tried on an uncomfortable smile as he furtively glanced at the empty seat across the table, then the open space beside her. "No worries," he said. "I can't remember my name half the time." He paused, his gaze focusing on the glass in his hands.

But he did remember her. She saw it in his expression and the way he clutched her empty glass. If she'd been a little younger, living a normal life in a normal world with a normal job, she might have been impressed. Jessie watched him, noting the courage slinking its way up into his mouth.

"Waiting on your boyfriend?" He asked finally, his voice quavering slightly.

She schooled her face, bludgeoned the grief and the rage into submission, before smiling coyly up at him. "No," she said. "He's —" Her voice stumbled. "We're not together anymore."

"Sorry to hear that."

His voice agreed with his words, but his eyes told a different story. He opened his mouth, hesitated, closed it, the courage he'd screwed up gasping for its last, desperate breath. "I'll get you that refill."

As he turned, Jessie snagged his order pad and pen from his apron, scribbled her phone number on an empty sheet, shoved it back into its hole. "Maybe after the holidays, when all this holly jolly crap has settled, give me a call." She winked at him, watched him weave his way through the press of bodies toward the bar, his step a little lighter.

Her smile vanished, washed away by the too familiar low boiling rage simmering in the pit of her gut.

A man slid into the booth across from her, clasped his hands on the table before him. He glared at her, his pale lips stretched into a tight line, the once bright and playful eyes she remembered sunken in and lusterless. Bruises colored his skin below his eyelids, snaked out cadaverous wrinkles that had once grasped life by the throat, but now tossed it accusingly back into her face, mangled and dead. Dreary silver splotches pocked his rumpled, flat black hair.

"Detective," she said. "Ben."

"Tell me why I'm here. And why I shouldn't just arrest you now."

Jessie snagged the arm of a passing waitress, watched Ben, before glancing up at the girl. "A Pina Colada for my friend," she said. "Double rum, Captain Morgan Spiced, one-hundred proof." She waited for him to decline her offer, smiled up at the girl and nodded. "Thank you."

The waitress scurried away.

"How have you been, Detective?" She paused, raking him with her gaze. He met her stare, hostility coiled like a viper ready to strike at the slightest provocation. "You don't look well," she said. "Gloria didn't leave you with much after the divorce, did she?"

"Screw this," he snapped, shoving himself from the booth.

"How's your investigation into Wynn's murder coming along?"

Hesitation.

Emotions she'd grown intimately familiar with over the past three years swamped his face. He screwed his eyes closed, sucked in a trembling breath. "You mean the investigation into the murder of my partner and best friend?" Fire raged in his eyes, his complexion burning red hot. "The murder you were complicit in and helped to cover up?"

"I—" The words burned to ash in her mouth, leaving behind a bitter and acrid taste that seared her throat with acid. She stared a moment at her hands as they worried each other on the tabletop. "Despite what you believe, I loved Wynn." She looked up, met his bitterness and fury.

"Like a black widow," he snapped back.

She snorted, pulled the briefcase from its silent and dark corner, and set it on the table. "I didn't kill Wynn," she said. "I do, however, know who did."

He frowned at her. "Is that a confession?"

Another snort, followed by an ironic smile. "Hardly," she said, gesturing toward his vacant seat. "I can give them to you."

"How? With that? What's inside?"

"Sit back down. Enjoy your Pina Colada," she said. "And you'll find out."

He hesitated, curiosity glinting from his eyes, like the cat. He sat, reached for the briefcase.

Jessie slid it from the table, settled it back into its corner on the seat beside her.

He scowled. "You better not be jerking my chain with this."

The background Christmas music died for an instant. The chaotic sea of incoherent conversation buffeting them faltered. Gary appeared beside their table, Old Fashioned and Pina Colada in hand. He stood over them for a moment, indecision splashed across his face.

Jessie smiled up at him, indicated Ben in the opposite seat. "An old friend from college. We still on after the holidays?"

Gary twitched a smile, indecision and confusion galloping across his face. "Uh, yeah. Sure," he said as he set the drinks down. "Got your number right here." He patted his shirt pocket.

Ben watched him walk away, wariness in his tired eyes. "A little young for you, don't you think?"

"Don't be a prick." She slid a manilla folder toward him.

After a brief hesitation, he opened it, his face suddenly blanching, his eyes going wide as he flipped through the contents. "Where did you get these," he asked, looking up, horror dripping from his eyes.

"Interested?" She sipped her drink. Black widow indeed.

He turned back to the photos, rifled through a few more, pulled one out, shoved it at her. "Who's that?"

Jessie glanced at the photo, the corner of her mouth twitching upward in satisfaction. "Her name is Tansy Harper. Seventeen. A priest named Michael Howe is her legal guardian. She currently resides at the rectory behind St. Jude's Parish."

Ben leaned forward, stared at the folder for a moment, the growing light behind his eyes predatory. "Who's—" he hesitated. "Whose head is she holding?"

"Jonnie Hallows," she said as she dropped a second folder on top of the first. "He is... he was," she corrected herself. "A drug dealer that dealt in... illegal exotic and rare concoctions."

Ben leaned back, crossing his arms, his eyes narrowing in suspicion. "Never heard of him," he said. "What are you playing at?"

Jessie snagged the first folder and its scattered contents, dropped them into the attaché case. "And you never would have," she said. "Jonnie and the organization he worked for aren't on any law enforcement radar, domestic or international." She shook her head. "And they never will be." She indicated the second folder. "I'd advise you to take a long, hard pull from your drink before you look at what's in there."

Ignoring her, he opened the folder, his eyes growing wide, what color remaining in his face draining completely away. He looked ephemeral, almost translucent as he stared at her, disbelief shining from his eyes. He reached for his Pina Colada, his hand shaking, barely managed to shove the straw into his mouth. He took a long, hard pull, nearly collapsing the straw before shoving the almost empty glass away.

I'm Dreaming of a White Christmas scratched a tinny tune from the speakers, the silken smooth voice entwining her in its dreamy melodic tone. She grasped for the artist's name, someone who had been an entertainment icon decades before she'd been born. Another name Cassidy would have known and used to cajole her into singing the song with her.

Less traumatic days when the bonds of friendship seemed unbreakable, no matter the crap their life threw at them.

Jessie shrugged the memory away, clutched the grief and bitterness close to her heart.

Ben watched her, his eyes wary. He slid a photo toward her. "Who and when."

Jessie glanced down. The Moreaus. Dead by their oldest daughter's hand. After she'd overdosed her with Ebony. Cassidy stood in the background, slumped over with dejection. Blood smeared the floor in a quiet sea of ruin.

Jessie suppressed the satisfaction worming across her face. "The Moreaus," she said. "Former... clients of the travel agency I worked for."

"Bullshit." Ben leaned back in his seat. "What kind of fricking game are you playing?"

"No game, detective. I assure you." She reached for the folder.

Ben snagged her hand, crushed it in his trembling grip.

Jessie winced, gave him what he looked for. "Let go of my hand. Please."

He gazed into her eyes, searching, lips pursed, brows furrowed. He let go of her hand. "This girl you told me about, Tansy Harper? She's responsible for this?"

Jessie shrugged. "In a way, yes." She paused, searching his eyes and what lay behind them, pointed at Cassidy. "But this is the person you want," she said. "She's the one behind everything, including Wynn's murder. Her name is Cassidy Kain. She's connected to Tansy Harper and Father Michael Howe."

"When?"

Jessie shrugged. "Jonnie Hallows? Last night sometime. The Moreaus? Early this morning."

Ben shook his head. "Impossible," he said. "We would have heard... something." His expression changed, slid into incredulousness. "Why?"

"Exactly." Jessie reached into the attaché case, slapped a pile of manilla folders and wrinkled envelopes onto the table in front of him. "I'm giving you the key to unlock the door into solving Wynn's murder." She paused, eyeing him with curiosity. "And more. If you're willing to open the door and walk through."

She watched him, the way he stared at the pile of folders and envelopes sunning themselves on the table between them, the hunger in his eyes and on his face. She recognized the look, saw it every time she gazed at herself in a mirror.

He glanced up, sudden cunning skipping across his face. "And what if I decided to use what you're giving me to investigate you?"

Jessie flashed him a sardonic smile as she leaned back in her seat, arms crossed. "Feel free," she said. "What I'm giving you will unlock the door to my secrets as well." She paused, made sure she had his full attention before continuing. "But before you start chasing rabbits, know that this offer is time limited. You have less than forty-eight hours to get what you need to solve Wynn's murder. After that—" She shrugged, slid from the booth, snagging the briefcase to her side as she stood, indicated the pile on the table. "Cinderella and everything surrounding her returns to its natural state of non-existence."

He shook his head. "Who are you?"

"Someone who loved Ellis Wynn very much." She walked from the table, winked at Gary as she strode past him and outside.

Misshapen, discolored snowflakes speckled the evening air, cast eerie shadows through the shivering streetlights. An occasional car slid past and down the nearly deserted street, splattering slush and ice against the curb. Scattered couples huddled into each other, hunching over in protection against the frigid and fitful breeze.

Jessie stood within the shadows of a shallow overhang, watching, waiting. She smiled, thinking of the last time she and Wynn were together, two days before his death, the decisions they made, the plans contemplated. All burned to ash by Navarro and his puppets.

Navarro had already paid. Peter was nearly done paying. Cassidy would pay. The ultimate price.

The doors behind her opened, belched out a small rowdy group of young, college-age men wrapped in the melodic embrace of too much alcohol and the spirit of the season. They brushed past her, snickering and laughing at their crude jokes made at her expense. One turned and leered. She leered back at him and winked, causing an explosion of drunken guffaws and back slaps as they continued their teetering walk down the slushy sidewalk.

The mood died.

Retrieving her phone, Jessie pressed the speed dial button for Peter Oliver as she strolled after the herd of drunken boys.

Peter answered on the second ring, his voice shivering slightly. "What do you want?"

Jessie smiled. "Are you at St. Jude's?"

A pause, accompanied by a muffled sound. "Yes," he said. "You fricking well know where I am."

Her smile grew. "And Marshall Stimson?"

"Yes. He, Bonnet and their crew were setting up their perimeter behind the rectory when I arrived." Silence wrapped in more muffled movement. "They have Cleary."

Jessie paused. Cleary's involvement had not been unexpected. But this... she worried her lower lip, allowing the allure of his fall to arouse the rage boiling in the pit of her gut with new possibilities. "And Cassidy?"

"Arrived a few minutes ago. Stimson has her."

She glanced at her watch. Slightly behind schedule, but what plan ever survived contact with the enemy? "Make sure Cassidy slips from Stimson's grasp. I need her in the wind. And hunted."

"And Cleary?"

"Collateral damage."

She heard the frustration in the rasp of his breath through the phone.

"How?"

"Surgical. But public. And loud." She smiled, allowed the fury to caress her heart with tender, trembling fingers.

"There's no way I'm getting into the rectory. Stimson's goons have it locked down tighter than—"

"I'll take care of it. Just be ready when the shit hits the fan." She switched the phone to her opposite ear as a couple strode past, embraced by the throbbing cold. "Any more questions?"

"How many people need to die to slake your thirst for—"

She hung up, sucked in a quivering breath as she gazed into the snow-swamped darkness, allowing the bulky flakes to swarm her face. She opened her mouth, licked the melting snow from her lips, blinked it from her eyes. A bashful wind teased her hair, scrubbed the lighter crystals from her face with flinty resolve.

A vague memory teetered at the edge of thought.

Another long ago, white-washed Christmas filled with wonder and purity. Her parents, eager for their little, precocious princess to amaze their friends and colleagues with her singing and dancing talent. The party after, filled with delight and the promise of new heights scaled and success borne on the back of their little girl. Finally, the nightmare monsters that followed later that night, the pain, agony, and madness that became her world.

It had been the last night she'd ever seen her parents alive.

Jessie blew out the breath, the promise of purity and wonder dying on the spear tips of the falling snow and the burning fire of her hate and wrath.

Peter's last words echoed through her mind. As many lives as it took.

She speed-dialed a second number.

A high-pitched hissing whisper answered.

"Where are you," she asked.

A pause. Low, distant voices. The phone muffled against an unshaven face. "Inside. Watching. As ordered."

"Kain?"

"Stimson is taking her to the back of the rectory. The apartment area." Scratchy silence. "Where Harmonie has Cleary."

Jessie smiled, allowing her imagination to carry her into that land of delectable sweetness. "Kain needs to escape."

"You didn't—"

"Plans change," she said. "Do we have a problem?"

A long, nervous delay. More muffled voices. The thud of boots against polished marble. The voices faded into memory.

"No." A skittish breath blown into the phone. "And Cleary?"

"Is on his own."

"If I'm caught?"

Jessie snorted. "Don't get caught. Make it happen. Sooner than later." She hung up.

CHAPTER 21
UNCOMFORTABLE REVELATIONS

AS WE NEARED the door to Father Mike's library, I slowed my stumbling walk, resisting Stimson's earnest push. I stopped at the door and tried to wrench my arm free. Stimson crushed my arm in his grip, threw me against the wall beside the door, rattling my teeth.

I tasted blood.

He leaned in, his breath hot against my face, a slow, quiet fire burning behind his eyes. "We're not going in there," he said, jerking me from the wall and shoving me back into motion.

Needle thin shadows followed us down the hall, sliding along the crease between the walls and the floor. Voices murmured at the bedraggled edges of my thoughts, teasing the frayed ends of the loose threads, pulling out the weave and the weft of my mind. Scattered light pocked the beige Berber like bomb craters, creating a chaotic minefield of glowing luminescence and murky dusk that exploded with each ill-timed step. The wall lamps sputtered and pulsed to the erratic rhythm of my thumping heart driving the staccato beat into a frenzy.

We slowed then stopped in front of the door to Tansy's apartment.

Remnants of Juzarine fae-daemon magic ebbed and flowed through the stuffy air.

I shuddered, tried to shake off the sticky webs.

Stimson grimaced and opened the door. "Ladies first," he said, and shoved me through.

I stumbled across the threshold and paused, allowing my eyes to adjust to the murkiness clinging to the room. Stimson closed the door softly, then stood tense and coiled beside me, clutching my arm again. His Touched abilities radiated off him, making him appear to glow with firelight.

He placed his hand against my back and shoved me forward.

I shook the remaining cobwebs from my mind, stepped from chocolate brown ceramic tile onto cream-colored Berber carpet. Fae-daemon power continued to hang in the claustrophobic air, its pulsating beat sluggish and nebulous in the murky light. A black stain soaked the beige carpet near the center of the room, roughly bracketed by the sharply angled outline of a masking tape body. Ebony-tinged dust motes drifted above the stained carpet, caught in a solitary shaft of moonlight slicing through the air from an uncurtained window.

I shuddered and licked lips gone suddenly dry before I dragged my gaze past the fouled carpet to a chair poised at the edge of the bloody sea. Cleary slumped in the chair, raspy breath rattling from his chest. Blood slimed his torn shirt and stained his trousers. His silver-streaked, fox-red hair lay flaccid in spoiled tangles over his elegant Errol Flynn face. Crimson-tinged sweat beaded on his forehead and knotted temples, greased down his bruised flesh. The stench of his vomit teased the unraveling threads of my own churning gut.

Harmonie stood behind Cleary, a bored smile creasing her

slender lips. She gripped the back of the chair, her bloodied and bruised knuckles framing his bludgeoned face. Dark irregular splotches, like paint haphazardly flung across a canvas, mottled her creamy-colored face, neck, and arms. Sweat gleamed across her skin, lending her super model complexion an ethereal appearance.

Beegle sat beside her, panting, his eyes and expression somber and quiet, almost accepting, his quiet whine drifting below the surface of the broiling tension.

Harmonie's smile widened for an instant, oozing contempt and indignation. She unclamped her hands from the back of Cleary's chair, wiped the sweat away with a mucked-up rag, squatted beside Beegle and scratched behind his ears.

She glanced aside at Cleary in distaste. "Your friend has much to answer for," she said, her French-accented English thicker and more syrupy than usual, laced with barely leashed fury. She graced Beegle's snout with a light, playful kiss and stood, discarding the rag onto a lamp table then turned her full, slate-hard gaze on me. "Do you share his sins?"

Outrage flashed into a firestorm. I growled and stepped toward her, my arms straining against the cables binding my wrists. "Cut me loose and I'll show you the true meaning of sin."

Before I could take a second apoplectic step, a steely hand clenched the back of my head, clamped bone-chilling fingers down on my skull. Blinding, sanguineous sunlight blasted into my mind, savaging my thoughts, and tearing at my memories. It undressed the truths, and the lies harbored there.

Stimson's hand followed my descent, drove my knees into the floor. I gasped and tried to wrest my head from his grip. He held firm, fingertips hooked into my flesh, his Touched power cruising past my shattered barriers, and enveloping my essence in a slow, strangled embrace.

A scream tore through the cocooning silence, the jagged-edged voice vaguely familiar.

Mine?

A night-shadowed mist surrounded me.

The corpse-shaped masking-taped outline at Cleary's bare feet began to glow. A misty haze rose from the floor, dripping quicksilver as it convulsed into an ephemeral shape that sagged on its knees. A Juzarine dagger stuck out from a heaving chest, angled upward slightly, casually asking for someone to hang their coat from it. Blood oozed from the wound. The bowed head began to lift. It floundered for a moment before finding its sea legs.

Father Mike.

I gasped.

Tansy floated over him, cloaked in a flickering sooty brume, ghost-like fists clenched at her side, eyes glittering with Blackhole oblivion. Ebony-fueled hatred rolled off her in tsunami-driven waves, buffeting my mind as they hemorrhaged rage. She reached down, stopped, and turned her eyes toward me, leering annihilation. The black abyss glowering at me shivered. Long-limbed fingers reached up through the bottomless depths blanketing her eyes, and tore back the gauzy, obsidian haze.

Stephanie Brandt scowled back at me from inside Tansy's eyes. A husky, axe-hewed voice whispered into the night, the words caressing my thoughts with acid-laced virulence. "Why did you kill us?"

I shook my head, tried to form my denial. I stepped closer, tasting the bile slathered over my cracked, sunbaked lips as I peered into the darkness and the mist-cloaked memory standing in front of me. I reached out. "Please," I breathed. "Don't."

Father Mike held up an unsteady hand, tears streaming down his cancer-sunken cheeks.

Tansy snorted and turned back to him. Snarling, she yanked the dagger from his chest and slashed it down and across him.

Sudden, searing pain gored me through my chest. I doubled over, feeling a second scorching agony tear through me. I reached out a shaking blood-stained hand, felt fire raging through my chest as I looked up into Tansy's swirling Ebony-soaked eyes.

A mania I had never seen before burned across her face, stretched her mouth into a terrifying sneer. She brandished the dagger, the bone blade dripping crimson.

My throat constricted as I mouthed words that scattered like wind-driven dust before falling to the floor on my side. Tansy's eyes dimmed for an instant, the rage banked to a slow burn. She looked down at me, recognition flashing across her face. Horror replaced the rage as she put a bloody hand to her mouth and screamed.

Glittering coal-black light exploded, blinding me.

The light and the vision vanished in the next instant, leaving me doubled over on my knees, my chest heaving, sweat dripping into my eyes. My forehead pressed into the bloody carpet where Father Mike had fallen. Where Tansy had stabbed him in the chest. Twice. With a Juzarine dagger. The frayed and frazzled edges of his slowly putrefying essence coiled rancid fingers around the fringes of my mind.

A wet tongue slathered slobber over my face, followed by a snout pushing its way against my cheek, nose, and mouth. I heard Beegle's whine from what seemed an impossible distance as someone, probably Stimson, yanked me up and dropped me into a chair, the sudden force jarring my teeth.

Voices argued, their words indistinct and unfocused, the volume reaching a crescendo before falling into uneasy silence.

"And Cleary?" Harmonie asked.

Another tense silence, but I felt Stimson's power throbbing in the space surrounding us. "Rouanet wants him," Stimson said. "Alive. And in one piece."

A hissed breath and a string of curses in French. "Cleary has much to answer for."

"And he will answer for his crimes," Stimson said. "But not at this moment. And not to you."

A fist pounded the wall. "This is not right."

"And I remind you that it is not you that determines what is right and what is not."

"Or expedient?" Harmonie said.

The door opened.

"Take the dog as well" Stimson said. "I can't have him interfering again."

"And you are named the 'sensitive' one." Harmonie's strained, fuming voice. Then a pause, followed by the scrape of leather against wood and ceramic. "Beegle! Heel!"

For an instant, I thought he'd refuse the command and stay to defend me. My instant evaporated when I heard claws clicking against the tile before disappearing through the open door. Stupid dog. When this was done, he was going to be grounded for the rest of his life, times three.

The door slammed closed, sucking out a part of my life with it.

Soft footsteps.

An urgent but gentle slap across my face.

Tepid water splashed into my face, causing me to sputter and gag.

I opened my eyes, tried to focus on the dank emptiness scowling back at me. A skull-splitting headache hammered my brain, throbbed behind my eyes. A coppery taste mired the inside of my mouth. I ran my tongue across the shredded inside of my cheeks, caressing the jagged wounds where I'd bitten through the flesh then licked lips caked with sticky, foul-tasting spittle.

"Wake up."

Hands clenched my arms, shook me like a dog worrying a rope, or a dead rabbit before throwing me back against the chair.

The world focused suddenly. Anguish seared my thoughts, driving chiseled iron spikes through my consciousness as memory flooded back, nearly flinging me from where I sat. A hand caught me by the shoulder, tossed me back into an upright position as a face consumed my world.

"Cleary?" I hacked.

"Focus."

Another slap, this one not as gentle, but more compelling and impatient.

The face blurred for an instant, shot back into focus as the hammer driving iron spikes through my brain faltered and fell, clunking against the floor with a sharp, metallic slap.

Stimson stared into my eyes, his face uncomfortably close, an obvious violation of my personal space, not to mention his raping of my mind. I rocked my head forward suddenly, met the soft flesh of his palm as it collided with my forehead and drove my head back with an almost neck snapping force.

"Don't force me to go back in there to get what I'm looking for," he snarled, punching my forehead with the tip of his finger. "Save us both the agony and just tell me where it is."

I shook my head, heaved out my churning gut, and watched in dismay as he easily sidestepped my vomit.

"You're an ass," I managed to slur as I spit a curdled wad of puke at him, tugging up an uncertain smile when it splat on his shoe.

He looked at it for a moment, shook his head and walked out of my life. Forever, I hoped. Disappointment, however, stroked my jumbled mind, when he reappeared and tossed a pitcher of water into my face.

I choked, spit the water back into him.

"Are you done?" Stimson asked.

"Go to hell."

"Not until you tell me where it is," he said, thrusting his face back into my personal space, his expression twisted with impatient fury. "Stephanie Brandt's Medusa Mirror. Where is it?"

Understanding scraped the last of the vaporous confusion from my muddy thoughts. I shook my head, licked my lips clean, and managed to meet his iron-forged glare. "I don't—"

"Cut the crap," he barked. His hand flew out, connected with my jaw, flinging my head sideways and cracking my neck. "Unless you really are the masochistic bitch you pretend to be." He paused, watching my eyes, his forehead creased in a thoughtful frown. "Which, if that is the case, you might find Harmonie a refreshing break from your usual torture routine." Silence invaded our space, quietly rolled tapping fingers across the top of my skull.

Having Stimson molest my mind had been bad enough. Harmonie, though, while not an Inquisitor, still possessed certain talents and skills I didn't want to intimately explore.

"Jessie Colemann," I whispered into the hushed stillness embracing us. "She kept it."

"What do you mean?"

"She still has it," I said.

"Shit!"

"Words," I said, managing a snorted chuckle at my own inside joke.

He ignored my feeble attempt at humor.

He stood up, pinching the bridge of his nose in frustrated anger. He looked at me a moment later, his expression dribbling frustrated compassion. "I barely managed to save you from being completely scorched because of Stephanie Brandt the first time. I can't do anything for you now." He paused, squatted down, his face level with mine. "Why didn't you trust me enough to tell me?"

I smiled back as best I could, tried to hide the wince at the end. "Despite what you might think, Marshall, the universe doesn't revolve around you."

"But I guess it revolves around you."

His unexpected and razor-sharp retort rocked me back. He glared at me, his lips clamped down so tight I thought they might actually be crushed by the force. The compassion lighting his flinty expression had been flash flooded away, leaving nothing behind but emotionless and dead bed rock. He stood and turned.

"I didn't know," I said at his back.

He spared me a look, his face carved in stone.

"Not until it was too late."

"That seems to be your SOP, Kain," he said. "Always too late and more than a dollar short." He stepped into the shadows near the door.

A body materialized from the darkness. Tall Skinny Guy.

"Angelo." Stimson whispered. "Watch her. If she so much as sneezes, shoot her." He spared me a no second-thought glance before slipping through the doorway, yanking it closed behind him. The door snapped shut, the click sounding suspiciously like the hammer of a gun being pulled back.

CHAPTER 22
ESCAPE FROM ALCATRAZ

I STARED at the closed door for a long, hard minute, shifted my eyes toward Angelo. He stared back with detached indifference, his hands crossed over his slender chest, dark chestnut-colored eyes devoid of anything even remotely resembling concern.

I tried a wan smile and tested the strength of the ties binding my wrists. They strained but didn't budge. Angelo snorted, shook his head.

How was I going to get out of this one? I couldn't even move my legs.

"At least you could tell me where you took my dog," I said, pleased with myself that my voice wasn't quavering as much as before.

Angelo remained tall, sleazy, and silent, the smirk squatting on his face dripping with hubris.

I shuddered as the last, barely remembered remnants of Ebony evaporated from the stale air hanging from the ceiling. The sibilant whispers faded soon after, slithering back into the ether.

I slumped in my chair, the corkscrewed tension unwinding enough that I could breathe again. I sucked in air, blew it back out, trying to ignore the dizziness dancing through my peripheral vision. The room swam for a moment before settling into a putrid caricature of Father Knows Best. My muddled memories stared at the blood staining the carpet in Tansy's front room, its ragged edge kissing the tips of my boots.

Father Mike's blood.

Shed by Tansy's hand.

No, not Tansy. Stephanie Brandt. Driven mad by the Juzarine, her Essence imprisoned in a Medusa Mirror for their continued macabre and sadistic enjoyment until nothing remained except a last pitiable breath left to wither and die.

My fault.

If I'd made sure she was dead before abandoning her body in the Nether Realm and to the Juzarine, we wouldn't be living this hellish party.

A shadow fell across me.

I glanced up, wished I could scrub away the tears splotching my cheeks.

Angelo looked down at me, his gangly mouth puckered in thought. He squatted, flicked open a knife.

I tensed, tried to think of an awesome "Everyone Was Kung Foo Fighting" move I could use to snap his needle-like head from his equally scrawny neck.

"But I didn't sneeze," I said, cringing at the desperation winding its way through my voice.

He smirked, delicately dragged the knife blade down my cheek, his dark eyes glinting with menace and a sewer-like delight that made me shudder.

"You know," he said as he held the blade against my throat. "You were quite the debutante back in the day." He paused, his eyes narrowing in fond reminiscence gone sour. "All of us boys had the hots for you, thought of nothing else except how to get into your pants." Another pause. He pressed the edge of the blade into my flesh. "What happened?"

I tensed, stared into his eyes, waiting for the killing stroke.

He stood suddenly, wrenched me forward by my shoulder, and slid the knife between my wrists. His breath dashed across the back of my neck, tickling the hairs. "Jessie sends her regards."

The door rattled open.

He turned as Cleary slipped through the narrow crevasse, chasing a raised suppressor. The sudden whispered concussion of a gunshot reverberated through the room.

Angelo's head popped back slightly. His hands sagged at his sides. Their grip went slack, dropped the knife as he folded into himself and accordion'd to the floor beside my chair.

"What the hell?" I snapped as Cleary closed the door behind him, limped over and put two more rounds into Angelo's chest.

"I'm here to get you out of this mess," Cleary said.

"Which Angelo was about to do when you offed him."

Cleary paused in his search of Angelo's body. "Why would he do that?"

"Because—" I began, bit back the words before I could vomit them at his feet.

Cleary pinned me back with a narrow-eyed glare, waiting for the punchline. After what seemed like an eon, he frowned and shrugged, returned to his search of Angelo's body. "Keeping secrets is going to get us both killed."

"Said every pot to every kettle." I snorted, narrowed my eyes at him, tried to imagine him burning at the stake for his hypocrisy, except that I'd be right beside him, both of us fried to a delectable extra crispy golden brown.

I ground that fantasy into the dirt, instead, asked. "Did you have to kill him?"

He slid my dagger from the inside of Angelo's jacket, stared at it before glancing up at me. "No witnesses."

"They'll think I did it."

Without responding, he pulled me forward, used the dagger to slice the zip tie, sheathed it before dropping it into my lap. "Yeah, sure. They'll think you used your incredibly supple and beguiling Houdiniesque abilities to slip from your bonds then kill your guard with a gun you conjured from behind your ear, making it vanish into thin air after the deed was done."

I shot him a snarky look as I rubbed the feeling back into my wrists, cringing as the blood rushed suddenly back into my hands. They screamed at me as the buzzing numbness faded, replaced by stabbing pins and needles that made them tremble as I threaded the dagger back onto my belt.

"How did you—?"

"Get away?" He looked at me and smirked.

Fiery crimson rings encircled the violet in his eyes for a heart-beat before vanishing, leaving behind a lurid afterglow that formed a knot in my throat.

I recoiled, my eyes wide with shocked horror. "Are you insane?" I hissed.

"Not yet," he said. "But Natasha is getting hungry. She'll need to feed soon, and I'd prefer not to be her main course."

He finished rifling Angelo's body. "Time to go."

"Not before I get Beegle back," I said.

Cleary snorted. "Why? That stupid dog threw you away for... what? A pat on the head and some doggie treats?"

"Like you?"

He stared, mock hurt flashing across his face and stood. "As a not so wise young smart-ass was once fond of telling me, sticks and stones." He winked, yanked me from the chair. "Time to move."

I turned him around, examined the ruin of his face, the swelling that dashed down from his left temple, nearly crushing his eye closed before wandering down the side of his face to the curve of his jaw. Blood crusted at the corner, leaked out to streak the side of his chin and neck. He seemed to list slightly to the left as well, like a sinking ship, the desperate crew unable to keep up with the flood.

"You look like crap," I said.

"We make a pair, don't we." He winked again, handed me Angelo's sidearm. "Just in case."

I stared at it for a moment, checked to see if Angelo ran hot, claimed the holster off his belt.

"Before we leave there's one thing I need to say to you."

Cleary turned back, his eyes questioning, impatience glaring at me with its arms crossed.

I punched him in the mouth. "Where the hell were you?" I shouted. "You were supposed to watch her. It's what I paid you for!" I clenched my fists at my sides, thought about punching him again.

He rubbed his jaw, scowling, fire and ice dirty dancing through his violet eyes. "Careful," he said. "You really want to do this now?"

I glared back at him, seething, blood boiling through my temples. My jaw trembled. Tears, despite my attempt to control them, squeezed out from my eyes, and rolled down my cheeks.

"Then here." He spread his arms in an open-wide invitation. "Take your best shot."

I shook my head. "You really are an ass."

He relaxed slightly.

I sucker punched him in the gut.

He doubled over, sputtering, astonishment riding across his face.

Before he could recover, I grabbed the back of his collar and kneed him in the groin.

He dropped like a bag of rocks, coughing and sputtering, his glowing, lobster-red face nearly touching the carpet at my feet.

I kneeled, touched my lips to his ear. "Yeah, I really do want to do this now."

He looked up at me, still panting, his bright red color beginning to fade.

"The shit had already hit the fan when I arrived." He stopped, sucking air for a few long seconds. He spit a wad of blood at my feet. Drool seeped from the corner of his mouth, pooling on the carpet below his face. After a few more unsteady breaths, he wiped his mouth clean with the back of a defiled sleeve.

"It was already done by the time I arrived. I found—"

"What?" Too late, after I'd spewed the words, I realized that maybe, I wanted to believe Tansy hadn't turned into the monster I knew she'd become.

He looked down at the floor, coughed and spat. "Michael's car was missing when I arrived. And then I found Michael lying in his own blood where you're standing." He tried to suck in a trembling breath, shuddered, turned his face toward me. Tears glistened in his eyes. "He was barely breathing. And Abbie—" He stopped, shook his head, slowly pushed himself to his feet, and leaned against the wall before straightening to his full height. He stabbed me with an angry look. "I found her in the hall, gutted."

The color drained from my face. My mind went back to the photo of Tansy holding up Jonnie Hallows' severed head. My stomach roiled. I thought I might be sick, managed to force the queasiness down. And then... I dropped to my knees and spewed what was left in my stomach onto the carpet beside Father Mike's sticky blood.

I huddled on my hands and knees, shivering, waiting for the waves of nausea and disgust to roll off me and my gut to settle.

Cleary's hand touched my shoulder. I slapped it off, glared up at him before shoving myself back to my feet, and finished wiping the goo off my mouth.

"And then what?" My eyes dripped a rage I wished I could use like a baseball bat to pummel him with.

Cleary regarded me with a cool, calculating look. "I called you, but you didn't answer." He shrugged, the movement helplessly frustrated. "And then Stimson and his hell hounds arrived before I could get out. Bonnet found me, despite my best efforts to avoid detection."

I waited for him to elaborate, gave up after the requisite decade.

"Can we go now?" He snapped. "Before they come back and the situation becomes even more interesting?"

"Tell me that Harmonie is still alive."

"Probably," he said. "She wasn't around when I escaped. As for the two Chasseurs watching me—" He shrugged. "Can we go now?"

I thought about belting him again, but as I watched him, I caught Natasha peeking out from behind his eyes, spied the nuanced strain lining his bludgeoned face. His control was eroding.

"Not without Beegle," I said.

He cursed, throwing his hands up in frustrated resignation. "That damned dog is going to get us both killed."

"You, maybe," I said. "Me—?"

I didn't wait for his response. Brushing past him, I toddled to the door, snatched it open. I looked back, gave Angelo one last sorrowful glare before stepping into the hallway and hobbling to where I hoped Harmonie had left Beegle. Father Mike's library, the only room at St. Jude's where he seemed to feel comfortable and safe when we weren't together.

I hugged the walls as I went, my hand gripping the butt of Angelo's pistol, praying that no one saw me. Cleary brought up the rear, grunting with each tortured step as he tried to keep up.

Our luck held, or maybe someone else had decided to watch out for me in Father Mike's absence. Either way, we reached the library without incident. I put my ear to the fading wood finish, heard only silence from within. Sucking in an uneven breath, I drew Angelo's pistol, opened the door and slid through the opening. Cleary followed me through the eye of the needle, closing the door softly behind us.

I stood just within the landing, scanned the room.

It looked like a hurricane had rolled through it. Books lay scattered across the floor. Desk drawers had been yanked from their homes, their contents dumped, then tossed in helter-skelter directions, the papers and notebooks they had embraced strewn chaotically over the top of the tumultuous piles.

A high-pitched baying shattered the silence, chased by a frenetic bark. Beegle stood in Father Mike's chair, his wagging tail thumping the back with the zeal of an over-caffeinated metronome. I smiled. If Father Mike knew Beegle was in his chair, he'd be furious, would probably order Beegle to be flayed, put on a spit and roasted. Beegle continued to stare at me, excitement in his brown eyes, his tail continuing to thump the back of Father Mike's chair.

I dashed to the chair and fell to my knees, weeping, my arms flung wide. Beegle whined, cast a distrustful glare at Cleary before shoving his snout into my face. I grabbed him by the scruff of his neck, pulled him into a crushing embrace. He slimed me with slobber and nipped my nose when I pressed my lips against his snout. He barked and bayed, his tail continuing to beat the snot out of the back of Father Mike's chair.

A shadow grew over me, dimming the silver-yellow light holding Beegle and me in its gentle and loving embrace. A hand touched my shoulder. I flinched, nearly tossing it aside before remembering who else occupied the room.

Cleary cleared his voice. "Now that you two have gotten reacquainted, can we be going?"

I gave Beegle one last kiss then stood and brushed past Cleary. I paused at the door. "Beegle, heel." The thud of a small, solid body bounced through the air, accompanied by the click of nails against the wood flooring. Beegle sat beside my leg, panting, his tongue lolling in an eager beagle grin. I glanced back at Cleary. "You coming? Or are just going to stand there and sulk?"

I opened the door and slid into the hall, Beegle padding silently beside me.

CHAPTER 23
FROM THE FRYING PAN

CLEARY FOLLOWED me into the hallway, closed the door softly behind him. "Where are we going?"

I thought about it for a long, undecided moment. The Warrens called to me. Mainly because of what Stimson had intimated during our first father-daughter talk in my kitchen. But also because it was the only place besides my mirror that I had access to the Nether Realm and the Juzarine. If Jessie had brought even one of their witches through the Nexus... I shuddered at the thought.

I needed to know if Father Mike was still alive. Other people in his cancer-ridden condition wouldn't have survived. But Father Mike was not "other people." Sheer will and drive would keep him alive until he knew Tansy was safe. At least I hoped so. But thanks to Cleary and his obsession with Houdini-like escapades and his current proclivity for a twitchy trigger finger, Stimson wasn't likely going to tell me what I wanted to know if I called him. That meant I needed my own eyes on him.

It also meant Stimson and Harmonie would most likely be waiting for me.

I cursed, caught Beegle gazing up at me with Father Mike disapproval. I narrowed my eyes at him. "Like you've never cursed before?"

"Are you talking to your damned hell hound?"

I hammered Cleary with a 'mind your own fricking business' glower.

"We're going to St. Raphael," I said.

"What? Why?" Cleary managed to swallow past the wad clogging his throat. "And you call me insane!"

"I need to know Father Mike is still alive. And St. Raphael is the only parish in Denver with the medical facilities capable of keeping him that way." I shoved back the sudden anguish knotting bitter talons through my chest. I hammered Cleary with a steely gaze. "Come or don't," I said. "At the moment, I couldn't care less. You've got your money, and I know that your time is valuable." I hesitated. "I also know that you've got unresolved, lethal business with Harmonie and Rouanet that you need to take care of."

I didn't wait for him to respond. I strode down the hallway toward the rectory entrance with Beegle at my heels. I heard Cleary's limping footsteps come behind me. He caught me just before Beegle and I turned the corner, and he whipped me around to face him.

His chest heaved, his mouth twisted with pain as it sucked air and blew it out again like an antsy whale.

I threw his hand off my shoulder and tried to turn. He caught my arm, spun me around like I weighed nothing, and slammed me against the wall.

Beegle growled and lunged for his leg. Cleary kicked him off, drew his pistol and touched it to my temple as Beegle prepared for another lunge. He hesitated, snarling deep in his chest, the sound rumbling through the space surrounding us like a growing earthquake.

"Tell him to back off," he whispered. He pressed the side of my face into the wall, pushed the muzzle of the suppressor harder against my skull for emphasis.

"Shoot me then," I said. "Beegle will rip your throat out before you can fire a second round."

Cleary snarled in my ear. "Your damned dog will die first." He drove his forearm into my neck and shifted his aim. "Don't think I won't do it."

The problem was, I knew he would.

I nodded.

Cleary released enough of the tension pressing my neck into the wall that I could swallow. And speak. I wheezed out a breath. "It's okay, buddy," I said. "Cleary and I are just having a brief discussion."

Beegle shifted his gaze from me to Cleary, his eyes blazing with fury. He trembled, his chest reverberating.

I nodded to him, managed a lopsided smile on the side of my face not smashed against the wall. "I'll be okay," I said.

Beegle glowered at Cleary one last time, curled his upper lip in a savage snarl, allowing the pale light to glint off his teeth. A promise. He backed up a step, sat, his snout lowered, lips still curled up, teeth glistening.

I heard Cleary swallow.

The pressure pinning my neck vanished. Cleary turned me to face him, put a hand on my chest. He touched the muzzle of the suppressor to my forehead. Beegle growled, the low rumble slowly swelling.

"I thought we had a deal," I said.

"We have a deal when I say we have a deal," he said. "And we have a deal when you tell me what is going on." He glared at me, his expression coiled to the snapping point. "No lies. No subterfuge. Just the damned truth."

"Jessie made a deal with the Juzarine," I said, pausing for a breath.

Cleary narrowed his eyes. He pressed the suppressor against my forehead. "What does that have to do with you?"

I hesitated, wondered if I could or should lie to him, decided that the truth might prick his dead ethics and morals with enough electricity to jump start their heartbeat. If maybe even for an instant. "She promised Navarro to them in exchange for a Medusa Mirror," I whispered. "Stephanie Brandt's Medusa Mirror."

The muzzle of the suppressor trembled for an eye blink against my forehead. "Why?"

I swallowed past the lump growing in the back of my throat, fighting back the rising tide of tears pressing against the dam I'd erected. "Why do you think," I responded, my voice trembling with grief-swamped rage despite my resolve to remain unemotional and in control.

He stepped away, lowered his gun, gaping. "No," he said. "It's impossible. Jessie and the Juzarine?" He shook his head. "She couldn't. She wouldn't."

I snorted. "Wouldn't she?"

"Tansy?"

I glowered at him, mouth set into a tight line, and snapped a nod.

"I can't... I won't. When?" The tail end of his denials dropped to the floor and shattered at his feet. He wiped his mouth with the back of a sleeve, turned, strode to the opposite wall, rammed it with his fist, and pinwheeled back. He continued to shake his head in disbelief.

I stood, rubbed my throat. "Probably before you found her with Jonnie."

"No," he said, still shaking his head. "It's impossible. The Shining Man—"

"Probably knows and is using that knowledge for its own sick and twisted pleasure." Its words haunted me from the depths of impotent hubris. How far would I be willing to go? What lines would I be willing to cross? Who would I be willing to sacrifice? To save Tansy and myself? I guess I was about to find out.

Beegle shifted his weight and stood. Another growl echoed low in his throat.

Hushed voices approached from around the corner, pursued a moment later by mouths, faces, and bodies.

Two Chasseurs stood in the center of the hallway, open-mouthed, eyes wide with astonishment, rigid with indecision. They recovered their wits quickly.

Both drew their sidearms simultaneously. One shouted. The other reached for the radio strapped to his shoulder.

The stifled concussion of a suppressed gunshot bounced through the hallway, echoed by the thunderous crack of an answering blast. One chasseur grunted, staggered back. His pistol flew from his grasp, tumbled to the floor as he collapsed. Beegle lunged at the second Chasseur as he fumbled for his weapon, latched iron-vise jaws around his forearm. He screamed. A gunshot detonated, the bullet pelting the wall beside Cleary's head.

He cursed, side-stepped from the wall, raised his gun. "Get your dog off him," he snapped.

A second shot exploded. The bullet ricocheted off the tiled floor, spitting ceramic splinters up into the air.

Beegle continued to maul the man's arm, dragged it down with his weight. The gun fell from his hand. Beegle let go. He straightened. Cleary fired. The man stumbled back a step into the wall.

Cleary aimed for a third shot.

I hurled myself into him.

The shot flew wild, the bullet tearing through a light fixture and into the ceiling, raining plaster and sparks down on us. I wrestled the gun from his hand, smacked the side of his head with the suppressor. It snapped off at the barrel, dropped into his lap. He tried to stand. I shoved the muzzle of Angelo's gun into his face. Blood oozed from the fresh gash I'd opened below his temple.

"Enough," I hissed. "Enough killing. Enough death." I glanced at the Chasseur leaning back against the wall. Blood swelled from below his collarbone, glittered through his shirt, staining the dark material an inky red. I turned my rage on Cleary and pressed the muzzle of the gun into his forehead. My finger began to pull back the trigger, slowly and with deadly purpose.

He grunted. "Go ahead," he said. "Do it. I'm dead already anyway." He looked down.

My eyes followed his. I gasped. Blood streamed from a hole in his side, soaking the silk. Crimson fire embraced his violet eyes. He grimaced, the strain tearing at the cuts and slices littering his chiseled face.

Crackling static stumbled through the space behind me.

"Shit," I muttered as I turned.

The Chasseur's hand fell from the radio microphone attached to his shoulder, quivered open-fisted on his leg.

Our eyes met.

Dread stalked his gaze, hunkered in the growing shadows. His breath stuttered in shallow staggering sprints that squeezed his chest like a soggy sponge. A last, quivering breath stumbled from his parted lips, its wispy edges curling into the air as it vanished into the bottomless depths of death.

I hung my head in frustration and anger. "Why?" I hurled at Cleary.

A smile tripped across his mouth. "No witnesses."

I snagged the radio from the second Chasseur, hesitated before offering a faltering prayer and closing his eyes.

"Feel better?" Cleary wheezed.

"You really are an ass," I said as I leveraged myself beneath his dead weight and hauled him to his feet.

He didn't resist. But he didn't assist.

"I told you to leave me."

"Like hell," I hissed back. "I paid you for a job. And you're going to fulfill the terms of your contract." I speared Beegle with an intense gaze, made sure I had his undivided attention. "Beegle," I said. "Scout."

He shook himself, huffed a whispered bark before scrabbling around the corner and down the hallway.

I turned up the volume on my stolen radio, heaved Cleary's weight onto my shoulder, and followed.

Almost immediately, intense, static-laced voices flooded the air, their clipped and hurried words tripping over themselves, creating pandemonium and bedlam before a snarled order throttled them into uneasy silence. Stimson's voice. Stern and iron-fisted, laced with his power, his single whip-cracked word took control.

Crackling stillness followed.

"Cassidy," Stimson said. "I know you have a radio. And I know you're listening. Whatever's happened, I know it wasn't you. Give us Cleary. Give yourself up." Snapping, crackling, popping. "Please. While I can still help you." Another pregnant pause, the spitting silence giving birth as I listened for the last of Stimson's impassioned plea for me to give myself up.

"I'll be waiting at the rectory entrance."

I stood in the center of the hallway, Cleary hitched onto my shoulder, straining with his zombie-like weight, the warm nuzzle of his blood soaking through my shirt. His sharp, iron-scented breath beat against the side of my face, flecking my flesh with bloody droplets.

Hesitation pinned me to where I stood as I began to heave my breath from the strain.

"Thinking about it, aren't you?"

I huffed a frayed sigh. "You deserve whatever they have waiting for you," I said. "But not today."

I pivoted his nearly dead weight right and staggered us both down the hall toward the nave.

"What about your insidious hell hound?"

"He'll find us."

"And if Stimson has people waiting for us in the nave?"

"I'm using you as a human shield."

He snorted, grunted, his side heaving. I spied an oozing stream of blood leaking from the corner of his mouth as I shambled us down the hall, using the wall every few yards to support his increasingly noodley body so I could shift his weight on my aching shoulder.

We reached the door leading into the nave several heart-thudding minutes later. The radio hanging from my belt had gone silent almost immediately following Stimson's plea, leaving us in a cocoon of stagnant quiet.

Leaning Cleary against the wall, I listened at the door. A stupid move, considering the door was too thick to allow me to hear anything short of the detonation of a nuclear bomb, and Stimson's people weren't as stupid as I wished to make them out.

I grasped the door handle.

"Are you sure about this?"

"Hell no." I pushed the door open, and dragged Cleary through, pausing long enough for the click of the door closing to echo hollowly off the silent walls.

CHAPTER 24

SOMETHING WICKED THIS WAY COMES

ADRIA PAUSED at the entrance to the hallway, listening to the melody of her thrumming heart as it beat in time to the discordant sounds pulsing from the radio in the front room behind her. Christmas music, entwined with the subtle promises of Christian themes. She felt an ache in her chest, a longing that skimmed just below the surface of her thoughts.

A smile flickered at the corners of her mouth, then fell—like a stone dropped into a still and silent pond—as the music ended, its ripples dying before their birth. Quiet whimpers and cries scraped the edges of her mind like roughly spun burlap. The stench of dread floated in the air, romping blithely with the Ebony haze clinging to the shredded fringe of desperation.

She glanced over her shoulder, eyes searching the night for the huddled shapes cowering on the snow sodden floor—wrapped gossamer and the desolation she'd quietly planted into their dreams. Her smile returned, faltering for an instant when the Essence of the one called Tansy, whose body she possessed, prodded her from the depths of the cage to which she had imprisoned her.

Adria gazed inward, stared at the Essence shackled to the bottom of the sea where she'd pinned it, watched with fascination as it struggled against the chains binding it. Leaning into the bowels of the abyss from which the Essence pined, she reached out, brushed the tattered edges with yearning, soothing and calming as she wrapped it into the false warmth of her embrace, and began feeding.

A window rattled, pelted by sleet, the needle-like crystals scratching against the ice dusted glass.

Adria shook herself, trembling with remembered delight as she licked phantom blood from her fingers, relishing the syrupy ooze. She grinned, gazing inward a few moments longer, savoring the terror peeking back at her from the nothingness anchored at the bottom of the pit.

Chuckling, she padded down the hallway of the modest three-bedroom 1970s ranch style home in bare feet, leaving behind a trail of sodden footsteps in her wake. She dragged her fingertips along the wall, relishing the sensation of the bumps and ridges, the reality of the physical to which she'd been reborn. Pausing, she brushed the glass of a picture frame, stared at the photos encased behind the pane. A lacerated memory crept from the bowels of the other's jigsaw thoughts. She frowned. Jimmy and Gloria Turner, their names a lusterless mist slowly evaporating under the rising darkness of Adria's need. Two of Cassidy's impossible successes, brought back to humanity after they had been deemed unrecoverable. Twins. Not yet five, smiling as they lounged in one another's arms, the nightmares coming into their young lives not yet a twinkle in the wrinkle of their future. Beside them, their mother, her bright eyes failing to conceal the troubled mind lurking behind them, the illness not yet exposed by the light. A man, standing behind the woman, arms draped protectively over her shoulders. He wore a frown heavy with concern as he glanced sideways at the woman. Their father.

Adria peered into his worried eyes, the lurking disquiet, hidden, but peeking out from behind the untruthful happiness on his face. She thought of her own parents. Her mother dead when she was just five. Killed when a drunk driver careened into her as she crossed the street. Her father, now also dead, but by her hand, his Essence the first she had fed upon after awakening in the Tansy body.

Further down, another set of framed photos, the mother absent, replaced by the woman in the front room exuding horror. Another name languished at the edge of the pit of forgetfulness. Molly Montgomery, Jimmy and Gloria's aunt. The name teetered for an instant, slid down into the depths, crushed into oblivion. Adria frowned, brushed the glass with trembling fingers, her mind grasping for the name of the woman once more until she looked into the haunted eyes of the girl standing beside her. Gloria Turner, who now stood over the woman, her aunt, and her brother Jimmy, her mind and Essence succumbing to the Ebony Adria had fed her.

The fifty-year old house creaked and groaned around her, pummeled by the gusting wind. She stopped and closed her eyes, listening to the snow as it clawed the roof and sides of the house, tearing tiny grooves into the wood and tar, seeking a way into the warmth where it could feed and grow.

She found herself in the girl's room, not unlike her own before she was stolen and cast from this world into the Nether Realm, trapped and held captive for the pleasures and indulgence of the creatures that had created what she had become. Smaller, the furniture less costly, simpler in its design, more functional than fashionable. Posters of teen actors and singers Adria no longer cared about, a small cedar writing desk, burnished to a subtle sheen, in the corner away from the small bed, its tops littered with papers and more photos, and lying beneath the turmoil a small notebook, its flimsy cover pasted over with stickers of hearts and kissing lips.

Adria picked it up, frowned as a memory from her life before tickled her thoughts. She'd once held a book like this, filled its pages with her musings and dreams, her one days and some days.

All gone now, ground into dust and ash by the terrors of her long imprisonment and torment at the hands of the Juzarine.

A torturous scream skipped down the hall, bludgeoned its way through the open doorway.

Adria shuddered, and grasping the notebook by its covers, ripped it in two, tossed the scattering pages across the room.

Returning to the front room, she watched in morbid fascination as the woman struggled to crawl across the blood-soaked carpet, her hand left behind and still bound with gossamer. Fascinated, Adria strode to the woman and knelt in front of her, examining her with clinical detachment.

The woman looked up, her face stretched into an agonized mask. Bloody tears rolled down her cheeks, fell from the cleft of her chin, splattering on her arm. She cringed when she saw Adria, swiped the air in front of her with her bleeding and handless stump.

Adria caught her arm, held it, looking from the stump into the woman's eyes, enthralled by the pain and staggering strength she saw. She lifted the arm up, pulling the woman into the air with it, forcing her to stand or lose her arm.

A soft mewling moan crawled across the carpet, rubbed its way between the woman's feet, cat-like and purring contentment.

Adria dragged the woman back to the center of the room and dropped her. She retrieved a chair from the kitchen and stabbed it into the carpet beside her. Then, lifting the woman, she dumped her into the chair and glared at her for a moment before walking into the kitchen.

The young girl, Adria pulled the memory of her name from the abyss; Gloria, stood near the back, cloaked in darkness and an Ebony haze. She swayed back and forth, humming a monotonous melody, her lank and tangled hair drooping over her eyes like a curtain waiting to be drawn back. She waved her hands back and forth in front of her face with chaotic grace, as if she were conducting an unheard symphony. She'd chewed her fingernails to their nubs, nibbled on her fingertips, staining them crimson in the grubby streetlight reflected through the cramped window straddling the kitchen sink.

The brother, Jimmy Truner, his name striding more comfortably across the littered back of Adria's thoughts, lay in a back corner, curled into a tightly woven fetal ball. He trembled, charcoal black steam slowly rising from his clenched body, mingling with the Ebony fog hanging in the air. He cried out, swatted at an invisible nightmare, curled back into his ball.

Adria would use him later.

She strode up to the girl, gently touched her forehead.

Gloria looked up through her eyelashes, enraged mania glowing from behind the gloom reflected from her eyes.

Adria smiled, gently shoved a Juzarine dagger into her tumbling hand, closed her fist around the handle.

Gloria shivered, gripping the dagger more tightly as she caressed it against her chest. A lunatic gleam shone from her gaze, lighting the gloom with an incandescent glow. Adria stroked the girl's hair, and pulled it from her eyes, delicately kissing her lips.

She leaned toward the girl, touching her ear with her mouth. "Sacrifice and feed," she breathed. "Then deliver my message to the one responsible for... this."

Gloria looked up, eagerness pulsing through her gaze. "Cassidy?"

Adria smiled and nodded.

A shiver galloped through the girl. Her knuckles shimmered white around the dagger she clutched in her fist. Her smile grew to echo Adria's. An unhurried nod. The languid grin tightening her mouth into a sullied thread barely visible in the stuttering light.

Adria peered through Gloria's eyes and into her soul, studied the black fire smoldering below the charred ashes of who she had once been. She grinned and stepped aside.

Gloria stood, her body convulsing into an unsteady step, pulling the chorus of ghostly whispers after her as she stumbled from the kitchen into the living room.

Grabbing Jimmy's ankle, Adria dragged him from beneath the table and across the floor toward the back door. He wept and whimpered, his nails trenching furrows into the cheap linoleum. At the door, she paused, listening. A faltering rustle skinned the shadows, chased by an abrupt, bone-scraping scream. Silence rushed into the vacuum, filling the emptiness with a dead tranquility.

Grinning, Adria yanked the back kitchen door open and tugged Jimmy Truner into the howling wind and snow.

CHAPTER 25
INTO THE FIRE

THE KEY LIGHTS WERE DARK, leaving only the emergency lights to weakly fill the dead space between fixtures. Emptiness glared back at me, making my stomach twist as we stepped from the south transept into the crossing at the front of the nave, the sounds of our scraping footsteps bouncing off the walls and tall, hidden ceiling.

As we turned down the center aisle toward the back of the nave and the doors leading to the parking lot, I felt an itch between my shoulder blades I couldn't scratch. I stuttered to an uncertain stop, tried to resist the pull coming from behind.

Dropping Cleary into a pew, I turned to face the crucified Christ hanging on his cross.

His body lay cloaked in shadow, but his face glowed sun bright in the light of a nearby emergency beacon. His shimmering gaze found mine, and tried to pull me toward him, beseeching me to forgive myself... and to accept his forgiveness and the salvation I had so long refused, but wanted more than life itself.

I stared, almost took the first step on that long-denied journey until Cleary's trembling hand found my arm. I flinched, stared down at his paling face, the dimming violet of his eyes slowly being overcome by Natasha's flaming Essence.

I tore my gaze away from him, peered through the inky blackness at the hanging Christ and the agony smeared across the sculpted face. The spell dissolved, leaving a black hole in the center of my soul, where my guilt crouched, feral and hungry.

I brushed the desolation aside, wrenched myself from Cleary's clutching hand, and heaved him from the pew and onto my shoulder again, grunting as I tugged him down the nave to the entry doors that led to the outside.

With my hand on the handle, I glanced over my shoulder.

No longer illuminated, the Christ's face lay veiled in dusky gloom, his luminous eyes gone dead. Unapproachable. Maybe forever. My heart lurched in my chest, and I felt the sudden tremor of my lower lip, bit it back, swallowed my grief and buried it.

Shaking off the last of the spell, I shouldered the door open and stepped into an incandescent winter night, the black velvet sky on fire with argent flames from the Fae Moon and a pin-pricked beach of glittering starlight.

A frigid wind tore at my hair, slipping frost-rimed fingers through the gaps in my shirt—arctic tips raising a field of goose pimples across my shivering flesh.

Cleary groaned, his shivering and chattering teeth rattling mine from the gums. "I can't," he said between clenched teeth. "It's too cold. Natasha... I don't have the strength."

"Fine," I said as I dragged him back inside and leaned his quivering body against the wall. "I'll be back as quickly as I can." Indecision grappled for my attention, grinning with foreboding—its twinkling eyes blinking pernicious doom. I shuddered, snatched his gun from his dead fish hand.

A sour look slipped over his drawn expression as he hunched deeper into his deflating body. "Don't trust me?"

"No," I said. "Where's your Land Rover?"

Beginning to shiver with intensity, Cleary gestured toward the doors. "The neighborhood across the street. Near the end of the block."

I sighed. That meant at least an easy two hundred yards of exposed running through the howling snow. I might as well have painted a glowing red neon target on my back that flashed an open invitation. "It's my Bronco or go home, then," I said, shouldering the door open. "It better be you I find when I get back."

He groaned, his eyes rippling beneath the closed lids.

I slid back into the teeth of the wolfish wind and picked my way down the steps to the parking lot.

A sea of glistening white dunes sprawled across the ice-sheathed blacktop, reflected an eerie glow into the frost-heavy air. The ash trees lining the edge of the parish property, their branches stripped bare by winter, reached spidery fingers into the fiery night.

A lone car drove past the parish, its headlights reflecting off the snow and ice clenching the street, disappeared at the end as it turned the corner into a sleepy neighborhood of small brick houses with single-car garages and miniature snow-carpeted yards.

I huddled in the moon-pale shadows clinging to the side of the parish, surveyed the silent winter desert spread out before me. My breath billowed from my mouth, roiled up into the air, before it vanished into the black hole of the night's forgetfulness. High-strung silence stared back, barren and stark.

A low whine snaking out from the deeper shadows startled me. I drew Angelo's pistol and peered into the night-shaded darkness. Another faint whine and a muffled woof hugged me. I smiled and holstered the pistol as Beegle materialized from the dark, shrouded in snow, his black snout whispered with silver and white.

I kneeled beside him, scratching him behind his ears, and nuzzled his snout. He leaned into my hand, his eyes dancing with delight, tail whipping the frigid air.

"I knew you'd find me," I whispered into his ear. "Ready for another adventure?" He slavered my nose and mouth with his tongue. I chuckled despite our present danger and shoved him off me. "Scout," ordered, pointing in the direction we needed to go.

He scampered off, snow spiting into the air in his wake as he vanished around the corner. He trotted back a few heartbeats later, sat and stared, panting. Steam rose in roiling puffs from his open maw, swirled through the moonstruck light before vanishing.

I arched a bow in question. He woofed his snuffled his response. I snorted back at him, smiled and shook my head. "Good boy," I said. "Let's go see what you found."

Beegle leapt from the snow back toward the corner. I followed him, gun drawn and held low at my side. We hugged the parish wall as best we could, tried to stay out of the light, using the darker shadows cast from the building for cover. W reached another corner that turned toward the back of the parish and the front of the rectory.

I peered around the corner.

The Order of the Four's Suburbans from earlier hugged the front of the rectory. My Bronco huddled nearby, an arm's length from the protective circle, looking lonely and forlorn in its empty silence. Snow-laced streetlight shimmered off the roof and hood, throwing argent sparks against the trampled snow.

Nothing else seemed to exist within that universe.

I stepped around the corner, froze as the hint of a feathery movement caught my eye.

A single Chasseur roamed the blackness between the Suburbans, scanning the leaden gloom as he wandered the shadows, armed with an assault rifle.

I melted back against the building, scraping my shoulder across rough-hewn stone and brick. I grimaced at the heavy touch of arctic-chilled rock pricking my flesh.

Where were the rest of Stimson's people? Had he pulled them back when I didn't respond to his invitation? Were they searching for us even now inside the parish? If they were, I needed to act quickly before they caught Cleary and Harmonie had another special talk with him.

On the other hand, the scene before me stank of trap. A single Chasseur left to patrol the perimeter? Not likely. More likely was that the Suburbans were ten months pregnant with backup and more than eager to birth its children at the slightest provocation.

The smart move would be to chance the coast-to-coast sprint for Cleary's Land Rover. But I'd never been that smart. Or that cunning.

Beegle peered up at me, his dark brown eyes glittering with eagerness. "Distract," I whispered.

Beegle barked, scampered from our hidey-hole and bounded across the parking lot, spraying snow as he shot through the drifting mounds, chased by the echoes of his baying and howling off the parish walls.

The Chasseur paused, looked in Beegle's direction, stumbled across a field of ice after him.

Beegle even had the balls to stop and wait for his pursuer as they struggled through the snow and over the ice. As they disappeared around the opposite corner, I waited, scanning the silence for the trap to be sprung.

Nothing.

After waiting an extra two unsteady breaths, I dashed through the grayish light, skidded to an uncertain stop beside the Bronco, heaving air, my hands trembling.

Nothing moved except the clouds scudding through the starlit sky, chasing the moonlight, and nipping at its tail.

I retrieved my spare key from underneath the driver side fender, faltered when I spied the Suburban that Angelo had dumped my belongings into. Avarice tugged my good sense, teasing it with childish taunts and jeers.

"Crap," I muttered into the night as I slid from the back of the Bronco and sprinted to the Suburban. As I skidded to a messy stop, something snugged my leg. I jumped and looked down. Beegle hovered at my feet. "Damn it, Beegle," I grumbled. He peered up at me, brown eyes glinting in the moonlight.

I opened the hatch, retrieved my Walther and Colt.

"Do not move."

My heart throttled into my throat as my fist wrapped around the grip of the Walther. The weight in my hand told me it was still loaded. But was it still hot?

"Turn slowly, hands where I can see them."

I obeyed, stared down at the laser dot punching the center of my chest.

Angry Olive-Skinned Italian Girl peered at me through the dimness; her assault rifle aimed at my chest. "Drop the weapons."

I noticed Beegle had vanished, and scanned the area behind Angry Olive-Skinned Italian Girl, but saw only emptiness in the wan silver light.

I swore under my breath that when this was over, I'd spring for that damned obedience training.

I tightened my grip on the Walther. "Or what?"

She flashed a humorless smile, deadly intent glinting from her eyes. "Or I kill your dog. And then we find your boyfriend and give him to the assassin."

"What dog," I said.

She glanced down, uncertainty dancing over her face.

"And as for Cleary, he isn't my boyfriend. In fact, I hate him more than you do."

She readjusted her aim on my chest. "Then we wait for the others to come out."

I shook my head. "Don't think so. I've got somewhere I need to be and you're burning my daylight." I blew out a breath. "Tell you what." I holstered my Walther and raised my hands. "You can have Cleary. Do whatever you want with him. Honestly, I couldn't care less. He's in the nave. But..." I started forward, angling my path toward the front of the Bronco. "I'm leaving. And you don't want to try to stop me."

In one swift practiced motion, she moved her finger over the trigger.

I spun sideways from her, drawing my Walther. Beegle launched himself from the darkness, baying. He slammed into her legs from behind and knocked her off balance.

A gun shot reverberated through the night air.

I aimed and fired at the center of her chest, the thickest part of her body armor.

Angry Olive-Skinned Italian Girl jerked back.

I fired a second round. And a third.

Her body jerked back twice before she sagged to the ground.

Beegle latched onto her wrist, chewed it like a favorite toy.

She screamed, tried to beat him off with her free hand.

He clamped down harder.

I heard the grinding crunch of snapping bones.

She dropped her rifle, tried to pull Beegle off her wrist, screamed again.

"Beegle, down!"

He savaged her wrist for another second, before letting go, and danced back as she took a swipe at him with a knife she'd managed to pull from her belt. He stood just beyond her range, teeth bared, and growling.

Before she could wind up for another swing, I punched the muzzle of my Walther into the back of her head. "Don't."

Hesitation. She dropped the knife.

I kicked it and her rifle into the freezing slush. Kneeling beside her, I kept my Walther pressed into the back of her head, feeling her tremble as she struggled to suck air into her throbbing chest. I touched my lips to her ear. "Remember this feeling. The next time you think you can take me."

I strode to the Bronco, turned to wink my goodbye to her in time to see the muzzle flash from across the street, watched in helpless horror as the front of Angry Olive-Skinned Italian Girl's head exploded, accompanied an instant later by a whispered thump.

Hunkering down beside the Bronco, I scanned the distant gloom hugging the street, but saw nothing, heard even less except for the harsh rasp of my frenetic breathing. Angry Olive-Skinned Italian Girl motionless, the churned frozen slush beneath her face growing black.

I yanked the driver door open, just managing to toss Beegle into the front seat as the rectory doors flew open, spewing out a skulking yellowish light and several armed Chasseurs.

A gunshot detonated through the air, the round punching into driver side fender. I squeezed off four quick helter-skelter rounds from the Walther. Bodies scattered. I slid into the driver's seat, fired up the Bronco. It sneezed a few times before the motor squawked awake. Hunkering down, one hand clutching the wheel, I managed to throw it into gear as I slammed my foot down on the gas. My baby squealed in protest before burning rubber through waves of snow and ice as more shots whistled past and thudded into the back hatch.

I slid the Bronco to a slippery stop below the nave entrance, hopped out and scrambled up the steps, wrenched the doors open. Cleary lay where I left him leaning against the wall. Blood wept from the hole in his side, pooling on the tiled floor beside him. His chest retched slow, agonizing breaths.

I aimed the Walther at his head. "Cleary?"

He snickered and glanced up at me. "Still here," he said. "Mostly. But not for long."

Expediency told me to leave him, let Harmonie have him. I never liked expediency. It was too... expedient. Cursing myself for the idiot I was, I hefted Cleary to his feet.

"Leave me," he muttered, pushing against my grip.

"Shut up," I said. "We have a deal, remember?" I shoved his hands away. "And I want what I paid for."

"Is that all?"

"I don't like Natasha."

I lugged him through the doorway, down the steps, propped him against the side of the Bronco, before folding him into the backseat as bobbing flashlight beams rounded the far corner of the building, harmonizing with the slap of boots through crusted snow and frantic shouts.

I chucked four more haphazard rounds into the snow-littered night, fumbled myself into the driver seat and flung the Bronco into gear, spinning snow into gold as we lurched into motion, bouncing over an embankment and into the street beyond.

CHAPTER 26
TIME FOR PLAN B

I PULLED A HARD LEFT at the first four-way stop, ignoring the angry blare from the horn of the pickup I cut off as it slid out of our way into the snow-banked curb, and continued to speed down the street. At the next intersection, I spun us around the corner and slammed the gas down into the floor as hard as I could. The Bronco fishtailed over black iced asphalt, almost careening into a tree as I sliced us over an icy embankment and through a snow packed yard into the next street.

The Bronco bounced and bucked as I gunned the engine again, bobsledding down the new street, sliding left around another corner, and slammed on the brakes. We skidded through unplowed snow and ice, coming to an uncertain stop near the end of the street.

I killed the engine, groaning inwardly while the Bronco rattled for several seconds before it expelled a final breath. Beegle gaped at me, demanding to know if I'd completely lost my mind. I gazed through the rear window, looking for pursuing headlights and listening for the rumble of roaring engines. Cleary lay across the backseat, eyes closed, breath raspy and harsh in the sudden silence.

Cloud-choked obsidian velvet embraced us, cloaking us from the feeble light streaming from the lonely streetlights standing watch.

"I think I lost them."

He cracked his eyes open. Crimson glowed back at me for an instant, went dark as quickly when he blinked, restoring the dulled violet of his eyes. "Or maybe they didn't follow us at all," he gasped.

I suppressed a shudder, wished I hadn't seen his eyes flip-flopping colors again. I didn't know what bargain Cleary had struck with the Shining Man for the Otherkind Mimic that called itself Natasha or how he managed to maintain control of it, especially now. Mimics were notoriously fickle, promising their human host a mutually beneficial symbiotic relationship. Eventually, though, no matter how strong the host, they always succumbed in the end, becoming cattle for the Otherkind.

The Order forbade Mimic bondings, destroying both host and parasite when discovered. Back in the day, Mimics and their hosts were burned alive, the only method known at the time that truly destroyed the Otherkind Essence inhabiting a human host. Today? A bullet in the back of the head before the barbecue.

The Order had been after Cleary since his defection to the Shining Man. And now, apparently, he was number one on their most wanted list.

And that tossed another nasty conundrum into my face. Did I take him back to the Shining Man or give him to Stimson and Harmonie?

I could let him bleed out in my back seat, but I'd just had the upholstery redone, and I didn't relish spending more cash I didn't have to clean up his mess. Plus, I didn't have a way to dispose of his body, which meant that Natasha would be free to infect another human Essence.

I could give him back to the Shining Man, but it clearly saw him as expendable.

My logical choice was to give him to the Order. I'd score a few points with Stimson that might keep me alive a little longer. Plus, I'd be doing my part to clean up the environment, making our polluted streets cleaner and safer, if just for a few minutes.

Cleary coughed and moaned. "Are you going to make a decision before we freeze to death?"

I glanced at him.

He lay across the seat, his hand clenched to his side. Blood soaked through the sleeves from his shirt I'd used for the pressure bandage, leaking out from around his hand, pooling on the seat and drooling down onto the floor.

My upholstery was toast, no matter what I decided to do.

"What would you do if it were me back there with a bullet in my gut?"

Silence. Followed by a pain-woven groan. I had my answer.

"Fortunately, I'm not you," I said into the darkness.

I grit my teeth, found my phone.

"You're still alive." Gracie's graveled alto answered before the echoes of the first ring melted into silence.

"Hey Gracie," I said. "You don't need to sound so surprised."

"You didn't get my best friend killed, did you?"

Beegle barked.

"Not yet," I said.

"Marshall Stimson and his posse were by earlier. He demanded to know what kind of trouble you'd gotten yourself into again. He seemed pretty worked up about it."

She paused. I felt the wheels turning, slowly and methodically.

"Why didn't you tell me about the Warrens and the Nether Realm?"

I rifled through the excuses I could give her, knew she'd know they were all bullshit. "Because if I told you, you'd want to come," I said. "I couldn't risk losing you." A sudden pain lanced through my chest, making me cringe as it twisted and wrung the blood from my heart. "Not like the way I've lost Father Mike... and everyone else."

I imagined her chewing her bottom lip.

"Someone else came snooping around for you," she said. I heard the rustle of paper, a muttered curse. "Name's Benjamin Shaw. CBI detective. Asking about you and Ellis Wynn." Another silence. This time, I pictured Gracie standing in her kitchen, empty hand on her hip, disapproval etched across her face. "Something you want to tell me?"

Benjamin Shaw chimed a distant bell. Wynn's former partner. It had been three years. Why would he come snooping around now? And how had he found out who I was and known where to find me?

Jessie.

"I don't know a Benjamin Shaw," I said, the lie souring in my mouth the moment I'd spouted it. I didn't know if she'd believe me or not, but at the moment, I had more pressing matters to attend to. "But I'll keep an eye out for him." If I survived the next twenty-four hours. "I need a favor."

I heard the muffled snort. "Of course you do."

"It's Cleary," I said, waiting. Silence hissed back at me through the line. She was going to make me say it before she told me to jump off the bridge I'd trapped myself on. "He's been shot."

"Dump him on the side of the road and leave the bastard to die. Better yet, put a bullet in his brain and be done with it. Make sure you get your money back from him first, though."

"I can't."

"Why?" She drew out the single word until it snapped in two.

"I need Andie."

For an instant, I thought she'd hung up on me. The silence stretched beyond the breaking point, churned the tension into a thick, syrupy paste.

"As long as I get to torch the bastard after she puts a round into his head. Meet you there." She hung up.

I glanced at Cleary in the rearview. His complexion was chalky white. Crimson oozed from the corner of his mouth and his eyes shimmered with fiery violet flames. If he died in the Bronco, I'd have to torch the car to prevent Natasha from moving on.

I loved my car.

Beegle snuggled against me and licked my face. I kissed him back, scratched him behind his ears.

"We're in a real pile of crap, aren't we?"

"Made a decision yet?" Cleary asked, his voice hoarse, his words slurring.

"Gracie thinks I should put a bullet in your brain and torch your corpse."

"Probably your best move," he said.

I continued to watch him through the mirror. "I think we'll stick with Plan B for the moment. Besides, if this works out, you'll owe *me*."

A weak, trembling smile and a flash of glistening ivory-colored teeth replied. I wasn't sure if it was Cleary or Natasha that answered.

I started the Bronco, waited impatiently while it sneezed and coughed to life. A wet, heavy snow piled up against the windshield, raking the windows with ice needled claws. A fitful wind rattled the glass, brushing aside the dusty flakes. I glanced through the passenger window as I put the Bronco into gear and went rigid for a haunted breath as I caught glimpses of nightmare shades wandering aimlessly through the frozen night, fire burning dimly from sooty, dead eyes.

Curious, Beegle levered himself so he could see out the window. His hackles rose, his throat and chest reverberating from the low, rumbling growl grinding up from his chest.

The empty souls of the perished, drawn to Cleary and the Mimic, were approaching us, driven by their hunger for what they had given away to the Otherkind in life.

Cursing, I slammed the gas pedal through the floor. Tires spun ice and gravel, the rear end fishtailing wildly until the tire studs remembered why they had been made. We lurched forward suddenly, plowing through drifting snow, and shot over a choked curb and down the street.

CHAPTER 27
FIELD TRIP

"DO you have to hit every damned pothole in the street?"

I glanced in the rearview mirror and grimaced, formed the words to an apology, but bit them back. If Cleary died in my backseat, I'd get a heartbeat, maybe two, before I became Natasha's next meal. I shuddered at the prospect.

Instead, I asked, "What the hell were you thinking?"

He licked blood-flecked lips, leaned his head back onto the seat and sighed, the breath hissing out in short, ragged bursts. "You'll have to be more specific," he said, his voice weak and thready. "I live... a very complicated life."

"Don't be an ass," I said. "You know exactly what I'm talking about."

Beegle yelped.

The Bronco slid through a patch of ice, wiggling its hips flirtatiously at a Toyota, nearly taking off its front end as we sloshed past.

"Sorry buddy," I said, not daring to meet Beegle's irate glare. Instead, I scratched him under his chin in apology. He grumbled but leaned into my hand, forgiving all.

I caught Natasha staring hungrily at me through Cleary's nearly colorless eyes, his face slack, the skin sagging around the pulsing iridescent embers swelling brighter with each sucking breath rattling his chest. I shuddered, turned my attention back to the treacherous, snow-choked roads, doing my best to avoid up close and personal conversations with the few other cars tobogganing down the streets.

A low moaning cough slapped the back of my head as I slowed for a red light. Sudden panic squeezing my heart, I gunned the Bronco, blowing through the signal, and earning an irate horn blast as a set of sun-bright headlights swept my port side. Crunching metal ground the air, setting my teeth on edge as I blasted down the street, slowing just enough to fishtail into the next right.

The street narrowed, grew less urbanized, the buildings not as gentrified. They hung back in the shadows, blank windows glowering with pent-up frustration as we passed by, slow burning anger reaching out with clawed fists to snag unwary travelers.

After six uncertain blocks, I slowed the Bronco as I approached a weathered, decomposing, three story charcoal gray brick building that had once housed thriving mom-and-pop shops on the ground floor, reserving the second and third floors for studios and apartments. Now mostly abandoned, the building huddled into its cracking foundation, scowling at the nearly vacant street and the memories of better times.

I pulled over to the curb, gritting my teeth as the Bronco staggered over splintered icebergs and the remnants of shredded tires.

Cleary groaned.

Snow dropped from an invisible sky, lay uneven, gray-tinged carpets across the potholed street and cracked and fragmented sidewalk.

I turned the engine off, waited while the Bronco rattled itself into an anxious silence. A hushed stillness enveloped us, draping the night with a crystalline cloak of ashen flakes reflecting jaundiced light cast from the sputtering streetlamps. I peered through the windshield and windows and tried to pick out Gracie's Mercedes SUV from the shadows, but I didn't see anything except the creeping darkness and swirling snow.

Where was she?

Another low moan shattered the anxious stillness. I looked at Cleary. His eyes were closed, but I felt the fetid fae-daemon power thrumming softly behind his lids, the growing hunger and craving for more than what had been promised.

I couldn't wait any longer.

I opened the door for Beegle. Then I dragged Cleary from the backseat and propped him against the grimed and jaded geriatric brick beside a nondescript locked doorway that protected a dimly lit entry and narrow stairway. I stabbed the buzzer button for an anonymous third floor apartment office.

After an infinite lifetime waiting in the swirling snow, the speaker crackled, spitting out an alcohol-sluiced voice. "Whoever the hell is down there. Go away." The connection snapped closed.

I grimaced, glanced at Cleary before slamming my thumb against the buzzer, kept crushing the button until the speaker sizzled with life again. "I said—"

"Shut up, you moron, it's Cassidy."

Edgy silence.

"Go away, I need no more of your crap on my doorstep."

The speaker died a second time.

Cleary coughed, heaved a wad of bloody spittle into the snow piling between his legs. He began to shiver, tried to hug himself with shaking arms.

Where the *hell* was Gracie?

I smashed the buzzer again, held it down to drown it. She didn't answer.

"Guess it's time to cut bait," Cleary whispered through chattering teeth, his voice cracking. He looked up at me, his eyes smoldering, the violet burning to ash as I watched. He shuddered and moaned. When he looked back up, something alien peaked through, ravenous hunger drizzling from his eyes. "Kill me. I can't—"

"Like hell," I said.

Cleary sagged into himself, his eyes rolling up into oblivion.

Cursing, I pulled the Walther, blew a hole through the door lock, and kicked the door in.

A darkness clambered over me, blotting out the sallow light falling from the streetlamp above us.

I turned.

Cleary grabbed me by the throat and drove me into the wall, his lips curled into a ferocious sneer, his eyes blazing crimson. He held me up against the frozen brick, my feet dangling, his fists slowly crushing my neck. Dark, rotting spots speckled my vision, dancing drunkenly through my eyes.

Beegle lunged at him.

Cleary caught him by the throat, harried my dog like a piece of festering meat before tossing him into the street. He vanished behind a swirling gray-white curtain, crying as he collided with the iced asphalt, and went silent.

Turning his wildfire eyes back to me, Cleary grabbed my left wrist and pulled the Walther against the bottom of his chin. "Don't look at me," he said between clenched teeth.

I struggled and writhed, my chest heaving into a vacuum as Cleary maneuvered his hand, pressing my finger back against the trigger while the hand wrapped around my neck squeezed until the spots swimming through my eyes blotted out the world, stealing my conscious mind and tossing me into never-never land.

Talons raked my thoughts, tore gouges through my soul, and reached toward my Essence.

A gunshot thundered from a growing distance.

I slammed into the ground, crumpling into a quivering heap, the world around me retreating into an endless night. The talons slid away, desperately scrabbling for footing through the scree littering the edges of my Essence as the shadowed gloom surrounded me.

A gentle wind caressed the side of my face with soft, inviting fingers, ruffling the loose, tangled ends of my hair and tickling the back of my neck. Shivers skipped down my spine, and I hugged my five-year-old self as I stared through the copse of trees bordering the back of our wide, open yard.

Silver Ash and Maple traipsed alongside Colorado Blue Spruce and Douglas Fir, holding hands with a few Ponderosa and Piñon Pines as they sidled up to the slender-bodied Quaking Aspens— their barren branches reaching skeleton fingers into the clear, late-morning December sky.

Snow lay in tattered blankets across the broken ground, creeping a few inches into the tree line before giving way to an uneven carpet of dead leaves and pine needles.

Audrey's delighted laughter capered out from between the trees as she looked for a place to hide, her favorite activity besides watching Sesame Street with our dad and eating our mom's home-made chocolate-chip cookies.

My turn to seek. I hid my face in the crook of my forearm, pressed it against the gnarled bark of the ancient silver ash growing in the middle of our backyard while leisurely counting.

"...Twenty-four. Twenty-five," I cried out, opening my eyes, and blinking away the spotted sunlight as I spun from the tree and gazed into what we called our forest at the edge of the lawn. "Ready

or not, here I come," I yelled as I ran to the edge of the trees to let Audrey believe I didn't already know where she'd hidden.

I stepped from the sunlight... into a sudden unnatural darkness.

Panic rose, snaking long slender fingers around my heart, and squeezed. I stumbled a few feet farther into the gloom, felt my chest constrict, and my heart stutter as I tried to suck in a breath of air that had suddenly vanished.

"Cassidy!" Audrey screamed. "Help me!"

Panic lost its reins, gave terror its head as I thrust deeper into the trees. I stumbled through fallen branches, over hidden rocks that snatched at my snow boots, threatening to tumble me to my knees. "Audrey!" I screamed back. "Baby Bear! Where are you?"

I staggered into a small clearing ringed by a chaotic circle of ragged and scarred Weeping Elms, their draping limbs scraped clean. In the center of the clearing squatted the shattered and scorched shell of a twin-trunked Canyon Maple.

A psychedelic phantasmagoria of rainbow colors swirled around the fractured tree, reaching out with wispy fingers, and slowly dragging Audrey into the center of the spiraling chaos.

I screamed, and lunged for my sister, grabbing her wrist as gnarled and clawed hands yanked her into the center of the tree, hauling me in with her. My ankle caught on a protruding root, twisted, and snapped.

I screamed...

And shot upright, listing suddenly to the right as my ankle gave out.

Unsteady hands caught me and tried to push me backward. I fought back in frenzied panic, striking the air with wild blows as a solid shoulder pressed me down into an overstuffed fabric chair, pinning my arms down. I tried to head butt the closest face. I missed but earned a string of curses.

"Hold her still!"

"I'm trying, damn it. You said she'd be out longer."

I vaguely recognized the hoarse, raspy voice, the hazy memory tap dancing upon my thoughts as they sluggishly built an image of a tanned, age-weathered face, framed by iron-gray hair, piercing dark gray eyes, and thin down-turned lips supporting slightly sunken cheeks. Gracie's voice echoed through the air above me.

I thrashed about in the grip of the hands holding me down, felt another hand grasp at my shoulder, followed by the stab of a needle. I bucked wildly to the side.

The jabbing needle vanished.

I shoved myself up, threw off the hands pinning me to the chair, stumbling a step forward, and face planted into a cold threadbare carpet that smelled of sweat-slimed socks, vomit, and too much bleach.

I gagged.

Sudden agony crunched through my nose and shot through my mouth, jarring the back of my throat as it sought to wipe out the astringent odor of ethanol and acetone.

More curses littered the surrounding air where I lay breathing torment. What strength I had fled screaming in terror into the dark.

My arms splayed out at my sides, I waited for the hands to return, haul me to my feet, and throw me back into the chair. Instead, only curses pelted me where I lay. The carpet pressing into my nose grew wet. I managed to lick my lips, tasted iron and salt, moaning with the realization that I had broken my nose.

Where was I?

I groaned, felt the soft touch of a shadow and leather boots against my cheek as leather-crinkled lips brushed my ear.

"You going to continue to act all batshit crazy or you going to let us get you back up and into the chair?"

"Gracie?" I mumbled.

"Help me get her up before she bleeds out on your filthy carpet."

Two sets of hands grasped me under the arms, pulled me up and dropped me unceremoniously into the chair.

Gracie's harsh expression filled my world. She scowled, glaring at me through squinting eyes, and nodded. "She broke her damned nose in that fall."

I heard a hard, flinty snort.

"Serves her right for being such a..."

"Andie?" I managed to slur.

Another face shoved itself into my narrow, groggy world. The same I'd seen in the Shining Man's office before she shot me up with Ebony.

She'd done it again. Why?

The agony slicing through my right ankle shrieked at me.

I groused, tried to slide from the chair. Hands gripped my shoulders, and pulled me back, strong and insistent, their grip telling me they weren't going to put up with any more of my crap.

Andie peered at my nose, shaking her head as she stood. "Sorry babe. Dust isn't going to fix that disaster." She glanced up, raised her brows in question.

I heard Gracie snort behind me, felt her lean over, the brush of her leathery skin against the side of my face.

"You going to behave?"

I swallowed, tried to remember how I'd gotten here. Wherever *here* was. I nodded.

Gracie's hands clamped down on my shoulders, dug her fingers beneath my collar bones.

Before I could react, Andie leaned in, grasped my nose, and twitched her hands.

A searing blade of fire sliced through my face. My vision swam, grew blurred behind a sudden hazy wall of red. Orange-red waves rolled across me, slowly slid away with the lowering tide. I blew a harsh breath out of my mouth, tried to stab Andie with white hot daggers that rolled harmlessly from my eyes and into my lap.

"You're welcome," she said, handing me a box of tissues, and stripped off surgical gloves that she tossed into a waste basket. She leaned against a nearby wall, arms crossed, dismay pulsing through her angry eyes.

Gracie came around to where I could see her, and snagging a metal folding chair, dropped into it.

"Where am I?"

They exchanged a look.

"You're at my place," Andie said.

I stared at her and frowned. "How...?"

A memory rose, slamming me in the gut with a sledgehammer blow. I scoured the room with my eyes, the panic rising in a tidal flood until they crashed into a shiny steel table cowering near the back of the room. A body lay on the table, draped by a leaden-stained sheet that glistened wetly in the brusque, sterile light.

"Cleary?" I stood, unsteady and shaking, my legs like melting butter. I caught Gracie and Andie exchanging a glance. Gracie gently eased me back into the chair.

"Don't," she said, her gritty, sandpaper voice soothing and tender. "He's gone."

I stared up at her, my vision beginning to blur. Tears rolled down my cheeks, dripped from the ledges of my chin. I shook my head. "But—"

Memory crept back from its asylum, hovered at the razor's-edge, stared up at me with stark, unadorned reality.

Cleary's hand crushing my throat.

Natasha tearing at my mental wards, grappling for a hold on to my Essence. The corruption wilting the life from my soul.

His free hand shackling mine around the Walther.

His finger pressing mine back against the trigger.

A gunshot echoing through the snowy silence.

Blessed darkness.

I wiped the tears from my face, screwed them from my eyes. I stood, forcing Gracie aside with a delicate but insistent hand.

Andie stood in front of the table. "There's nothing I could have done to save him," she said, her knife-edged tone not unkind. "Not after he—"

I chucked Andie from my path with a hard look, stood at the edge of the table. I stared down at what had been Alastair Cleary, my mentor, my first lover, my enemy. I reached for the sheet covering his head. Andie grabbed my arm. I tried to pull it from her grip, but she insisted, and I realized I didn't have the strength.

"The Mimic is still inside him," she said.

I frowned at her, grimaced at the memory of Natasha's gangrenous touch, the withered fringes of my Essence still dribbling corruption, and wondered how Cleary had managed to keep the Mimic at bay all these years. I shuddered, fell back into the chair. "He was supposed to keep Tansy safe while I—"

"While you what?" Gracie turned her diamond-hard gaze on me.

I folded my hands in my lap, wondering what the hell I was doing, what I could do now that Cleary was dead.

Andie washed and dried her hands, leaned against a wall, glowering spikes through me. She glanced at Gracie. "Did she tell you what she's got herself into?"

Gracie sighed. "She told me enough," she said, her dissonant tone dragging glass shards down my back. "Unless she'd like to dump another fifty into that tip jar." Her flinty gaze stripped off the last shreds of the secrets clinging to my pride and inability to forgive myself.

I wilted, my strength spent. Tears thrust weepy fingers through my eyes, as they pried the stones from the dam. Water seeped through the cracks, gained momentum, grew into a flood. I slammed the floodgate closed, refusing to let the rising tide loose, and stared at the table where Cleary lay, unable to meet either of their stares.

My hands shook in my lap, clawing at each other like starving hyenas, trying to tear the flesh from their fingers. Images flashed through my mind, stark and razor edged.

Tansy cowering on her knees in front of the Shining Man, her body beaten, bruised, and bloody, the key to her humanity locked behind the iridescent glass of the Soul Mirror leering from its desk. The Ebony-flamed mania blazing from her eyes as she held up Jonnie's severed head to the security camera. Marshall Stimson raping my mind with the supersensory memories of Tansy stabbing Father Mike.

Stephanie Brandt seething from behind Tansy's vacant eyes, her mocking and shrieking laughter driving blue-hot spikes through my heart.

"Why did you kill us?"

Tears burst from my eyes, poured down my face, the flood fed by snot gushing from my nose. Lightning flashed through my torn and tattered ravings. I stared into the light, begged for forgiveness. For redemption. The tormented face of the crucified Christ scowled back, hurling accusation and condemnation.

I sucked a ragged breath and between howling wails, gasped, "Jessie... Tansy... Stephanie Brandt—"

Gracie touched my shoulder. I flung her hand away, doubled over, threw myself into the back of the chair and screamed.

The echoes of my shrieking died. Andie and Gracie stared. Silence pressed down with a crushing weight. I wiped the snot streaming from my nose, managed to dump out words between the belching sobs, "Tansy is the monster the Shining Man coerced me into killing."

A hissed curse slithered through the air.

"What the hell did you bring to my door?"

"Zip it, darling," Gracie said, "You think the Shining Man cares one wit about who or what gets caught in the crossfire of its games?"

Andie pointed a quivering finger at Cleary's sheet-shrouded body. "No, but it cares about that. And it'll be coming for what belongs to it."

The Mimic.

The reason Cleary betrayed the Order to the Shining Man. Even now, I didn't understand why he'd done it. I wondered if anyone knew for certain. Guess his reasons didn't matter anymore.

I hocked the grief up from my throat. "Burn the body."

Gracie laughed. "Seems I told a young hothead of a girl to do just that."

"I thought I could save him."

"And that's your problem, little lady, isn't it?" Gracie stood over me, her whip-thin shadow blotting out the sterile light blazing down from the ceiling. "Look at me."

I didn't want to, but Gracie was the hurricane you couldn't ignore.

Gracie's eyes blazed. Her Touched abilities, rarely let out, hummed with discordant voices as they embraced me.

I tensed, expecting what Jessie and I snarkingly called a 'Gracie whooping,' the tongue lashing she beat us with during our early days when we purposely slogged through the crap just to see how many swarms of hornets we could piss off. Instead, a compassionate warmth enfolded me, smoothed away the fear, the regret, and the self-crimination that dogged my every shuddering breath.

She knelt, pried my clenched hands from my lap. "You can't

salve your guilt by saving every other soul." She squeezed my hands, her power caressing me in its grandmotherly embrace. "There's not enough of them in any world that can do that."

"She's my sister," I said.

"She's not," Gracie said, the force of her words shocking me with their sudden, uncompromising truth.

I tried to yank my hands from her grasp. Her grip tightened, almost painful in their intensity to hold me captive.

"I understand your connection to the girl," she said, her tone softening, but still tempered with steel. "But Tansy Harper is not your sister. And though you may think of her as family, at the end of the day, she's not your blood." She paused, watching me with an intensity that made me squirm like a worm trapped on concrete when the sun hit it. "She's never wanted to be here," Gracie said. "She's never wanted you to be her sister or her protector." She stopped. I waited for the final blow to hammer my self-righteous self-reproach into mush at my feet. "Or her rescuer."

"Father Mike," I said.

Gracie shook her head, lips pursed with the final nail of regret as she handed me my own hammer to pound it into the lid of the coffin of my making. "You are two of a kind," she said. "Driven by guilt and remorse over the outcomes of events you neither instigated nor could ever hope to control."

She slid her hands from mine as she stood and stared down at me, her stern, wizened face swirling with grandmotherly concern. Her power drew back, settling behind a well-practiced mask.

Emptiness flung itself at me, twisted my soul into tightly wound knots that squeezed out what little self-empathy remained, tried to soak up the bitterness crouching at the sliver of the open doorway.

"So you think I should abandon her to her fate?" I said. "You think I should let the Shining Man win? Take Tansy's soul for his own?"

My bitterness surged through the gap and charged up the hill, hell bent on sweeping away any resistance dug into the high ground.

Gracie stiffened. "You got the Medusa Mirror?" She narrowed her eyes, bludgeoned me with raw, unsalted truth. "You can get the Medusa Mirror?"

I opened my mouth, prepared for my next strike, snapped my jaw closed, the fury powering my rage suddenly writhing at my feet. I watched it die an ugly and agonizing death. "No," I said, reluctantly, even now, almost unable to accept the truth. "Jessie destroyed it."

"Then the best you got for Tansy is a bullet." Gracie towered over me, her shadow cloaking me in the gloom of my doom. An uneasy silence filled the gap between us. She continued to glare down at me, her blistering gaze pummeling me back into the hole I'd crawled out of. "Here," she said. "I'll spare you the guilt and give you the bullet." She dropped the magazine from the pistol she carried and ejected the chambered round, the sharp metallic clack of the slide being racked back thwacking the inside of my desperate thoughts. She deftly caught the round and dropped it into my lap, turned and strode from Andie's apartment.

CHAPTER 28
WHERE DEMONS NO LONGER FEAR TO TREAD

AN ETERNITY PRESSED down on Adria as she crept through the shadows of a disused, centuries old tunnel below St. Michael's Parish. Millennia of earth and stone throbbed with forgotten power. Smoke-like tendrils snaked through the stuffy air crowding the narrow passage, scraped the roughhewn walls carved from native rock, dripping yearning and hunger. The gateways barring the Veil of Order separating the Nether Realm from the human world shivered with anticipation, their siren song alluring and enticing, entangling Adria's thoughts. The rotting essence of Tansy's body quivered, straining toward the magic and its pull as she dragged the blade of her Juzarine dagger across the throat of the Noble Knight of the Order she'd ambushed.

She sighed, her quiet breath ruffling the hairs on the back of the man's neck as she held his weight in her embrace. He convulsed. Once. Twice. Went still, his blood wet and warm on the dagger's blade. His body sagged in her arms. Kissing the lobe of an ear, Adria allowed the man to slide from her grasp to the floor, where he lay in a growing scarlet puddle that reflected the crystalline light raining down from the ceiling.

A faded and worn plaque, the lettering lusterless and dreary, almost unreadable, peered at her from the wall, the words carved into the weathered bronze clinging hungrily to the waning witchery that had once given the Order of the Four dominion over the gateways in this place.

Adria scuffed trembling fingers across the inscription, mumbling, "The Shield of Michael the Archangel. St. Michael's Parish." She smiled. Dipping her fingertips into the blood of the dead Noble Knight, she smeared it over the dying plaque, kissed the dingy letters, the abrupt sting of waning enchantment sizzling through her lips. The Tansy Essence squirmed from the pit of its confinement, went still.

"Soon, my beloved. Soon," Adria crooned as she pressed her hand against the bronzed slab.

Stone shuddered. The sound of bone scraping bone echoing through the confined space. Dust and debris showered down from the low ceiling, varnishing the ends of her tangled and tattered hair. A narrow, darkened stairway materialized, the steps winding up into deepening darkness. Adria strolled up, bare feet patting the pitted stone steps, fingertips grazing the uneven walls. Ghostly voices trailed her up the stairs, whispering memories of a stolen childhood and a nightmare world driven by chaos.

Minutes later, she stepped out from the top of the stairwell into a waiting room of a modern St. Michael's Parish, its foundations forgotten, the distant memories of witchery and wizardry buried beneath centuries of progress and enlightenment.

A second Noble Knight turned at the sound of her entry, the young woman's expression frozen with surprise, hands fumbling at her belt for a panicked grip on her sidearm as Adria slid the blade of her dagger into her heart. The girl shuddered, hands falling limp as Adria dropped her and sheathed her blade, staring for a heartbeat at the youthful beauty frozen forever in a mask of death.

She knelt, touched the woman's face, wondering, if she'd been given the chance, would she have grown into her own beauty as well.

Reflected snow light glinted in through the storybook framed windows, dancing timidly at the edges of the liquid chandelier light from above, its tender caresses mocking the horror glowering from the center of the room.

The discordant chorus of whispered voices pecking at the frayed edges of Adria's thoughts dimmed as she stepped through the sea of red spreading over the marbled floor, reveled in its hot, steamy touch, the squelch of her wet feet across the tiles echoing off the incandescent paneled walls. A glimmer of hunger trailed after her, pulling at its leash, eager to feed, its foggy tendrils crawling over the girl lying dead behind her. It paused, wrapped the body in its gauzy cloak, and fed.

Adria stopped, clothed herself in her own comforting embrace, shivering as her power lapped up the last of the fading Essence behind her.

A low, feeble cry rustled from the depths of the despair to which she'd tossed Tansy's Essence, chained and shackled, no longer able to reach beyond the blackness in which it existed. "Patience, my love," Adria cooed. "Soon you will know the power and the freedom that I now know." The cry quieted, settled back into its prison, the chains shackling it falling silent.

The cloying fragrances of myrrh, black pepper, sandalwood, and frankincense drifted through the silence surrounding her, reached out shyly, its loving touch walking shivers down her back. A warding meant to dampen the fae-daemon power swirling through her blood.

Ineffectual and naïve.

Adria stood before two floor-to-ceiling doors fashioned from yew, closed and locked, bound in iron, their burnished surface dull and lusterless despite the light glistening through the frosted windows. She smiled delicately as she reached up to brush tremulous fingertips along the door's silken surface. Power ached within the wood, yearning for her to release it. She touched an iron band, sensed the memory of enchantment bound into the metal, its energy withered and decayed, the protection it once promised dead.

The Touched woman who had released her Essence from the Medusa Mirror into this body waited for her on the other side of these doors, shrouded in a unique power. Corrupt and impure, born of a blasphemous union between fae-daemon Essence and the human soul. Trapped between two worlds, belonging to each, exiled from both, wishing to unleash death and destruction, but unable to accept the consequences.

Another smile creased her lips as Adria leaned forward and tenderly kissed the iron. It quivered at her touch, raging over its impotence, before collapsing into sullen frustration. Humankind had forgotten so much through the eons. Neglect, disbelief, disuse, what they called enlightenment. All were guilty. But worst of all was their hubris, their total reliance on their intellect and rationality. Two sides of the same failed coin that would ultimately spell their doom.

Adria pushed the doors open.

Flickering darkness glowered back at her as she brushed across the threshold into an ornately decorated office walled with cold, lifeless wood, its spirit rotted and decayed. A forest of candlelight wavered through the uncertain gloom, the prancing flames fluttering, their chalky light paling at her sudden appearance.

Basil-laced holy water lay strewn over the granite-tiled floor, a circle meant to prohibit her, blistering the bottom of her feet as she strode into the room and across the darkly glinting sea separating her from the woman. She stopped amid the heaving ocean, allowed her flesh to sizzle and boil for a moment before striding through the barrier onto the cool and inviting marble tiles beyond. Incense hung in the air, the tattered haze chased with nettles, sage and thyme.

Archaic, fatigued human magic once used to repel her Makers and protect the Fallen, those spawned by the Creator in his image. To have been perfect and without transgression, but who instead chose their own path, trampling their preeminence underfoot, treating it as if it were smut and swill, and thus were cast out from Paradise to fornicate and multiply, blighting their world like locusts with their filth, corruption, and licentiousness.

And yet, the Creator still loved them, yearned for their return to his eternally open embrace. While her Makers, the fae-daemon, languished in the Nether Realm, begging for him to accept them back into his fold, but receiving nothing from their anguished cries except cold, heartless, and silent denial.

Adria paused, drew in a long, slow breath, reveling in the stinging memory of the holy water, how it scalded her flesh, and tickled the bones beneath. She drew her dagger, held it at her side. And waited.

The woman, cloaked in twilight, arms crossed, leaned against the edge of an aged olive wood desk, the polished planks glinting secretively in the swaggering candlelight. On the desk beside her, hunched a bronzed, leather satchel, its skin wrinkled and sagging with age.

A Touched girl just entering her womanhood stood to the woman's right, shrouded in shadow, the reek of cold steel clinging to her slender form. She trembled, fear sluicing from her like a dense rain.

Adria wrinkled her nose, baring her teeth in a feral snarl.

"What do you want," the Touched woman leaning against the

edge of the desk asked, her voice edged with steel and tempered with fire and violence.

Her Redeemer.

"You were expecting us," Adria said, her voice woven with bloodthirsty ferocity.

The Touched woman pushed herself from the edge of the desk, walked behind it. "I thought you might come by," she said. "What do you think of our reception?"

Adria shrugged. "Inadequate," she said. "You have forgotten much throughout the eons. More than you thought you ever knew."

Silence.

Fear quivered through the air.

Adria closed her eyes, tasted the disquiet, savored the sour tang as it slid down her throat. "You fear us."

"What do you want?"

She opened her eyes, focused on the inky form of the leather satchel huddling near the center of the desk, felt its whispered call, its longing desire. "We have come for our Medusa Mirror."

The rustle of leather against cloth.

The growing stench of dread entwined with the dead caress of steel from her left.

"Your Medusa Mirror is mine until you fulfill your task. A pause, followed by the whispered hiss of an impatient breath. "As we agreed."

"Half-truths. Distortions. Deceit." Adria drew closer, pointed her dagger toward the satchel, her hand trembling, the voice of the other imprisoned inside rising from the blackness grazing her thoughts, urging and exhorting, driving her forward. "Give us our Mirror."

"No."

The word reverberated between them, driving echoed spikes into her skull.

Adria screamed, reached out with her empty hand. Faedaemon magic surged from her, snuffing the candlelight. Darkness swelled, enveloping them in pitch-black oblivion as lightless tendrils crawled forward, oozing past her toward the Touched woman behind the desk, then, disintegrated into dead, skeletal fingers that withered and evaporated into dust scattered by a hot, dry wind.

Adria gasped, her chest heaving as she collapsed to her knees, driven to the floor, her Essence suddenly... impotent.

The Juzarine dagger dropped from her limp fingers, rattled against the cold, hard, polished tiles.

Light flared, banishing the darkness.

The Touched woman stood in front of her, bathed in the flickering light of three candles, their flames tickling the air with the heady scents of basil and thyme. Smoke trailed toward the ceiling, vanished in a dim haze. She stared down at Adria, her expression cold-blooded, her gaze remorseless, and nodded.

A short, balding man Adria had not noticed hobbled from the blackness, stood beside the woman, his eyes hollow, the gleam behind his scrutiny blazing with an animalistic curiosity. He knelt and touched the floor near her, muttered words in the ancient, sacred language.

Adria stiffened as light flashed, burning through the dark, surrounding her in a circle that sucked the breath from her chest. She shrieked, collapsed into a puddle inside the middle of the flaming circle. The Other voice from inside scrabbled up from its prison into the light, clawing its way upward, pulling power from her, draining the life from her paralyzed Essence. She curled up inside of herself, panting, sweat drooling down from her temples, and dripping to the floor beneath her, sizzling as it struck the marbled stone.

The woman knelt and laid the satchel gently on the floor in front of her. Smiling, she reached inside and pulled out the Medusa Mirror.

Candlelight glinted from the glass, casting an eerie reflection of Adria's contorted face back at her. She uttered a strangled cry and shoved herself to her knees, her hand scrabbling for the dagger that lay beside her.

"The more you struggle, the more pain you will endure," the woman said.

Adria howled, wrapping her hand around the dagger's handle, then collapsed again, her strength sapped by Tansy's surging Essence.

The woman chuckled, slipped the Medusa Mirror back into the satchel. "The choice is yours, of course," she said. "Complete the task set before you and when you are finished, I will destroy your Medusa Mirror in your presence." She nodded toward her. "And the body you inhabit shall be yours. Her Essence entwined with yours in a lover's eternal embrace. Forever."

Gasping, her chest heaving, Adria pulled her head from the floor. "Release us."

"Your oath first, I think."

She hesitated, strained against the bonds shoving her into the floor, collapsed back into the tiles. Her hand opened. The dagger rolled from her palm, clattered against the floor. "We agree," she said from between clenched teeth.

The woman leaned forward, eyes glittering intently. "Your oath," she said. "Swear it."

Adria spewed a tired breath, nodded. "We swear it."

The woman stood, the satchel at her side as she nodded to the balding man.

He uttered the sacred words, stepped back. The incandescent fire writhing from the surrounding floor sputtered and died, plunged her back into the night.

The weight crushing her to the floor vanished.

Adria staggered to her feet, the Juzarine dagger finding its way into her hand. Pushing Tansy's voice back into the darkness of its despair, she crushed it, flinging it down into the abyss as she lunged toward the woman, slashing the air with the bone blade.

The woman stood motionless, watched as the dagger's blade sliced the air toward her neck, stopped a hairsbreadth from her flesh.

Adria strained against the warding, her glare locked with the woman's amused gaze.

"You cannot harm me," the woman said. "Or those under my protection, unless I release them." She leaned forward, hammered Adria with her gaze. "Finish what you have sworn to complete. Then and only then will you be allowed to obtain what you seek." The woman blew out the candles and strode from the room with the balding man and girl trailing after her, leaving Adria standing in enraged silence and darkness.

CHAPTER 29
WRAITHS IN THE MIST

WITHOUT REALIZING IT, I found myself on the floor, collapsed into myself, knees shoved into my chest, arms hugging my legs as my star imploded. I clutched the 9mm round Gracie dumped in my lap, my mind encouraging it to explode in my hand. Tears stormed down my face and pooled into a soggy, wet muddy bog.

The whispered thud of clawed feet thumped toward me from the chasm of forgetfulness. I sucked in a ragged breath, another form of guilt thudding through my chest. I dragged my face up, smeared away the streaming tears. How had I forgotten about him?

Beegle stood in front of me, bleeding forgiveness, his depthless brown eyes overflowing with an unconditional love I didn't deserve or could ever earn. I tore a grateful smile from the pit of my self-loathing as he nudged his nose up under my arm to kiss my cheek. The touch of his wet, warm nose against my face dug out a quick and quiet laugh. I dragged him into my lap, crushed him to my chest and opened the floodgates again. He licked my face and settled into my arms, his head shoved up under my chin.

The quiet scrape of fabric across metal tugged at my attention.

I looked up. Andie leaned over the lip of her surgical table, hands planted at the edge. Blood smeared the stainless steel shine, staining her fingers. She met my stare, her expression turbulent, the winds of her anger continuing to churn through her eyes. Cleary continued to lay motionless on his slab, shrouded in his blood-stained self-righteous sacrifice. I wondered if his last-minute selfless act would be enough to erase the bloody sins blackening his hands.

Probably not.

"You're welcome," Andie grunted.

I twitched under the force of her spiraling ire. "Thank you," I said as I buried my face into Beegle's scruffy neck.

"Now get out," she said. "And don't come back. Ever."

I flinched, the sting of her words punching me with the force of a slamming fist. I pried my face from Beegle's scruff, poured a measure of courage into my empty cup as I met Andie's gaze. "I'm sorry."

She snorted, shoved herself off the table. "You aways are." She turned her back on me. "Now please leave so I can clean up your mess. Again."

Another spear thrust through my heart. Another bridge burned. Did I deserve it? Probably. Did I want it? If you'd asked me that question two years ago, I'd have said yes. Relationships and the people that inevitably came with them were too much work, left too much collateral damage in their wake, were too impossible to maintain when your life was not much more than a chaotic mess.

Now? I didn't know. But I suspected I was going to miss the people cluttering my life at this moment, especially if I kept using them as cannon fodder. As much as I didn't want to admit it, constantly hanging out with just me, myself, and I was becoming an impossible lifestyle to sustain.

I lowered my chin to give Beegle one last kiss on the top of his head, hoped the bridge I'd just incinerated could be rebuilt someday.

If there was a someday left to me after the next few hours.

I shoved myself to my feet and managed a miniature smile when Beegle threw an indignant glare at me before padding over to Andie and nuzzling her leg.

She ignored him for a moment, before kneeling and kissing the top of his head. "You don't deserve him," she said, stood and shooed him out the surgical room door.

He trotted past me into the front room where he lay down near the front door, his expression watchful but relaxed in that carefree beagle way. I smiled at him despite my desolate mood. "People keep telling me that," I said. "It's probably true, too." I looked at her. "But despite his wandering eye, he always comes back home. Probably because I keep feeding him."

Andie looked at me over her shoulder, a dim spark of forgiveness glittering behind her ire. "You need to leave," she said. "While you still can."

Trepidation pranced through the churned earth waiting beside my grave. "Who did you call?"

She bit her lower lip, held my gaze for an instant before turning back to the surgical table and its physical and metaphysical occupants. "People you don't need to be messing with at the moment. Now get out. I have work to do before they arrive."

I waited, hoping for more, my feet urging me to do what we'd been told to do, but refusing to give into their passive aggressive whining. The emptiness between us stretched to the snapping point. My feet decided to take matters into their own hands, began propelling me toward the front room. I resisted for an instant, finally gave in, pausing at the doorway, hoping for something more than 'I'll have my people call your people and we'll do lunch.'

"Don't do anything stupid," I said.

She snorted. "You mean more stupid than you?" She hesitated, smoothed the stained edge of the sheeting with slightly trembling hands, tucked the frayed hem beneath a death-gray hand. "Stay alive."

"C'mon Beegle," I said. "We've got work to do."

I hobbled down the stairs, wincing with every step as I used the wall and handrail to steady my unbalanced gait. With everything that had gone down since Cleary's selfish soul cleansing and Gracie's 'Come to Jesus' soul whooping, I'd forgotten about the wood chipper Cleary had rammed me through. Beegle limped awkwardly beside me, his nails scraping the worn wooden stairs with each stilted step.

Caliginous-draped memories fluttered at the ragtag periphery of my mind, tormenting me with jumbled jigsaw images.

Distant shrill giggles echoed through my head, the kind of hushed frenetic snickering and whispered chortles that romped through a young teen girl's birthday party and sleepover. Pitchy, raven eyes swirling with Ebony gloated at me through a shaggy mist. Gnarled hands blistered with oozing sores and peeling desiccated flesh clawed at the shoulders of a young girl, pressing her down into a steamy, writhing mud. Tears flooded down her grimy, mud-smeared cheeks as she reached toward me through the undulating mist, bludgeoning me with her silent cries while I took the coward's way out.

The gauzy vapor separating us evaporated for an instant, allowed the grinding words the girl flung at me to dash through the sudden gap.

"Why did you kill us?"

Beegle barked.

A glacial, arctic wind pummeled me, rocking me back against an ice-rimed wall.

The images haunting my memories scattered.

Snow littered the air, jitterbugging through the darkness.

Gracie leaned against the side of my Bronco, arms crossed, parched breath blowing steam. Snow canopied her tan leather fedora, dripping slender icicles from the brim onto her bony shoulders. She shoved herself off the Bronco and doled out an abrupt, fond smile for Beegle then slammed me with a grim stare.

"Took you long enough to drag your sorry butt down here," she said. "We got us a small problem."

Beegle skipped up to her, wound his blocky, beagle body around her legs, sat and yipped up at her. She fished inside her coat pocket and dropped a doggie biscuit in his direction. He snapped it from midair, swallowed the damned thing whole then stared up at her with fond expectation.

I gaped, suddenly remembering where we were standing, scraped the gathering snow and ice from my shoulders, and shook it from my sulking and tangled hair. "I thought—"

"That's your problem," Gracie said. "You think too damned much at the wrong damned times. Keep that crap up and you won't survive much longer." She nodded her chin past the back of the Bronco.

The outline of a shadowy form materialized as I squinted into the flickering night, reluctantly dragging the feathery touch of coiled fae-daemon and Ebony fueled power with it. I shuddered, tensed at the rasping scrape of dull razors edging their way down my back.

Shimmering midnight sneered back at me through the smoldering snowfall.

I staggered a step toward the approaching form, drew the Walther and held it at my side.

Beegle snarled, then limped to stand between me and the glistering doom slithering through the gray-cloaked darkness.

I heard Gracie scrape a boot through the ice-glazed tundra behind me. She clasped my shoulder, gloved fingers squeezing it in warning. "Don't," she whispered into the blanketing silence. "It's what Jessie wants."

I sucked in a frozen breath, heaved it from my knotting chest. "It's my fault she's doing this," I said.

A cacophony of hushed voices twisted through the silence separating us, their dissonant sounds writhing snake-like into my thoughts.

Familiarity knocked, cracked the door open to memory and peered out from behind the cobwebs. "Dylan?" I breathed in horrified disbelief.

A faint, desperate mewling scratched its way through the bitter arctic air. I held my breath, wondered if I'd imagined the sound, my hand tensing on the grip of the Walther. The discordant voices trailed after, their weft and warp, wrapping my mind in tightening strands of terror. The mewling came again, crawled up to my boots and sat like a ravenous rat, waiting with impatience for me to play with it.

I shook Gracie's hand from my shoulder, ignoring her warning curses, and dragged myself toward the stumbling body. The whimpering continued, louder, more insistent, pulling me toward it. The approaching form grew more distinct, the hazy edges more defined and angled. Snow twirled in a chaotic tornado between us, playing hide-and-go-seek with the tall, lanky body standing a few feet from me.

I glanced at the Walther hanging from my hand, wondered why it suddenly felt heavy and cumbersome in my numbed grip. Despite the dragging weight of Gracie's warning and growing trepidation, I managed to haul myself forward another step. The wind gusted, rattling against me.

The mewling staggered into the wind, its shape warped, its mood hungry and feral.

I hesitated, pried the Walther from my side, tried to suck in a steadying breath as the body listing in front of me grew more defined.

I gasped, my gut twisting and churning, unable to decide whether to spew out butter, or curl up on itself into twisted and turning knots.

Dylan Davies, a child I'd recovered from Juzarine captivity three years ago, stood a few steps from me, his ashen face slack and dead, empty eyes shimmering with Ebony. Drool dripped from his sagging mouth, pooled at his bare feet, spitting steam into the dead air.

A new agony ripped its way from my soul to settle hungry and angry at the base of my heart. "Ah Dylan," I breathed. "What has Stephanie done to you?"

"Stephanie, Adria, Tansy," He mimicked, leering at me, his lean face twisted into a gruesome parody of the streetwise teenager he'd become, the spark of humor in his eyes corrupted and riddled with a putrid stench that made me want to gag.

"They are waiting for you," he said, his words slurred, his voice flat and lifeless. The empty light in his eyes shifted. His expression growing contemplative for an instant before sliding back into a catatonic stare. "You will not save him, though," he muttered. "Like you could not save any of us. In the end." He shuddered, the flat, barren look behind his eyes shifting for a moment. The leer reappeared. "Why did you kill us?"

Tears blurred my vision. "I didn't have a choice," I said. "She was already gone."

Before I could reconsider my actions, I shoved the Walther against his forehead.

He giggled the same high-pitched squeal I'd heard from Emily.

I pinched my eyes shut and squeezed the trigger.

When I opened them, Dylan lay in the snow, his eyes glaring up at me in blank and empty accusation.

The wind coughed and spit snow, dusting trails of iced pebbles across my boots. The hissing voices melted away, leaving behind a crushing silence that slowly pressed the air from my chest until only desolate hollowness remained. The stench of corruption wafted through the air, curdling the virgin scent of the spiraling snow.

I stood where I'd shot Dylan, shaking and staring down at the nothingness glaring back up at me, still clutched in the obsessed claws of vengeance. Even in death, Dylan's tortured expression remained caught in the crushing grip of Stephanie's madness.

Footsteps crunching through frozen snow and ice startled me from my stupor.

I spun, brought the Walther up, rage swiping away the guilt-ridden grief clutching my heart.

Gracie stopped a few steps away, hands raised, her eyes blazing with that damned, motherly, 'I told you to leave it alone,' glower. "Careful, girl," she said as she reached across the chasm and slid the Walther from my quivering grip. "Don't want to be blowing holes through the only person left who might want to help you." Her quick smile dripped warmth and acceptance, despite my continuous hot-headed recalcitrance.

Beegle sat beside her, tongue lolling, his boundless brown eyes overflowing with beagle wisdom, compassion, and grace.

For me.

I deserved none of it.

Maybe that was the point.

The ear-grating reverberations of distant sirens echoed through the shivering air.

I glanced up as a heavy curtain dropped back to cover a third story window. Andie's apartment. She'd tried to warn me as well.

Would I ever listen?

Why ruin perfectly good disfunction?

"We better be moving," Gracie said as she touched my arm, and began guiding back toward the Bronco. "Gunshots in the middle of the night attract the wrong kind of attention, even in this part of Denver."

Beegle woofed his agreement as he brushed himself against the back of my legs, forcing me into a staggering walk.

The sirens grew louder, their discordant echoes bouncing off the emptiness clinging to the surrounding buildings.

The creak of an old and tired hinge broke the fractured calm enveloping me as insistent hands shoved me into the front passenger seat of the Bronco. Metal slamming into metal followed, muffling the ripening sounds of the approaching sirens.

More metallic caterwauling squealed into the claustrophobic space pushing in on me. Beegle's hot breath washed across the back of my neck, accompanied by a sloppy and wet kiss that tickled goose bumps down my shoulders. Gracie materialized behind the wheel of the Bronco.

The engine protested with curmudgeonly ire before groaning to life.

I touched Gracie's arm as she shoved the Bronco into gear, began crunching from the curb. "Dylan said that I wouldn't be able to save him."

"Save who?"

I sucked in a startled breath.

Images of Father Mike lying prone on the floor in the middle of Tansy's front room, blood slowly pooling beneath him, soaking into the carpet, bashed the side of my head. Realization bludgeoned the last of the cobwebs clinging to my grief-stricken thoughts. I cursed. "Father Mike," I said. "Stop the car."

"Are you flipping out, girl?" Gracie shook my hand from her arm, cranked the wheel hard left. "The police are going to be here any moment, and we need to be gone when they get here."

I grabbed the wheel, jerked it right until it hit the stops, pulled us hard to starboard. The Bronco bounced against the ice-bound curb, tried to ride the crystalline whitecap glittering in the headlights. "I'm driving."

Gracie slapped me with a flinty glare.

I shoved my door open and slid into the dancing wind. "Do you trust me?"

Gracie snorted. "No."

I yanked the driver door open. "Stupid question," I said as I pushed her shoulder. "Move."

Another 'you've lost your mind' grimace contorted her withered face.

I continued to shove against her shoulder.

Undulating red and blue lights flashed off the hunkering buildings, staining the piled and slushy snow, escorted by the approaching bone-grinding crunch of tires, and the blaring roll of sirens.

"Please."

Shaking her head, Gracie skimmed across the seat, her sudden absence sucking me in behind the wheel.

As the first police cruiser drifted around the street corner behind us, I killed the Bronco's lights, gunned it into a lurching, unsettled forward motion. We jumped the curb onto the sidewalk, snaked around the next corner and bounded back into the street as the pursuing headlights swept the building behind us.

CHAPTER 30
HOUSTON, WE HAVE A PROBLEM

SILENCE SETTLED between us as I navigated the slush frozen roads toward St. Raphael, a three-story Denver Commandery safe house and emergency medical facility in the center of downtown Denver within spitting distance of trendy new high-rise apartment buildings and the burgeoning Denver financial district.

Though the Commandery operated and maintained several safe houses and medical facilities throughout the Denver metro area, St. Raphael was the only location that could provide the kind of emergency medical treatment Father Mike would require.

To maintain its cover in the neighborhood, the facility also provided limited walk-in urgent medical care for the locals.

I twitched a glance at Gracie.

She stared out the windshield, expression stony, mouth clamped into a thread-slender line. She clasped her hands in her lap, the veins wandering over their backs forming steep ridges across the liver-spotted flesh.

"Have I told you this is a bad idea?" she said.

"You have."

She looked at me, her eyes shoving me against the door, grabbing me by the collar, and shaking me, rattling my teeth. "What makes you think Tansy will be here for Father Mike?"

"Stephanie," I said.

"No difference between the two," she replied. "Not now." She hesitated. "Maybe never."

Those last words drove a spike into my heart, corkscrewed through it, then yanked it from my chest, still beating, pumping blood into the space between us.

She tunneled over Beegle, made sure I couldn't look anywhere else except into her eyes. What I saw made the hairs at the nape of my neck do a jitterbug. "You better start facing that truth before you get everyone killed. Or worse." She continued to stare, the weight of her gaze crushing what little hope I still held into a pulpy mess at me feet.

I shivered, and shook her glare off, retrieved the mushy mess from the muck, squished it back into my stuttering heart, before shoving the whole gooey mess back into my chest. "I have to try," I said. "If not for Tansy, then for Father Mike." I paused, sucked back a snarling sob before it could wring my chest into an unending highway of contorted knots. "I can't believe I've lost her. Not yet." I pursed my lips. "But if I have, Father Mike is all I have left. I can't lose them both. Not together. And not like this. I can't let Jessie win."

"And the Shining Man?"

That caught me by surprise. I'd forgotten about the Shining Man. I wondered if it were involved in Jessie's shitstorm to slice and dice me into tiny bite-sized chunks and then feed me to the blood-enraged sharks. Was the Shining Man that shark? Unwitting or not, it didn't matter. Not really.

"If Jessie loses, the Shining Man loses.

Gracie grunted, unconvinced. "You're playing some pretty long odds."

I bit back my exasperation. "She started with Father Mike. He's the shell holding all of us together. Me. Tansy. Jessie. There's no one else. He's all that's left. And he's the easiest target. She'll be there." Pretty lame, but there it was, stripped of its dark and corrupted veneer to writhe in its final moments of agonized death.

Gracie turned her attention back to the snow plastering the windshield before the wipers flung the sloppy mess into the endless dark. "You got a plan?"

"I thought we could barge in, guns blazing, take the first-floor staff out before they had the chance to raise the alarm. Slaughter the rest when we reach the surgical recovery floor. Then wait."

That managed to pull a smile out of the old bat. "You been watching way too much Rambo."

If Commandery safe house security protocols hadn't changed, the entry doors would be rigged to repel anything not totally human, which, unfortunately included people like me... and Gracie, unless we had a passkey that disarmed the trap.

"You still have your Commandery security badge," I asked.

"Do bulls have balls?"

"Depends." I turned the corner, urging the Bronco slowly past the building as snow fell in heavy wet flakes that choked the streets with a clinging slush that even the Bronco struggled to churn through.

Dim white light leaked from the edges of drawn and closed blinds covering the second- and third-floor windows. Double glass sliding entry doors stared into the night as we drove past, the building's own brand of darkness glaring from behind their frosted panels. The curb in front of the building was barren, except for the snow piled against it.

Stephanie's voice sighed through the snow-suffocated gloom, caught me by the throat and squeezed.

I slammed the brakes, skidded into the curb across the street.

Muted laughter glided through my mind, the knife blade sliding between my thoughts before slicing through my consciousness. I shuddered, grappling my head between shaking hands, my face screwed into a contorted spring ready to snap. I heard Beegle's whine from a distance, the scrape of his nails digging into the seat, followed by a needle-sharp grunt from Gracie.

My world vanished, cloaked in an impenetrable wall of midnight. Smoky tendrils snaked out of the void, coiling around my mind, pressing savage, violence-roughened lips to the edge of my soul.

I blasted out a strangled cry, threw my door open, and staggered into the teeth of the wind-driven snow.

"Cassidy, girl, no—" Gracie's warning cry snatched at me, grazing the back of my thoughts as I sloshed across the street.

Snow scraped my face, tangled rigid flakes into my hair, and yanked at me with playful malice. I stumbled at the curb and collapsed, the grime-mucked ice stabbing my knees. The cackling continued, roped a noose around my neck, and dragged me forward.

Hauling myself up, I lurched over the curb, tugged my way toward the sliding doors, paused for a heartbeat as I glanced at the dead badge scanner and the shattered glass glittering from the piling snow and strewn across the entryway inside. I drew the Walther and shouldered my way through the splintered maw of the doors. Snow spiraled in after me, sucked into the tornado-like wake of my passing.

Pallid, sallow light greeted me, its scraggy edges scraping the darkness clinging to the walls. Blood-splatted counters rose from the shadows, shriveled bodies slumped over the tops, drained of their Essence, the memories of their anguished cries floating on the stilted silence.

The Ebony-laced noose tugged at me, urging me toward the stairwell.

Two more bodies sagged against the floor at the base of the stairwell door, their emaciated eyes empty, and soulless.

I stopped and stared, my mind blank except for the Ebony fog corkscrewing through my thoughts. Another yank on my leash. My hand found the stairwell doorknob. The click-clack of nails slapping the tiles behind me spun me around, the Walther sweeping up in a deadly arc.

Beegle stood a few paces away, his dark eyes glinting in the dusky light. He looked at me and sat. A flinty grunt from the front of the lobby pulled my attention from Beegle. Gracie straddled the threshold, a sawed-off single-barrel pump action twelve gauge clenched in her fist. I frowned. *Where the hell had she hidden that?* I wondered.

Our eyes met. She grimaced and shook her head.

The Ebony noose collaring my neck jerked me more insistently toward the stairwell. Stephanie was growing impatient. "I have to," I said. "It's what I came for."

"It's what she wants," Gracie said as she hefted the shotgun.

"If something else comes through this door besides me, blow it away." Without waiting for an answer, I whistled at Beegle. He scrambled to his feet and trotted over. Raking Gracie with one last glance, I opened the door, motioned Beegle through, following as he scrambled up the steps.

We tumbled into the third-floor hallway a few minutes later. There we stood and listened. My breath was a grim rush through my ears, and the Ebony draped sinuously around my mind like a cat. Emergency lights glowered from the ceiling, casting an eerie light on the sallow-colored walls. The mournful reek of blood and bowels staggered drunkenly through the air. Blood pooled around a lone body slumped over the medical station desk.

A high-pitched keen slithered from the end of the hallway, snaked its way up my spine, and stabbed me in the back of the head. I shuddered, tried to control the pain mushrooming in my brain. Another forlorn wail followed.

I drew the Walther and flicked a glance at Beegle.

He stood next to me, trembling, his gaze burrowing through the darkness.

I nodded at him.

Curling his lip in a silent snarl, hackles standing at attention, Beegle crept down the hall. I slid along the tiled wall a few steps behind him, sweeping the corridor with the Walther. An unnatural cold seeped from the wall tiles.

We reached the end of the hall. Room 536.

The piercing moan languished for a moment, its tone less insanity, more lament, the sound hickory-dickory-docking up and down my spine.

The room was on my left, the door cracked open. I glanced through the rectangular vision panel. The room was darkened except for the faint greenish glow of instrument lights behind the privacy curtain. I hesitated, listening for any sound or movement, but I heard only torturous silence. The door handle tickled my flesh with the dull scrape of debased fae-daemon power wrapped in a bow of Ebony. It wormed up my arm, sat on my shoulder, all teeth and bestial hunger.

Beegle nudged my leg.

I shoved my hand at him, ordered him to stay put, and hoped he'd comply. Sometimes, I just never knew.

He sat, growling deep from his chest.

Another low moan sounded.

Sucking in a quick breath, I shoved the door open and stepped into the room, pausing just inside the threshold. The door swung closed whisper quiet behind me, cutting off Beegle's annoyed grumble.

A languid rustle greeted me as I stepped around the privacy curtain.

Rank power washed over me, tickling the back of my neck as it giggled its way down my spine, chasing goose bumps helter-skelter across my body. I swallowed down the pulsing urge to turn and run screaming from the darkness.

Silence wrapped me with an almost suffocating embrace. I moved deeper into the oppressive gloom. Nothing moved or breathed except the throbbing fae-daemon power reverberating through the darkness.

The faint scrape of a hysterical giggle, followed by a sucking sob danced in front of me. I swept the sludge-thick air with the Walther.

"Cassidy?"

Recognition driven heebie–jeebies skipped up and down my back and arms.

My heart hammered my chest. My pulse pounded through my temples. Something warm and wet crawled up my throat from my stomach. I pushed it down, and stepped back, hugging the wall, as my right hand searched for the light switch.

Sterile white light flickered from the fluorescent ceiling lights, settling into a dull throaty hum that scraped the center of the room with a feeble, covetous stuttering gleam.

A shadowy figure huddled in a chair beside the bed holding a limp, gray-tinged hand attached to the cadaverous arm of a lifeless body.

My heart sputtered to a dead stop as panic blasted my mind, wrenching my body, and twisting my gut. I sagged against the wall, my hands numb. In the distance, the clatter of the Walther on the cheap floor tiles knocked on a door. A gut-wrenching punch decapitated my legs. I collapsed.

I was too—

"Cassidy?"

The rawboned voice scraped across my anguish, dragging my head up. I squinted into the murky darkness, focused on the jittery figure in the chair. Twin pools of pitch-black flames glowed from the needle-like face, pricking my chest with knife blades, and piercing my sluggish mind.

"Gloria?"

One of mine. From a few years earlier. Around the time I brought Dylan Davies back from Juzarine captivity. Like Dylan, Gloria Turner had been classified as a Lost One, unrecoverable because of the time spent in the Nether Realm.

A high-pitched squeal-like giggle slithered out from the chair, causing my jaw to clench.

"We have been waiting for you. Why did it take you so long?"

I shuddered, discovered that I still had a heartbeat and legs. I pushed myself to my knees, dragged the Walther from between my legs, and brought it up in a trembling grasp. Insistent scratching from the other side of the door nagged at my attention. I knew I should open it to let in what was scraping at it, but my brain's clutch wouldn't release so I could shift it out of first.

Gloria's tight lined face grew out of the darkness, lunacy masking her expression. And her eyes... Not even Emily's eyes had glowed with that kind of madness.

Something dark stained her lips and chin, dribbled down the sides of her neck, and settled on her bare shoulders. She clenched and unclenched her left hand in her lap in a spasmodic hypnotic motion. Like she was trying to grasp something just out of reach.

I swallowed back my dread.

She tensed and unfolded herself from the chair, continuing to grasp the dead hand.

My gaze focused on that hand, crept up the arm, settled on the sunken, shriveled face. Relief thumped panic in the side of its head.

Not Father Mike.

But not better.

Molly Montgomery, Gloria's aunt and guardian.

I snaked my way to my feet, took a tentative step toward Gloria.

She dropped her aunt's hand, continued to clench and unclench her hands at her waist, fingers unclasping and darting out, as if she were trying to grab something. "Please do not come closer," she said. "We do not want you to disturb her."

I stopped, felt my mouth go dry, licked the webs of fear from my lips, and frowned. "Disturb who?"

"Molly." Her gaze darted down to her feet. She shook her head, mumbled, looked back up. "She is sleeping now."

The ceiling lights sparked, stuttered to life, splashing an anxious pall across the bed.

I peered through the sputtering gloom, conjuring an image of what I imagined Gloria saw, continuing to clasp the Walther at my side. "We'll be quiet," I said. "Let her sleep."

Gloria nodded and twitched a confused smile. "She did not want to come with us. She wanted to tell you what we were doing. But we could not let her tell you. She would have ruined everything."

Her glowing eyes looked down for an instant, rose, peered into mine, went unfocused and faraway. Found their way back.

"Why did you kill us?"

I shook my head. "I didn't—"

She stepped towards me.

I bumped against the wall behind me, and brought the Walther up, the spear tip of the laser trembling against the center of her chest.

"I did not want—" she paused, shook her head. "But she made me."

The pain reflected from her eyes tore my heart from my chest. "Molly tried her best to keep you safe."

Gloria giggled. "Not Molly, silly. Them."

"Who?"

"They have him."

My heart stuttered. "Has who?" I asked, but I already knew the answer.

Gloria wagged her head and began to hum the same jarring melody I'd heard from Emily and Dylan. She stopped. "*Why* did you kill us?" She took another step toward me, squeezing her eyes closed, and pounded her forehead with her palm. "Make it stop." She opened her eyes. "Please."

"Gloria—"

"They have him," she said. "They are waiting for you to come and save him. They said that if you do not come—"

Sand coated my mouth. It scoured my throat, blew wind-driven dunes through my gut. "Where are they?" I asked. "Where did they take Father Mike?"

"Where it all began, silly," she said, her voice dripping honey-laced venom.

The Warrens.

Gloria rocked herself suddenly and screamed. "Make it stop!" The Ebony glow in her eyes faded, the lunatic expression on her face smoothing over.

"Cassidy?"

"Gloria?"

"Kill me. Please."

"I—"

She took another step toward me.

The scratching against the other side of the door grew more frenzied.

I gave the step she took, scraped my back against the wall, the Walther shaking in my hand.

Raw, fae-daemon power skinned over me.

"If you ever cared for me. Even a little. Please. You would do this for me." She banged her palm against her forehead again. "Please. I can't... I can't get them out."

Ebony clung to her, wrapping her in a snailing cloud of midnight

I reached out to her. "Gloria," I said. "Look at me. Focus on my voice. I can help you."

A whimper limped from her. She shook her head, and squeezed her eyes closed, screwing her face into a clenched agonized mask. "It is... too late."

Her eyes flew open, pulsing with power, Ebony glittering through the confused light. "They are waiting for you to come."

Gloria hunched over, hugged her stomach, and clenched her jaw. "Please make it stop. Make them stop." She looked at me. "Kill me. Please."

I shook my head. "I—"

"Kill me!"

She charged me, arms flung out, fingers curled into savage claws.

Guilt ripped through my heart and soul. I squeezed the trigger as Gloria reached for my throat. The explosion reverberated through the small room, echoing off the walls, and slapping me hard.

She jerked back, white-knuckled her fists as a murderous snarl tore itself from her throat.

I put two more rounds into her chest, put a final round into the center of her forehead.

Gloria stood still for a long silent moment, her hands still glued into fists. The Ebony flashing from her eyes sparked and spit for an instant then dimmed and died.

Contentment dribbled from her fading eyes, chased by acceptance, and embraced by gratefulness before she collapsed to the floor.

Tears sprang from the dead wells of *before*. I slumped to my knees in front of her, allowed myself to cry, dropping the Walther as I jammed myself into a fetal ball, the sobs wracking my body.

A long dead memory I had killed and buried tore itself from its grave, slunk into my consciousness, whispering into the back of my mind in Stephanie's terrified voice, *why did you kill us?*

CHAPTER 31
SECOND CHANCES

ASHEN GRAY LIGHT filtered between the drawn window blinds above my head, limped across the floor. The shadows cringed at dawn's touch, jerked back, inch by bloody inch.

Gloria lay on the floor beside the bed, soulless eyes glaring blankly at the sputtering ceiling lights, the final dredges of Ebony swirling through her veins drying into lifeless dross. Molly's withered arm draped over the edge of the bed, curled fingers casting skeletal shadows over Gloria's sunken face.

I sat, back pressed against the wall, knees drawn to my chest, my arms hugging them tight, and my head lowered, staring blindly at the floor. My tears had long since dried, leaving behind a desolate landscape of guilt and self-reproach. My body ached, muscles too strained to relax, my thoughts wild and untamed, and filled with darkness, death... and blood.

Beegle lay at my feet, head between his paws, wise brown eyes staring up at me with concern, attempting to cleanse my blackened soul with compassion, grace, and forgiveness.

I didn't remember opening the door to let him in.

I ignored him. I didn't have the strength to accept his grace, chose instead to wallow in an acid bath of self-deprecation, blame, and guilt.

How had it come to this?

Three of my kids dead. Otherkind abductions gone cold, the stolen children classified as Lost and Unrecoverable. Abandoned. Cases closed. Until I defied my masters, their authority, and the odds. I recovered them, damaged, no longer quite human, but given a second chance. The crowning achievements of my capricious time as a member of the Order of the Four and the Denver Commandery.

All there were dead by my hand.

Guided artfully by the two children I couldn't save. Stephanie Brandt, abandoned to her fate to save my sorry ass. Tansy Harper, a girl I considered to be my sister, but who didn't want to be saved. Not by me. Not by Father Mike.

Their union was conceived by the person who had ultimately saved me and who I ultimately betrayed, Jessie Colemann. She'd gleefully told me what she had set in motion, and she hadn't been subtle or coy. Every step had been taken with the breakneck speed of an out-of-control and fully loaded semi careening down an ice-packed mountain road that wouldn't stop until it slammed full force into its intended target.

Me.

Why did you kill us?

My drunken thoughts sludged back to that fateful moment in the Nether Realm last year when I'd put two rounds into Stephanie Brandt's chest and the blade of a Juzarine dagger through her heart before limping bludgeoned and bloodied through the failing Nexus and back into the human world. Too late, I'd discovered that the Juzarine had Changed her. And when I finally found her, she'd become more fae-daemon than human, becoming more alien by the moment.

I'd had no choice, had I?

Which is what Navarro had intended when he chose me for her Recovery. Though, I wasn't supposed to come back from that mission, either.

Except, Stephanie's Essence survived, allowing the Juzarine to collect it and imprison it into a Medusa Mirror.

Guess the joke was on both of us.

Enter Jessie Colemann stage right blazing with a lust for vengeance against Navarro and me for—what?

Ellis Wynn

So much blood. So much death. More to come.

I snorted a dejected sigh and shook my head. *C'mon Cassie, better get your shit together, or more will die.*

Beegle looked up, eyes glinting with sorrow. He whined, scooted closer, and lay his chin on my boot. I scratched the top of his head. He sighed, thumped his tail against the grime smearing the floor.

My thoughts strayed to St. Jude's, the crucified Christ hanging from the sanctuary wall. I imagined his gaze burning with anger, the forgiveness so freely offered before forgotten and trampled beneath the feet of his rage.

Why did you kill us?

I conjured the memory of Tansy's expression as she held Jonnie's severed head up to the surveillance camera in his apartment. The madness glittering in her eyes, the unhinged joy dripping from the grin stretched across her face. The lust for more blood and death carved into her expression.

I'd created that as much as Stephanie had. As much as Jessie. Probably more. Maybe Father Mike and I should have listened to Tansy and given her the release she pleaded for. At least when she'd gone mad, she'd have been in her element. Someplace safe for us.

Or maybe not.

It didn't matter. Did it?

I sucked in a heavy breath, blew it out.

Beegle raised his head from my boot, whispered a growl.

I looked up, reached down to snag the Walther from between my knees, held it in my lap.

The door whispered open.

The staccato beat of careful footfalls attached to an outlined figure slipped over the threshold. A taught string of crimson light shot through the air, spun round the edge of the privacy curtain.

I tensed, wondered if Stimson had found me again.

He had. In a way.

Harmonie Bonet brushed past the curtain, painted my chest with a flaming spear tip.

My thoughts unfocused and blurred. They tried to slide off the road and into a ditch. My grip on the Walther tightened, but I didn't move.

She stood in the center of the room, feet planted shoulder width apart, her eyes searing holes through my chest to the dregs of my shattered soul.

I huffed an *"I don't really give a shit"* breath and casually brought the Walther up to my knees, finger on the trigger.

Harmonie raised a brow, quirked an amused lopsided smile as she stepped closer.

Beegle rose enthusiastically to his feet, tail whipping the air in a frenzied greeting.

Her smile grew, fire and ice glittering through her eyes. She nodded toward Beegle.

He bounded toward her, baying in delight. He skipped around her three times like a puppy before settling beside her leg.

She knelt and scratched the scruff on his neck, suffering a few frenetic and sloppy licks to her face.

Stupid dog.

"I don't think he likes you," I said.

Harmonie smirked and stood, holstered her pistol. "A lot better than you." She glanced at the carnage beside the bed. "Stimson would like a word."

"You think I give a shit?"

She shooed Beegle back to me. "You probably should... give a shit, yes."

I wrapped an arm around Beegle's neck, kissed the top of his scraggly head. "He sent you to kill me."

"That was one scenario we discussed, yes."

"And if I decline to speak with Stimson?"

"Then yes. I *am* here to kill you."

I snorted. "Why is it always ultimatums with you people?"

"Black and white, babe. It's what keeps us alive."

"Yeah. Right." I shoved myself to my feet, and holstered the Walther, stretching tired and cramped muscles. Beegle hugged my leg, brown beagle eyes intent on Harmonie. "I won't go unarmed."

She stepped aside and motioned me past. "I'd be disappointed if you did."

I walked past her through the door into the hallway and toward the stairwell. Harmonie followed, a step behind. We met two stone-faced Chasseurs at the door. Harmonie touched my shoulder.

"What?"

"You're in the middle of some pretty heavy shit. Shit you won't survive on your own. Do yourself a favor for once. Be civil. And don't burn down the house while you're still inside."

I flashed a snarky smile. "Yes, Mom," I said, marching through the door and down the stairs to the ground floor.

Stern, aseptic light flooded the lobby. The sliding glass doors were wrenched closed, the shattered glass scraped away and replaced by plywood boards screwed into the frames. Dark grease spots blackened the tiled floor beside the stairwell door, the only memories of the two bodies I'd stepped over earlier.

Glass littered the floor, mingled with melted snow and mud. The two bodies lying over the reception counter had been removed as well, leaving behind dark blemishes in the stark fluorescent glow.

"Where's Gracie?"

"Safe." Harmonie pinned me with a disapproving look. "You shouldn't have involved her."

"She involved herself," I said.

Harmonie studied me for a moment, frowning. She shrugged. "Regardless." She shoved my shoulder, followed me through the lobby doors into a grim December morning.

Gloomy gray clouds choked the sky, nervously spitting shredded sheets of sleet, and pelted the ground with white, frozen pebbles. A bitter wind skipped through the frosty air, stirring the grounded sleet into firestorms of tiny white tornados.

My boots crunched bone-chilled ice as I walked toward a black stretch Suburban parked across the street, hemming in my Bronco. I scanned the block in both directions, wondered at the complete lack of traffic and city life surrounding the safe house. I stopped a few paces from the left passenger door of the Suburban and looked at Beegle. He looked up at me, an inquisitive expression flashing across his face. I smiled and kneeled, buried my face in his hair as I stroked his back. "Guard my back. If I'm not out in a few minutes, kill everyone."

He woofed at me.

I chuckled and stood, nodded at Harmonie.

She stepped past me to the Suburban, opened the passenger door, and invited me inside with a flourish.

I peered into the dusky gloom before sliding into the back of the Suburban and sat in the center of the bench seat facing Marshall Stimson. Harmonie followed, closing the door and plunging us into a deeper darkness as she settled into the seat beside him.

I sat in silence, my hands clasped in my lap, and stared through the tinted rear window between Stimson and Harmonie, like a coiled spring ready to snap.

Stimson shattered the spun glass silence. "May I offer you a drink?"

I glanced at him, swallowing my trepidation. I kept my hands folded demurely in my lap. Nodded.

Smiling, he opened a cabinet set into the door to his right and pulled out two chiseled glass tumblers and a bottle filled with a rich amber liquid. He poured two drinks, handed me a glass.

I took it, stared for a moment into the shiny amber liquid, and sniffed. Bourbon.

He smiled apologetically. "I'm afraid it's all I have."

I flicked him a nervous smile, slammed back my drink and held the empty glass in my lap between my hands. He sipped his, set the glass down on the tray in the door.

I stared longingly down at my lap, wishing I had another drink. "What do you want?"

"Ridding our world of the Otherkind would be nice, but for the moment, I'll settle for an end to your mess that doesn't include a world-ending apocalypse."

I looked up. Harmonie stared at me. Stimson examined me from behind a cunning expression. "I didn't start this," I said, realizing I sounded more like a petulant ten-year-old than the world-savvy Otherkind Hunter I'd believed I was.

His expression inscrutable, Stimson retrieved my glass, and refilled it, handing it back to me. I clutched it in my lap, stared into the dark indistinct reflection that hovered on the gleaming surface of the bourbon.

"Although that point can be argued, I won't disagree with you," Stimson said. "But you were warned and now people are dead. Mine. And yours."

I clenched back the grief, refusing to allow the tears to blow through the dam. "I know." It was the only snarky comeback I could think of. "And I'm sorry about your—"

Stimson waved my lame apology away, ire flashing across his face. "Save it," he said. "You have more important things to worry about at the moment, like ending this shitshow before more innocents die because of your petty and selfish disagreements."

I gaped. Petty and selfish? My mouth opened, acid dripping from my lips, the words loaded and ready to strafe him, blow bloody holes through his self-righteous crap.

He continued to glare back in challenge, daring me to utter a single contradictory word.

"I pulled your butt from the flames last year," he said, draining his glass, and depositing it back into the cup holder. "This time, you're going to have to do it yourself. I can't be seen to interfere."

Which meant that Archbishop Sébastien Rouanet, Grand Master of the Order of the Four, the man holding Stimson's leash, had thrown the Denver Commandery to the wolves.

If it had involved anyone else but Tansy, I would have done what was being demanded without a second thought.

But it was Tansy.

The wind billowing in my sails died, leaving the tattered and ragged canvas hanging limp.

"I can't kill her," I said. "She's my sister."

"She's not," Stimson said. "She's an unfortunate you recovered from the hell of Juzarine captivity whose parents couldn't accept the fact that their little girl never truly or completely came home.

Michael should never have taken her in." He reached for his glass, hesitated, before leaning back in his seat. "It's an occupational hazard."

"Like Stephanie Brandt?"

"Collateral damage." Harmonie, her tone unemotional, and cold-blooded.

"Which part," I challenged. "Her abduction and captivity by the Juzarine or that I was sold out by my people and meant to die?"

"I didn't know," Stimson said. "And you never said anything to the contrary."

Because I didn't know until after it was too late. And when I finally did know...

A year wasted combing the Nether Realm searching for Stephanie Brandt's Essence, hoping to end what I hadn't ended when I'd killed her. She'd been an innocent victim, the bait used to lure me to my death. What Harmonie had called collateral damage.

Turned out, neither one of us wanted to die that day.

Stimson reached across the abyss, pried the empty glass from my grip. He studied it, watching the paper-thin light leaking from the ceiling as it glinted off the finely chiseled crystal, pure and undefiled.

Was there such a thing in our world as true innocence?

Stimson set the glass back in the cubby beside its twin and closed the door.

I stared at Harmonie. She glared back, her eyes flint and steel, striking each other, sparking the flames that would burn what remained of my world to ash before trampling it into the ground, buried forever beneath the scorched earth if I didn't do it first.

My regret over Stephanie thrust the tip of the dagger blade

through my heart. It twitched, stopped for an instant, stuttered back to life, limping from beat to faltering beat.

I thought about the nights I'd lain awake over the past year, second guessing my decision to kill her, obsessing over the *what if's*, wondering what might have happened if I'd ignored the logic, tried to bring her back at the cost of my team's lives and probably my own.

I thought of Howard Brandt and his obsession with recovering his daughter after learning that she might still be alive, wondered what he would think if he knew the real reason for her loss, what she'd become because of that reason, what she was now capable of. Then I knew suddenly in the deep dark pit of my own obsession that he was dead, a victim of his own obsession. I wanted to grieve for him but couldn't find the space to shove more self-deprecation into my guilt.

No matter what I did now, Stephanie and Tansy were the gaping and bleeding wounds I'd carry to my grave and beyond.

"I need your decision."

Did I have a choice?

If I did nothing, Jessie and the Shining Man won.

If I killed Tansy, Jessie and the Shining Man won.

No matter what I did, I was screwed six ways to Sunday.

"I can't say it's been a pleasure." I slid over without waiting for a response, opened the door, and slipped out into the gnashing teeth of the December winter. I slammed the door closed.

Beegle stood beside me as we watched the Suburban pull away, frozen exhaust billowing through the heavy, wet snow dropping like bird crap from the ashen sky. The sun had vanished, hidden behind an impenetrable wall of snarled black clouds.

I stared up into the snow, and blew slow heavy breaths, watching the swirling clouds dissolve into a hazy mist before vanishing into the cascading wall of white. I sensed Beegle hovering beside my leg, felt him shiver, and the quick cadence of his breathing.

I knew what I needed to do, knew I had no choice, and knew what was waiting for us at the Warrens. But I still wanted to believe that I could save Tansy. Save Father Mike. Hell, even save Stephanie. Somehow. But my options had dwindled into negative numbers.

I looked down at Beegle.

He stared up at me and woofed quietly into the thickening snowfall.

I smiled, kneeled down beside him, and ruffled his coat, I laid a gentle kiss on the top of his head. "Then let's get going. We're burning daylight."

I shoved him into the front seat of the Bronco, slid in after him, and kicked it into life. It sputtered in protest for a few seconds, stretching and popping its joints before settling into a rumbling purr; a lioness waiting patiently in the brush for the kill.

My phone rang.

I knew the number, didn't want to answer it, did anyway.

"I thought you never wanted to talk to me again," I said.

Peter's harsh breath skipped through the line, brushed the edge of my cheek. I shivered, the memory of that touch still scraped raw and bleeding, too much water under that vaporized bridge.

Silence.

Then.

"Stephanie Brandt's Medusa Mirror is still intact," he said. "If you want to save Tansy, meet me. You know where. I'll leave the light on." He hung up.

My phone refused to leave the side of my ear. I sat, gawking through the snowbound windshield, trying to fathom the meaning of his cryptic call. A trap? The truth? Did it matter?

Why hadn't Jessie destroyed Stephanie's Medusa Mirror? If she hadn't, she might dangle it like a carrot in front of me, enticing me to believe there still might be hope for saving Tansy. And Peter Oliver would be the perfect treat to lure me into her web.

I finally remembered to breathe, sputtered the air from my lungs, the warmth and humidity fogging the glass beneath the frozen snow.

My brain twisted around, thrusting images of Emily, Dylan, and Gloria into my thoughts. Tansy came and went, passing through on her way to Hell for an eternity.

Beegle forced his snout under my arm and managed to slap my face with a wet tongue.

The leering memories melted, leaving behind a black hole emptiness that threatened to pull what light remained into the dark oblivion of nothingness.

The Bronco hiccupped, throwing me out of my daze. I leaned over and smacked Beegle's snout with a wet one as well, kicked the car into motion, spinning snow, ice, and frozen slush against the drift-choked sidewalk.

The main roads, though plowed, well... sort of, were ice-packed, slippery and fickle, making driving treacherous. And slow going, which gave me time to think about all the infinitely messy ways what I was walking into could go wrong. I ran through each of the myriad scenarios and came to the same conclusion every time.

I looked at Beegle and raised a brow in question. The expression he threw back agreed with me. I shrugged. Guess it was time to slam through that door and dance where angels never ever wanted to tread.

CHAPTER 32
WHERE ANGELS HAVE NEVER TREAD

I STOOD on the porch leading to the narthex of St. Michael's Parish. Snow swirled around me, slicking the roughened, dark surfaces of the black oak double doors glowering down with disapproval at me and Beegle. My frosted breath churned through the roiling mist, its edges shredded by a frantic wind before vanishing into distant, half-remembered memories. The sun—more myth than truth—hunkered low behind the seething clouds.

Wind-driven ice stung my face and eyes. The stench of corruption heckled the immature morning, slithered across the ice-slicked concrete, and crept through my thoughts and memories, coaxing my mind into a conscious dream.

Ebony-borne power crouched in the crevices, silent and watchful, its pitchy touch scraping the back of my nerves raw.

I shuddered, my hand creeping to the butt of the Walther resting at my hip. Beegle snarled, his hackles stiff and erect. Silence embraced us and shielded us from the winter desolation scattered across the empty parking lot behind us.

My mind turned to Peter and his revelation, the trap that more than likely waited for me on the other side of the doors. I still could turn away, confront Stephanie and find a way to save Tansy on my own.

Which, without the Medusa Mirror, more than likely meant killing Tansy. Order of the Four lore told me that there could only be one Medusa Mirror. That without that Medusa Mirror, exorcising the Chimera was impossible. Now, Peter had told me that Jessie hadn't smashed the Medusa Mirror. If it were true and I could take it from Jessie, I could use to free Tansy of Stephanie's Essence.

My instincts screamed at me to run, that what waited for me on the other side of the black oak doors that led into the bowels of St. Michael's Parish was a trap, one more twisted game conjured by Jessie to torture me.

But I had to try.

My thumb found the door latch and pushed down. I shoved the door open, stepped across the threshold.

The door closed behind me, the slap of the latch catching startling me. Beegle snapped at the sound, his agitation overwhelming me like a swarm of hornets.

Shadowed light greeted us, guarding the way into the nave. Unbalanced Touched power tickled the numbed edges of my mind.

I looked down.

A wintry and sooty mist hugged the stone tiled floor, seemed to shiver with delighted anticipation. Power echoed from the fog and cooed seductively as it stroked my soul.

Wrapped in shadow, I stood in the narthex, staring down the center of the nave toward the sanctuary at the opposite end. White-yellow light from a million tiny suns danced off the polished tan-gray marble floor, reflected against the stained-glass windows lining rough-finished gray walls. Burnished light oak pews marched down either side of the nave, stopping a few feet from the dark gray marble steps leading up to the sanctuary and a rough-hewn snow-white marble altar.

Jessie stood in the center of the sanctuary. Beside her on his knees cowed Peter Oliver, his hands bound behind his back. His chin hugged his chest, body stretched to the snapping point, his bent form embraced by the wavering shadows cast from the flickering candlelight.

The crucified Christ hung from his cross behind her, agony and torment bleeding from his eyes. Unable to help myself, I looked into those tortured eyes, and nearly collapsed where I stood, remorse and shame pounding the nails binding the Christ to his cross into my chest and through my heart. I sucked back a sob and tore my blurring vision from the affliction ripping his soul apart. Then I saw the Medusa Mirror seething from the marble altar.

Before I could stop him, Beegle charged down the narrow aisle toward the altar, the echoes of his raging snarls bouncing across the emptiness.

As he approached the platform, Jessie raised her arm and aimed a pistol at him. A gunshot detonated through the sanctum. Beegle yelped, dancing back, and slipped between a row of pews as another gunshot splintered wood where he'd stood seconds before. He continued to bay and bark from cover, his pain-laced and frenzied snarls reverberating back and forth across the walls.

Screaming outraged curses, I drew the Walther, stepping from the shadows cloaking the narthex, and fired a round. Pristine white marble splintered beneath the Medusa Mirror, the ricochet reverberating through the enclosed space.

Jessie laughed and stepped behind the altar, waiting as I rushed toward her, my unsteady steps thudding off the marble floor. I slowed a few feet from the bottom step and glanced into the veiled darkness between the pews that Beegle hid behind. He returned my look, whimpering. Blood streaked the hair near his shoulder and snaked down his front leg.

I turned my attention toward Jessie, lungs heaving, my heart skipping against my chest. The tableau reminded me of a climactic scene from "A Fist Full of Dollars". I stopped at the bottom step leading to the sanctuary, wished I'd thought to wear the iron door taken from a wood stove before facing my nemesis.

"I'll admit," Jessie said, her words resonating through the space between us, "that I did not anticipate this." She gestured toward Peter and the Medusa Mirror with her pistol. "It is, however, the unexpected in our lives that make living and breathing worthwhile." She arched her brow. "Wouldn't you agree?"

I took the bottom step, my hand clenching the Walther.

Jessie tensed. "Carefully consider your next move," she said.

I retreated, and lowered the Walther to my side, flicked a glance at Peter Oliver. "So, what's the play?"

Peter stiffened. He didn't turn, sparing me the trauma of staring into his expectant and accusing eyes. I knew what they would say. I was torn. Too many oaths sworn. Too many agreements. Too many debts. And though I was torn, if forced, I knew my priority. What I would sacrifice. In that moment, I was glad he didn't turn around. I didn't need the distraction as my mind swirled around the possibilities and their inevitable conclusions.

A shrewd smile skittered across Jessie's lips. She lifted her shoulder in an ambivalent and dispassionate shrug. "I thought that was obvious," she said. The smile vanished, chased away by a deadly earnest that sent a shiver down my spine. "This is your Kobayashi Maru. Your impossible situation."

I started to raise the Walther but stopped when Jessie pressed the muzzle of her pistol against the back of the Medusa Mirror.

"Cass," Peter hissed.

He twisted around. The left side of his face looked like it had been beaten with a bat. His left eye, bloodied, black and blue, had swollen closed. His mouth wasn't much better.

I blew out a breath, held his glare for a few seconds, looked at Jessie.

She flung back my stare, her eyes wild with a mad gleam that set my teeth on edge. I felt something knocking insistently on the door to my mind. My soul skittered away from the sound, its hackles raised.

Voices hissed around me, snaked across the grain of my soul, ravenous, fangs bared to pierce my flesh and feed.

Ebony and quicksilver fire licked the stones around my boots, crept up the sanctuary steps, splintered tendrils clinging to the marbled pavement as it spread.

I shook off the feeling, tried to focus on Jessie.

"What do you want?" I demanded.

She snorted. "I thought that was obvious. I want you to lose."

My eyes strayed to the Medusa Mirror.

Jessie grinned. "You want this."

I nodded, choked down the sand scouring my throat, desperation grabbing my heart and squeezing until it popped.

"Then take it."

A shadowed shape slipped past me, collapsed my leg like a folding hinge.

Peter Oliver surged to his feet, lunging at Jessie as Beegle shot toward her.

A gunshot roared into the emptiness.

Peter head snapped back. He tumbled over, lay on his face, blood flooding the floor beneath him.

Beegle latched onto Jessie's wrist, using his weight and momentum to spin her around. The gun flew from her grasp.

She screamed, and catching Beegle by his throat, wrenched him off and flung him into the wall behind the sanctuary. He slammed into the tiled stone and crumpled at the base, breathing, but unmoving.

I gasped, stumbled forward, the echoes of maniacal laughter bouncing through my thoughts. I snagged the corner of the altar to steady myself and stared into Jessie's blazing eyes. Spider webs of grasping darkness cloaked her face.

She tangled her fist into my hair, yanked me from the podium, spun me like a top, and drove her fist into my gut, punching the air from my lungs. I collapsed, my hand clutching her shirtsleeve. She seized my throat and hauled me off the floor, then pitched me down the Sanctuary steps.

I lay on my back, gasping and sucking blood up my nose into my mouth.

Darkness danced through the shadows cloaking the corners of the chancel, grasping at my consciousness. I felt myself slip and begin to tumble into oblivion. I fought it back.

Ebony-invigorated Touched power throbbed. It stabbed at my mind with keen-edged steel, slashed at the edges, and the world unraveled. I began sliding into an abyss where I would be lost for eternity.

Jessie's rage filled my swimming vision. She kneeled and wrapped iron-like fingers into my collar, then hauled me from the floor. I stared into her cold-blooded eyes. Ebony swirled behind the rage, fueling the firestorm until it consumed every breath I sucked into my starving lungs.

She hurled me into the nearby wall.

I bounced off and crumpled to my knees, my world spinning in chaotic circles and insane colors. She rose over me again and cracked the back of my head against the oak paneling, then flung me up the sanctuary steps and into the altar.

It rocked imperceptibly. The Medusa Mirror jostled toward the edge, where it balanced for a heartbeat before tumbling over.

I reached for it, caught a corner of the frame, heard the crack of glass. My heart shriveled.

Jessie soared over me, snatched my hair, and landed a left cross into my jaw.

I dropped to the floor in a heap, tried to crawl away as she clamped her hand around my right ankle, and dragged me back, where she picked me up by the back of my tactical belt and shirt collar, and bashed me back down into the floor.

Her boot rammed into my stomach; she flung me onto my side against the front of the altar. I discovered the Walther lying a fingertip from my quivering hand, fumbled for it.

She stomped on my hand, pinning it to the floor.

I screamed.

Steel flashed above me, thrust downward toward my face. I jerked my head sideways, barely avoided the knife blade as it singed the edge of my ear and plunged into the hard wood flooring.

I drove the heel of my right hand up under Jessie's chin.

A hissed gasp exploded through the air above me.

She let go of the knife, lurching back. I brought my knee up, driving the heel of my boot into her groin. She grunted, folding over slightly. Leveraging my leg up, I used it to shove her off me.

Jessie staggered back, doubled over, gasping and retching, a hand protectively cradling her groin.

Managing to find the Walther, I dragged myself back a few feet, and rolled onto my back, sucking air through what felt like a straw. Tears stung my eyes and blurred my tunneling vision. I fought back the nausea churning through my stomach; the dizziness causing the room to spin like an insane merry-go-round.

Jessie looked up, chest heaving. Her gaze harpooned me, eyes glinting with churning blackness and malevolence. Touched power pulsed from her, vibrating through the air between us in buffeting waves.

I shook my head, the Walther a leaden weight in my hand. I dragged a handful of air into my lungs. "Please," I wheezed. "Don't do this."

She cracked a ragged grin, yanked the knife from the floor with her left hand, and slid a Juzarine dagger from a boot sheath with her right, the double-edged bone blade burnished snow-white, glinting with lethal Juzarine magic that would warp and corrupt my Essence until nothing remained except an empty shell, waiting to be refilled with a fae-daemon consciousness.

I slid away, found the wall of the chancel, used it to leverage myself unsteadily to my fee. I leaned against it, trying to calm the fire reverberating through my chest with every breath.

Jessie's gaze flicked to the Walther clenched in my wobbling hand. "Have you no honor?"

"More than you."

I double tapped her in the chest. Added two more rounds for insurance. Me? Petty?

She staggered back, collapsed to her knees.

Holstering the Walther, I stumbled to her and pried the Juzarine dagger from her grasp I grabbed the top of her head, and paused for a breath, staring into her eyes. "We were better than friends," I said. "Closer than sisters."

She spit blood into my face. "Until you stole my life from me."

I drove the dagger through the side of her neck. She gasped, her breath gurgling in her throat as the fire burning in her eyes flickered and died.

I stepped back, and fell to the floor, gasping and wincing as slivers of agony speared my body.

A low breathy hiss filled the space between us. I felt the touch of hot desert-dry fingers caress my mind. They wrapped themselves around my thoughts, teasing and cajoling before sliding away and evaporating.

I shuddered and heaved a terrified breath before crawling to where the Medusa Mirror lay. Horror cremated my hope as I traced bloody fingers along the crack running diagonally through the glass from corner to corner.

Ancient Otherkind lore babbled that the mirror was now useless, its parts not worth saving.

But it was all I had to save Tansy.

I'd find a way.

I shoved myself to my feet. Lights danced through my swimming vision and tore pieces from the ragged edges of my consciousness as I stumbled to where Beegle lay. He looked up at me, whimpering. Blood oozed from his shoulder, stained his hair black. I hugged him and kissed the top of his head.

"I need you, buddy," I said. "I need you now more than ever."

We limped together across the platform, stared down at Peter, his head soaking in an ocean of blood. Regret slid across my heart. More blood on my hands that I could ever clean off, no matter how hard I scrubbed.

My vision swam through a black and stormy sea as I stumbled through the narthex and leaned against one door, sucking air and wincing with every breath.

I gazed at the cracked Medusa Mirror, then glanced at Beegle, grimacing as I shoved my way outside into what might be my last day on Earth.

CHAPTER 33
REDEMPTION

I NUDGED the Bronco through the snow onto the scorched-earth driveway leading to the Warrens, easing it to a hesitant stop near the decaying garage. Heavy metal grunge throbbed from the walls and shattered, blacked-out windows of the ramshackle house.

To the Mundane world, the Warrens was the quintessential horror movie haunted house; an abandoned early twentieth century Tudor-styled house nestled deep within a remote ten-acre wooded canyon, accessible only by a pothole-pitted dirt road where a guy hoping to get laid might take his equally horny date.

I sat in the Bronco, staring at the house, heart hammering, throat dry, skin cold and clammy despite the heat blasting from the vents. I dialed Gracie again and grimaced as it went to voicemail—for the sixth time.

Harmonie had said that Gracie was safe, which in Order dialect meant that she'd been removed from the equation and there would be no cavalry riding over the hill coming to my rescue. It looked like I was doing the stupid horror movie cliché on my own: walking alone into the haunted serial killer house.

Beegle panted softly beside me, licking his wounds clean. He whispered a woof to let me know he was ready to rock and roll. I didn't like the idea of dragging him into the wood chipper with me, but without Gracie, I didn't have a choice.

And then there was the cracked Medusa Mirror.

I didn't know if it would still pull Stephanie's Essence from Tansy's body, if it would fracture when I tried to use it, or if it would jerk Tansy out of her own body with Stephanie. Hell, I didn't know if it would do anything at all.

But I had to try.

My final option was putting a bullet into Tansy. And I wasn't going to do that, no matter what happened.

I helped Beegle out of the Bronco, and we crunched through crusted ice and refrozen snow to the base of three rotting wooden steps. Their paint had peeled away decades ago. They led to a crumbling wraparound cedar deck, once sheltered by a shake-shingle roof.

I stared up into the shadows embracing the front door.

Slightly out of tune fae-daemon power throbbed through my bones, grating against my nerves and soul. I'd sensed the same power bubbling from Emily, Dylan, and Gloria, their Essences infected by Ebony, soured and rotted, their souls festering with Juzarine magic.

I made sure the Medusa Mirror was secured inside my coat and drew the Walther.

Watching my footing, I climbed toward the deck, pausing with each mournful creak, breath held. My heart tapped my ribs with a hard, insistent knuckle. Despite the cold, sweat rolled down my temples beneath my hat. Beegle followed, his nails tapping the wood in harmony with my creaking steps.

Facing the door, I used my teeth to pull off a glove. I touched my right hand to the warped and frozen wood. The door thumped to the beat of the music from inside. Fae-daemon power wound through the thumping beat. It tried to twist my thoughts away from what I came to do and toward a desire to forget why I was here. Go inside. Join the fun.

I shuddered, slid my hand to the door latch, and pushed the handle down. The latch disengaged with a hushed, cranky clack. I pushed the door open, cringing at the pig-squealing hinges. Beegle slid through the narrow opening, and stopped a few steps inside, head down, scruff standing at attention. I felt the grind of his growl at the back of my jaw.

My skin crawled as I crossed the threshold and brought the Walther up. The heavy metal grunge slammed into me, trying to shove the air from my chest. Dust and swirling snow hung heavy in the grasping darkness. Dimmed sunlight clawed its way into the room past the tattered edges of the blacked-out windows, clinging to the rotted baseboards.

I stepped past Beegle into the front room.

Stephanie knew I had come. I felt it in the change in timbre of the power snaking through the house. It wrapped around me like a hunting python and tugged at my thoughts, trying to form an image that dissolved into mist almost as quickly as it formed. I shook my head to clear it of the stray cobwebs that continued to cling to the edges of my mind.

The room slowly materialized around me. A combination of debris from the crumbling house and discarded garbage littered the floor. A ragged-looking rat rooted through a pile of rotting food and beer cans in the far corner.

I took a slow deep breath to calm my thudding heart and stepped past a pile of jettisoned fast food bags and wrappers further into the room. I switched on the Walther's laser, using it to paint anything that might be a target. A gaggle rats scattered from Beegle as he blazed the trail across the room, their glowing beady eyes tasting my flesh with goose bumps that ran races up and down my arms.

Controlling another shudder, I pushed my back against the far wall and used the hesitation to calm my racing heart before I turned the corner to lunge deeper into the crevasse. Beegle a step ahead to my right.

I took a quick breath, and stepped away from the wall, sweeping the darkness with the laser, the light reflecting off a shattered mirror hanging on a nearby wall. A hallway. Crap. I hated hallways. They were close and cramped. Nowhere to go, made it hard to fight. And run away.

I swept to my left.

Deeper darkness stared back at me.

A closed door sat at the end of the hall, slightly off its hinges.

I swept to my right.

More darkness. More doors. One on the left, another at the far end. No indication which direction might be better. Guess I should have explored the ground floor better during my previous visits instead of focusing on the basement and the Nexus pinned to one of its crumbling foundation walls

Paper. Rock. Scissors?

I turned right and stepped into the hall. Noticed Beegle had hesitated.

Odd and erratic fae-daemon power boiled up into a roiling hurricane in front of me. I tried to step back. My foot caught something sticking up from the floor, twisting my ankle in its grasp. Thunder slammed into me. The door at the end of the hall blew off its hinges, glancing off my shoulder before I could turn out of its way.

The Walther flew from my grasp, disappearing into the darkness as I spun like a top and slammed into the floor on my hands and knees, doing my best to protect the Medusa Mirror. I sucked dust and debris as it rained down from the disintegrating ceiling.

Beegle howled and bayed, shooting past me, snarling in the closed distance. He suddenly yelped, and went silent, followed by the dull thud of a solid shape into the floor behind me.

An instant later, an anvil-heavy foot smashed into my back, hurtling me into the floor. I shoved my hand between the mirror and the rotting wood, cringing from the sudden, stabbing pain, gasping for air that suddenly didn't exist.

Fingers tangled into my hair, peeling me from the floor. Fiery breath scorched my cheek and neck. A hand wrapped into my coat and flung me through the air. I slammed jackhammer hard into a wall, collapsing into a quivering pile of flesh and bone. I tried to muscle myself up, instead flopped over face-first into chaotic piles of garbage and filth.

My legs. Where were my legs? Why did they keep deserting me in my hour of need?

I tried to suck in a gasping breath. Black, pinpoint lights swirled through my eyes. My lungs finally remembered to work. A quick sucking breath filled my chest. I rolled to my side, trying to blink away the swirling lights as hands shot down out of the darkness, and jerked me back to my feet, slamming me into the wall, careening the back of my head off crumbling plaster and wood. I tasted blood. I'd bitten my tongue. Hard.

Stephanie's glowing Ebony-gorged eyes burning and boiling with hatred bore into mine.

She spun from the wall and hurled me through the hallway entrance and across the front room. I crashed into a far wall where I crumpled to the floor in a boneless heap. My chest heaved, groveled at the feet of the breath that still refused to fill my panicked lungs.

Heavy steps approached, dragging a slow menacing hiss with them.

Where was Beegle?

Move damn it! Move!

My body refused to cooperate.

I lay in a heap, unable to even groan as the footsteps stopped in front of my face. Grimy, and torn toes wriggled playfully in my wheezing breath.

Despite my growing terror, I still couldn't move.

If I survived this, I really needed to ask for a refund.

A hand snatched my foot, dragged me from the wall, across the offal-littered floor to the basement door, and paused.

The squeal of rusted hinges harangued my jumbled mind, followed by a bashing kick to my ribs that launched me into a chaotic tumble down the stairs, that dumped me face down into a pile of rotting food and rat crap. An army of roaches swarmed out from beneath me, disappearing beneath other piles of slop and swill before I could draw a shuddering breath. A foot wedged itself beneath my ribs and shoved. I flipped onto my back where I lay in the middle of my own body puddle.

Pain pulsed through every space I could feel. My stomach boiled. If I had anything left, I would have spewed its contents across the debris-littered floor.

A deeper shadow materialized from the darkness, straddling me. Tansy's face shoved itself into my blurred vision, blowing stale blood-tinged breath across my face. I hacked and coughed, spit bloody slobber into the eyes glaring into my own.

Instead of curses, I heard the high-pitched giggle of a teen girl.

My heart lurched.

Hands grasped either side of my head and drove it into the floor as a lithe body settled itself on my stomach. It leaned down, knobby knees ramming themselves into my upper arms, and pinning them to the floor. The glittering charcoal-black eyes I'd seen in the hallway, bore into mine, the pale light illuminating the face that framed them.

"Baby Bear?" I rasped, obliterated hope impaled upon the spearhead of desolation. "Fight it. Please."

Tansy's face leered, the eyes glowing brighter for an instant.

"We thought you might not come," she said. Stephanie-voice.

Spittle drooled from her gaping mouth, wept onto my face, and jogged down into the corner of my mouth.

"I'm here now," I said, the last of my strength leaking out through the gaping hole in my soul.

A hard slap snapped my face to the side.

Her blood-grimed fingers clenched my chin, dug into my bloody cheeks, forcing my head back to where I had to stare into Stephanie's eyes scowling from Tansy's face.

Was I too late?

A horrid leer split her thin mouth. She let go of my chin, leaned down into my face, her grimy hand slithering into my coat, and snagging the Medusa Mirror.

I grappled for it with unsteady, sweat and blood-slick hands.

She drove the back of my head against the floor again, and leaned closer, her chapped, split lips kissing my ear.

My hands slipped down to my sides, numb, my fingers no longer obeying my brain's commands.

She continued to straddle my body, pinning my arms to my sides with legs stronger than anything I'd ever known, and slid the mirror from my coat. She gazed at it, careful to avert her gaze from the cracked glass, her hands tenderly rubbing the frame.

"Thank you for bringing this to us," she said in a sing-song tone that scraped the hackles on the back of my neck.

She giggled, the sound shivering against my ear, then

backhanded me, the force of the blow splitting my lower lip, and drawing more blood from my throbbing tongue.

A frail moan dribbled through the dank air from the opposite end of the basement.

Stephanie stood, her glowing eyes boring through mine for another heart wrenching moment before looking past me into the shadows. "Another one you won't be able to save." She giggled again, kicked me solidly in the ribs, doubling me into a knot as she skipped toward the source of the moan.

I managed to roll to my side, blinking the tears from my burning eyes.

Stephanie crouched beside a rotting office chair, one wheel missing, causing it to cant to the side. She gripped a Juzarine dagger. Father Mike slumped in the chair, bound by gossamer, his head lolling against the slow rise and fall of his chest.

My breath caught. "Father Mike?"

His eyes fluttered open, focused for an instant. He opened his mouth, forming silent, tortured words. Stephanie slapped the side of his head.

"Stop!" I screamed.

She looked at me. "Why?" She looked back at him, the light in her eyes dancing with malevolence. "Is this not why you came? To participate in your final destruction?" She looked at the Medusa Mirror and smiled, the expression distant and loving. "We have endured this prison for so long. But now we will be free. Forever." She set the Medusa Mirror, glass side down amidst the scattered wreckage strewn across the rotting concrete. Standing, she raised her foot

I hauled myself to my knees, I snatched a piece of concrete and flung it at her, hitting her in the face.

She shrieked and staggered back, tripping over Father Mike's leg and dropping the dagger. As she fought to untangle herself, I dragged myself to my feet and limped toward the Medusa Mirror. Stephanie hissed, her Ebony-laced eyes gleaming.

Grasping the back of the chair with a gangly hand, she heaved herself toward me. I pivoted, staggering as she plunged into me, knocking me away from the Medusa Mirror. We grappled, slamming into the floor and rolling through the garbage, her hands crushing my wrists. I head butted her. She howled and released my wrists. I leveraged a knee beneath her and shoved. She fell back and splayed over the floor, giving me the chance to crawl for the Medusa Mirror.

As soon as my hand latched onto the frame, she caught me. Then she dragged herself over me, her hands grasping and yanking it from my grip. Cackling with delight, she sat up, raised the mirror over her head. My hand grasped for the Juzarine Dagger. I drove it into her chest.

Her eyes went wide, her arms drooping. The Medusa Mirror dropped onto my chest, as she fell over onto her side.

I scrambled out from beneath her, and snatching the Medusa Mirror, dipped my finger into her blood. I smeared it across the frame, grabbed her by the hair and forced her to look at her reflection.

She screamed, bucked in my grip, tried to turn her face away, but I held firm. I wouldn't let her turn away. The basement went suddenly dark and silent. Stephanie stopped her wild bucking and went utterly still, her eyes clearing, the Ebony fading away.

"Baby Bear?"

"Cassie?"

Blowing out an enormous sigh, I smashed the Medusa Mirror into the floor, realized suddenly that there was too much blood.

Tansy groaned.

I grasped the handle of the dagger in her chest, tried to scream for help, but the words fled, leaving me gasping for breath

My vision blurred. The back of my throat burned. My hands trembled around the dagger's handle, wanting desperately to yank it from her chest. I resisted the urge.

Where the hell was my phone?

"Don't die on me, Baby Bear. You're not going to die on me."

Her breath wheezed, gasping in short, quick bursts. She wrapped her hands around mine and squeezed.

"Tansy?"

"Thank you," she said.

Her hands loosened, falling away as the life fled from her eyes.

An instant later, they went blank.

A contented smile stuck to her mouth.

I screamed.

CHAPTER 34

GARAGE SALE SOUL

I SHOULDERED open the doors to Three Bears Bar and Grill, a trendy Otherkind dive, with Beegle nipping my heels.

Hunkered watchfully in the center of the hip LoDo nightlife scene, Three Bears provided a façade of legitimacy for Numen Galére activities, including dealing Dust to human Otherkind Wannabes, and the trafficking of human children.

Dark. Narrow. Cave-like. Mahogany wood flooring and walls. Plush, overstuffed black leather open booth couches. Cushioned, plush black leather backless seats, embraced between low squatting small round black marble tables. Toward the back, more traditional nosebleed-high bar tables and leather-backed stools.

Behind the bar, bottles of every conceivable kind of alcohol, laced with Dust, lined the mirrored wall, backlit to sparkle and entice. In the center, an ordinary antique cherry-framed mirror stared out hungrily, waiting for the press of bodies to occupy its morbid fascination.

Everything needed for unprotected and unremembered intimacy.

People aware of the Otherkind's existence in the human world

—dissatisfied, impatient, convinced they deserved more or simply wanted more—frequented Three Bears. Not the fringe. Not the disenfranchised. But the successful. The trendy. The entitled.

They believed the Otherkind would give them what they thought they deserved, or more of what they already had, but that never seemed to be enough or good enough. And by the time that cherry popped, it was too late. They were either Otherkind chattel or wished they were.

A disgruntled hierodule stood behind the bar, spit shining glasses while his partner spiked the booze with Dust. The hierodule looked up at my approach, his pinched expression warping into impatient displeasure. "We're closed," he said, his voice paved with gravel and potholes from a too many pack-a-day habit.

I strode to the bar, slapped down a grimy white canvas bag dripping scarlet-stained gore, clotted blood and a grayish ooze I didn't care to identify. I dropped the fractured Medusa Mirror next to the bag as I winked at the bartender and sidled onto the stool, hooking my boots into the barstool legs. I leaned forward and pressed my knees into the black leather padding skirting the bar.

His frown drew the corners of his whip-thin mouth down to touch the angled curves of his pencil-sharp chin. "What the hell—"

I fired back a sultry smile. "I have an appointment," I said. "Tell the Shining Man that Cassidy Kain is delivering his FedEx package." I leaned over the top of the bar, scanned the bottles squatting behind the bullpen, and scowled, tapping the vibrating marble with an impatient fingernail. "Got any AsomBroso Añejo while I wait?"

The double doors at the back of the bar opened, birthing the grim-faced Solitary still wearing its hem-tattered forties gangster film-era glamour. It paused just this side of the threshold, its glinting, crimson-tinged eyes scanning the room, and settled on me sitting at the bar.

It smiled, unsheathing a line of jostling virgin white teeth honed to razor-edged points. The smile faltered when its gaze swept over the blood-scummed bag and broken mirror, regained its grandeur a moment later.

"Miss Kain," it said. "How nice of you to join us this morning. And thank you for arriving on time."

Fury seethed below the surface of my meticulously composed veneer as I glided off the stool and snagged my show and tell goodies. "I have the items the Shining Man intended for me not to deliver."

A mischievous glint winked behind the Solitary's eyes as it stepped aside and motioned me through the doors.

I strode past it through the doorway into a slender, elongated corridor blazing with a radiant montage of effervescent color.

Beegle barked and whined. I cringed, unprepared for the visual assault on my senses, the hairs at the nape of my neck trembling as they decided to join the fun. I heard the Solitary chuckle, the noise grinding through my gut.

Another set of doors opened, sucked us through their yawning maw and into the maelstrom, vomited us out the other side into the Shining Man's office.

The Shining Man sat back against the edge of its desk, arms crossed, and a condescending smile plastered across its slender, bloodless lips.

Beegle sat on his haunches, quivering with enthusiasm a couple of leaping steps from the Shining Man, growling with an intent menace that would have cowed a raging lion.

It glanced up at my approach, waved a nonchalant hand at Beegle, who shivered for an instant before standing at attention and slamming it with a dangerous growl. The Shining Man raked Beegle with an irritated glare the dog ignored.

"Miss Kain, please tell your dog to stand down."

"No."

Irritation flashed across its face. "We have business to conduct. Business that cannot be discussed over your... dog's poor manners."

For a moment, I considered unleashing Beegle on it. But I knew the Shining Man was toying with me, testing me. And I didn't want to lose Beegle.

"Beegle. Down."

At first, I thought he might choose to ignore me.

"Please."

Beegle stopped and sat, his gaze intent on the Shining Man, one lip curled up to display his teeth.

"Thank you."

I met its bottomless gaze, calmed my stuttering heart, despite the leisurely boiling fear bubbling from the floor of the chasm where I'd tossed my soul.

It continued to manifest the same blue star-bright illusion I'd witnessed on our first meeting nearly forty-eight hours earlier. The enchantment rolled and shifted as if teased by a frisky wind, revealing an inimical expression one instant and obscuring it the next.

I cleared my throat and focused my quivering gaze past its writhing face, noting the disdainful, patronizing expression it flung at me like a challenge. Despite the gauntlet at my feet, I stayed calm, throttling the urge to drive my dagger through its heart—if Otherkind even had hearts.

The shrieking silence yawning between us lifted the hackles at the back of my neck. Unable to remain respectfully quiet, I shifted my eyes and bludgeoned it with my gaze. "Can we get on with this? I have some personal matters to attend to."

"Of course," it said. "I believe you have a delivery for—"

I tossed the canvas bag at its feet.

It splat against the carpeted floor, rolled, coming to an uneasy rest at the toe tips of the Shining Man's wingtips. Goo trailed the bag, sliming the carpet, and riddled the tops of the Shining Man's shoes with dark, sticky splotches.

It arched a brow, picked up the bag, and peered inside. A malevolent grin creased its lips. "And the Chimera?" It asked as it dropped the bag onto its desk behind it.

I clutched the blood-stained frame of the Medusa Mirror in my fist, the rage scalding my mind as it weaved acid and hatred through my clenching thoughts.

"You knew." It wasn't a question.

An insouciant shrug brushed my accusation aside. "Whether I was or was not aware of what you are accusing me of is of no import," it said. "And is of no concern to you."

The subtle tone that slithered beneath its statement delivered a cautioning shock of electric pin pricks through my gut.

I chose to ignore them.

"You knew." I hacked the accusation from the mangled stump of my grief.

"The Chimera," it said.

Klaxons clamored through my mind.

I didn't care.

Its gaze shifted, peered behind me, roamed back. A gratified smile crept over its mouth, kindling a searing flame behind its vacillating eyes. "You are distraught," it said. "But I am curious." It paused, the look it probed me with brimming malicious delight and callous disregard. "How many of your personal lines did you trample? How far down into the abysm did you crawl?" The smile creasing its mouth grew. It leaned forward slightly, nailed me with a blistering look. "How much of yourself did you sacrifice to... save the girl?"

The sound of the steel trap door snapping shut jarred me. This time, I listened. But too late.

My hand swept my hip for the Walther.

Immense fae-daemon power flooded over me, and through me. Fire seared down to the roots of what I was, burned to cinders what I thought I had been, what I thought I could be, what I thought I would never be.

My foundation shifted, tilted precariously, flinging me into absolute nothingness.

My vision blurred.

Tears washed through my eyes, dropped steaming into the snow at my knees between where my hands had sunk through an icy crust. The prancing light faded into a maddening swath of nightmare rainbow colors as a river of memory ebbed and flowed past me. Blurred images shimmered like razor-edged points of light that danced off the caps of surge-driven waves.

The webs of time shrouding the images quivered, began to tear away, showed gaping holes that shivered and shifted in the breath of an invisible wind. In one, a glistening remembrance materialized.

A five-year old me and my twin sister Audrey, imprisoned and chained in a cage of gossamer. An indistinct figure clothed in shimmering fae-daemon power stood behind our cobwebbed prison.

Memory screamed at me to turn away, to keep the secret locked away. I shoved it aside and ripped the door from its hinges, peering into the glittering clouds cloaking the form. Sun-blinding golden eyes rose to meet mine. An unhurried smile crept across twig thin lips, turned the corners up to touch the luminous eyes hooded beneath translucent lids.

I screamed.

The shifting daylight returned, cloaked by shadow and cunning gamesmanship.

I was on my knees bent over in the snow, my hands buried to my forearms in the trees behind my childhood home. Frigid cold stung my flesh and seeped in through my tactical pants. I'd lost the Walther somewhere in the blinding blanket of white slowly sucking me into oblivion. Hot tears streamed down into the snow below me, tiny steamy tornadoes swirling into the air where they struck.

Beegle had vanished.

I sucked breath into a chest that felt like it had been crushed against a granite cliff, and I managed to raise my head enough to find those same glittering golden eyes gazing down at me from an impossible height.

"You," I hissed into the stinging air.

Frosted breath swirled before me for an instant before evaporating into extinction.

A wicked and sly smile reached down, grasped my chin, forced my head up to meet those eyes and the pernicious evil that cavorted behind them.

"Just so," it said, the words the sound of my soul being ground into the filth.

I tried to rise, shove myself from the snow, fling myself at the monster that had destroyed my childhood, and sent my life careening into the crevasse I now inhabited. But my body wouldn't obey my mind. After a moment of struggling, I collapsed back into the snow, my panting breath sand blasting ice from the crusted snow beneath.

My world swirled with tornadoes of chaos, the colors and visions melting into a canvas drenched and sodden with nightmare hues that catapulted blazing harpoons through my heart, pinning it to my disintegrating soul.

My vision swam, the spiraling melted crayon colors lying flat and lusterless between my hands where they clutched ineffectually at the vomit-grimed carpet beneath me.

Beegle cowered beside me, his eyes wide with terror, a steady quiet whine sliding from his throat.

A shadow consumed the light surrounding me.

Firm fingers grasped my chin, caustic and insistent, forcing my eyes up. The Shining Man squatted in front of me. Power whirled through his shimmering eyes. It reached out, fondled the edges of my soul. I quivered at the touch, tried to shy away from it. It let me go. My gaze dropped, focused on the bile-engorged puke spattering my arms and hands.

"We are more alike than you would care to admit."

"I'm nothing like you."

I felt the indifferent shrug, heard it stand. "Perhaps."

Rude and surly light slapped me as his shadow withdrew. My chest continued to heave; my heart sledge-hammered against it, drove my pulse with flash flood force.

"I confess I find your naiveté refreshing. Even after all that you have seen and experienced, you still nurture that spark of innocence my kind longs for."

I managed to lift my eyes to meet its gaze. "Let me up and I'll shove my innocence through your fricking heart."

Its whimsical chuckle lit the surrounding air with virgin humor.

"One day. Perhaps. But not today."

It twisted, set the fractured Medusa Mirror on its desk, retrieved a smaller, less ornate mirror, dropped it in front of me.

Tansy's Soul Mirror.

"As agreed," it said. "Tansy Harper's soul for the Chimera and the rogue noble knight."

It buttoned its coat, paused, curiosity bathing the sinuous expression capering across its misted expression. "And a gift."

The Juzarine dagger it had confiscated during our initial conversation materialized beside my trembling hands. I reached for it, hesitated. Fae-daemon power spider-crawled from the bone blade, stinging my fingertips. I tiptoed my hand back and glanced up.

The Shining Man watched me, malignant fascination gleaming from its eyes. "The weapon has been restored to its original condition," it said. "Accept the gift or not. Your decision matters little to me. Although the consequences—" It chuckled, the lust leering down from its shifting face spidering across my flesh. "Shall be delicious."

Its gaze lifted.

I vanished from its universe.

"Please escort the young lady and her canine companion out."

Rough-hewn flesh carved with callouses snagged my arm, hauled me to my feet. Against my better judgment, I grasped the Juzarine dagger and Tansy's soul mirror, clutched them to my chest.

The Shining Man paused at the door. It didn't turn, but I saw the lascivious look pass over its face before it let itself out and closed the door behind it.

CHAPTER 35

WHERE NO ONE WANTS TO KNOW YOUR NAME

NEW YEAR'S EVE.

THE END OF AN OLD LIFE.

The promise of a new one.

That's what they were selling.

I wasn't buying.

A light snow floated down in wisps of fluffed cotton candy from a dark, brooding sky that dusted the frozen ground at my feet with virgin white. As I stared unseeing, the snow gently laid an uneven alabaster shroud across the churned earth of Tansy's grave.

The frosted air chimed lightly with the fragile crystalline melody of spun glass. A shiver flickered down my spine. I hugged my coat more tightly around me as I blew out a swirling cloud of tension. My body sagged slightly inward as the twin sisters Heartbreak and Melancholy fluttered down to either shoulder. They eyeballed me curiously, took turns pecking away the last dead, rotting remnants of the armor I'd used to protect myself from them.

My heart lurched in my chest. I heaved another dark, listless breath, felt the pressure churning my gut ease for a New York Minute before it settled back down into another building storm. I swiped the tears off my face, wondered how badly I'd managed to smear my makeup over the past hour standing and staring down at the finality battering my soul.

A timid smile trembled the edges of my mouth as I pictured Tansy glaring at me with scowling disapproval.

Even with the emptiness and the longing that throttled her heart and soul, Tansy had been all about the primping and the presentation. I lost count of the times she stopped me in the hallway at St. Jude's, her face screwed into a disapproving frown, her critical gaze telling me in no uncertain terms I couldn't leave looking like a despondent serial killer.

"I'm not going to a party," I complained. 'I'm hunting.'

Her frown would deepen as she grabbed my arm and steered me back toward the depths of her apartment, where she sat me down in front of her mirror and hovered over me like a mother hen fretting over her socially inept chicks.

"Doesn't matter," she'd quip. 'I can't have my big sister be seen looking like she'd just crawled from the gutter. Even if she is hunting.' She'd spin me to face the mirror and the horror of my appearance, and lean over my shoulder, her disapproving reflection tenderly patting my cheek in grandmotherly fashion. "I have a reputation to maintain." She'd wink at me from the mirror before trying to turn the proverbial thistle into the rose.

Beegle whined impatiently beside me.

A tremor skittered up and down my spine. I shook it off, glanced down at him. He squinted up at me through the thin veil of snow fluttering down around us. I shifted my umbrella to shade him from the snow. He panted approvingly and returned his gaze to Tansy's grave.

I blew another sigh, shifted my rheumy gaze over to my dad's grave, tried on a brief, grief-ridden smile. He would have loved Tansy. Would have treasured her more than I had. Would have taught her everything that he never had the chance to teach me.

Or Audrey. My eyes wandered to her empty grave. She and Tansy would have been fast friends from the moment they'd met. They were the two clichéd peas in the pod, and I wished they'd had the chance to know each other.

"Miss?"

The unexpected, bashful question startled me. I'd forgotten about the cemetery grounds keeper waiting for me so he could finish his job. I turned toward him, flashed a demure smile.

"A few more minutes?"

He looked up at the wistful snow wafting down from the brooding sky. When his eyes turned back to me, his expression had softened, and I wondered how often he'd lived this exact scene. After a fleeting pause, he nodded.

"Take as long as you need." He motioned toward his cart parked on the path at a respectful distance with a nod of his head. "I'll just be over there. Come get me when you're ready." He trudged back to his cart. I noticed he was shivering.

"Thank you. I won't be much longer." I turned back to Tansy's grave.

The service had been brief and perfunctory. Attended by myself and the priest I'd cajoled into performing the rights. Father Mike had asked to attend. I had insisted otherwise. Tansy's possession and her death by my hand had changed something in our relationship. At least for me. Despite everything he'd done for us, despite my love for him. Too much pain. Too much regret. Too much second guessing our decisions. And there was the cancer. Still present. Not as aggressive after the Ebony. But moving. Slowly. I didn't know if I could face his death a second time.

The priest, clearly wanting to be anywhere else except where we stood, muttered the prescribed words, flicked me with a glare, and said, "My condolences for your loss." Didn't bother to bless Tansy's grave before stalking off to somewhere warmer and more appropriate to his station. Probably a nearby bar. Grand Inquisitor of the Order, Marshall Stimson, respectfully disguised as an anonymous mourner accompanied by Harmonie Bonet, had stood quietly at a polite distance, near the tree line, and nodded to me before melting back into the trees.

I felt eyes on me, so I glanced up.

A man I didn't recognize, but who conjured indistinct and hazy memories that evaporated into mist when I grasped at them, stood within the tree line where Marshall and Harmonie had stood. He watched me, his eyes trying and failing to express some compassion. Instead, his steady gaze wore craftiness and calculation, littered with a dogged certitude and laced with the same cold-blooded venom Jessie had wrapped herself with after Wynn's death.

I sucked in a trembling breath, and matched his stare, my hand snaking to the Walther beneath my coat.

I guess old dogs weren't the only ones that couldn't learn new tricks.

He studied me for a few seconds longer before vanishing into the shadows.

Hesitant footsteps crunched through the frozen turf behind me, stopped a step away. My heart stuttered for an instant, settled back into a faster, more anxious beat. A hand touched my shoulder. Though I swore I wouldn't react to his touch, I stiffened.

"Cass."

"Shouldn't you be dead?"

Chagrined silence, escorted by a dash of guilt and self-recrimination. His hand slid from my shoulder.

"Probably," he said, and blew out an arid sigh.

"Why aren't you?"

His shrug ruffled the back of my neck. Beegle grumbled his disapproval.

"Luck," he said. "The capriciousness of ballistics. Your stupid daemon dog. My hard head." He paused, ruffled his hands into his coat pockets. "Divine intervention."

Beegle glared at him, let him know that this stupid daemon dog wouldn't make that dumb mistake a second time.

I grunted, thrust my hands into my coat pockets. They grouched at me, insisted I set them free to stroke the stubbled cheek they knew and remembered so well. I clamped down on their mutiny, crushed the coup d'état, and curled them into tightly wound fists.

"Cass."

I knew that tone, its lilting melody, the hypnotic beat that could convince a zombie to go vegan.

I closed my eyes, tried to chew through my lower lip. "Don't say it."

"I'm sorry."

"I told you not to say it."

"I had to."

Famous last words.

"How are you doing?"

"How do you think I'm doing?"

I sensed the quiet sigh that gently nagged the hair on the back of my neck, the hesitant lift of his arm, his hand reaching for my shoulder again.

I stepped out of range, attempting to find a way to hate him for his culpability.

"If you need—"

Silence. Followed by a self-conscious shuffling of feet through the ice-stiffened grass.

"I don't."

His hand found my shoulder, remained longer than normal. He began to turn me toward him.

"Please. Don't," I said.

When he pulled his hand away, it felt like he'd punched a hole through my heart.

An explosive sigh blew across the back of my neck, tickled the earrings dangling from my ears. Tansy's. Another bobble she'd spent the better part of her teen years trying to get me to wear.

He stepped beside me. I glanced sideways at him. He hunched down into his coat, shoulders shrugged, hands stuffed into his pockets, icy breath swirling from his nose and open mouth. I thought of kissing that mouth again, cursed myself for the fool I was. I didn't need more of that baggage.

"So you're finally free."

A sad smile touched the corners of his mouth. He shrugged. "Are we ever truly free?"

More unicorns and rainbows.

"What about you?" he asked. "I've heard rumors."

A cynical smile curved the corners of my mouth. "What have you heard?"

Silence greeted my question.

We both knew the answer. Knew it was better left unspoken.

He stuttered a breath, brushed a frozen tear from my cheek. "Please be careful," he said. "I don't think you truly understand the hornet's nest you're walking into."

I shrugged. "Don't really have a choice," I said. "You and Jessie took that away from me."

He winced.

Regret tried to pry its way into my heart. I pushed it back, threw it on the ground, and stomped it dead.

Beegle whined insistently again, nudging my thigh with his head.

"I need to finish this."

He turned his gaze toward the churned foot of Tansy's open grave.

The Soul Mirror winked at us through the snow-misted light. Swirls of emerald vapor swayed beneath the glass, pure and undefiled by the profaned and perverted essence of Stephanie Brandt that had seduced, warped, and then corrupted Tansy, made her vulnerable to Jessie and her vengeance.

Peter looked at me. "Do you want me to stay?"

I shook my head. "I'd rather you didn't."

The hope in his eyes flickered and dimmed. He pursed his lips. A reluctant understanding settled over his face and darkened his expression.

I smiled at him, reached up, and stroked his stubbled cheek. Most of the swelling remained, determined to hang out until after the fat lady sang her third encore. The bruises had faded, were now an intoxicating shade of enraged blue and an over ripe mottled banana yellow.

He took my hand from his face. Turned it over, touched his lips to my palm. I closed my eyes, bit my lower lip. My heart quivered.

"Please don't," I said. "Those passing ships are already sunk and forgotten."

An almost inaudible lament brushed against my mind.

My eyes opened, caught the sadness as it slid from his gaze, touched the corners of his mouth, and vanished.

He gave my hand back.

I took it, glanced fleetingly at my palm where his lips had touched it, shoved it into my coat pocket. My own sad smile slipped across my face for an instant before sliding off.

"See you around?"

I nodded, waited for him to trudge through the frozen grass up the sloping rise to the parking lot peeking out from behind the row of frost-kissed shrubs. I watched him dwindle into the late morning haze until he crested the rise at the edge of the cemetery and disappeared.

I blew out a heavy breath, then knelt and looked into Tansy's Soul Mirror. The glass reflected a face I barely recognized. Dark, haunted eyes stared back, the fires burning behind them struggling to remain lit. The lips cracked a weary smile that quivered with exhaustion before crumbling, snuffing what little light remained behind the eyes.

I sighed and drew my dagger, shielding it from the casually impatient glances the cemetery caretaker tossed at me from his cart. Leaning down, I brushed the mirror with a kiss, allowing an errant tear to splatter the snow-stained glass.

"Hey, Baby Bear," I whispered, my voice quivering. "I hope you find the peace you searched for." I paused, jerked back the flood threatening to overwhelm the flimsy dam I'd piled up against the rising tide. "I'm sorry I couldn't find it for you." I slammed the pommel of the dagger into the mirror, smashing the glass.

A hushed breath shivered from the fragmented slivers, spiraled into the falling snow, tinting the glinting flakes emerald green before dissolving into wishful memories.

I waited for the tinkle of the crystalline bells to fade before wiping snot from my nose, dropped the shattered mirror into the hole and stood. I turned, and sheathing the dagger, nodded at the caretaker. He stared for an instant, curiosity flashing across his blunt face.

Walking over, I leaned into him, slid a C-note into his gloved hand. "Just fill the hole," I said. "Don't gawk. I'll know."

His face paled. He cleared his throat and nodded.

I smiled. "Thanks."

"Of course, miss," he said, his voice quivering slightly through the frosted air.

After one last longing glance at Tansy's grave, I plodded up the slow rise toward the parking lot, following Peter's footsteps. Beegle trotted beside me, his tags jingling in time to his waltzing gate.

As I crested the lip of the hill, I stopped to brush off the snow littering my bangs.

The man who'd watched me earlier from the trees leaned against my Bronco, hands stuffed into the impatient warmth of his winter coat. A gauzy carpet of melting snow blanketed his head, dripped from closely cropped silver splotched, black hair and down his temples. Mirrored sunglasses hid his eyes, but not the grim determination carved into the granite of his expression.

Beegle growled, the rumble deep in the pit of his chest.

The man shoved himself from the side of my Bronco and removed his sunglasses to regard me with sunken, lusterless blue eyes that might once have been sun bright and playful. Dark circles bruised the washed-out skin beneath his eyelids. Wrinkles that resembled cracked, sunbaked earth crouched behind the circles clinging to his eyes.

I pulled my hands from my coat pockets, turned the palms toward him.

He nodded his acknowledgment and flashed a badge. "Cassidy Kain."

Not a question.

"Depends," I said.

"On what?"

"On who's asking."

Another succinct, compact nod, as if he were intimately acquainted with the type of subterfuge I flung at him. He reached into his coat, handed me a business card. "Detective Benjamin Shaw, Colorado Bureau of Investigation."

I glanced at the card, crossed my arms. Beegle curled his lip and growled a quiet snarl.

Detective Shaw tensed. "Cute dog," he said.

"Can I help you, Detective?"

His gaze lingered on Beegle for another moment before returning to me.

The wind shifted, puffed a blast of swirling snow between us, dragged the whoosh of lunch traffic through the lot. Crows squawked in the trees surrounding us, their raucous calls dripping shivers down my back.

The detective cleared his throat. "I'd like to ask you a few questions."

Foreboding settled on my shoulder, cawed into my ear. "About?"

"Ellis Wynn's murder." He motioned to an unmarked sedan parked a few spaces away. "If you wouldn't mind following me to the station, we could talk under more hospitable conditions."

I managed not to flinch as the jaws of the bear trap snapped closed.

"Actually," I said, my tone turning icy and inhospitable. "I do mind. I just buried my sister, in case you were too focused to notice. And I'm really not in the mood to spend the rest of my afternoon sequestered in a CBI interrogation room. Enjoy the rest of your New Year. Detective." I began to reach past him. "If you'll excuse me—"

He gripped my arm, leaned in, his expression suddenly hostile, his eyes lit with the same vengeful fire that had burned behind Jessie's gaze.

"I know you were responsible for Ellis Wynn's death," he hissed. "And I'm going to prove it."

Beegle stepped beside his leg, growling, the rumble vibrating deep in the foundation of his chest.

The detective looked down. "Call your dog off."

"Let go of my arm before you lose your leg." I allowed my gaze to slide down. "And possibly other body parts as well."

A moment of biting silence embraced us, the void punctuated by Beegle's increasingly violent snarls.

Shaw relaxed his grip.

I wrenched my arm free, brushed past him, and yanked the driver door open. "Beegle!"

Beegle chucked one last furious snap and leapt into the front seat. I followed him in.

Shaw grabbed the door as I closed it, held it in a vise, his gaze flaming. "Don't get comfortable," he said. "Wherever you are, I'll be there. Whenever you look over your shoulder, I'll be there." He paused, spittle dripping down his chin. "You may not have physically pulled the trigger, but you were responsible, nonetheless. And I'm going to make sure you pay."

I started the engine. The Bronco gasped and gagged for a moment before settling into its normal rumbling purr. "Have a good day, Detective." I put it in gear and smashed down the gas pedal. I smiled as the Bronco roared from its parking spot, dragging the detective a few feet before he could release his grasp.

As I turned from the lot, I stared out the passenger window. Shaw stood where I'd abandoned him, arms at his side, the hem of his winter coat billowing in the coughing wind, his expression dark and determined.

Memory flashed its sudden burning starburst.

I stood in Ellis Wynn's apartment, blood trailing down my chin from a split lip. More blood oozed from my nose. I felt the bruise rising from an eye as it began to swell. Rage spasmed through my chest, strangled my thoughts and the reasons I'd confronted Wynn instead of ending him into senselessness. I clutched a 9mm pistol at my side, knuckles straining. My arm shook, struggling to ignore my brain and obey my outrage and put two rounds into his chest and a third into his head.

Wynn glared up at me defiantly from where he sprawled on the floor, his nose and mouth bloody, his left cheek swollen and stained a ghastly shade of rotting blueberry and mottled yellow gray.

"Why?" I asked.

He snorted, wiped the blood from his chin with the back of an unsteady hand. "Because no one should be allowed to function outside or above the law. Your Order has done both for far too long."

"Jessie's part of that world. My world. Our world."

He blanched, shoved an elbow beneath him.

The 9mm in my hand rose.

His eyes narrowed. "And she wants out."

"You're lying."

"Am I? Ask her yourself what she wants."

I hesitated, uncertainty chewing a ragged hole through my tilting world. "No one gets out," I said. "Ever."

"Are you going to kill me?"

I laughed. "No," I said as I holstered the pistol. "But you're going to walk away from this. You're going to walk away from Jessie." I squatted in front of him. "In fact, you're going to resign from the CBI and you're going to disappear so that not even Jessie can find you."

A pause. Thoughts tossed across his mind. Possibilities imagined. "And if I don't...walk away from this or Jessie?"

"Then you'll both die." I stood. "You're choice. If you truly love her, I know you'll make the right one." I strode from his apartment before he could respond.

Turned out, he wasn't allowed to make that choice.

Neither was I.

A song rolled out from beneath the tattered carpet of my thoughts. *I'm Henery the Eighth, I Am,* sung by Herman's Hermits, released as a single in 1965.

Second verse, same as the first.

————

The story continues in book 2 - Revenge

She was forged as a hunter. Now she's forced to protect.

Cassidy Kain, once an agent of the Order of the Four and now enforcer for Denver's fae-daemon kingpin, is caught between shadows—hunted by the law, hated by the Order, and chained to the Shining Man's will.

When a bestselling author vanishes, Cassidy uncovers a secret darker than any story: Desiree Ladrona and her writing group stole the power of a Juzarine Muse. Now the Muse is free, murdering them one by one in the twisted style of their own novels—and Desiree is next.

Protecting Desiree means defying the Shining Man, outpacing Detective Benjamin Shaw's investigation, and confronting a supernatural predator who mirrors Cassidy's own sins. At a Denver literary festival, where the Muse plans to consume the imaginations of thousands, Cassidy must decide: destroy the Muse, deliver her to the Shining Man, or sacrifice herself to save the city.

In a world where every story has a price, Cassidy must choose between vengeance, servitude, or sacrifice.